THE RIO AFFAIR

A WORLD WAR TWO NOVEL

STACY LYNN MILLER

SEVERN RIVER PUBLISHING

Severn River Publishing
www.SevernRiverBooks.com

ISBN: 978-1-64875-630-6 (Paperback)

ALSO BY STACY LYNN MILLER

Hattie James WWII Novels
The Songbird
The Rio Affair
The Secret War

Lexi Mills Thrillers
Fuze
Proximity
Impact
Pressure
Remote
Flashpoint

To find out more about Stacy Lynn Miller and her books, visit
severnriverbooks.com

To Leslie and Allison.
My daughters and keepers of my heart.
They teach me every day that love is unconditional and enduring.

PROLOGUE

Rio de Janeiro, Brazil, March 10, 1941

Frederick Ziegler held this morning's edition of Rio's only English daily newspaper in his hands, stewing over the front-page headline: "Plantation Massacre: Missing Women Found." Though the story didn't mention the enchanting Hattie James, he was confident she was behind Heinz Baumann's death, which could not have come at a worse time. The Americans were close to reaching an agreement with the Brazilian government to build a naval base in Natal and establish a foothold in the South Atlantic, and Baumann was supposed to stop them. The urgent summons awaiting Frederick when he arrived for work at the Swiss Embassy early this morning, which now had him rushing back home in the back seat of his government sedan, meant panic had set in with his unofficial superior—the one that mattered.

His driver slowed at the gate of his mansion and pulled into the courtyard. Frederick recognized the luxury black sedan at the far end of the curved driveway and its chauffeur methodically polishing the back fender. That vehicle arriving unannounced meant that more than his livelihood as an ambassador rested on him picking up the pieces Baumann had left behind.

Once parked at the main entrance, Frederick ascended the steps and was met by the maid, holding the silver tray with his daily mail. "Thank you, Isabella." He took the stack of envelopes and offered the servant his briefcase.

"You have a visitor from the German Embassy, sir," Isabella said in English, with a thick Portuguese accent. "I have him waiting in the study."

"Very good."

The woman bowed her head and waited for him to pass.

Once inside, Frederick surmised the visit was designed to send a message. They minimized in-person contact to avoid being noticed together, so coming here implied that what his guest had to say was more important than the risk.

He ascended the grand sweeping stairs and pushed open the double doors at the top landing, revealing a handsome room. The Swiss Embassy had spared no expense in securing housing for his posting in Rio. The mansion was spacious enough to host sizable events, and the interior craftsmanship rivaled that of any ambassador's home he'd visited in his thirty-year diplomatic career. His favorite features were the twelve-foot-tall ceiling and top-to-bottom built-in bookshelves in rich teak wood, giving his office a stately feel.

A man was seated in one of his plush leather armchairs in front of his Georgian-style mahogany pedestal desk, reading the book Frederick had left on the end table next to the armchair. Someone else reading the novel he had not completed felt like a violation of privacy. Like the world he shared with the author was no longer his private oasis.

Frederick spoke in German. "How can I help you, Mr. Wagner?"

"Heinz Baumann's death was ill-timed," Strom Wagner said in German as he came to his feet to shake hands.

"I could not agree more." Frederick circled his desk and sat in his tufted leather rolling chair.

"What does it mean for our plans?" Wagner retook his seat.

"It has set us behind, but we still have nine weeks. I'll relocate assets from São Paulo and continue where Baumann left off."

"Berlin is breathing down my neck. Control of the Atlantic shipping lanes rests on you doing this right."

"I am quite aware, Mr. Wagner, but I assure you we will get another man in place." Frederick sounded more optimistic than he was. It had taken months for the shipboard position to open. Baumann's insider had been working there for days, ready to set the explosives when the time came. However, this man had died alongside Baumann. Given the time-frame, getting another agent aboard that ship would prove challenging, perhaps beyond Frederick's ability.

"I can't stress the importance of this mission." Wagner stood and buttoned his suit coat. "Keep me informed."

"Of course." Frederick walked Wagner out the front door and watched him enter his waiting sedan. As Wagner drove off, Frederick felt the pressure of Berlin's grasp tighten around his throat. With all eyes upon him, this might be his final assignment.

1

The same day

Having divided loyalties was never good, particularly in the spy game. He never expected to be caught in the middle and cursed the day he signed up for this job. Two weeks ago, he would have never doubted the sanity of his actual mission, but Hattie James had a way of getting under anyone's skin in a magical way, even from a distance. However, no matter how unpleasant the circumstance, he would do what needed to be done to protect the Fatherland.

After pulling the sedan into the back alley and parking in the shadows cast by the surrounding two-story buildings, he waited for the delivery truck to pass, dipping in the seat to prevent being seen before exiting. Broad daylight was not ideal for his task, as the possibility of someone spotting them, even off the principal traffic route, was high. However, waiting until darkness came was impossible. Heinz Baumann's logbook had a good chance of being there, but not for long.

He cursed German efficiency. Baumann had served as the SS intelligence section chief in Rio de Janeiro, collecting information on shipping and enemy military activities in the vital capital city for the last five years until his death yesterday. To Baumann's credit and detriment, he had kept meticulous records on every facet of his extensive intelligence-gathering operation. His journal was now in the hands of an FBI agent and destined for an American diplomatic pouch unless intercepted.

The dry cleaner shop's back door was locked but required only a stiletto knife, special training, and elbow grease to open without breaking it. A curious blend of the odors of cleaning solvents and freshly laundered fabrics with a starchy undertone wafted out. Deeper inside, between the crammed rows of hanging clothes in plastic bags, a whiff of warm, moist air from the steamers working their magic on wrinkled items remained faint throughout the industrial end despite the machines not operating.

He'd arrived during the traditional lunch hour when the shop was closed and employees were away. The store would not reopen for another fifty minutes—enough time to finish the job. He slowed, hearing humming coming from the front. Sunlight poured through the entryway to the storefront, where staff greeted customers, so the window blinds were wide open. An attack would have to be swift to minimize the chance of a passerby driving or walking past seeing him in action.

He hugged the wall and inched closer on the balls of his feet until Nala Cohen came into view. She was at a tiny desk behind the customer counter, watching the traffic while eating lunch. She was a short, unimposing woman of average weight, but her training as a spy made her a stealthy threat. Speed and surprise were his only hope of success.

After tightening his grip on the stiletto's pearl handle, he moved swiftly, closing the distance to Cohen in seconds. With his right hand over her mouth, he sliced her throat with the knife in his left and dragged her from the chair in one smooth motion. Her hands went to her throat, but it was too late. Blood oozed from the wound, pooling on the polished concrete floor as Cohen convulsed and gurgled her last ounces of life. Once she stopped moving and he was sure she was dead, he wiped the blade clean on her dress, returned the knife to its secret compartment in his jacket, snatched Cohen's keys from her skirt pocket, and entered the cluttered business office. The entire space was a functional dry cleaner shop, but it was only a front for the true purpose of the building that lay behind a hidden opening accessed by using the key now in his hand.

After raising the wall calendar hung near the gap between two rusty filing cabinets to expose the keyhole, he inserted the small, star-shaped key. The American agent inside would pose a more significant challenge than Cohen. Butler was muscular, well-trained, armed, and would have advance notice once the door began its arc while opening. The element of surprise would not be an advantage this round.

He drew a pistol from his waistband. Predicting every second would count, he cocked the hammer back to shave off the extra time needed to apply added pressure to fire double action. The door would swing inward to the secret room from left to right. He stood as far left as possible, readied his gun in one hand, and clutched the key hanging from the keyhole with the other.

"The things I do for my country," he mumbled before taking three calming breaths to stabilize his aim.

He turned the key.

A click.

Instead of waiting for the door to complete its steady arc, he rushed forward and shoved it open with his right shoulder. This exposed a clean, orderly office the same size as the cluttered one. Butler, the only one inside the room, was seated in his usual chair along the left wall. The man wheeled his sidearm toward the commotion.

He applied light pressure on the trigger before centering on the target, sending a bullet flying toward Butler. It winged his target in the shoulder short of him finishing his pivot. Butler grunted and flinched, providing the extra second needed for the next shot.

A direct hit in the chest.

A dark stain on his white shirt formed and expanded at a rapid pace. Shock consumed Butler's wide eyes, foretelling his inevitable demise through a third blast between the eyes. The force arched Butler back, and he dropped limp to the floor, lifeless in a growing pool of blood.

His focus shifted to locating the motive for coming here and committing these two murders. He painstakingly searched the area, but Baumann's logbook remained elusive. Time was running out. The store was supposed to reopen soon, which meant the shop's staff would return to work sooner. "Think, you idiot. It has to be here," he mumbled, skimming both hands through his hair and scanning the room. The only thing unchecked was

Butler's body. He rifled through the man's pockets, discovering a collection of three keys on a ring. A close inspection determined one was the key to this room, and another was identical to one on Cohen's set, which likely opened the building doors. The third key was shaped like the one for the secret office but was much smaller. He was sure it unlocked a hidden compartment, but where? Nothing stuck out after the search.

Anger built as precious time ticked away. If the contents of Baumann's logbook reached the United States, Germany's intelligence gathering in the Western hemisphere would be decimated, as would their long-fought battle for control of the Atlantic shipping lanes, and every sacrifice he'd made for the last few years would have been for nothing.

He bent and clutched Butler's corpse by the lapels. "Where is it?" he screamed in Butler's face, half expecting a dead man to give up the hiding place. His hope was slipping away, but when he released his hold on Butler, something on the floor beneath the table caught his attention. He focused on the tiny, round metal object and determined it resembled the keyhole used to enter the secret office.

He turned toward the lifeless Butler. "You sneaky little cuss."

The third key fit the lock perfectly, and within seconds, he opened a hidden compartment in the subfloor containing the black journal and stuffed it into the waistband at the small of his back.

After carefully waiting until a delivery truck had cleared the alley, he wrapped the bodies in bedspreads and tossed them into the sedan's trunk. He scrambled to sop up the bloody mess left behind, using customers' garments and tossing the last bit of evidence into the luggage compartment. Once satisfied that no one would suspect two murders had occurred there, he drove away.

But he wasn't done in town. The next stop wasn't part of the mission but was payback.

He went to the heart of the Lapa district well before the waterfront ignited with vibrant nightlife and tourists and partygoers filled the streets, but time was becoming critical. The nightclub was due to open in a few hours, which meant other staff would arrive soon. His opportunity for revenge would be gone if he didn't act quickly.

He parked on the vacant side street. The front door was usually locked at this hour, so he circled to the secondary entrance employees used for cigarette breaks and left unlocked for deliveries. He passed refuse cans and empty produce crates and stopped to pet the cat that took up residence in this area and sometimes the corridor inside.

"You need to stay outside today, girl. Now, go." He shooed away the stray with his hands, earning an agitated meow before she darted farther down the street.

He entered the club. When the door closed, the hallway grew dark, but the stale scent of cigarette smoke led him to the dining area. The room was occupied only by empty tables and chairs and the echoes of the sad stories of many of the drunks who called this place home every day when the doors opened for business.

Only the overhead lights near the bar were on, but light streamed through the bottom gap in the kitchen door, suggesting the owner had recently arrived and was still dealing with the daily produce and meat deliveries. A noise from the other side of the door confirmed his suspicion. Since that area had no direct exit, only windows for ventilation, the conditions could not be more perfect.

After scurrying behind the bar, he grabbed two bottles of the high-end Cachaça, a distilled sugarcane spirit made of seventy-five percent pure alcohol. He had enjoyed this potent spirit a night or two too many, but tonight, it would serve a different purpose.

He poured liberal amounts on the counter, around the door, and tracked it to both exits. After piling dozens of dining linens in strategic locations and soaking them in the liquid to maximize damage and entrap the owner, he stood at the mouth of the corridor, sparked his lighter, lit an alcohol-soaked cloth napkin, and dropped it onto the route of flammable liquor. A trail of flames marched toward the bar and branched off into two tracks. One hurried to the entrance, while another screamed in the kitchen's direction. Every pile of linen burst into a fiery ball, and charry smoke started filling the room, choking out the air.

When the kitchen door opened, it was too late for the owner. The blaze had engulfed the paths to the doors. There would be no escape. Delighting in the sight, he watched as the woman covered her face before he slipped further into the corridor. He calmly walked to his car, smiling at the sweet taste of revenge in his mouth.

The thorn had been plucked.

He drove north out of town, through the tall mountains, and took a dirt road off the main highway, stopping in the tropical forest where there was no guardrail and the shoulder disappeared down a sheer drop. After stuffing the blood-soaked linens into the bedspreads, he popped the trunk, removed Butler's and Cohen's bodies, and rolled each one off the cliff. Momentum took them down the jungle wall until the trees and shrubs enveloped them in their protection, never to be seen again by humans. The cougars or jaguars would feast on them tonight, leaving no trace.

Completing his job created a dilemma: being loyal to one side seemed like a betrayal to the other. He wasn't sure how long he could sustain the status quo and knew he must choose sides soon.

2

The next day

A warm body lay sleeping inches away, but Hattie James had never felt lonelier, more trapped in the bed she'd made for herself. She leaned against the headboard and hugged her knees to her chest, taking care not to wake David while she pined for the one thing she could not have and likely didn't deserve. In twelve days, Maya Reyes had woven her way around Hattie's heart so tightly it hurt to breathe without her there.

Someday, she thought, hoping for a day not too far away when Maya would no longer blame her for bringing Heinz Baumann into their lives and for her sister's death two days ago. Intellectually, Hattie understood Anna's passing was not her fault. She had no way of knowing Baumann was looking for her father, nor how sadistic he was, when she agreed to infiltrate his inner circle. But Karl was involved in a dangerous spy game, and Hattie should have seen the signs or at least been leery, which meant she should have been better prepared. It was a mistake she vowed not to repeat. Perhaps when she could forgive herself, Maya could as well.

Clanking noises from down the hallway meant Eva was in the kitchen, preparing breakfast. Hattie closed her eyes, put aside her mother's diva moments she'd witnessed over the years, and fondly remembered family breakfasts in Washington, DC, when she was a child. Her father always wanted something substantial, with sausage, eggs, toast, cheeses, and fruit, and her mother obliged, but with a Brazilian twist, substituting tapioca crepes for bread and introducing tropical fruits.

After sliding from bed without disturbing the man beside her, Hattie put on a robe, gargled mouthwash in the bathroom, and let the sound of one of her records playing guide her to the kitchen. Her mother was at the island, stirring something in a mixing bowl and swaying to the beat.

"I didn't know you listened to my music," Hattie said, going farther inside.

Eva was startled but spouted a smile when she looked at Hattie. "Good morning, sweetheart. It's one of my favorites. I like the shifting time measures at the bridge and chorus."

"I do, too. It lets the song build. That's why I prefer to open with it."

"It really is a mood setter. I can see why you chose it."

Hattie spied her mother's empty mug on the island before stepping toward the counter next to the refrigerator. "More coffee?"

"Please." Eva stopped stirring, padded to the range, and poured a fraction of the mixture into a frying pan heating over a blue gas flame. "You're up early. Would you like a crepe?"

"I'd love one."

"Are chorizo and egg okay? I'd be happy to make you something else."

"No, no. That's fine, Mother." Hattie filled the cup and placed it next to her mother.

"What about David? Shall I make him some?" Eva worked her wizardry at the stove, adding the correct portions of meat, egg, and cheese.

"He's still out. He had a hard time falling asleep last night."

"Is that the excuse they give these days?" Eva giggled. "You better save some of that for after the wedding."

"Mother, there are some things I refuse to discuss with you." Hattie rolled her eyes. "If you can't respect those boundaries, perhaps now that I'm making a decent income, it's time for David and me to find our own place."

The effort to perpetuate the impression that she and David were engaged while living under Eva's roof was tiresome. The charade of them dating in New York was much more manageable, as the pretense was only for public consumption and ended at the threshold of her apartment. However, in Eva's home, they had no privacy except at night when they closed the door. Everything about their daily life, from the bathroom to the shared dresser, had to promote the lie that they were in love and preparing for a wedding, down to the toothbrushes hanging from the same stand.

"I'm sorry, Hattie." Eva's expression turned sheepish as she flipped her creation onto two plates. "I didn't mean to make you uncomfortable." After returning the pan to the stovetop, she squeezed Hattie's hand, squinting with sadness. "I want you to feel that you and David can stay here for as long as you'd like, and I promise to abide by whatever boundaries you set."

Hattie expected some bumps as they got to know one another again, but she had never seen her mother so remorseful over something said in jest. Her reaction bordered on desperation, making Hattie's throat swell with compassion and regret.

Eva had visited her daughters yearly after divorcing Karl, Hattie's father, spending the summer months in the States, but she had lived by herself in Rio since 1929. She likely filled her days with teaching and evenings with potential suitors but woke every morning to an empty house. It must have been challenging for her to have her family so far away.

Then an image flashed in Hattie's mind that tempered her sympathy for her mother. It was a horrible memory of the reason Eva was alone and why Hattie's younger sister had no mother nearby for her teenage years. Hattie had learned a critical lesson when she caught the woman in bed with another man: infidelity was a choice with a never-ending ripple effect. It hurt everyone around Eva, and Hattie only now saw how it wounded Eva the most. However, it was an injury of her own making. It didn't matter that Eva believed Hattie's father had turned into a Jew-hating Nazi. Nothing justified breaking her vows. She should have left him long before that.

Nevertheless, Hattie returned Eva's gesture by squeezing her hand. "I'm sorry, Mother. I shouldn't have been so cross. Perhaps the ordeal at the plantation is still weighing on me."

"Heavens." Eva pursed her lips. "You were kidnapped, drugged, hunted for sport, and one of you didn't make it back alive. It was a bloodbath, with a dozen slaughtered like hogs. I would guess the nightmares would weigh on you for years." Her eyes shimmered with watery sadness, pulling on

Hattie's sympathies again. Just two weeks ago, the woman had reunited with Hattie. They were on the verge of a new relationship when Heinz Baumann, a sadistic man searching for Karl, almost took Hattie away forever. It would have been a hard pill for anyone to swallow.

"I suppose it will." Hattie hugged her mother before wiping her tears away. "Let's not start the day like this. You've made some beautiful crepes. Let's have breakfast. Then you can help me pick a song list and wardrobe for my debut at the Golden Room this Friday." She grabbed their coffee mugs.

"I'd love that." Her mother straightened her posture, transforming into the confident Eva Machado who once sang to thousands. She garnished her creations with homemade salsa and fresh fruit and joined Hattie at the table, but she popped up seconds later. "I forgot to get the paper."

Hattie gestured for her mother to retake her seat. "You cooked. I'll get it."

"I squeezed some maracuja this morning. Would you like some?"

"Please. I've missed having passion fruit with breakfast. We don't get it often in New York."

"I remember." Eva padded to the cabinet and took out two small juice glasses.

"I'll be right back."

Hattie exited through the front door and walked on the ambling paver pathway through her mother's lush courtyard garden. The colorful palette of pale yellow, vibrant orange, and ocean blue flowers mixed among the thick greenery had all spread their petals for the day and were pointed toward the sky, soaking in the warm autumn morning rays. Hattie had never seen a gardener during her two-week stay, yet the expansive space remained well-tended by her mother's preservation. Hattie suspected Eva's time caring for the flora was another outlet to counter the loneliness.

She opened the weighty wooden gate, collected the rolled newspaper from the ground a few feet away in the driveway, and slid off the rubber band. After unfurling it, Hattie discovered a photo of Heinz Baumann under the headline, "Lobo do Rio."

"Very fitting," she said, suspecting the story would have legs in the local papers for weeks.

The media had labeled Baumann the Wolf of Rio after four of the missing ladies were found alive in cages on his plantation, along with the massacre of Baumann's German workers, whom Hattie's father had left for the police to find. The latter was a ruse to mislead investigators into thinking a gang from the favela had killed the Nazi spies as retribution for kidnapping and murdering their women. Karl's plan seemed to be working.

Hattie closed the gate. While retracing her steps through the courtyard, she flipped the paper over to read the headline of the second story below the fold, "Fogo mata um." Recognizing the picture of the building, she stopped in her tracks before reaching the door. The Halo Club marquee, still intact atop the corner entrance, stuck out among the charred remains of the other half of the structure. The words above the image said that the fire had killed one.

"Maya." Hattie threw a hand to her chest, thinking the worst. Her ragged breathing and rattled state prevented her from fully comprehending the article written in Portuguese. She dashed inside the house. Her pulse thumped faster by the time she reached Eva at the kitchen table and shoved the paper into her face. "What does this say? Please tell me it wasn't Maya."

Eva caught her bearings and focused on the newspaper. "What? Baumann?"

"No." Hattie's hand shook as she pointed to the picture below the fold. "The Halo Club. Someone was killed in the fire."

"Let me see." Eva grabbed her reading glasses from the tabletop and scanned the article under the heart-stopping image. "The story says the fire started early yesterday afternoon before the establishment was scheduled to open. Firemen found one body in the rubble, but it was too badly burned to identify at the scene."

"Dear God." Hattie nearly fainted from her shallow breathing. "I need to use your phone." She didn't wait for permission before lifting the handset from the wall and asking the operator to connect her to one of the few numbers in Rio she had committed to memory—Maya's home phone. "Pick up," she repeated, but the knot in her stomach only twisted tighter as the call continued to ring. Hope let her hang on for twenty rings before she flicked the receiver hook three times and asked to be connected to the Halo Club in the Lapa district.

The operator returned seconds later, explaining in broken English, "I'm sorry, miss, but that number is out of order."

"Thank you," Hattie said calmly and hung up the phone, but she was anything but calm. A person died in the fire, and Hattie could not reach Maya, who always arrived at the club hours before opening to set up for the day. Hattie turned to her mother. "I need to go down there."

"I can take you." Eva pushed up from her chair, but Hattie put up her hand in a stopping motion.

Hattie was an emotional wreck, and having to bottle it up during the car ride might cause her to burst at the seams. She wasn't prepared to explain her deep connection with Maya, a woman she'd known for only two weeks.

"Stay. I'll wake David."

Ten minutes later, once Hattie roused him from bed, David closed the garage door, hopped into the driver's seat of Eva's Ford Deluxe, and coasted down the hill to the main road. He squeezed Hattie's hand after shifting into gear and was at speed. "We'll find her."

Hopefully alive, Hattie thought. "Go to her house first." Her voice shook.

Perhaps Maya was still sleeping or had drunk herself into a stupor overnight after her life's work burned down, but that thought was likely the peak of hopeful thinking. In the twelve days Hattie had known Maya and seen her running a bar and holding up under her sister's disappearance, Maya never took a drink. In fact, Hattie didn't even know if she was a drinker. Not being one would make sense. A club owner would not last long if they drank the profits.

Downtown traffic was frustratingly thick, but Hattie hadn't spent enough Tuesday late mornings in town to know if it was typical for this time of day. David turned onto Maya's street, but her vehicle was not where she typically parked it overnight. Unfortunately, Hattie didn't know whether to take it as a sign that she had already left for the day or had never made it home yesterday.

Her temples throbbed with her anxiety while David parked their sedan at the curb. The instant he set the parking brake, Hattie flew out the car door and up the concrete walkway. She pounded on the door loud enough to frighten a cat sunning on the neighbor's windowsill. Twenty seconds was sufficient time to hear whether Maya was coming, so Hattie removed the small cutout of wood siding below the threshold and fished out the key Maya kept there. Her hands shook so much that she missed the lock twice. Hattie cursed, steadied herself, inserted the key, and opened the front door. The entry hall was shadowy, which meant the window blinds hadn't been raised for the day to let in the sun.

"Maya!" Hattie called out, hoping there would be motion deeper in the house. She eased down the hallway and peeked into the kitchen but found it empty. The living room, Maya's darkroom, and Anna's room were also unoccupied, so she continued toward her last hope of finding Maya at home. After easing the main bedroom door open, she shouted Maya's name again but discovered the bed was immaculate and the bathroom had no sign of being recently used.

Maya wasn't there.

Hattie plopped on the mattress with a heavy heart, closed her eyes, and ran her hand across the bedding. Only four nights ago, she and Maya had made passionate love between those crisp white cotton sheets. Flashes of smooth skin, gentle curves, and sultry eyes forced her breath to hitch. Hattie had dated a dozen women secretly since moving to New York and was even in love once, before Helen Reed broke her heart. Each woman she encountered romantically netted a lasting impression, but her night with Maya was unparalleled. It was raw and erotic and, at times, sweet, tender, and even silly. The juxtaposition of extremes was more intoxicating than all the world's vodka.

Hattie rejected their end or Maya's potential demise in the fire. "It can't be over." Calmer and more determined to find the woman she refused to let go, she pushed herself from the bed and left through the front door, returning the key to its hiding place.

Once in the car again, she said to David, "She's not there. Let's go to the Halo Club."

He squeezed her hand and drove.

They pulled onto the street facing the club within minutes, and Hattie's jaw dropped at the sight. After David parked, Hattie opened the passenger door and exited the car numbly, smelling the charry aftermath. The destruction was devastating, but the picture in the newspaper didn't do the damage justice. The front of the nightclub was intact, but only a skeleton outline of the back half remained. The bar, kitchen, dining room, and stage where Hattie once performed were gone. It was all gone.

"My God." Hattie's knees buckled, but David rushed to her side and supported her by her elbow. A disturbing image of fire surrounding Maya, leaving her no avenue to escape, filled her head. She hoped whoever died in here was overcome by the smoke long before the flames consumed them.

"I got you," he said.

A small crowd of gawkers taking in the extraordinary sight had congregated on the corner. There were no signs of police or firefighting activity, nor was the rubble roped off to keep out looky-loos. The only effort to deter pilferers was a plank of wood nailed across the front doors. It was a sad spectacle that brought Hattie to tears.

After a moment, she gathered herself. "Let's go around to the side."

"Sure." David tightened his grip on her, but Hattie patted his hand.

"I'm fine, really." She shook off his hold. Whatever truth awaited her, she wanted to face it on her own two feet.

The smell of ash and smokey remnants grew stronger as they approached the building. When they passed the last untouched section of the wall, movement from within the remains caught Hattie's eye, giving her a surge of optimism. The object moved again, but Hattie made out the shape of the cat that used to frequent the trash cans behind the club.

Hattie bent at the knees and encouraged the animal to come closer. "Come here, girl." But the creature would have nothing of it and scurried off when a loud crack sounded deeper inside the ruins. Hattie looked up and grabbed David's arm before she fainted.

Maya was combing through the rubble.

"Thank God," Hattie croaked.

Maya stopped and pivoted in their direction. Soot covered her face and arms, and she looked exhausted. Her long, brown hair was uncharacteristically stringy, and her slacks and dark blue blouse were smudged with ash. It was hard to tell from this distance, but Hattie swore her chin was quivering.

"You're alive!" Hattie shouted, slumping with profound relief.

When Hattie lifted a leg to scale a section of burned wood, Maya yelled, "It's not safe! I'll come to you!" She trekked toward Hattie and David, making several twists and turns through the debris until she reached them on the sidewalk. She wiped off a layer of dust that had collected on her pant legs.

"I came as soon as I heard." Hattie stretched to embrace Maya, but the woman pulled back.

"I'm afraid there's not much left to see." Maya sounded accepting of the horrible circumstances besieging her, which was worrisome.

"What happened?" Hattie asked. "Was it a kitchen fire?"

"No. The fire captain said it started near the bar."

"That makes no sense. Did you have something plugged in?"

"No." Maya placed her hands on her hips and ran a hand through her stringy hair. "I can't think what might have ignited it."

Hattie reached out tentatively and touched Maya's elbow. "I read someone was killed. Who was it?"

"Nessa. She was taking on extra hours to help prepare for opening." Maya threw a hand over her mouth, stifling a sob. "If I hadn't been at the grocer dealing with a wrong order, I could have helped her out."

"You don't know that." Hattie stepped closer and placed a hand on Maya's shoulder. "You could have died as well." Maya didn't back away, so Hattie let her hand linger. Maya melted into the gentle touch momentarily before regaining her composure.

"I guess I'll never know." Maya lifted a piece of debris and picked up a water pitcher but threw the cracked vessel back into the ashy pile. "There's nothing left to salvage."

"Do you have insurance?" David asked.

"Yes," Maya said, "but I'm not sure how it works when they suspect arson."

"Arson?" A sickening feeling swept over Hattie at the fear that this might have been connected to her father or the events at Baumann's plantation. "Who would set fire to the Halo Club?"

"I don't know."

"How will you survive?" Hattie asked.

"I'll be fine. My house and car are paid for. I'm more worried about my employees and what will happen to them. Some can't afford to miss a single paycheck."

"If there's anything I can do to help."

Maya gave Hattie an angry look. "You've done enough helping. Now I'm planning my sister's funeral for Saturday." She stopped mercifully short of delivering the gut-wrenching blow of laying blame for Anna's death at Hattie's feet again.

Hattie pushed back the emotion swelling her throat. Moving beyond the hurt between them would be a greater challenge than she had expected. Maybe leaving Rio was for the best. If not for Agent Butler breathing down her neck by threatening to jail Hattie's sister and brother-in-law if Hattie didn't flush out her father—one of America's most-wanted fugitives—she would pack her things and broken heart, return to New York, and take her chances at rebuilding her career in a city that considered her the daughter of a traitor. But she knew Butler and thought she knew Maya. He would tighten the screws to achieve his desired outcome—Karl James's head on a pike. Until that changed, she would remain patient, concentrate on performing at the Golden Room, and keep trying to break down Maya's walls.

3

Friday, three days later

Hattie stood in the wings of the famed Golden Room stage, smoothing the front of her sophisticated white floor-length gown. It was adorned tastefully in sequins designed to sparkle in the lighting. When her mother let her "shop" from her vast wardrobe collection at home, Hattie never thought she would steer her toward this stunning dress. It was fit for a royal wedding, and she felt like a million bucks in it.

She peeked around the curtain to eye the main room. The two-tiered music hall was trimmed with brass and gold finishings. A raised section started past the ornate bar, ringed the room on three sides, and was divided by a polished wood railing, giving those elevated tables an unobstructed view of the stage. The packed room was awash with men and women adorned elegantly in tuxedos and formal gowns, eating from fine china, drinking from sparkling crystal glasses, and smoking expensive cigars and cigarettes. The chatter of hundreds of conversations created a loud hum.

Hattie focused on the center near the front and found her mother at tonight's table of honor. Eva had dressed in a glittering black dress also fit for a ball and had styled her long brown hair to gather above the neck, exposing her bare upper back. She had chosen black, not white, to not stand out as much, telling Hattie, "This is your night to shine."

Butterflies in Hattie's stomach swarmed when the lights in the dining room lowered, and the room quieted slowly. Her heart raced, making her acutely aware of every little noise in the space. She could not remember the last time she was this nervous before a performance, but she attributed her anxiety to what she considered to be at stake. Tonight marked her official entry into the Brazilian music world and Rio's high society. Eva had held those honors for decades, so Hattie suspected the expectations were elevated. Disappointing the crowd would mean letting down her mother and herself.

A male voice came over the loudspeaker and announced in Portuguese and English, "The Golden Room and Copacabana Palace are proud to present the American songbird Hattie James."

The arched curtain retracted from the middle, revealing the entire band and David at the piano on the right. Hattie emerged from the wings onto the stage and into the blinding lights. The audience roared with shouts, whistles, and deafening applause. She gave David's hand a tight squeeze before she passed.

"Your hand is sweaty," he said. "You got this."

Hattie swallowed her anxiety when the crowd howled even louder as the musicians began to play. She stepped up to the microphone stand at center stage a few feet from the edge and broke into her first song. She never imagined Rio as the location for her comeback after her US career stalled following the sensational news of her father giving national secrets to the Nazis. However, she was glad it was here, on the same stage where her mother had captured the hearts of thousands of Brazilians.

Her musical choices tonight were overladen on the ballad side, containing a hint more sadness than in her past performances. With the horrific ordeal at Baumann's plantation, Anna's death, and the Halo Club burning still weighing heavy on her, she feared her energy might not carry her through to the end of the show. But when her show was over, Hattie felt redeemed by the standing ovation and her mother's beaming smile.

David offered his hand when she stepped toward the wings. "You were amazing," he said. "Just when I thought you couldn't get any better, you pull off a performance like that."

Hattie kissed him on the cheek. "It was good being up there. When I performed with Maggie last week, I realized I'd forgotten what it was like to sing with a full band behind me." She missed her friend and their friendly competition as RCA's top two best-selling female singers.

"You belong up there."

"So do you." Hattie squeezed his hand before letting go. "Despite not speaking the language, you did great with only three band rehearsals."

"Music is the universal language." He shrugged.

"I suppose you're right," Hattie said. Otherwise, how could Hattie have sung to an international audience in English and received a standing ovation? She slid her arm around his as they descended the stage stairs and reentered the main dining room through the employee door.

The crowd was respectful, acknowledging her with more applause but allowing her to join Eva and the three men at the table of honor without stopping. One man was Frederick Ziegler, the Swiss ambassador Eva introduced at the Golden Room the night Hattie sang with Maggie Moore. Her mother had appeared smitten by Frederick throughout the show, and now she greeted Hattie with an impassioned hug. "Sweetheart, that was perfection. I couldn't be prouder."

Hattie sensed the motherly pride, wishing she had felt more of that during her childhood, not like she always came in second to Eva's singing career.

The men stood to greet and congratulate Hattie. Eva introduced two as Brazilian diplomats. Both congratulated her, and one asked if she would be interested in performing at his daughter's wedding. Between the FBI lurking over her shoulder, the aftermath of the Baumann Plantation nightmare, and the Halo Club being destroyed, Hattie's life was in turmoil. Committing to anything beyond her Golden Room contract might constitute too much, so she declined.

Ziegler was the last to address her. "Another stellar performance, Miss James. You will undoubtedly be Rio's sought-after act this year." He turned to Eva and bowed a fraction before returning his attention to Hattie. "And your mother, of course." He certainly had the diplomatic thing rehearsed.

"Thank you, Mr. Ziegler. I'm glad you enjoyed the show."

David held out a chair for Hattie, and Ziegler did the same for Eva.

Eva waved to their waiter.

He scurried over and placed a steaming teacup and a small honey container in front of Hattie. "Your tea, Miss James."

"Thank you," she said, fixing her drink to taste.

The man reached inside his black tuxedo jacket and pulled out a single stem of edelweiss. "A gentleman asked I give you this, miss. He seemed rather taken by your performance."

Hattie took the flower and glanced around, searching for her father, as no one else would have given her that particular bloom. She suspected he had left like he'd done when he first saw her at the Halo Club. She returned her attention to the waiter, holding the edelweiss like a treasured heirloom. "Thank you. If you see him again, please pass along my gratitude."

The server nodded and scurried off to another table.

David remained quiet, but Eva pursed her lips, giving Hattie the side-eye. Edelweiss was not natively grown in Brazil, and to Hattie's knowledge, the only place to get one so fresh was from Eva's indoor flower room, where she grew her favorite plants. She'd obviously put it together that Karl had sent the gift and wasn't happy about him staying in contact with Hattie.

David refilled everyone's champagne glasses while Hattie stuck to her tea. The conversation among their group was pleasant, with the group discussing music, food, their travels, and their fondness for gardening.

"You must see Frederick's garden, Hattie," Eva said. "He showed it to me yesterday. Goodness, it's so lush and well maintained. I absolutely loved it."

"That's a grand idea," Ziegler said. "You and David should join Eva and me at my estate for lunch tomorrow. I'd love to show you the grounds."

Hattie's chest tightened as she remembered the pressing event she had to attend the following afternoon. "I appreciate the offer, Mr. Ziegler, but David and I have the funeral of Anna Reyes tomorrow."

Ziegler acknowledged by tilting his head slightly. "Ah, yes. You must pay your respects to the plantation victim who didn't survive."

"Thank you for understanding. Perhaps next Saturday." Hattie sensed tears coming, but falling apart in front of a group of Rio's elites on her opening night would not be a pleasant sight. "If you'll excuse me a moment." She pushed back her chair, grabbing the edelweiss.

"Of course." Ziegler stood, as did the other men at the table.

Eva looked concerned.

David pulled back Hattie's seat. "I'll come with you."

"Please stay," Hattie said before whispering into his ear, "I need a few minutes alone."

David nodded his understanding and kissed her on the cheek.

Hattie sensed his stare all the way to the bar. He likely suspected what she was feeling—the weight of her sorrows threatening to consume her, driving her to seek solace at the bottom of a vodka glass. Minus her longing to reconnect with Maya, he would have been accurate. She could not show up at Anna's funeral drunk or looking like a hungover wreck. Her respect for Maya and for herself would not allow it.

She eyed an empty stool at the end, silently thanking her mother for helping her select a dress that gave at the thigh and waist, making it easier to move. Climbing onto it was a snap. She acknowledged the man in a military uniform seated beside her with a polite nod before admiring the gold and brass accents along the bar top and at the back wall.

Moments later, the bartender appeared and placed a napkin in front of her. "Great show, Miss James."

"Thank you, Thomas." She accented his name correctly.

"What will it be?" he asked.

"Soda water, please."

"You got it." As he fixed her drink, the conversation between Mr. Costa, the restaurant manager, and the head waiter five feet away grew animated.

"What's up with them?" Hattie wagged her thumb in their direction.

"Senhor Costa fired the assistant manager tonight for being late again, so it's chaotic behind the scenes."

"Interesting," Hattie said, surmising a job opening of that caliber at the Copacabana Palace was a rarity. The head waiter appeared agitated as he left. When the manager turned to walk away, Hattie called, "Senhor Costa, do you have a moment?"

He looked flustered but came to her. "Yes, Miss James? Has everything been satisfactory?"

"Top-notch," Hattie said. "This might be outside my purview, but I understand the assistant manager position has opened up."

"Yes, it has."

"I know the perfect candidate. She's—"

"She?" Costa's dismissive tone suggested he didn't think a woman could run an establishment of such elegance as the Golden Room, which was infuriating.

"Yes, a woman. Maya Reyes is an experienced nightclub owner you would be lucky to have. In fact, my mother highly recommended her when I first arrived in Rio, and I was honored to perform at her club. I'd still be working there if it weren't for this week's horrific events. So, if you want to please me and Miss Machado, the least you can do is meet with her."

Thomas stood quietly behind the bar, drying a glass while watching this exchange with a slight grin.

Costa appeared browbeaten. His new headliner and the most influential woman in the country had cornered him into an untenable position. He might be ostracized from Rio's elite circles if he didn't take the interview. "Of course, Miss James. I'd be happy to see her. Have her call the club reservation desk Monday to schedule an appointment with me."

"Thank you, Mr. Costa. You won't be disappointed."

He spun on his heel and marched away, flagging down a waiter and berating him for some error with the food.

Thomas placed the glass on the back counter before leaning an elbow on the bar in front of Hattie. "I've never seen him agree to anything."

"A little fear never hurt anyone." Hattie laughed.

"I'd say he was up to his neck in it," said the uniformed man with a slight Texas drawl. Hattie turned, and he tipped his cocktail toward her in a show of respect. "You lassoed him like a bulldogger out of the chute."

Hattie laughed. "Like a what?"

"You know, the cowboy who wrestles the steer to the ground."

She laughed harder. "If there's one thing I learned from my mother, it's how to handle men with little regard for women."

"Well, I'd say she did a bang-up job. Where are my manners?" He stood and extended his hand. He was slightly over six feet tall, with more muscle than average. His short sandy hair was similar in color to hers, but his square jaw made him quite striking. "Lieutenant Commander Leo Bell at your service, Miss James."

They shook hands.

"It's a pleasure to meet another American in Rio, Commander Bell. I wasn't aware the United States military was in Brazil."

"Just me and the Marine guards at the moment. I'm a naval attaché assigned to the embassy. I arrived a few days ago."

"What does a naval attaché do?"

"That's a dandy question. As far as I can tell, I give my advice to a bunch of bigwig diplomats who pay me no mind."

"That doesn't sound very satisfying."

"I'm not sure yet, but I get to travel and meet the most beautiful women." Bell waved the bartender closer. "May I buy you a drink?"

"Please, call me Hattie. Just soda water for me tonight, but thank you."

"Hattie it is. You know, it's funny meeting you here. I saw you perform with Maggie Moore at the Copacabana club in New York City. When I read you were headlining at the Copacabana Palace here in Rio, I had to come."

"That was a fun show. In fact, Maggie performed here last week and cajoled me into joining her on stage."

"I'm sorry I missed it. That must have been some performance since you're a regular here now."

"I like to think it was."

"Come now, Hattie. Don't be so modest. When it comes down to it, I traveled five thousand miles just to see you perform."

Hattie liked this man. He was polite, amusing, and easy on the eyes. However, his friendliness, particularly since learning she had been surrounded by spies most of her life, made her wonder if he had come tonight for a reason. Still, she laughed. "You sure know how to make a girl feel special."

"Well," he said with an adorable smile, "if there's one thing my daddy taught me, it's how to treat a lady with respect."

"I'd say he did a bang-up job, Commander Bell."

"Please, call me Leo."

"Leo it is."

David suddenly appeared and placed a hand on Leo's shoulder. His jaw was set, and he didn't look happy. "Hey, pal, that's my seat."

Leo focused on David's hand before looking him in the eye. "Now, that's not a polite way to say hello. How about you try that again, pal?"

"David." Hattie softened her tone to defuse the tension between the men. "This is Commander Leo Bell. He's a naval attaché at the US Embassy."

"I don't care who he is. That's my seat." David didn't take his eyes off Bell.

"I've been sitting here for the last hour," Leo said, "so that makes it my seat."

"Hattie is my fiancée, so any seat next to her is mine."

Leo rose from his chair and stood toe-to-toe with David, towering over him by several inches and likely outweighing him by forty pounds of muscle. "I beg to differ."

The manager approached. "Is there a problem here, gentlemen?"

"I was telling this mac here—" David started, but Hattie interrupted.

"There's no problem, Mr. Costa. We're having a pleasant conversation. Isn't that right, Mr. Townsend?" She pivoted to him, pelting him with eye daggers until he lowered his defensive posture.

"That's right, a pleasant conversation," David said.

Hattie turned again to the club manager. "Please put Commander Bell's bill on my tab to make up for any misunderstanding."

"I'll see to it, Miss James." Costa looked sternly at David before walking away and whispering something to the bartender.

Hattie refocused on Leo. "It was nice meeting you, Leo, but I'm afraid I must return to my party."

Leo gave a polite nod. "It was a fine pleasure meeting you, Hattie."

"I'll leave a note with the manager that if you come back to see another of my shows, he's to seat you at a proper table."

"That's mighty kind of you."

David offered Hattie his arm while narrowing his eyes at Leo. He led her toward their group. "What the hell, Hattie?"

She spoke softly, keeping her smile plastered and acknowledging fawning guests as she passed. "I should ask you the same thing. What's the matter with you, marking your territory like that?"

"What was I supposed to do? Everyone at the table saw you laughing with him and looked at me, expecting me to do something."

"So you pick a fight with a man twice your size who did nothing wrong?"

"Let's talk about this when we get home," he said as they stepped closer to their table.

"Trust me, we will." Hattie reached their table and acted like nothing happened. "Mother, have I told you that you look stunning tonight?"

"Thank you, sweetheart, and so do you."

Hattie kissed her mother on the cheek. "I'm going to change out of your beautiful gown so I don't ruin it. I'll be right back." Hattie turned her attention to the men across from Eva, who had stood at her arrival. "Gentlemen, it's been a pleasure. If you'll excuse me?"

"Of course," Ziegler said. The others bowed their heads.

Hattie weaved through the music hall and entered the employee-only area through an unmarked door. The corridor was less fancy than the room she left but not as run-down as some dives she had worked at while climbing the ladder.

A golden star with her name blazoned in bold black letters adorned her dressing room door. Below it, in smaller cursive, were the words "The Palace." She paused to take in the moment. Seven weeks ago in New York, she lost her recording contract and agent on the same day, starting the downward spiral of her singing career. She'd gone from the top to the bottom in record time, but tonight, that star proved her persistence and hard work had paid off. Hattie James was back. Breaking into the international market was no longer a someday goal. She was in it, headlining at South America's most prominent nightclub. The only thing that could have made this moment more perfect was having Maya by her side to witness it.

Hattie refocused, tempering her pining but not letting go of it. Doing so would be impossible, and trying would break her.

She slid inside, closing the door behind her. The dressing room was plush, with a soft, comfortable couch, a wet bar in the corner, a walk-in closet for her stage costumes, a large, well-lit vanity, and a personal restroom. She'd brought in several of her favorite products, but the Palace provided a stylist from their on-site salon to do her hair and makeup before the show. That woman knew exactly how to bring out Hattie's best features and make her feel like a star. However, one feature of the room stood out— her private enclosed patio with a locked gate leading to a reserved parking spot five feet away. The pampered experience was out of this world.

After placing the edelweiss on the vanity, Hattie unzipped her gown, slipped it off, and added it to the hanger she'd left on the coffee table when she changed for her performance earlier that night. The light inside the closet automatically came on when she opened the door.

She yelped, clutching the dress to her body. "Father, what are you doing in there?"

"I needed to talk to you." Karl was dressed in a waiter's uniform.

"Not in my underclothes." Hattie wagged her index finger at the first set of garments hanging on the rod. "Hand me my clothes."

"These?" Karl lifted the hanger with a blouse and a pair of slacks.

"Yes, now turn around."

Someone knocked, and a muffled voice came from the other side. "Are you all right, Miss James? I heard a scream."

"I'm fine!" Hattie shouted, tiptoed to the door, and locked it. "I dropped something."

"Ring the front desk if you need anything."

"I will." Hattie dressed quickly. "You can turn around, Father." She handed him her stage gown to hang on the rod and snatched the low-heeled black pumps from the closet floor after he stepped out. Balancing to slip on her shoes, she asked, "What's so important that you broke into my dressing room?"

"What was Frederick Ziegler doing at your table?"

"He was Mother's guest. She saw him at the club a few weeks ago and said they go way back."

"This can't be a coincidence." Karl looked worried. "He may be Swiss, but our conversations over the years led me to believe he's more loyal to Hitler than Switzerland."

"You're saying he's a Nazi?"

"I can't say for sure."

A rattle on the doorknob grabbed her attention. David called out from the hallway. "Hattie? The door is locked."

"I'm dressing. Give me a few minutes!" Hattie shouted. She turned toward her father, speaking softer. "This place is like Grand Central Station."

"I better go. Keep an eye on your mother and don't trust Ziegler."

Hattie squinted in concern. "Do you think he's dangerous?"

"All Nazis are. I love you, sweetheart." Karl kissed her on the cheek, slipped out the patio door, and disappeared into the night.

Hattie touched the spot her father kissed, and whispered, "I love you too, Father."

She slumped onto the couch to stop her head from spinning. Three weeks ago, she was singing in a dump without the prospect of ever singing at an A-list club, was resigned to living a life alone with only a broken heart as company, and had thought spies only existed in movies. All that had been turned upside down when she stepped foot in Rio. She was a star again, would do anything for Maya Reyes, and had turned into her father, seeing spies everywhere.

"Breathe," she told herself. "You'll get through this."

4

The next day

Ascending the stairs to the Church of Our Lady of the Candelária in Rio's Centro district brought back unpleasant memories from Hattie's childhood. The last time she stepped foot inside a church, she was nineteen. Her mother, a devout Catholic, dragged Hattie and her sister to mass every Sunday when they were kids, but once Hattie witnessed Eva breaking her wedding vows, she never returned, choosing to believe in a higher power in her own way.

This cathedral was more magnificent than the one she frequented as a child in Washington, DC. The Baroque architecture grand façade flanked by two tall bell towers and adorned with statues of saints and intricate stone carvings rivaled pictures she'd seen of any European cathedral.

She and David followed a group of funeral-goers through the imposing entrance of massive wooden doors. The interior was equally impressive, with high ceilings and abundant natural light streaming through large windows. Sophisticated frescoes and gold leaf detailing gilded the walls and vaulted top. The main altar was an elaborate work of art with more sculptures of religious figures. A casket surrounded by candles and flowers was at its center.

Mourners dressed smartly in suits and conservative dresses paid their respects in a somber atmosphere, filling the six pews closest to the front. The air held the scent of incense, adding to the reverence of the occasion.

Hattie picked up a flyer with Anna's photo at the entrance. The text was written in Portuguese, but she discerned it was an obituary of Anna's brief life. It also listed the short schedule of events, including the service at one, a graveside burial at three, and a reception at Maya's home at five.

Hattie and David walked down the center aisle between the pews. She recognized many of the faces as employees of the Halo Club. Several more were unknown to her, but she suspected they were Maya's and Anna's friends or neighbors. Heads turned, and mourners from the nightclub muttered their excitement at seeing what they considered music royalty among them. Hattie found it unsettling when the people she worked with treated her like a queen after she appeared at the Golden Room, acting giddy around her and bowing when she walked past. It mortified her that they were doing the same at Anna's funeral.

The sound of camera shutters snapping pictures meant Hattie had become a spectacle, and staying would be challenging. However, she wanted to pay her respects before leaving. She approached the altar and saw Maya in the first pew. The absence of anyone sitting with her brought into clarity the fact that Maya was now truly alone in the world. It broke Hattie's heart. She wished they were on better terms, if not as lovers, at least as friends, so she could comfort her and carry some of her burdens.

Hattie paused, coming even with Maya's row. Maya's head was bowed. She looked like a shadow of her once vibrant self and appeared lost. Hattie kneeled before her, clutching her hands. Their gazes met. Maya's tear-filled eyes were bloodshot and puffy from days of unbearable grief. When Maya's lips trembled, Hattie choked back her own tears.

Hattie squeezed. "I'm afraid my coming is creating a commotion among the staff, so I won't stay, but I want you to know I'll be whatever you need to help you get through this."

Maya threw a hand over her mouth and sobbed. "Please stay."

"Of course I will." Hattie rose, sat on the pew next to Maya, and wrapped an arm around her shoulder.

David settled beside Hattie.

The priest spoke at the podium, expressing gratitude for everyone's presence to honor Anna Reyes. For the next hour in that church, Hattie was the rock Maya needed, reassuring the grieving woman when she looked lost during the solemn hymns and bolstering her when she wept at the speeches. Hattie had become the companion she hoped she could continue to be long after this day ended.

At the cemetery, when Anna's casket was lowered into her resting place, Hattie served as Maya's legs when Maya's knees buckled. When the mourners paid their respects by adding a single rose stem to Anna's grave and shaking Maya's hand, Hattie remained by her side and took Maya's cues. She held her hand whenever Maya reached for hers. Wiped Maya's tears with her thumbs when she looked into her eyes. Embraced Maya whenever her shoulders crumbled. Hattie was the partner she'd dreamed of being, if only for that afternoon.

Later at the reception, each mourner brought a dish of food or drink and laid it on the table Hattie and David had set up in Maya's living room. David stayed there, helping serve guests throughout the two-hour gathering. Hattie remained by Maya's side, tending to her needs and acting as the gate-keeper for the well-wishers so Maya was never overwhelmed. It helped that most of the visitors were starstruck with Hattie, allowing her to dominate the conversation when Maya wasn't up to it.

It was nearing seven, and Maya's obligations to the community would soon end. Many people had left after gracefully paying their respects. The front door opened again, and Hattie suspected more guests had exited, but the one person she didn't expect to see at Anna's funeral reception entered the room. She snapped her head toward Maya, who was speaking in Portuguese with a woman.

When the woman kissed Maya on the cheek and stepped away, Maya redirected her attention to Hattie. She looked tired. "Is that it?"

"Not yet. Brace yourself." Hattie rubbed Maya's arms. "I'll ask him to leave."

Maya craned her neck toward the room's entrance. Her eyes turned fiery. "What the hell is he doing here?"

"I don't know, but I'll tell him he's not welcome." Hattie moved to step toward their new visitor, but Maya pulled on her arm.

"No, I want to hear what he has to say."

The man eyed the remains of the lovingly prepared dishes on the table but took nothing.

A Halo Club employee approached Maya. Hattie recognized her as a cook who worked in the kitchen but couldn't think of her name. Maya greeted her with an affectionate embrace and spoke in Portuguese. At the same time, Hattie kept her eye on the uninvited guest, who walked about the room, studying the modest furnishings. The inspection felt intrusive.

Maya and the woman embraced tenderly, their eyes teary, until the woman said goodbye and departed.

The man made his way to Maya. He acknowledged Hattie and spoke in English. "Miss Reyes, I came to pay my respects."

"Respects?" Maya said in a scoffing manner. "If you had shown your respect by doing your job when I first came to you, Chief Inspector Silva, my sister might still be alive."

"We had no way of knowing her disappearance differed from the hundreds who go missing daily and return days later."

Maya's eyes narrowed, and her tone was sharp. "It didn't take much for us to piece it together. We talked to people you should have interviewed."

"We can't change the past," Silva said. "I came to say that you and Miss James have been cleared of any wrongdoing in the plantation massacre."

"That's very nice of you to wait until my sister's funeral to tell us we won't be charged with killing the people who kidnapped us, hunted us like wild animals, and shot my sister. You deserve a prize for showing such kindness." Maya's face flushed red with mounting anger.

"Perhaps this isn't the time for this, Inspector Silva," Hattie said, positioning herself between him and Maya to prevent the melee she saw coming.

"Perhaps you're right, Miss James. Good day, Miss Reyes." Silva bowed his head and walked away, snatching a dessert from the table on his way out.

Once the door closed, David appeared in the living room. "That's it. Everyone is gone."

Hattie turned to Maya, her anger melting into sadness. "I can stay if you'd like, maybe help put things away."

Maya's lips trembled. "Please stay."

"Let's get this place cleaned up," Hattie said.

Within an hour, Maya, Hattie, and David had rearranged the room to its original configuration, stored the rest of the food in the refrigerator, washed the dishes, and tagged containers with their owner's name for return by next week.

"At least you won't need to cook for days," David said, tossing a dish rag over his left shoulder. "By the way, I love your darkroom setup. Are you a professional?"

"My father was," Maya said. "I dabble in it."

"Did you take the photos of Anna that were in the church?"

"Yes." Maya let out a long, breathy sigh. "I did."

He patted her shoulder. "Your mailbox looked like you hadn't gotten to it in a while, so I put everything there." He pointed toward the counter in a little alcove near the back door.

"Thank you." Maya picked up the stack of mail and flipped through the envelopes, stopping on a particular one. She opened it and read the letter. Her jaw set, and her head shook. "It figures."

"What is it?" Hattie asked, stepping closer.

"The insurance company is holding payment on my claim for the club until the fire department concludes its arson investigation."

"And when will that be?"

Maya clutched the page, crumpling the middle. "It says to contact the fire chief or Inspector Silva at police headquarters for more information."

"For heaven's sake." Hattie flapped her arms in frustration.

"That man will haunt me forever."

"Not if I have anything to do with it." Hattie extended her hand. "May I take the letter?"

Maya held it out but squinted in curiosity when Hattie took it. "Why?"

"My mother has a great influence in this town. I'll have her speak to someone who can light a fire under the fire department to wrap up their investigation and get you that insurance money."

"I..." Maya's eyes filled with tears again. "I don't know how to thank you."

Hattie rubbed Maya's arm. "Don't you know I'd do anything for you?"

"I..." Maya averted her eyes. "Thank you."

"Until that check comes in and you can rebuild, you'll need to work. The assistant manager position at the Golden Room opened up yesterday, so I talked to the manager, and he wants to interview you."

Maya jerked her head back. "The Palace won't hire a woman to run that club."

"Well, this manager has agreed to meet with you." Hattie held back that her mother would ostracize him if he didn't. "Mr. Costa said to call the reservation desk on Monday and ask to schedule a meeting with him."

"I don't want you pulling strings around town helping me, Hattie."

Hattie took Maya by both arms and looked her squarely in the eyes. "I know leaning on me today doesn't mean you're over being angry at me for bringing Baumann into our lives, but I won't let that stop me from doing what's right. The Golden Room needs a good assistant manager, and I can't think of anyone more qualified than you."

"I don't know, Hattie." Maya closed her eyes, rubbing her forehead. "It feels like I'm taking advantage of your celebrity."

Hattie sighed at Maya's reluctance. "I signed a six-month contract with the Palace with an option for an extension. Frankly, having someone of your caliber at the helm, watching my back, would put me at ease."

Maya shook her head again.

"Just take the interview. See what Costa has to offer. If you're uncomfortable with the terms, don't accept."

"It doesn't feel right." Maya pursed her lips. "Me getting a job while the rest of my employees are out of work."

"As the assistant manager, you would be in a hiring position and could transform that place into the country's most woman-friendly nightclub, just like you did with the Halo Club."

Maya formed a slight grin. "Some of my people would faint if I got them work at the Palace."

"Maybe they would stop bowing and treating me like royalty."

Maya let out a little laugh. "That will never happen."

"Well, it's worth a shot."

Minutes later, David went to the car, and Hattie and Maya stood in the hallway with their heads lowered, delaying an awkward goodbye.

"Thank you for staying today," Maya said. "I couldn't have gotten through the day without you."

Hattie raised Maya's chin with an index finger. "Anything for you."

The moment would have been ripe for a kiss a week ago, but Hattie hesitated to rush things. Instead, she hugged Maya and wished her luck for the interview. She walked out the door hopeful yet wishing she could have done more to heal Maya's broken heart.

5

Six days later

Hattie fed off the audience's energy to make the final note of the set the strongest of the evening. Her mother, seated again at the table of honor, was the first to her feet, a sign Hattie's performance had improved, as had their relationship. The standing ovation from the packed house intoxicated her, and Hattie raised her arms in pride before bowing to showcase her gratitude.

The curtains closed. While David remained on stage to help clean up with the band, Hattie walked down the back corridor toward her dressing room. Halfway there, a familiar voice called out, "Awe-inspiring show tonight, Miss James."

"Thank you, Mr. Costa. I've been working on mixing up the set list and arrangements to keep the performances fresh."

"I could tell. If the crowds hold up, we might want to renegotiate your contract to add a second show on Friday and Saturday nights, especially during the peak tourist season from December through April, if we agree on your extension."

"Do you really think we could sell out two shows a night?"

"And then some. Hotel reservations from the United States tripled after we placed ads in American newspapers announcing you were performing here in residence."

Hattie laughed, thinking RCA Records and Howard Price, her former talent agent, could shove their doom and gloom predictions. They'd said no housewife would want to buy records sung by the daughter of an accused traitor. However, Costa's report proved them dead wrong. Not only would they put out good money for her music, but they were lined up, willing to travel over five thousand miles to watch her perform. If this came to fruition, Hattie would have to consider hiring a local agent to negotiate on her behalf.

Europe was the next logical step, but with war waging there, that would have to wait. That made securing a recording contract her immediate objective. The only question was where. If she accepted a deal in Brazil, she would likely be expected to record in Portuguese or Spanish to cater to the Latin market. However, her language skills were weak, and her accent would make her a laughingstock, leaving English the way to go, which limited her choices. RCA Victor was out after the owner fired her. Deca Records in London was top tier, but the war made it unavailable. That left only Columbia Records in New York City for national exposure, but they might not be interested after RCA's hatchet job on her.

Hattie sighed. Her options to take her career to the next level were few, but she would remain patient. She continued down the hallway to her dressing room, plopped onto the plush couch, and kicked off her shoes. If she didn't have to return to the dining room and visit with her mother, she would pull her bra off and settle in for a long nap.

After several minutes of quiet, a knock drew her attention. "I have your tea," the muffled voice called out, bringing a smile to Hattie's lips and ridding her of exhaustion.

"Please come in." Hattie sprang to her feet as the door opened, and she circled to the front of the coffee table.

Maya walked in, carrying a teacup and a small container, and handed them to Hattie. "I brought the honey separately as you asked."

"Thank you. The bartenders tend to over-sweeten the drinks." Hattie placed both items on the tabletop, added the right amount of sweetener, and stirred with a spoon from the cup saucer. She took a sip to coat and soothe her vocal cords.

"I know." Maya sighed. "They were taught to prime the pump to entice the guests to order desserts. I've told them to stop the practice and scale down to traditional ratios, but retraining everyone will take some time."

"Look at you." Hattie laughed. "Only three days and already making sweeping changes."

"I refuse to manipulate the customers."

Hattie had kept her distance while Maya got oriented with the new job, and tonight marked the most they'd spoken to one another. Maya still seemed detached and emotionally flat.

"Which is why I know you'll make the best assistant manager the Golden Room has seen." When Maya shifted to leave, Hattie put her teacup down and turned her by the arm. "Any progress on the investigation or word from the insurance company? It's almost been two weeks since the fire."

"Still ongoing." Maya moved again to go, but Hattie grabbed her arm once more.

"Talk to me, Maya. I know you're still hurting." She stepped closer and chanced caressing her cheek. "Let me help you."

Maya's breathing deepened, which Hattie took as a sign of yearning, but she reassessed when Maya jerked her hand away. "I can't do this, Hattie. Anna's passing is still too raw in my heart, and I still—"

"Blame me." Hattie closed her eyes to the truth. It still stung deeply.

"I don't know if blame is the right word, but I associate you with her death. When I see you, I relive her being shot over and over again."

"It will get easier. I promise." Hattie forced a slight smile to prevent giving in to the tears threatening to overtake her. "If you need me to keep my distance, it will be the hardest thing I've had to do, but I will."

"I think that is for the best." Maya dipped her head and walked toward the door.

When she put her hand on the knob, Hattie called out, "I'll wait for you, Maya Reyes, for as long as it takes."

Maya glanced at Hattie and held her gaze for several beats. The longing look in her eyes gave Hattie hope that time would heal Maya's heart and bring her back to where she belonged.

Once Maya left, Hattie changed out of her dress and slipped on a comfortable pair of slacks, a tasteful white blouse, and her favorite flats. Her selection was a little underdressed for the Golden Room, but her ninety-minute high-energy show in three-inch heels had her toes throbbing. She would rest her tired feet and put on her happy face for the remainder of the evening.

After removing her stage makeup and applying some powder and rouge for a natural look, she returned to the dining room. Instead of going straight to her mother's table, she veered off to say hello to a familiar face she had seen in the crowd during her performance.

"It's good to see you again, Commander Bell. I see the manager gave you a much better seat tonight."

He stood, offering her the chair beside him. "That she did, but why so formal, Miss James? What happened to Leo?" he asked in his distinctive Texas drawl while giving her a playful wink.

She sat. "Perhaps it's the uniform."

"Well, next Friday night, I'll have to break out the old civilian suit my wife insisted I pack. That should fix things right up."

"Actually, Leo"—Hattie emphasized the man's name—"I'm quite fond of the uniform. You stand out in a crowd of black suits and tuxedos."

"Now I'm not sure what to wear."

A waiter came by and filled the extra water glass on the table.

"I take it your wife didn't accompany you to Brazil."

He sighed. "No, and she wasn't too happy about me leaving for six months."

"I can tell you miss her." The melancholy in his voice told her so.

"Yes, I do." Leo raised his cup of amber liquid and sipped. "Tell me, Hattie. What brings you to Rio besides singing at the Copacabana Palace?"

That was a loaded question, one Hattie couldn't answer truthfully. She could not blurt out that the FBI coerced her into flushing out her father, the accused traitor who gave secrets to the Nazis, but she could talk about the other reason.

"I needed to kick-start my career again after the bad press about my father, so I came here to follow in my mother's footsteps."

"Ah, I read about him. It's good to hear you didn't run and hide like I did."

Hattie cocked her head. "What did you hide from?"

"My father, like you."

"What did he do?"

"He's a drunk who shot and killed my mother when I was seventeen, so instead of hanging around for all the whispers and being called the son of a killer, I joined the Navy. Figured I wouldn't come across anyone from El Paso aboard a ship."

"I'm sorry, Leo. People can be cruel."

"Which is why I figure you have a mighty tough road ahead of you back home. I can't blame you for coming here." Leo gestured toward the table of honor in the room's center. "That's your mother, right? She's beautiful."

"Yes, Eva Machado. She's a Brazilian singing icon."

"Well, you *do* take after her, and I'm sure she's a force to be reckoned with like you."

"I don't know about me, but that's an understatement about my mother." Hattie laughed.

"I know you'll be back on top in the States once this thing with your father blows over."

"I had doubts after RCA and my agent dumped me because they feared the bad PR, but the manager told me tonight that American bookings for the hotel are up after they ran ads in the major markets about my performing here regularly."

"See." Leo tipped his glass. "The sins of the father won't affect you like they didn't me."

"I'll drink to that." She clinked glasses with him.

Leo glanced to his right. "Don't look now, but your fiancé is hot under the collar again."

"That's my cue to join my family." Hattie pushed up from her chair. "It was great seeing you again, Leo. I really enjoy speaking to another American."

Leo also stood. "Please don't take this wrong, but I hope to see you again. It sure is nice spending time with someone from home."

"Next week, then?"

"Count on it." He tilted his head and smirked before saying, "Give my best to David."

"You're bad, Commander Bell." She turned toward her mother's table.

David's eyes were narrow, and his arms were folded across his chest. Her mother appeared equally annoyed by the friendship she'd struck up with Leo Bell, and Hattie could see their point. On the surface, it would seem that Leo was trying to make a play for her, and she was reveling in the attention. However, she didn't get that vibe from Leo at all. He never crossed any line, even before David clarified their engagement. Either he was really like David and was more interested in men, he had some other sinister motive to make his way into her company, or they were simply two Americans enjoying each other's company in a foreign land. Hattie wanted to believe the last option, and something about his sense of easiness told her she could.

David and Ziegler rose when Hattie approached their table.

"That was another amazing performance," Ziegler said.

"Thank you. I'm glad you enjoyed it."

Eva stood, giving her a cross look, one reminiscent of childhood when her mother was about to give her a lecture. "Excuse me while I use the ladies' room. Hattie, join me," Eva said more as a command than a request.

Here we go, Hattie thought, but she knew it was better to get this over than let it fester. When they were out of earshot of the table, she whispered to her mother, "Let's take this to my dressing room."

"Good idea." Eva's tone was sharp.

Hattie increased her speed, almost marching toward the backstage door as her ire built with each step. She would have argued with her mother in the corridor if not for some band members lingering nearby. She turned the knob to her dressing room and walked inside but didn't hold the door for Eva. Once it closed, she spun on her heel and placed her balled-up fists on her hips. "I've done nothing wrong."

"You're making a fool of David."

Hattie set her jaw and came close to cracking her back teeth from clenching so hard. If her mother only knew the truth about her and David, Eva would see that she wasn't interested in Leo in the least, not to mention that he had a wife and appeared to be a man of honor. Leo would never cheat on his spouse like Eva had.

"We are merely friends, Mother. He's a naval attaché working out of the US Embassy. He was surprised to see me performing in Rio, so we started a conversation. Plus, he's married."

"A wedding ring doesn't prevent him from straying."

"And you would know all about that." Hattie's words came out sharper than intended, and she instantly regretted letting her past resentments bleed into their argument. When Eva's expression went blank, Hattie realized she'd hurt her mother profoundly and had to repair the damage she'd created. "I'm so sorry, Mother. I didn't mean to lash out like that."

"Whether you meant to makes no difference, but it shows I still have much work ahead of me to earn your trust and respect."

Hattie hated to admit it, but Eva was right. The three weeks they had spent together hadn't entirely erased a decade of resenting the woman and despising what she had done. Nonetheless, Hattie needed to learn how to let go of the past. She dipped her head. "I don't want to fight with you."

"Fighting is the last thing I want."

"Believe me when I tell you that Commander Bell has made no advances. I can tell he misses his wife desperately, and I have no interest in him other than entertaining conversation with another American."

"All I ask is that you consider how it makes David look. He appears weak if he doesn't step in."

"I will." Hattie sighed at the truth of the matter—she could never tell her mother she was pining for Maya Reyes, and David would prefer to make a play for Leo if the man was so inclined rather than fight him to keep his honor intact.

"You still sound angry," Eva said. "Maybe we should postpone our lunch tomorrow with Frederick."

"No," Hattie snapped back. Since her father sneaked into her dressing room last week and expressed his concern about Ziegler, she'd been waiting for a chance to learn more about him, and going to his home would provide an opportunity for her to snoop. "I've been looking forward to it. If he's going to spend more time with you, I should get to know him better and see where he lives, don't you think?"

"I do, and that makes me very happy, sweetheart. Thank you."

6

The following day

The Gávea neighborhood hosted many of Rio's upper crust, including the man Eva had become smitten with in recent weeks. As they drove through the area, Hattie noted every estate was large, fenced off, and landscaped with lush, inviting greenery. She now understood part of Mr. Ziegler's allure. As an ambassador, he lived in luxury and ran in elite circles, two things Eva was always drawn to.

Today's lunch could not have come soon enough for Hattie since Eva had continued to see him socially. This was her opportunity to dig up something about the man her father had warned her not to trust.

David pulled their car up to the double-panel wrought iron gate and pressed the button on the pole-mounted speaker. The walk-through entryway to the right was also made of black polished bars.

A man's voice sounded through the crackly box. "Posso te ajudar?"

"Eva Machado, Hattie James, and David Townsend to see Mr. Ziegler."

"Please pull to the steps, Senhor Townsend."

The gate parted in the middle, allowing David to drive forward. The courtyard was as lush as the street side of the property, accenting the magnificent neo-colonial mansion, highlighted by dark red brick and a pillared entryway painted a crisp white.

When David aligned the rear passenger door even with the stairs, a man dressed in a black-and-white servant's uniform emerged from the front door, descended the stairs, and opened the car door.

"Good afternoon, Miss Machado," he said in a European accent that sounded German. The Swiss had a sizable Germanic population, so it was expected.

"Hello, Riker." Eva slid from the back seat, accepted his hand, and gestured for Hattie to join her. "I'd like you to meet my daughter, Hattie James."

"It's a pleasure, Miss James."

"Likewise, Riker." Hattie let him help her from the vehicle while David circled around from the driver's side. She thought it interesting that Ziegler had local and Swiss servants, attributing the mix to balancing the needs of maintaining a large household and the security requirements of a foreign ambassador.

"I left the keys in it," David said. "Shall I pull it forward?"

"I'll park it, Mr. Townsend, and will wash it before you leave, as I care for all the cars of Ambassador Ziegler's guests."

David acknowledged with a nod and offered Hattie his arm. Riker guided them inside the mansion. White marble tile, a mixture of rich woods, and a tall ceiling welcomed them, as did the smell of fresh paint.

"This is magnificent, Mother," Hattie said.

"This is only the appetizer, sweetheart," Eva said, turning to Riker. "Where is Mr. Ziegler?"

"In his study, miss. I have instructions to take you to the patio for refreshments before lunch. Mr. Ziegler will join you in a few minutes."

"I know the way." Eva waved off Riker, freeing him to go about his duties. She diverted around a hallway with ladders and tarps and led Hattie and David through an exquisite hall accented in more rich wood and white fabrics. The room was large enough to host a banquet. They passed the music room, where a baby grand piano was the centerpiece, and exited the building through double French doors to a covered patio. Multiple fans with bamboo blades operated by a belt-and-pulley system dotted the cover's underbelly, generating a comfortable, gentle breeze.

The back garden was even more elaborate than Eva had described, with tall palms, full greenery, and a rainbow of flowers outlining a meandering concrete path. An ornate fountain fed into a lushly edged two-foot-wide stream that circled a perfectly manicured lawn accessible by a wood-and-stone footbridge.

"My," Hattie said.

"The intricate design is breathtaking, isn't it?" Eva asked.

"It is."

A servant stood behind a table, offering a variety of hot and cold beverages. David asked for a cola, and Hattie and Eva requested limonada Suíça. It was Hattie's favorite growing up, especially when Eva blended the whole lime and skin with sugar and condensed milk.

They strolled to the end of the patio with their drinks, taking in the garden's grandeur.

"I thought this location would be ideal for a wedding." Eva raised her free hand, palm forward as if framing the area for a picture. "The grass would be perfect for the ceremony, and the grand hall could host the reception."

"Mother," Hattie said, lacing irritation in the one word.

"I know I'm overstepping, but this is only a possibility for you to consider. I spoke to Frederick, and he's happy to offer his estate for the big event."

"Please, Mother. I won't be pressured into planning a quick wedding." Announcing her fake engagement to Eva when they first arrived to justify David traveling to Brazil with her seemed logical at the time, but Hattie now realized it was a colossal mistake. Trying to stop Eva from overplanning a wedding that would never happen was as futile as using a broken umbrella against a hurricane.

"I'm only asking you to think about it."

"I see Eva has shown you my tropical oasis," Ziegler said, emerging through the French doors.

The echo of her father's warning prickled the hair on Hattie's arms.

Suspecting Ziegler's Nazi ties, she needed to confirm if his interest in her mother was genuine.

He shook David's and Hattie's hands before kissing Eva on the cheek. Hattie had seen several men greet Eva like this in public, each an innocent show of affection. However, this one lingered a fraction longer, and Eva practically melted into the kiss. It was nice seeing her mother happy, but somehow, it seemed wrong with anyone but her father and particularly unsuitable with a possible Nazi.

"It's a beautiful garden, Mr. Ziegler," Hattie said. "And so is your home."

"Call me Frederick. Please excuse the mess. We're making some improvements for next month's gala."

"Gala?" Hattie asked.

"Yes, in honor of my posting. It's tradition to invite host country dignitaries and other embassy missions to a new ambassador's home." Ziegler glanced at Eva. "And your mother has graciously agreed to perform that evening."

"That's wonderful, Mother."

"I hope you're hungry," Ziegler said. "With your mother's input, the cook has prepared all your favorites."

"I am. Mother insisted we skip breakfast."

Frederik gestured toward the nearby servers and directed his guests to the patio table. Within moments, two servants brought out the first course. The food was delicious, and the conversation was enjoyable. When the topic turned to Ziegler's time in the United States, David asked, "Is that how you met Hattie's father? I understand you frequented his social parties in Washington."

"Yes," Frederick said. "That's how Eva and I first met. She was a force even back then." He leaned closer to David as if he was about to reveal a secret. "This woman could seduce a room with her voice and have every man hoping to take her home. I'm not ashamed to include myself among the captivated."

David glanced at Hattie. "Now I know where Hattie gets it from."

Hattie and Eva blushed, and Ziegler laughed. The idea of men fantasizing about taking her mother to bed while still married to her father made Hattie uncomfortable to the point she could not concentrate on the conversation. Images of sweaty hands pawing Eva with her father in the other room looped in her head like a poorly produced B movie.

"You two are much alike," Ziegler said to Hattie. "Perhaps you might consider joining your mother on stage at my gala next month."

The suggestion instantly pulled Hattie back. She had never considered performing with her mother, and the idea made her uneasy. Hattie envisioned Eva dominating every song. She would play Abbott, her mother's straight man, while Eva would play Costello, getting all the applause.

Eva smiled. "What a great idea. Many of the younger guests would love her."

"That's a kind offer, Frederick, but I can't take the time off at the Golden Room," Hattie said, hoping to decline without being rude.

"It's on a Monday," Eva said, "to coincide with his birthday. Aren't Mondays your day off?"

Hattie grinned, smothering a cringe. "It is. Let me think about it." She felt cornered with all eyes upon her, but she focused on why she came here. With Ziegler busy with Eva today, Hattie would have her opening to explore. She never considered herself a snoop before learning that her father was an operative, not a boring diplomat who would never hurt a fly as she had thought all her life. However, since the FBI had thrown her headfirst into the deep end of the spy world, she had become curious about everyone and everything.

She turned to Ziegler. "May I use your restroom?"

"Of course." He waved over a female servant. "Please see Miss James to the upstairs powder room." The woman nodded. Frederick returned his attention to Hattie. "We're repainting some downstairs areas this week, so the hallway is blocked."

"Thank you." Hattie wiped the corners of her lips with the cloth napkin and placed it on the table before rising from her chair. David and Frederick also politely stood for her exit.

The servant guided Hattie through the house, giving her a glimpse of more rooms, including a stately formal dining room with a palatial gold-and-crystal chandelier. They climbed the broad, sweeping staircase from the grand hall she had seen earlier to the second-floor landing. The doors to every room were closed except for the double set nearest the stairs.

Hattie peeked inside as she passed, noting the room was an ample study, but the open glass French doors leading to a balcony at the far end caught her eye. The view of the garden it offered must have been spectacular.

The servant guided her halfway down the wide marble-floored hallway decorated with tables staggered along the walls. Fresh flowers adorned each and appeared to have come from the property. The woman stopped at an ornate teak door between two lit wall sconces. "I'll wait for you here, Miss James."

"I'll find my way back," Hattie said, hoping to snoop for a few minutes alone.

"Of course, miss." The woman dipped her head in respect and hurried down the stairs.

Hattie entered the powder room. It was as elegantly detailed and furnished as the rest of the house. White subway tiles rose four feet up the wall as wainscoting and were topped with a chair railing. Paisley wallpaper in brown and gold tones was above, stretching to the coffered ceiling trimmed in an intricate wood design. The toilet sat between two colonial pillars, resembling a throne.

While conducting her business, she felt like a queen and was reminded of how uncomfortable she was when the Halo Club staff treated her like one. Hattie was accustomed to extra attention from her celebrity, but the royal treatment was too much. After finishing, she washed her hands with the creamiest shea butter soap she'd ever used and wiped them dry with a fluffy cotton towel. This was opulence piled upon opulence.

Hattie exited, retraced her steps toward the stairs, and slipped inside the open study doors. She supposed finding Hitler's portrait or the Nazi flag hanging from a wall might be too wishful. Unfortunately, the room appeared like any other stately home office. The faint, sweet aroma of top-grade cigar tobacco lingered in the room. She strode directly to the balcony for the bird's-eye view of the luxurious back garden. It was more spectacular from a higher vantage point, with the intricate design coming into perspective. Tremendous thought had gone into the balance of patterns and color and fastidious care into its upkeep. Her mother was right about this spot being the ideal location for a wedding. It was a tropical dream.

Even the mixed scents of the flora seemed sweeter and more potent from her elevated position.

Hattie took in the storybook setting once more before reentering the study. She scanned the room's architectural details and furnishings, impressed by how each item complemented the other in color, size, and style. Most decorations had a museum feel to them, but Hattie was drawn to the personal touches on the desk and framed pictures hanging on the wall directly behind it.

The eyeglasses lying open atop a black journal and the well-used ivory pipe propped in its hand-carved stand made of the same precious stone said this space was not merely for show. Ziegler conducted business of world consequence in this room, but for whose benefit? Hattie wondered.

Her gaze drifted to the images hanging behind the desk, and she stepped forward to inspect each one. Ziegler appeared in every photo, posing alongside other men. She surmised the subjects were all important diplomats or government officials. One contained horses with a group of men dressed in matching sporting uniforms, making her believe they were at a polo match. She gasped when she focused on the man with his arm slung over Ziegler's shoulder.

"Baumann," she whispered.

Ziegler and Baumann looked younger, so the picture must have been taken years earlier. During her singing lessons with Baumann's daughter, Hattie had gotten the impression that she and her father had been in Brazil for four or five years. However, this photo appeared much older, perhaps from ten or more years ago.

Hattie racked her brain to figure out how Ziegler might have known Baumann before. Eva's suitor was a diplomat and had likely traveled the world for decades, but Baumann was a Nazi SS officer who owned the plantation as a cover for his clandestine operation. Their long-term association only made sense if Ziegler was stationed in Germany at one point.

"What are you doing in here, Hattie?"

She was startled and turned, discovering David behind her.

"Your snooping is going to get us in trouble," he said.

She bobbed her head left and right, looking over her shoulder. "Did a servant come up?"

"No, I told her you could show me which door so she could stay downstairs."

"Then look at this." She waved David forward and pointed at the photo of the polo match. "Isn't that Baumann with Ziegler?"

He squinted at the image. "It looks like him."

"It is him, but how did he know Ziegler?"

David shrugged. "Frederick is an ambassador. They likely ran in the same circles in Rio."

"Look closely," Hattie said. "This picture is at least ten years old. Elsa mentioned she had only been in the country for a few years, so Baumann and Ziegler knew each other well before Rio. Baumann was a Nazi officer. I bet Ziegler is, too." Given Eva's resentment toward Karl and her suspicion that he had become a Nazi, Hattie hoped this would be enough for her to doubt and break up with Frederick.

"But Ziegler is Swiss. Aren't they neutral?" David asked.

"I learned from my father that Switzerland has a strong German population. I'm sure many of them are sympathetic to the Nazi party."

"That's a leap, Hattie."

"Maybe, but I don't trust him." And neither did Hattie's father.

David looked over his shoulder toward the double doors. "We better head back before someone finds us here."

"You're right." Hattie slid from behind the desk.

They walked down the sweeping staircase and were met by Eva's smooth singing voice and music playing. Hattie guessed her mother and Ziegler had moved to the music room. They were at the doorway within moments, watching Eva seated at the piano, serenading Ziegler, who sat nearby, sipping from a brandy snifter. He was practically undressing Eva with his eyes, something Hattie could never unsee and should have never witnessed.

When Eva finished her song, Hattie stepped forward, prompting Ziegler to come to his feet. "I hate to cut this short, Mother, but I must get to work early to review a set change."

Eva glanced at Ziegler with puppy dog eyes. They had seen one another six or seven times since reconnecting at the Golden Room three weeks ago, and each time, Eva had made it home at a decent hour, giving Hattie hope their relationship hadn't progressed to the bedroom. After seeing that picture of Ziegler with Baumann, Hattie wanted it to stay that way.

"We can drop you at the house first," Hattie said.

"I think I'd like to stay a little longer. Frederick can have someone drive me home."

"Remember, you have an early day with church tomorrow," Hattie said. If tossing in a dose of Catholic guilt didn't keep them apart, nothing would.

Eva gave Hattie the evil eye.

"I'll ensure she gets home," Ziegler said, shaking David's hand. "Thank you for joining me for lunch. It was a pleasure."

"Likewise," David said.

When Ziegler shook Hattie's hand, she knew she had lost the battle over her mother. "I appreciate the invitation, Frederick, and hope to see you soon at one of my shows."

"I'm sure we will." His use of we didn't escape her. Ziegler was going out of his way to make it known he considered himself and Eva a couple.

Once outside, Hattie hopped into the front seat of Eva's sedan with David behind the wheel. She had a bad feeling about Ziegler and an even worse one about her mother likely sleeping with him tonight. Eva had left her father, believing he had turned into a Jew-hating Nazi. What would she do if Hattie's suspicions about Ziegler were correct after giving herself to him?

The back of her neck tingled as David drove through the gate and onto the main boulevard. She had a sinking feeling that Frederick Ziegler would prove more sinister than Heinz Baumann.

7

The following day

When Hattie woke, the other side of the bed was empty and the house was conspicuously void of recorded music playing and fresh smells wafting aimlessly in the rooms. She checked the Big Ben alarm clock on the night-stand, noting it was almost eight in the morning, dressed quickly, and wandered into the kitchen. It was unoccupied. Her mother attended the church service at nine, so Eva should have been dressed and making break-fast by now. Nothing would have kept her from going to mass unless she didn't feel good.

Hattie took the hallway to Eva's bedroom. The door was ajar, but she knocked lightly while walking in to not startle Eva if she were ill. Two steps in, she discovered the bed empty without signs of having been slept in overnight. She called out her mother's name, holding on to the last sliver of hope that she was in the bathroom, but received no answer. Hattie dipped her head at the thought of Eva spending the night with Ziegler. Perhaps if she had aired her concerns about him yesterday instead of leaving, Eva would have seen what Hattie saw in him. However, they were likely lovers now, and her mother would now view him through that prism. It would be a monumental challenge to convince her otherwise.

When she returned to the kitchen, Hattie discovered David fixing a pot of coffee. He wasn't a cook, but as a bachelor, he had mastered brewing a cup of joe in his New York City apartment.

"How about I make us something to eat?" Hattie said.

"I was hoping you'd say that." David laughed.

"How do eggs over easy, toast, fruit, and some sausage sound?"

"Very American. If you can throw in some hash browns, you'll make a friend for life."

Hattie laughed. "I thought we already were friends for life, but I'll see if she has any potatoes."

For the next half hour, David helped her make their first hearty breakfast since arriving in Rio. She'd found two aging potatoes in the pantry and had to cut away some bad spots, but she'd saved enough to make two servings and season them with a combination of her mother's spices.

"This is really good, Hattie," David mumbled without waiting between bites. Bits of hash browns swirled in his mouth.

"Did my daughter cook for her future husband today?" Eva appeared at the kitchen entrance and placed her handbag on the island, still wearing the same clothes she had worn yesterday.

Hattie gave her a stern look but pushed back on the disappointment bubbling to the surface. "Must I establish a curfew for you, young lady?"

"That would be quite the role reversal." Eva laughed.

"Are you hungry?" Hattie asked, but she already knew the answer.

"Thank you, sweetheart, but I ate at the mansion. I have just enough time to change and drive to church."

"I suppose you'll stay late for all those extra Hail Marys you'll have to recite."

"Hush." Eva swatted the air and grinned. "I'll be a few minutes." She disappeared into her bedroom suite.

While Eva was dressing, Hattie debated whether to broach her suspicions about Ziegler since it was clear that they had become lovers. However, the longer Hattie delayed the conversation, the deeper Eva would fall for a man unworthy of her trust.

She waited long enough for Eva to make herself decent but knocked on her door when she would likely be putting on her makeup for the day. "Mother, do you have a moment?"

"I have a few minutes. Come in while I freshen my face."

"Thanks." Hattie sat in Eva's reading chair with a direct line of sight to her mother sitting at her vanity in a conservative dress with a high collar, applying her eye shadow. "What do you really know about Mr. Ziegler?"

A slight smile formed on Eva's lips as she wiped the facial cream from her face. "It's lovely of you to be concerned, but Frederick and I go way back. He's a widower with three adult children and five grandchildren, and he has spent most of his diplomatic career in the States, Europe, and now Brazil since last month."

"I know he's Swiss, but does he have ties to Germany?" Hattie asked.

"I think his family was originally from Austria. Why do you ask?"

"When I was at his home yesterday, I found a photo of him with Heinz Baumann."

"Well, Frederick is an ambassador, and Baumann was an important businessman in Rio until that horrible night on his plantation."

"No, Mother. The picture I saw was taken at least ten years ago. They were playing polo and looking all chummy. Doesn't it bother you they've known each other for some years?"

Eva shifted in her seat. "What are you getting at?"

"We know Baumann was an SS officer and ran a spy ring. It's not too far-fetched to believe they were associates."

Eva jerked her head back. "Come now, Hattie. The man is the Swiss ambassador. They are a neutral country. There is no way they sent a Nazi to represent them."

"What if they don't know?"

"I think you're overreacting, sweetheart. Being acquainted with a Nazi doesn't make you one. Knowing your father would have taught you that."

"He says he isn't a Nazi and that we have to trust him." Hattie amplified her voice, feeling the need to defend her father.

"And you believe him just like that?" Eva had spent the last fourteen years believing Karl had become something to revile. Hattie's father offered no proof other than his word that he wasn't. The government could have presented a mountain of airtight evidence against him, but Hattie would have believed in the man who raised her. She'd loved him unconditionally all her life and knew him to be a good man despite the lives he'd taken protecting her.

"Yes, just like that. He's my father." Hattie wished she could have said her father had reason to believe Ziegler was loyal to Nazi Germany, not Switzerland, but that would only make Eva dig in deeper.

Eva finished applying her makeup and sprang from her chair. "I think you have a problem seeing me with a man who makes me happy."

"That's not true, Mother," Hattie lied. Like every child of divorced parents, despite what Eva had done, seeing either parent with someone else made her uncomfortable. However, deep down, she wanted to see her mother happy.

"I know you've hated me for years and blamed me for breaking up the family."

"I still have difficulty with your infidelity, but—"

Eva lowered and shook her head. "Your father and I hadn't lived as husband and wife for years. Germany changed him. It doesn't excuse what I did, but that was the only time I strayed."

Hattie reached out, raising her mother's head by the chin. "I was going to say what you did was wrong, but I can also see you held on as long as you could. Your marriage was over in your mind."

Eva's lips quivered. "Thank you."

Hattie realized that talking to her mother about her concerns with Ziegler without concrete evidence was misguided. Doing so had only raised Eva's defenses. Hattie needed more information before bringing up the subject again and knew no better way than to return to his mansion. "I'm sorry I upset you. How would you like it if we both sang at Frederick's gala?"

"Really? You would sing with me?"

"I would be honored to sing with you, Mother."

Eva pulled Hattie into a tight embrace, swirling Hattie's guilt for having an ulterior motive. "Oh, sweetheart. You have no idea how happy this makes me."

"Then we must create a set list and choreography."

"We can start today," Eva said, almost giddy.

"After church." Hattie laughed.

Eva glanced at the clock on the wall. "Oh, meu Deus! I'm going to be late."

8

Five weeks later

The past few weeks had been quiet, with no more surprise visits from Karl and no word from John Butler, the FBI agent no longer pressuring her to flush out her father. She sang to a packed house every night she performed, a sign that her celebrity in Brazil was growing.

Since she had agreed to sing with her mother at the gala, Hattie and Eva practiced the songs they'd selected whenever their schedules allowed. They had differing choreography ideas but worked together to create an impressive show for Ziegler's guests, where both shared the spotlight equally. Ziegler had sent a sedan to Eva's house to collect them for tonight's big event, but Hattie insisted on driving separately so they could leave at their convenience.

David pulled Eva's Ford Deluxe through the gate of Ziegler's estate and slowed at the parade of luxury vehicles queued to drop off their passengers. The valets ushered partygoers from their auto to the welcoming red carpet, where they climbed the few stairs to the mansion. Most cars hurried off with their original drivers, but other attendants were also available to take the cars away.

Torches lined the driveway, stirring vivid memories of the horrific night

Baumann and his men hunted her, Maya, and Anna on the plantation. The sadistic game had started when they emerged from the cold, dank basement cells into the compound, with the area aglow from torches like tonight, lighting a path toward the coffee fields. Hattie remembered how her feet flopped in the oversized sandals their captor had thrown at them and how the unevenness of the rocky dirt road was magnified under the flimsy shoe bottoms. But mostly, she recalled the feeling of terror as she dragged Maya and Anna by the hand into the darkness, fearing for their lives. That night, she dreaded, would haunt her until she died.

When it was their turn, David inched up to the drop-off spot. A man dressed smartly in a black tuxedo and thick glasses opened the passenger door, and Hattie accepted his hand to exit. "Good evening, Miss James," the man said in a heavy Portuguese accent.

Hattie pushed back the unnerving memories and put on her stage smile. "Thank you. My, this is quite the Rio affair." She swiveled her head around, taking in the elegant potted floral decorations and velvet stanchions lining both sides of the entry steps. More torches lined the front of the house, giving it a tropical appeal.

"We are pleased to have you as our guest." He leaned in closer and spoke softly to her. "I hope to sneak in to hear you sing tonight. My wife used to wait tables at the Halo Club before it burned down, and she tells me you put on an amazing show. I work nights, so I never got to see you."

Hattie's throat thickened at the mention of the nightclub. Her relationship with Maya was on the mend, but she still had much repair work to close the chasm between them. She had yet to see Maya outside of work but remained hopeful they would be in each other's arms again.

Hattie touched the man's hand. "Your wife? What is her name?"

"Monica."

Hattie remembered her. Monica was a petite waitress who had gushed over her the day after she performed at the Golden Room with Maggie Moore. "Yes, Monica. She's a sweet woman. Is she here?"

He nodded. "She's a server inside."

"Thank you." Hattie patted the attendant's arm, thinking she would have to find his wife tonight and say hello.

While another valet drove off with their car, David joined Hattie at the curb, stuffing the claim check into the breast pocket of his new tux. He offered his arm to Hattie, and they entered the mansion. The vestibule was overflowing with flowers, some of which Hattie recognized from her earlier visit as having come from the lush back garden. Jazz music was playing, and Hattie noted several small speakers had been installed there and down the corridor to offer a consistent sound while moving toward the banquet hall. The Swiss Embassy had spared no expense for tonight's event.

A server greeted them with a tray filled with champagne glasses. David grabbed one, but Hattie asked she be sent sparkling soda water served in the same type of glass. The waiter whispered to his coworker, who scurried down the hallway.

Hattie and David continued deeper into the house. The ballroom was teeming with men in dark tuxedos and women in formal gowns. The dresses were in various colors and designs, but they all had one thing in common—elegance. Each was made of delicate fabric and adorned with fine trim and shimmering accents. Eva had helped Hattie select a gown for tonight that would fit right in with the crowd, and Hattie felt right at home with Brazil's elite.

A stage had been erected at one end of the room, where a band played the jazz Hattie had heard when she first arrived. Tables decorated with white tablecloths, elegant china and crystal, and colorful flower center-pieces dotted the room's perimeter, leaving the center open for dancing near the platform and mingling closer to the staircase.

A server caught up to them and handed Hattie a glass of sparkling water in a champagne flute. She thanked him and asked him to assign someone to refresh her drink in the same fashion throughout the evening. Appearing to imbibe in Ziegler's refreshments should avoid the obvious stares and silent questions.

Hattie scanned the room, looking for her mother among the sea of sparkling gowns, but Eva stood out in her silk floor-length white formal. Her bronze skin contrasted against the pure palette, creating an even more exotic appearance. A stylist had fixed Eva's dark hair and makeup earlier tonight at home, as she had Hattie's, making her look stunning with a refined weave at the back of her head.

Ziegler was next to Eva, conversing with a handful of uniformed dignitaries while holding a champagne glass in one hand and gesturing with the other. Hattie recalled the picture she'd found of him with Heinz Baumann and her father's caution that Ziegler may have had more loyalty to the Third Reich than to Switzerland. She cringed when he rested his hand on the small of Eva's back. Her gut told her he was at least a Nazi sympathizer, and the idea of him touching her mother intimately made her blood boil.

"There's Eva," David said, encouraging her toward her mother with a squeeze of his arm.

Hattie nodded and walked with him, counting how long Ziegler kept his hand on her mother's backside. Eleven seconds was far too long for her liking, but when she reached their group, she silently thanked her years of performing and having developed the ability to appear upbeat when she felt precisely the opposite.

"Hello, Mother."

Eva spun, and a sweet smile stretching to her eyes overtook her. "Sweetheart." They embraced before she turned to the others. "Everyone, I'd like you to meet my lovely daughter, Hattie James, and her fiancé, David Townsend."

It was just their foursome following a brief conversation with the Italian military colonel and diplomats. Ziegler mentioned he would host a smaller reception for Brazilian business leaders and asked if Hattie would perform with her mother again.

"That's a splendid idea," Eva said.

Performing with her for free tonight because Ziegler was ... Hattie hated to think it ... her mother's lover ... was out of goodwill. However, a second event in as many weeks was taking advantage, but her mother was too lovestruck to see it.

"I'm afraid I won't have the time, but I have a favor to ask. I saw an acquaintance working as a valet out front. Would bringing him inside to see tonight's show be possible?"

"Of course. I doubt anyone will leave while you're on stage." Ziegler waved over a server and explained the request after Hattie described the attendant with the thick glasses. He looked at his pocket watch and returned it to its hiding place in his tuxedo vest. "It's about a half hour before I'd like to start the entertainment."

"We better get going," Eva said. "Frederick has set aside a room for us to prepare for our performance." She linked arms with Hattie and guided them to the sweeping staircase. A muscular man wearing a tux tight around the arms stood in front of a velvet stanchion at the bottom, preventing guests from going upstairs. Eva addressed him. "Evening. My daughter and I are ready to change upstairs."

The man glanced toward Ziegler, and Hattie followed his gaze. Ziegler issued an affirmative nod, and the man unclipped the rope and let them pass. Hattie understood the need for security at a gathering with so many high-ranking officials but was perplexed why her mother needed permission to go upstairs when she had spent several evenings and nights there and presumably had the run of the place.

They ascended the stairs. The double doors to Ziegler's study were closed. Hattie wished they were open so she could do more snooping. Eva led them down the hallway to a room next to the powder room Hattie had used during her earlier visit. The ample bedroom had a vanity with a variety of supplies to touch up their hair and makeup. Their stage dresses hung from two full-length mirrors in different corners. Two glasses and a water pitcher with ice were centered on the dresser.

"It looks like he's thought of everything," Hattie said.

"Frederick is very thoughtful," Eva said with a smile.

Hattie bit back the snarky retort she had in mind. "Which one is mine?"

"Closest to the window."

They had stylish outfits tailored specially for tonight's event. One had black on the left and white on the right; the other mirrored the colors. Both ended an inch below the knee and were cut looser at the waist than their formal gowns to make performing easier.

They changed and took turns at the vanity while chatting about the nuances of their planned performance. Eva turned and wrapped her hands around Hattie's when they were done. "Before we go on, sweetheart, I wanted to tell you how much working with you the last few weeks has meant to me."

"I've enjoyed it as well, Mother." Hattie had observed how her mother dissected every song, recommending when to hold a note, take quick breaths, and use vibrato. Her ideas on the harmonies were a master class in music instruction. The passion her mother put into her preparation was like nothing Hattie had seen, and she developed an even more profound respect for Eva's talent and expertise. She could see how Eva rebuilt her career twice, moving back and forth from the United States. Anyone with that much genius, who poured that much of themselves into a single performance, was destined to succeed. Hattie had a long way to go before reaching her mother's level of talent, but she had the Machado grit and would never stop striving.

Eva wiped a tear that threatened to fall. "I couldn't be happier connecting with you this way, nor prouder to be on that stage with you."

Hattie snatched a tissue from a box on the vanity and dabbed it around her mother's eyes. "We need to stop this mushy stuff. Otherwise, we'll have to do your makeup all over again."

Eva laughed. "I suppose you're right." She turned toward the mirror, checking herself. "We better get going."

They exited the room and descended the stairs. The guard unclipped the rope to let them pass. Eva got Ziegler's attention in the ballroom and gestured that she and Hattie would take their positions at the far entrance. She guided Hattie down a hallway and entered the kitchen. Its size rivaled that of Maya's nightclub but was equipped with all the newest appliances and conveniences.

A man in a tux and thick glasses speaking to a server caught Hattie's eye. He was the valet she had talked to earlier. When they locked gazes, he tugged on the server's sleeve. The woman turned. It was Monica from the Halo Club. Hattie approached and squeezed their hands. "It's so good to see you, Monica."

Tears were in the woman's eyes. "Miss James, it's an honor."

"Nonsense." Hattie focused on her husband. "I see you've been pulled inside. I hope you enjoy the performance."

"I'm certain I will, Miss James."

Ziegler's voice came over the loudspeaker, the cue that Hattie didn't have much time before he made their introduction.

Hattie spoke to them both. "I'm not sure if you know, but Miss Reyes is now the assistant manager at the Golden Room. I'll leave your names with her. When you can arrange a night off together, I want you to be my guest for the dinner show."

"We couldn't," Monica's husband said.

"Yes, you can. Consider it done, and if you want to work at the Palace, let Miss Reyes or me know. We'll try to bring you both on."

"You're a godsend, Miss James." Monica squeezed Hattie's hand and was about to let go when Hattie hugged her.

"We're Halo Club family," Hattie said. "We stick together."

"...Eva Machado and Hattie James," Ziegler said over the speaker to a welcoming applause.

Eva tugged Hattie's hand. "That's our cue."

Monica's husband slung an arm over his wife's shoulder, and both had beaming smiles.

Hattie entered the ballroom with her mother to hoots, whistles, and a roaring ovation. While climbing the stairs, Eva said softly to Hattie, "That was very sweet of you in there, Hattie. You have a big heart."

Hattie winked at David, sitting at the upright piano at one end of the stage. She and Eva stepped up to their microphones in the center, the spotlights blurring the view of most of the audience. This marked the first time Hattie and her mother had appeared on stage together, and its importance suddenly hit her. She had spent over a decade despising everything about her mother for what she had done to their family. However, two months ago, she had learned the truth surrounding Eva's betrayal and that neither parent was to blame for the broken marriage. Putting their painful past behind them was long overdue.

While they waited for the applause to settle, Hattie placed a hand over her mic, grabbed Eva's hand, and, for the first time in twelve years, said, "I love you, Mother."

Eva's expression pinched with surprise, and she pressed her hand against her chest. "I love you too, sweetheart."

And for the next hour, Hattie and Eva put on the show of their lives. It was skillful and graceful and, at times, playful and powerful. They even threw in a bit of humor, playing off their age difference and mother-daughter dynamic. It was a night Hattie would never forget and always consider the standard bearer of what a performance was supposed to be—a piece of her heart.

Hattie felt like she was floating on air as she left the stage. She had followed in her mother's footsteps since she was a teenager, striving to become a professional singer, but this was the first time she had connected with Eva in the profession they shared. Not until tonight, seeing the pure joy on her mother's face, could she admit it was something she always craved.

They walked hand in hand through the kitchen and upstairs into their changing room, where Eva collapsed into tears on the bed with her face buried in her hands.

Hattie rushed to her side. "What's wrong, Mother?"

"Absolutely nothing." More tears fell when Eva met Hattie's eyes. "For the first time since I can remember, nothing is wrong."

Hattie's heart broke for the woman and for Hattie's part in abandoning her. She had thought Eva had deserted her family, but she was off the mark. Hattie and Karl had deserted her. Olivia was the only one who had stood by Eva all this time, making Hattie feel ashamed.

She kneeled before her mother and laid her head in the crying woman's lap. "I'm so sorry for hurting you."

Eva's sobs slowed as she caressed Hattie's hair. "My weakness brought this on." She raised Hattie's head by the chin until they locked stares. Her eyes swam with pain, regret, and unmoving love for her daughter. "Learn from me. Never lose your way. Stay strong, know your center, and always cling to it."

Hattie had never felt closer to her mother and was never prouder to be Eva Machado's daughter. Love for Eva swelled in her throat, forcing her to croak out her words. "I will."

Eva released a long, deep breath as if cleansing herself of the past. "We must go. Frederick is expecting us to mingle with his guests."

They changed, and Hattie let Eva use the vanity first to tame her hair and touch up her makeup. When it was Hattie's turn, and she saw the dark streaks of mascara on her face, she realized it would take some time to make herself presentable again. "I'm a mess. You should start rubbing elbows. I'll be right behind you. Could you have a server bring up some hot tea? I have a tickle in my throat."

"Of course. I love you, sweetheart." Eva kissed Hattie on the forehead and left the room, taking full, confident Machado strides. She, too, was floating on air.

Before wiping the smudges from her face, Hattie took a moment to study herself in the mirror. When she turned fifty-five, years from now, she would feel fortunate to have as much beauty and strength as her mother. She laughed, thinking the FBI's strong-arm tactics to get Hattie to Rio had resulted in some good. Hattie had found her mother again, and Eva had her daughter back.

Now that Hattie's makeup had regained its flawless appearance, she decided to go downstairs to get some tea since it had yet to arrive. In the hallway, she heard muffled voices from somewhere on the floor as she approached the staircase. Since the guard prevented guests from accessing this level, Ziegler must have permitted them to go upstairs.

Hattie couldn't resist the chance to snoop around, so she followed the sound, discovering they emanated from behind the double French doors at the top of the stairs. The conversation was in English. She recognized one voice as belonging to Ziegler, who spoke clearly, and thought the others could have been the officials from the Italian Embassy she met earlier. However, their thick accents made understanding what was being said difficult. The discussion focused on a ship with a hundred on board and had something to do with planting evidence to sever diplomatic relations between the United States and Brazil. Someone mentioned assassination, canceling the naval base near Natal, and said, "Sink."

Hattie gasped. People inside that room were planning to sink a passenger ship and blame the United States. She had to tell someone and turned to run downstairs but stopped as a sense of dread soured her stomach. She'd been caught.

"What are you doing there?" the guard from the base of the stairs said in a threatening tone as he climbed to the top landing. If he meant to intimidate her, it was working.

"I...I..." Fear took root. Hattie shook, unable to speak.

"Why aren't you with your mother?" The man stepped closer, grabbing

Hattie by the arm hard enough to form a bruise. His hold was like a vise, and the pressure kept rising, making Hattie think she might not leave this mansion alive.

"Is everything all right, Miss James?" A woman's voice came from the stairwell.

Hattie snapped her stare, discovering Monica climbing the last stair, carrying a drink tray. Her timing could not have been more perfect. "Yes, yes. I was waiting for my tea. Is that it?"

Monica squinted in confusion, but Hattie pleaded with her eyes. "Yes, Miss James. The hot tea you asked for."

"What were you doing at the door?" The guard jerked Hattie's arm.

"Should I have had the server knock on every door to find me?"

The study door opened, and Ziegler appeared. His expression was hard to read, but he clearly wasn't happy. "What's going on?"

"I'd asked for tea from the kitchen, and your brute started manhandling me." Hattie rubbed her arm once the guard released it. "I think I'll be bruised tomorrow."

"That's enough, Mr. Lang. We'll talk later. Return to your post." Once Lang bowed his head and descended the stairs, Ziegler turned his attention to Hattie. "Are you hurt? Shall I call a doctor to examine you?"

"No, I'm fine," Hattie said, but she was nervous as a cat. Her only advantages were Monica standing beside her and the crowd downstairs. Even if Ziegler suspected Hattie was up to no good, he could not act without raising suspicions. "Mother is expecting me." She faced Monica. "I'll take my tea downstairs."

Hattie hurried down, not waiting for a response, and Monica trailed. The guard eyed her with suspicion at the bottom, but Hattie shot him a look of disdain. The way he handled her, combined with what she overheard, bolstered her father's conjecture that Ziegler wasn't who he seemed. He was, at the very least, working with the Axis powers.

Once past the brute, Monica said to Hattie as they walked, "Are you okay, Miss James? Shall I get Mr. Townsend?"

"Thank you, Monica, but I'll be fine."

"But he shouldn't have touched you like that."

Hattie stopped and took the teacup from the tray. "I appreciate your concern, but it was a misunderstanding." Though she knew the incident had likely put Ziegler onto her suspicions. "Please return to your duties and come to the Golden Room sometime soon, won't you?"

"I will, Miss James." Monica turned and disappeared down the hallway.

Hattie entered the ballroom and located David and Eva standing together among several dignitaries. Her mother was in her element, hobnobbing with high society, but staying to mingle was the last thing on Hattie's mind. She and David had to get away and decide what to do with the information she learned upstairs.

9

The following day

A nagging feeling that something was off hung with Hattie during the drive into town. She'd called the number to the Cohen Dry Cleaners, the front for the local FBI operation, first thing this morning, but the operator said the phone had been disconnected and there was no forwarding number. She thought it odd that Agent Butler or Nala Cohen hadn't reached out to give her a new way to contact them about her father. Then again, nothing the FBI did was normal. Nonetheless, she had to get information about the plan to sink a passenger ship she overheard at the gala last night to the right people to stop it.

David parked their car around the corner from the dry cleaners. He and Hattie walked the rest of the way and discovered the shop was closed. Two signs were posted in the window. One was written in cursive, and the other was printed with "Aviso de Despejo" blazoned across the top in bold letters.

"What do they say?" David asked.

Hattie read the sign. Her Portuguese had gotten much better over the last month. "One is an eviction notice. The other says the store is closed permanently and says to go to the shoe shop to claim any items that had been dropped off for cleaning."

"That's odd," David said. "Did Butler say anything to you about moving locations?"

Hattie pulled a pen and paper from her handbag and jotted down the number. "No, he didn't." Looking down the block, she noticed other businesses on the same side of the street were open. "Let's ask someone at the shoe store."

The shoe repair shop was two stores down. When they entered, the bell affixed to the door sounded their arrival. The customer area was short and narrow, like at the dry cleaner store. A counter with shelving above it covered the length of the far wall and contained stacks of shoes, shoeboxes, and a stock of Shinola and Jet-Oil shoe polish. A four-foot-long mechanical lathe with buffing pads on both ends sat in front of the shelf.

The hammering sound she heard when she walked in stopped, and a man appeared in the doorway from the back room. He welcomed them in Portuguese. Hattie asked if he spoke English, but he replied no, so she talked to him in his native language.

"Do you know why Cohen Dry Cleaners is closed?"

"Ah." The man wiped his hands on his apron. "You're here to pick up your dry cleaning."

"No, sir. I was curious. I've used them before."

The man shrugged. "No one has seen the owner for seven weeks. The staff kept the shop open for some time, but when the rent was due, they couldn't pay. The landlord kicked them out, and the eviction notice went up. He takes it over in two days."

"And you've held on to the unclaimed items?" Hattie asked.

"It seemed like the right thing. Only one suit is left."

"This might sound strange, but would you mind showing it to me?"

He shrugged again. "I don't see the harm." He vanished into the room, reappearing moments later with a man's outfit wrapped in transparent plastic. Hattie could not be sure, but the outfit resembled the one she'd seen Agent Butler wearing several times. "Want it?" he asked. "I don't think anyone will claim it after all this time."

"Yes, I would." Hattie draped the garment over her arm. "Thank you, sir. I appreciate your time."

Once on the sidewalk and walking toward their car, David said, "What did he say? And what's up with the suit?"

Hattie explained Nala's disappearance and how the shoemaker agreed to hold unclaimed garments until the customers retrieved them. "This is the only one left, and he doubted anyone would claim it."

"Why did you take it?"

"I thought it might be Agent Butler's and could lead us to what happened to him and Nala."

"Why do you care?"

"I find it strange that they disappeared around the same time I gave them Baumann's logbook."

They reached the car and got in, closing the doors.

"Well, they're no longer breathing down your neck to hand over your father," he said. "If they're gone, we can go home after your contract with the Golden Room ends."

"Maybe," Hattie said.

A quandary formed as she thought about David's point. If the FBI was done with her, her sister would be safe from being railroaded into a conviction for aiding her father. She laughed, thinking Olivia was the only family member who hadn't helped Karl in some way after his escape. Hattie and Eva had seen him multiple times, yet neither had turned him in to the authorities. But Hattie refused to leave Rio until her father was clear of all the charges against him. Then there was Maya. She and Hattie had been through so much in their short time together, and Hattie needed to see their relationship through, no matter what it took.

She ripped off the sheer plastic wrap over the suit and recognized the fine light brown pinstripes woven into the dark gray suit. "I think this is Butler's. He wore one like it." She rummaged through the pockets but found nothing. However, an envelope was stapled to the hanger, so she opened it, discovering a business card. It had only a set of numbers printed on it.

"What is it?" David asked.

Hattie cocked her head, studying the card. "Do you have a half-real coin?"

"Yeah. Why?" David dug into his pants pocket.

"I think it's a phone number. We should call it." Hattie tossed the suit in the back seat and opened her door. "There's a payphone nearby. Come on."

They dashed across the street, jaywalking between passing cars, and hurried to the corner. Hattie lifted the receiver, inserted the coin, and asked the operator to connect her to the number on the card. The call connected after two rings.

"Embassy security," a man said, using a distinctive Texas accent.

Hattie hung up the phone.

"Well?" David asked.

"Take me to the US Embassy."

David drove to the Botafogo neighborhood on São Clemente Road, the heart of Embassy Row, and parked two blocks from their destination. He was quiet during their walk to the guard shack at the entry gate. Despite Hattie's reassurance in the car that this was strictly a professional visit, he clearly wasn't happy about this trip.

After showing their passports to the armed Marine guards, they entered the magnificent colonial-style building inside the American compound. Two dozen people were seated in rows of perfectly aligned chairs in the middle of the waiting area, and four creaky pulley-operated ceiling fans swirled the air beneath them. Three embassy clerks sat behind a counter stretching the room's width, helping visitors.

Hattie and David queued in the five-person-deep line for the reception desk. It moved quickly, and Hattie displayed their passports when it was their turn. "Hattie James and David Townsend. We need to speak with Lieutenant Commander Leo Bell, the naval attaché assigned here."

The clerk was pleasant. She referenced a piece of paper with a list of names, picked up her phone receiver, and spoke to Leo before returning her attention to Hattie. "Commander Bell will be right out. You may have a seat if you'd like."

"Thank you." Instead of sitting, Hattie stood with David near the wall, where the American flag and framed photos of President Roosevelt and the secretary of state were. Hattie remembered seeing Cordell Hull once in the

State Department building, but her father had nothing positive to say about the man other than he was "a politician through and through."

Minutes later, Commander Bell appeared in the corridor, wearing a khaki uniform with a matching tie. His smile lit the room. "Hattie, it's good to see you." He turned to David and shook his hand. "And you, David. What brings you two to the embassy?"

"May we speak somewhere private?" Hattie said.

"Of course. I'll take you to my office." Leo escorted them to the security desk, where an armed Marine issued them clip-on visitor badges and inspected Hattie's purse. "Follow me."

Leo took them deeper inside the building and up a flight of stairs. The hallways were busy with men and women carrying folders and coffee cups, and several whispered Hattie's name when they passed. She wasn't sure whether she was being recognized as a famous singer or as the daughter of an accused traitor.

Leo led them to an office at the end of the hall and closed the door. He offered them some water, and both accepted. The workspace wasn't stately like Hattie's father's at the State Department, but it was clean, uncluttered, and furnished with a metal desk, a bookshelf, and two guest chairs. A framed picture of a woman on his desktop was his sole personalization.

Hattie picked up the photo. The woman resembled Helen Reed—the ex who broke her heart—with her wavy blond hair and dimpled smile. "Is this your wife?"

"Yes, Beverly."

"She's beautiful." Hattie returned the frame to its spot and sat in a chair. David and Leo followed.

"What did you want to discuss, Hattie?" Leo asked.

She handed him the business card from the suit she recovered from the shoe repair shop. "I found this in some dry cleaning."

Leo examined the card, and his eyes widened with surprise. "Did you call this number about an hour ago?"

Hattie nodded. "I did." She retrieved a second business card from her handbag and gave it to Leo.

He read the card and leaned forward in his chair. "Who gave this to you?"

"Nala Cohen did on my first day in town. She introduced me to Agent Butler."

"So that line about kick-starting your career was a pile of manure."

"Not exactly. The FBI tanked my career by running one news article after another in the papers about my father until they cornered me into coming here to search for him."

"So you've been working for them," Leo said.

"Not willingly, but that's a long story." Though her involvement at Baumann's plantation was kept out of the newspapers, she expected him to ask her about it since he knew about Agent Butler. The fact that he didn't likely meant Butler never passed along the information before his disappearance. "I came today because the dry cleaner shop is closed, and I haven't heard from Agent Butler in nearly two months. Do you know where he is?"

"No, I don't."

"When did you last hear from him?" she asked.

"I can't discuss that with you, Hattie."

She shifted uncomfortably in her chair, realizing getting anything out of him would be more complicated than expected. "Then who can? I have vital information that must reach the right people."

"Wait here." Leo exited the office, closing the door again.

"What do you plan to tell them?" David asked.

"Not everything," she said, and he nodded his understanding that she would not reveal things about her father. Silence passed between them for several minutes until Hattie said, "You're upset."

"I can tell he has a crush on you."

Hattie laughed at the unlikelihood. "He's devoted to his wife."

"I'm sure he is, but I'm still right about the crush. There's no denying how he looks at you."

"I think it's more about being starstruck than anything else."

"We'll see."

The door opened, and a man wearing a white business shirt with sleeves rolled up to his elbows walked in with Leo. The man was shorter and heavier than Leo and projected a bureaucratic air. Hattie thought she recognized his face as one of the many diplomats she met last night at the gala.

David and Hattie stood.

Leo made the introductions. "This is Jack Lynch, the deputy ambassador and chief of security. I've explained your situation."

Lynch shook Hattie's and David's hands. "It's a pleasure to meet you." He sat behind the desk while Leo remained by the window. Hattie and David reclaimed their seats. "I understand you have some information to pass along."

"First, when was your last contact with Agent Butler."

"About two months ago. Why?"

"I gave him something and need to know if it got to the right people."

"When did you give it to him?"

"The day after the massacre was reported."

"I last saw him at least a week before that event. What did you give him?"

"A logbook detailing the Nazi spy operation Heinz Baumann ran out of his coffee plantation north of town."

Leo's eyes widened again.

Lynch cocked his head back. "You were involved in the massacre?"

"I was nearly his victim, but I found the book in his office before the police came, and handed it over to Butler at the first opportunity. It was written in German, but from what I could glean, it would help understand how the Nazis collected intelligence in Rio."

"If that's true, it's concerning that Agent Butler never had it couriered to the States in a diplomatic pouch." Lynch rubbed his smooth-shaven chin. "I suppose there's a chance he might have made other arrangements to get it out of the country."

"I hope so," Hattie said. "Now for the other matter. I was performing at a gala last evening."

"Yes," Lynch said. "I was there. You and your mother were quite entertaining."

"Thank you." Hattie acknowledged the compliment with a polite nod. "While upstairs changing, I overheard Frederick Ziegler speaking to someone in his study. They talked about an assassination, sinking a passenger ship, and blaming the United States to stop a base from being built in Natal."

"You're sure they said Natal?"

"Very sure."

"What ship? When?" Lynch's eyes widened with curiosity. The urgency in his voice suggested that she had indeed stumbled onto something important.

"They didn't say."

"Who was Ziegler talking to?"

"I believe two men from the Italian Embassy."

"Is there anything else?"

"I'm afraid not. That's all I heard."

"Thank you for the information, Miss James." Lynch stood. "I'll forward your report through diplomatic channels."

Hattie wasn't sure what that meant, but she was sure he was holding something back. And what was with "diplomatic channels"? Bureaucratic red tape would slow any action. "How long will that take?"

"I'll send your concern in the next pouch, so it should reach the State Department in two weeks."

"Two weeks?" Hattie tossed her hands in the air in frustration. "I heard them say a hundred people would be on board that ship. Something needs to be done about it today."

"I can inform the Brazilian Foreign Ministry about your allegation, but there's little they can do without a specific threat."

"Pathetic."

"Yes, well." Lynch adjusted his tie, adding a smug lift of his nose. "Your country thanks you."

Once Lynch left, Hattie wasn't sure whether he was a bureaucrat slow to act or was sly and holding something back.

Leo closed the door and folded his arms across his chest. "Well, I'll be darned, Hattie. You are full of surprises."

Hattie shook her head. "I'm trying to do the right thing, but I doubt I did any good."

"From what I can tell about Jack, he's a by-the-book kind of guy. I'll do what I can to ensure the proper people know about this."

"Thank you, Leo. I appreciate that." Hattie trusted Leo to do what he could, but that didn't preclude the State Department bureaucracy her father had complained about for years from derailing Leo's effort to stop the attack.

Once they exited the embassy and she and David were heading home, she mentally listed everyone who knew about that logbook. Baumann and his men were all dead. Agent Butler and Nala Cohen were missing. Maya, David, and her father knew Hattie's intentions, but none had a reason to retrieve the book. Maya had no stake in its contents. David was there when Hattie gave it to Butler and viewed turning it over as a way to escape this mess. Her father had given her the book as leverage with the FBI. Unless Butler and Cohen had turned into traitors, or one turned on the other, only one possibility remained: someone else must have followed them from the plantation to the dry cleaner. The back of Hattie's neck tingled. No one around her would be safe until she discovered who had the logbook.

10

By the time they reached the house, Hattie had convinced herself that another bad actor had been responsible for the missing logbook, and Ziegler was the likely suspect. When David pulled into Eva's garage, a dark brown delivery vehicle came up the driveway and stopped behind them. Hattie got out. As she walked closer, she noticed the official-looking blue-and-gold emblem on the door with "D.C.T." written diagonally across it and "Telégrafo" below it.

A man wearing a gray uniform exited the driver's side, and Hattie approached, greeting him in Portuguese. "Good afternoon. May I help you?"

"Yes, I have a telegram for Miss James."

"I'm Hattie James." She wondered who would write to her at her mother's house and worried it might have been a coded message from the FBI.

Once he handed her a sealed envelope, David gave him a few reals, and the man tipped his cap in appreciation and drove back down the hill.

David closed the garage door, and they entered the property through the garden gate. Hattie secured her purse over her shoulder before sliding her finger under the envelope flap and pulling out the yellow slip of paper. The telegraph company logo and today's date were printed at the top of the letter. The communique was addressed to Eva's home via Washington, DC,

United States, bolstering her fear of the FBI having sent it. She drifted her focus to the bottom and was relieved to see her sister's name.

Hattie read the text. "Couldn't stand it any longer. Needed to see for myself that you're okay after what happened. Will arrive at Port of Rio on SS *Brazil* on Mother's Day, Sunday, May 11th. Traveling alone. Love, Olivia." She stopped before reaching the front door and reread the words to absorb her sister's message. Olivia was coming to Rio by passenger ship in thirteen days. By ship. To Rio.

"My God." Hattie flew a hand over her mouth, terrified Olivia's ship could have been the one Ziegler had talked about sinking in his high-stakes game of sabotage. Her legs wobbled, but David buoyed her by her arm.

"Are you okay?" he asked.

"It's Olivia." Hattie showed him the telegram. "She's coming to Rio via ship and could be in danger. She could be Ziegler's target."

"That's a long shot, Hattie. You don't know if Ziegler's talk was merely speculation. Even if it was something sinister, ships arrive in Rio daily."

"Cargo, but not passenger ships, not with war waging in Europe. This can't be coincidence." Hattie gathered herself. "I need to call her husband and make sure no one convinced Olivia to get on that ship."

"You're overreacting, Hattie."

She gave him a stone-cold look, making it clear he was lucky she didn't tear his head off. After everything she'd gone through with Baumann and her father's warning about Ziegler, she'd come to a natural conclusion— Ziegler was using Olivia as a pawn to find her father and the lists he had safeguarded with her. But David didn't know about her father's visit, so Hattie held back her anger.

"I can't stand by and do nothing. My sister's life could be at stake." She marched inside, picked up the phone receiver in the living room, and plopped on the couch. "Hello, operator? I need to place an overseas radio call to the United States."

"What number, miss?"

Given the time and day, Hattie assumed Frank would be at work. "Wait." She fished through her purse, pulled out her little address book, and flipped to the section labeled "W" until she located Frank Windom's direct line at his office.

The operator told Hattie to hold after she relayed Frank's name and his direct line. The dreaded waiting. Radio calls from Rio could take seconds or hours to connect, depending on the availability of circuits and operators along the route. She bobbed her leg up and down, hoping her nervous energy would somehow hurry things along.

Fifteen minutes went by before the operator returned. "I have your party, miss."

"Hattie?" Her brother-in-law's voice crackled over the radio connection.

"Frank?" She spoke loudly to overcome the static. "I just got Liv's telegram. I can't believe you let her come to Rio."

"What was I supposed to do? You know how Liv gets something in her head and can't let it go. She convinced herself that you and Eva weren't telling her the whole truth about what happened on the plantation. Letting her go was the only way for us to get an ounce of peace."

Hattie regretted sharing the ordeal with Olivia because of this reaction, but it was better than hiding more secrets from loved ones. However, her sister's instincts were right. As Hattie had with her mother, she had omitted the part about her father being there and saving her and Maya by killing those people.

"Did anyone talk to her about me or the incident? Maybe suggest she come to Rio?"

"I don't think so. Why would you ask that?"

Hattie prepared to tell another lie to avoid worrying Frank. "It's such a long trip. I'm worried about her traveling alone."

"She's not alone," Frank said.

"I'm confused. Her telegram said—"

"When I saw her off in New York, she bumped into an acquaintance heading to Santos on a church mission. That made me feel better about putting her on that ship. Besides, there's security all over. Some political bigwig is aboard."

"That's good," Hattie said, but both bits of information made her more suspicious. "Who was this missionary?"

"A woman. Her name is Heather."

Man or woman, Hattie would not put it past the FBI or the Nazis planting someone into Olivia's life to follow her and flush out their father and those lists. "All right, Frank, I'll pick her up at the docks and send you a telegram so you'll know she arrived safely."

"Thank you. That's a load off my shoulders."

Hattie finished the call and slumped further into the couch. She still could not be sure whether Ziegler engineered Olivia's passage onto that ship, and her encountering an "acquaintance" was too much of a coincidence for Hattie's liking. These revelations decided it. Hattie needed to learn more about Ziegler's plot. Otherwise, she would not rest easy about her sister's safety, and her gut told her that Baumann's logbook might hold the key. The only problem was that she wasn't sure who to trust for help.

Hattie excused herself and pretended to use the bathroom while deciding who in her inner circle she could trust with her life...and her sister's. She wasn't sure whether the missing logbook and the possible ship sinking and assassination were related, but after having her world turned upside down, coincidence surrounding the Nazis was an unlikelihood.

After flushing, she fished out the rolls of film from her dresser containing the photos she'd taken of the book before turning it over to Agent Butler and stuffed them into her purse. She returned to the living room, where David was still sitting on the couch.

"I need to go for a drive and clear my head." She hated lying to him, but she felt this was one secret she had to keep from him.

He rolled his eyes and sighed. Since Anna's funeral, he had been quiet about Maya, but Hattie suspected that was because intimacy was off the table since Maya still held her at arm's length. "Just say you're upset and going to her, hoping to get closer."

"Fine." Hattie extended her hand palm up and stared him in the eye. "May I have the car keys? I need to be with someone who won't say I'm overreacting."

"She still blames you for Anna's death." He dug into his pants pocket and handed her the keys.

"Which is why I haven't pushed things."

"Don't be long. Your mother will be back from her studio in a few hours."

"I won't."

Hattie drove downtown in the afternoon city traffic and parked near

Maya's modest home. She stared at the front door, remembering the times she stood there with Maya when Anna was still missing, wondering how to console her and hoping for a first kiss. Then, one night, when Hattie felt her lowest after encountering her father, she came here seeking comfort and found it in Maya's arms. That night of passion and Maya's willingness to show her vulnerability had flipped Hattie's world around, erasing the pain of Helen Reed's past betrayal. Hattie had learned to trust someone with her heart again, and Maya was worth waiting for while she worked through her grief. Hattie was taking a chance by coming here, but she refused to shrink back behind her walls while her sister might be in danger.

She walked to the door, carrying her purse with the film, and knocked. Maya had seemed more like herself since starting work at the Golden Room. Her bright expression had returned when speaking to guests or other employees, but when Hattie entered her orbit, the lines on her brow grew more prominent as a sadness stole her smile.

Maya opened the door, offering another sad look. The hurt and pain were still in her eyes but much softer than it had been in the previous weeks. They stood in silence for several moments, the longing between them drawing an invisible, undeniable lifeline.

Hattie finally said, "May I come in? I need a favor."

Maya remained quiet, but her eyes said she was torn over opening her heart again. Without a word, she opened the door wider, letting Hattie into her home.

The living room had changed dramatically since the funeral reception. Maya had different furniture and decorations. The items all appeared new and sleek with the times, but the room lacked the homey feel it once held with pieces collected over the years.

"My, this is different," Hattie said.

"I couldn't live with the memories, so I packed up some things and gave others away."

Hattie ached for her. Everyone mourned in their own way, but she recognized how daily reminders could be too painful to endure. "I'm a firm believer in fresh starts." Maybe it wasn't the smartest thing for Hattie to say while she still sought to rekindle their connection. It was a virtual invitation for Maya to push her away.

"What's the favor?" Maya dipped her stare, but Hattie didn't know what to think of her reaction. Unsure, she couldn't discern whether this marked their end or a new beginning.

"I had hoped you could develop some film for me, but if you gave your equipment away—"

"No, I still have everything, but I'll have to get some boxes down from the attic."

"If you're not up to it, I'll understand."

"No, no. It's fine. What do you need developed?"

Hattie lowered her gaze, knowing the topic she was about to raise would surface horrible memories for them. "Remember the logbook my father handed me that day?"

Maya became stiff and only nodded.

"I gave it to the FBI, but now the book and agents are missing, and I fear their disappearance is connected."

"What does that have to do with the film you need me to develop?" Maya asked.

"Before I gave the book to Agent Butler, I took pictures of it." Hattie opened her purse and removed four rolls. "It's all right here."

"Why can't you simply give the film to the American Embassy?" Maya asked.

"Because I need to see what's on those pages."

Hattie explained what she had overheard at Ziegler's mansion the night of the gala, the tepid bureaucratic response she had encountered at the US Embassy, and her fear that the ship her sister was sailing on might be Ziegler's target.

"I know this is a lot to ask, but if Olivia is in danger and there's a chance I can save her, I need to try." Hattie placed the rolls in Maya's hands and cupped them, knowing she would understand her motivation.

Maya's lips quivered. "All right, I'll help you."

There was an eerie similarity between Hattie's and Maya's quests to save their sisters, and Hattie felt her uneasiness.

"Thank you, Maya." Hattie squeezed Maya's hands containing the film, sensing that more of the chasm separating them had filled in, narrowing the gap.

She helped Maya retrieve some boxes from the attic and set up her darkroom again in the spare bedroom. After hanging the blackout curtain over the window and stringing two levels of clothesline from wall to wall, Maya installed the red light in the ceiling socket.

Over the next few hours, Hattie watched Maya meticulously develop the negatives and then expose the photographic paper, develop, fix, and wash it, and hang each photograph to dry. When they worked together at the Golden Room and were alone for brief moments when Maya delivered her hot tea after her performance, Maya still kept her distance. Otherwise, guests and other employees kept them at arm's length. But, in the privacy of Maya's darkroom, awash in a scarlet glow, Maya didn't pull back once—an encouraging development.

When batches of photos had dried, Hattie stacked them in their precise order according to the logbook page numbers to make room for more. In the end, they developed nearly a hundred pictures.

"What do you plan to do with these?" Maya turned off the red light and opened the curtains, letting sunlight bathe the room again. "The pages are written in German."

"I'll have my father translate them."

Maya gave a bitter laugh. "A lot of horrible things happened at that plantation, and he was obviously part of it. I wouldn't trust him to tell you the whole truth."

And the rift between them returned.

"He's not like that, Maya."

"I know he raised you, and you love him, but what do you really know about the man? You had no idea he was mixed up with Baumann and the Nazis."

Maya made good points, but the last few months had taught Hattie that Karl could weave intricate lies. She laughed, realizing she was much like him. She'd been living a fabrication all her adult life, hiding her sexuality. And after the FBI had dragged her into the world of spies, she'd learned to wrap lie after lie around half-truths to make her stories believable and easier to remember. It was all to protect her family, and she believed her father was doing the same thing—lying to protect the ones he loved.

"I hear you," Hattie said, "but I have to trust he would provide a full and accurate translation when his other daughter's life might be at risk."

"Suit yourself." Maya finished cleaning her work area while Hattie watched. The sense of want and longing she'd gotten from Maya when she first arrived was gone, tossed out with the remnants of the developing solution. But Hattie was accustomed to the setback. It was the same story since the funeral—two steps forward, one step back—but at least she still felt them making progress.

Hattie followed Maya to the kitchen, carrying the stack of photos and negatives in two thick envelopes. Maya poured them some lemonade and sat at the small aluminum dining table. Hattie joined her, sipping the drink and thinking about what she should do next about the photographs. Her apartment in the States and hotel in Rio before moving in with her mother had been ransacked several times, so she didn't want to risk keeping them at Eva's home.

"I have another favor to ask."

"What now?" Maya sounded annoyed, but Hattie had to push.

"Can you hold on to these until I can get them translated? Keep them in a safe place where no one can find them?"

"You can't do that at your mother's?"

"Probably, but I trust you the most." Hattie reached across the table and clasped Maya's hand.

Maya squeezed and visibly swallowed before pulling back. "Yes, there's a loose floorboard under my bed. I can store them there."

"Thank you, Maya." Hattie drank more of her lemonade. "I've been meaning to ask about the insurance claim on the Halo Club."

"They paid out on Friday"—Maya's expression turned long—"but it's not enough to rebuild."

"What do you plan to do?"

"I don't know. I have ninety days to clean up the mess. Otherwise, the city will condemn the property and take it over."

"Have you considered a bank loan?"

"I doubt anyone would loan that amount to a woman." Maya took their empty glasses to the sink.

"You have time." Hattie stood, resisting the urge to reach for Maya, but she formed the beginning of a solution to Maya's dilemma in her head. The specifics weren't clear, but she knew it would bring them closer together. "I'm sure things will work out."

The sound of one of Hattie's songs playing and the heavy, earthy aroma of black beans, pork, and rice cooking hung in the hallway when she walked into the house through the private entrance. She smiled at the familiar smell. After dropping off her purse in the bedroom, Hattie entered the kitchen, discovering her mother and David preparing the evening meal. Eva was dressed casually in slacks, chopping kale to put into the steamer, and David was peeling a fresh orange for a side dish, sending its zesty citrus scent into the air.

"Hi," Hattie said. Both heads turned when she approached the stove and inhaled fragrances rising with the steam from the deep pot. "Umm, feijoada. My favorite."

"I'm glad you made it in time for dinner, sweetheart." Eva flung a dishtowel over her shoulder. "Did you find anything you like?"

"No." Hattie looked at David with questioning eyes.

"I warned you the women's bathing suits here aren't like the ones in New York," David said, adding a furtive wink so only Hattie could see.

"And you would know this how?" Eva asked, swatting David's arm.

"I have eyes," he said, shrugging.

Hattie mouthed "thank you" to him. The lie was innocent enough to be believable. She wasn't sure if she had it in her today to tell another one after the promising day with Maya.

Hattie turned to Eva. "Mother, did David tell you I accepted Frederick's invitation to sing with you at his party next week."

A smile grew slowly on Eva's lips until she was beaming. "That's wonderful, sweetheart. We can discuss the song selection over dinner."

The meal was delicious, and the conversation was pleasant, with Eva and Hattie agreeing to cut three songs from their earlier appearance together to shorten the performance. The best part of the evening was that Hattie didn't have to concoct any stories to cover where she'd been or what she'd been doing. The only blemish on the evening was not telling Eva about Olivia coming. Until she was sure her sister's ship wasn't in danger, keeping her worry in check during her mother's daily gushing over the impending visit would be impossible.

After saying goodnight, Hattie tossed and turned for an hour in bed. Her mind drifted between worry for Olivia, the stumbling blocks to getting into Ziegler's study to learn more about the sabotage plot, the many lies she had to keep track of, the secrets her father had entrusted her with, and the closeness she experienced with Maya today.

Hattie gave up trying to sleep and slipped out without waking David next to her. After grabbing David's satchel, which contained the one source of distraction she could try to mitigate, she tiptoed to the living room and turned on an overhead light. She pulled out the sheet music her father had gifted her on Christmas Eve, removed the rubber band around it, and placed the stack on the coffee table. She laid out the twenty songs in four rows of five, staggered so she could see all the song titles. Her father had said each held special meaning to him and to never let them go. They had to contain the lists Baumann had killed several women over, but how?

Hattie picked up one set and studied the lyrics, notes, and stanzas but wasn't skilled enough at reading music to discern abnormalities. She examined a second, a third, and a fourth but yielded the same results.

"Can't sleep, sweetheart?"

Hattie snapped her stare toward Eva's voice. She entered the room, wearing her silk robe and slippers, and made Hattie feel like she'd been caught sneaking into the house an hour after curfew. "No. How about you?"

"Menopause. What's your excuse?"

"I have a lot on my mind."

"Nightmares again?"

Hattie was still haunted most nights by her ordeal at the plantation, but she wasn't up for the lie. "Not tonight."

"Anything you want to talk about?"

"Not really."

Eva peeked over Hattie's shoulder. "Picking new songs for the Golden Room?"

"No. Father gave me this collection of sheet music for Christmas, and I was studying the titles." Her explanation wasn't complete honesty but was the closest she'd come to it when cornered since arriving in Rio. Telling the truth, as incomplete as it was, felt refreshing. Maybe her mother would have some insight into the selection.

"Let me see." Eva sat beside her and scanned the sheets. "What an odd compilation."

"I thought so too, but it was very thoughtful." Or sly. They held secrets her father entrusted to her. Once Karl answered her signal to translate the logbook, she would not let him leave until he told her why.

11

Four days later

Hattie performed Thursday through Sunday, each evening wearing a stem of edelweiss from her mother's indoor garden—the signal for her father to know she had to speak to him. However, her call went unanswered. Karl had said he would watch over her and come whenever she needed him, but after four nights, she worried something may have happened to him or he might have moved on. Both possibilities frightened her.

She'd woken every day, anxious to read the newspaper to learn if his body was found or if a passenger ship had been sunk somewhere in the Atlantic, but she could no longer stand by and do nothing. Since the FBI tossed her into the world of spies and Nazis in Rio, she had taken comfort in knowing her father was lurking in the background, but tonight, as she prepared to perform at Ziegler's party for local business leaders, she had a sense of being marooned. Nevertheless, she decided to take advantage of every opportunity to learn more about Frederick's plan to sabotage a passenger ship.

After flushing the toilet in the upstairs powder room and washing her hands at the sink, Hattie removed from her handbag the Minox micro-camera Agent Butler had given her to spy on Baumann before his disappearance. This event wasn't as formal as the gala, so she had selected a stage dress that covered her cleavage, allowing her to stuff the camera into her bra between her breasts. She adjusted it with two fingers to ensure a bulge didn't show while performing. Now, she was prepared to snoop at a moment's notice.

Hattie returned to the guest room, discovering Eva applying the finishing touches on her makeup. "Ready to bring the house down again, Mother?"

Eva placed her tube of lipstick on the vanity and fluffed her hair. "Ready." She stood from the bench and locked arms with Hattie. "Let's knock 'em dead."

As it was during the gala, the other upstairs rooms were closed, and the same guard controlled access to the second floor. The muscular man lowered the velvet rope at the base of the stairs, allowing Hattie and Eva to pass. They entered the kitchen, and Hattie touched Eva's arm when she saw Monica loading a tray of finger food for the partygoers in the ballroom.

"I'll be a moment, Mother." Hattie stepped to the counter, and Monica smiled. "I was so glad you and your husband came to the Golden Room as my guests on Thursday. Did you two enjoy dinner and the performance?"

"Yes, Miss James, everything was wonderful. I think Javier is a little in love with you."

Hattie laughed. "The way he held your hand all evening, I have a feeling he only has eyes for you." Ziegler's voice came over the loudspeaker in the adjoining room, announcing Eva and Hattie to the stage. Hattie hugged her. "I gotta go."

For the next forty-five minutes, Hattie and Eva wowed the group of businessmen with David playing piano. Hattie recognized some of them from previous performances at the Golden Room, but they appeared more relaxed and let loose with a few hoots and hollers. Throughout the show, Ziegler's gaze remained fixed on Eva, undressing her with his eyes in a crowded room of Rio's elite. The man had no shame.

After the performance, Eva was in her element, mingling with the guests. She controlled the conversation and strategically touched an arm here and there, raising Ziegler's eyebrows several times. Flirtation was part of maintaining the allure and keeping people returning for more shows or buying more records. As Hattie knew from personal experience, it was a balancing act of grasping how far to take it without encouraging the recipient. However, knowing when to push it led Hattie to meet Helen and other women. As the evening wore on, Hattie realized her mother had it down to a science, but she doubted she ever took it beyond the boundary of appropriateness, at least with a fan.

When a large group of businessmen cornered Eva and Ziegler, Hattie whispered to David. "I'm heading up." That was his cue to keep an eye on the guard, and if the brute looked like he might head upstairs, David's job was to distract him. She squeezed his hand and tried to let go, but he held on, locking eyes with her. His message was clear. He had her back, but she needed to be careful.

She walked to the staircase and spoke to the guard. "I need to change."

The man unclipped the stanchion and allowed Hattie to pass. She climbed at an average pace. After reaching the top landing, she tested the knob to Ziegler's study. It was unlocked, so she eased the door open, praying it didn't creak. Once inside, she closed it, slowly releasing the knob to avoid making noise.

The glow from the first-floor lights through the balcony's glass doors softly illuminated the dark room. A faint, sweet smell of cigar smoke hung in the air, suggesting Ziegler had been in the office before tonight's party.

Hattie crept her fingertips along the wall, searching for the switch, and came across it. The overhead brass chandelier came to life, casting the room in warm yellow light. She strode directly to the desk. The tray next to the ivory pipe contained fresh ash. She opened the leather portfolio at the desk's center. Several papers written in German were inside. Hattie understood only a few words, but it appeared to be from the Swiss Embassy. Unsure what might contain helpful information, she removed the camera from her bra and snapped a picture of the sheets.

She opened the top drawer, noticing pens, pencils, paper clips, writing paper, and a letter opener. Another drawer had tobacco, a cigar cutter, and nail clippers, but no papers. Turning her attention to a lower file drawer, she pulled on it but found it locked, which drew her interest. After grabbing the opener from the top drawer, she attempted to force the lock but had no luck. She tried picking it with a paper clip but yielded the same result.

"Think, Hattie," she said, running both hands through her hair and scanning the contents of the top drawer again. She hadn't much time before the downstairs guard would question why she was taking so long. When her gaze settled on the nail clippers, she recalled her father breaking into his desk drawer with a pair after losing the key. That should have clued her in that her father had skills beyond those of a diplomat. She grabbed the clippers from the top drawer, spun the attached file out, and inserted it in the lock. After several jiggles, raking the file back and forth like her father had done, the lock turned.

"Thank you, Father," she said softly while opening the drawer.

There were a handful of hanging files. Hattie thumbed through them, but nothing stood out. The size of the desk made her suspect the drawer should have been twice as deep despite having extended it fully. A knock on the back of it sounded as if it might be hollow, so she wiggled the rear panel until it came loose, revealing a hidden cubbyhole. A leather roll was inside. She untied the straps, discovering it was a document pouch. Several pages were written in German. Her pulse picked up when she flipped to a diagram of a ship's lower compartment. She gasped at the last page, a map of Guanabara Bay near Rio.

"This is it," she said, snapping pictures of the map and each page in the bundle.

With three pages to go, a loud knocking from somewhere on the floor startled her.

"Hattie?" David shouted from somewhere close by. "I'm having the car pulled around. We're leaving in ten minutes."

A second voice sounded closer. "Where is she?"

"I told you I'll hurry her up," David said, followed by stomping and a series of noisy thumps.

Hattie finished taking the photos, rolled up the documents, returned them to their hiding place, and rushed to the door while stuffing the camera into her bra. She turned off the overhead light, casting the room into darkness, and debated what to do next. Despite Eva being Ziegler's lover, getting caught in his office after last week's close call the night of the gala would not end well. She twisted the knob. Rapid breathing and a racing heartbeat made her dizzy, but staying there was not an option, so she inched the door open until the glow from the hallway poured inside.

She peeked outside. No one was in sight, but Hattie wasn't out of danger yet. She raced to the guest room and changed into her slacks, blouse, and flat shoes at breakneck speed. After grabbing her purse and throwing her stage dress over her arm, she hurried to the corridor and downstairs, discovering David holding a hand to his back at the bottom landing and a man kneeling beside him. A small crowd had gathered with Eva at the forefront, looking concerned, and Ziegler was beside her.

"My God, David." Hattie rushed to him, placing her hand on his shoulder. "What happened? Are you all right?"

"I tripped down the stairs because of this ass." He gestured toward the guard. "He couldn't wait one damn minute for you to change out of that stage dress. I told him the zipper gets stuck sometimes."

"Are you hurt? Is anything broken?" If he injured himself seriously while protecting her, Hattie would never forgive herself.

"Just my pride." David straightened and turned stiffly to the man speaking to him.

"Follow my finger," the man said to David, moving his index finger from one side of his field of vision to the other.

David complied and said, "I'm fine, Doctor."

"Are you sure?" Ziegler shifted and focused on the doctor. "Should I call for an ambulance?"

"There's no need, Herr Ziegler," the doctor said, turning to David. "You might be a little sore tomorrow, but if it doesn't resolve within a few days, you should see your physician."

"Thank you, I will," David said. "I apologize for the commotion, Frederick."

"Nonsense," Ziegler said. "I'm glad you're unhurt."

"Hattie and I are heading home," David said.

After saying goodbye to Eva, Hattie and David had the valet bring up the car, and they drove away.

"Are you sure you're all right?" Hattie asked.

"I'm fine. I faked stumbling and controlled the fall." He glanced at her after turning onto the boulevard. "Did you find anything?"

"I think so." Hattie patted the micro-camera stored in her bra. "I found a roll of documents in a hidden compartment in his desk that contained a map of the bay. Everything was written in German, so I'll have to get it translated."

"Who do you have in mind?"

"My father could, but I don't know how to locate him." Hattie had yet to tell him about the edelweiss Karl had told her to use to signal him. She wasn't sure why she had held that information back other than it was her only connection with her father. "Maybe Commander Bell can help."

"Do you really want to give this to the embassy?" David said. "They weren't much help when you brought them your suspicion last week. Besides, you're not even sure what you have."

"You have a point. Perhaps I'll ask my mother if she knows someone who can translate something from German."

"And what will you tell her when she asks why?"

"You're not making this easy, David."

"My job isn't to make things easier for you. It's protecting you."

"And I appreciate that, but the priority is to develop the film."

"Where will you go? You can't just walk into the corner drugstore with possible sabotage plans," he said.

Hattie considered telling another lie, but he would figure it out eventually since he knew from being at Maya's house after the funeral that she dabbled in photography and developed her own photos.

"Maya."

"Are you two on good enough terms for such a big favor?"

"We'll see." Hattie couldn't tell him she had already called on Maya for the same favor regarding Baumann's logbook. Combined with what she had held back about her father, Hattie questioned why she kept so many secrets from David when he had protected her long before the FBI insinuated itself into her life. Instinct told her she might find a way out of this mess when she realized the answer.

12

The following morning

David insisted on driving Hattie to Maya's home, citing she would be in danger if anyone suspected what she had. But that meant things could get tricky if Maya let on that she'd done this last week for Hattie.

Hattie stood on the stoop after knocking, feeling her nerves build at the possibility of David figuring things out about the logbook photos. The door opened, and Maya appeared, looking surprised at seeing Hattie at her doorstep. A brief grin of satisfaction formed on her lips before her gaze shifted to David standing behind Hattie. A long look of disappointment replaced her smile.

"What are you two doing here?"

"May we come in?" Hattie said.

Maya invited them into the house. Once the door closed, Hattie drew her into a hug even as Maya tried to pull away. "It's good to see you," she said before whispering into her ear, "He doesn't know about the other film. Please play along." She hoped Maya understood. Otherwise, Hattie would have to tell another lie to cover her tracks.

Maya pulled back and narrowed her eyes in curiosity. "It's good to see you, too."

"I have a favor to ask," Hattie said.

Maya gestured for Hattie and David to sit. "What is it?"

Hattie pulled the micro-camera from her handbag and placed it on the table.

"What is that?" Maya fixed her gaze on it, cocking her head slightly.

"It's a camera the FBI gave me to get photos of Baumann's plantation."

Hattie repeated the story she told Maya last week about overhearing a sabotage plot at Ziegler's mansion during the gala and her fear that her sister's ship bound for Rio might be the target.

Maya nodded and appeared interested, making it seem like she was hearing the account for the first time, and Hattie was never so grateful.

"The camera?" Maya gestured her chin toward it. "You took pictures of something?"

"I performed at Ziegler's again last night and sneaked into his study. I found a hidden compartment in his desk and discovered what might be the sabotage plans, so I took pictures of them."

"Might be?"

"They were written in German, so I can't be sure."

"I take it you want me to develop the film."

"Yes. I can't trust taking it to the drugstore, and I don't know anyone else who can help me." Hattie squeezed Maya's hand, pleading and expressing thanks for not giving away the secret about the logbook photos.

"I'm low on photo paper." Maya raised her eyebrow. It was a reminder that they had nearly depleted her entire supply last week. "How many pictures did you take?"

"Ten."

"I think I have enough," Maya said before turning to David. "Come. Wait in the kitchen while Hattie and I develop the film. I'll pour you some fresh lemonade."

Once David was settled at the small dining table, Maya guided Hattie to her darkroom. The blackout curtains were still up but open, and the clotheslines they had strung last week were still hanging.

"You kept everything up." Hattie had thought she would have taken the equipment down as soon as she left last week since Maya had sounded determined to escape the memories.

"I hadn't gotten around to taking them down."

In the months Hattie had known her, Maya never put off a task, and her procrastination could have meant one of two things. She could have been struggling to find the mental energy to take down the memories, or it could have been a good sign that she might soon come to terms with Anna's death. Hattie chose to believe the latter and smiled.

Maya placed the Minox on the counter and examined it. "Interesting. I've never seen a camera this small."

"It was easy to conceal." Hattie pointed to her cleavage.

Maya laughed and blushed. "Can you show me how to open it?"

Hattie pointed to the release button on the door housing the film, grazing Maya's finger, but Maya didn't pull away. It was another good sign, but a quandary formed whether to push the touch further. Hattie considered a caress on the cheek or a gentle stroke of her hair but settled on a second graze of her thumb, keeping it in place while she studied Maya's hand. Despite being strong and calloused from hard work, it had a delicate, erotic caress. It was something Hattie never knew she craved until meeting Maya Reyes.

Their gazes met, and Hattie recognized the battle in Maya's eyes. It was plain she was struggling with associating her sister's death with Hattie, yet she still felt the bond between them. Hattie could not risk losing the progress they had made, so she looked away before Maya could.

"Just keep this button pressed and slide the door open."

Maya rewound the film and pulled out the cassette. "This is so small."

"Can you develop it?"

"I think so. The hardest part will be making the negatives." Maya prepped the developing tank and solutions and had to get creative with the reel to hold the film in place since it was so narrow. After processing the negatives, she held them up to inspect them. "This is odd."

Hattie stepped closer, so they touched shoulder to shoulder.

"Only the first frame was exposed, and it appears it was exposed multiple times."

"What?" Frustration built quickly as it sank in that the pictures she had taken were no good. "How could that happen?"

"It means the film advance lever was loose or defective. Did you drop the camera?"

"No, I was careful with it."

"Let me look at it." Maya inspected the device, pulling on various pieces. "It's broken."

"Since I didn't drop it, what else could have caused that?" Hattie asked.

"Wear and tear, but this thing looks brand-new. It almost seems like it was tampered with."

This was no coincidence, which frightened Hattie. Someone didn't want her to take more pictures with that camera. There was no telling when it was sabotaged since Nala Cohen gave it back to her with a fresh roll of film the day after the plantation massacre. Nala, Agent Butler, and David were the only ones who knew she had it. Nala could have sabotaged it before giving it to Hattie, but that made no sense. David had ample opportunity every night since she hid it in her underwear drawer. Agent Butler or any number of people had plenty of opportunities to sneak in when Eva's house was unoccupied. Or the lever could have simply been faulty.

"Thank you for trying, Maya."

Maya put a few things away on the shelf above the counter and turned to Hattie. "Wish I could have helped."

"But you have." Hattie stepped closer and, without thinking, caressed Maya's cheek. Knowing she had gone too far, she was about to retreat, but Maya melted into her touch. The one step backward she had expected was replaced by several steps forward. The pull connecting them pulsated in the silence. It was more potent than the days leading up to their first kiss, and Hattie missed the sensation. She needed their emotional intimacy back, to be vulnerable in the other's arms again.

Hattie licked her lips, preparing them for the kiss she desperately wanted, and inched her head closer until their mouths were a breath apart. She felt the steamy exhale from Maya's breathing and was sure Maya wanted this, too. The pull was now in control, and Hattie had no intention to stop.

She pressed their lips together in a tender, emotion-filled kiss. Desire flowed between them like a whisper caught in the breeze, floating on their passion for one another. As she prepared to deepen it, a tear from Maya fell on Hattie's cheek, breaking the spell. Hattie pulled back to see tears streaming down Maya's cheeks, so she wiped them away with her thumbs.

"I don't know how to stop the pain of losing her," Maya said.

"Time will do that for you." Hattie kissed her cheek and stepped back. "We better get going."

They returned to the kitchen, where David sat at the table, reading the newspaper and sipping lemonade.

"That was quick," he said.

"The camera was broken," Hattie said. She explained more about the advance lever but didn't express her suspicion that someone might have damaged it on purpose.

"What do you plan to do next?" David asked. "Time is running out."

This entire situation was a nightmare. Olivia's ship would reach the Port of Rio in four days. Now that her pictures were a bust, she had to return to Ziegler's study and get her hands on those plans long enough to take photos with her personal camera, which would be tricky. Ziegler didn't have another social event scheduled before then, and Hattie was sure the guard likely said something to him that would make him suspicious of her. She hated to think it, but if her sister's ship was the target, her only hope of saving Olivia rested on convincing Eva that Ziegler wasn't the man she thought he was and that her other daughter's life was in danger.

"Talk to my mother."

13

Eva danced to Hattie's record while cleaning the kitchen after the breakfast she cooked for Hattie and David. She had listened to her daughter's records over the years, studying the arrangements, the lyrics, and Hattie's artistic choices throughout each song. Eva would have made different choices, but that was rooted more in habit than her having her professor's hat on and correcting her student. And if Eva were honest with Hattie, she would tell her that her stylistic selections suited her voice better than what she would have recommended. She realized the teacher had much to learn from her long-ago pupil.

Her phone rang, and Eva answered it. "Olá."

"Hello, Miss Machado." The woman spoke in Portuguese. "This is Sonja Rodriquez. My daughter, Elizabeth, has an appointment with you after school today, but I'm afraid she's sick and must cancel."

"I hope it's nothing serious." Eva finished the call, learning the girl had a minor stomach virus but should be better for next week's lesson. She moved to her home office to annotate the cancelation in the girl's record and confirmed her appointment calendar was clear for the rest of the day. Wednesdays were always her lightest day of the week since most schools in the city held football practice that day for the upcoming Friday matches. If Hattie hadn't gone into town with David, this would have been the perfect day to take her daughter to Rio's bustling shopping district on Rua Ouvidor and walk the enchanting mosaic sidewalk on Avenida Rio Branco before stopping for lunch. Eva wanted to share more of Rio with her daughter and hoped Hattie would stay long enough to get to know the city as she did.

Eva retrieved the wineglass she'd left on her desk the other night and placed it in the dishwasher. David had left his spare reading glasses on the kitchen table, so she picked them up and put them on the dresser in the room he shared with Hattie. As she turned to leave, she noticed the satchel Hattie had out last week when she could not sleep. It was sitting on the floor against the dresser.

She recalled some of the song titles Hattie had said Karl had gifted her and remembered laughing at a few as they brought back several fond memories of better times when they were a family. Some titles escaped her, so she opened the tote and pulled out the bundle of sheet music that resembled the ones Hattie was looking at that night. She laughed again at some songs and was perplexed by others. One caught her attention. Hattie had sung "Cheek to Cheek" with Maggie Moore on stage at the Golden Room, but Eva hadn't heard her sing it since. Those two had done a masterful job with that song, and Eva thought it would be the perfect addition to the set list she and Hattie had put together for their performances at Frederick's parties.

Eva grabbed the song collection, went to her office, and sat at the upright piano she kept in the house for practice. After setting up the sheet music, she started playing "Cheek to Cheek" and was having fun with the song when she noticed something odd printed between the lines in the stanzas. She stopped and examined the sheet more closely, discovering a series of markings that should not have been there. They could have been imperfections created during the printing process, but Eva noted the sequences were different on the exact spot from page to page, which made her curious. She pulled out another sheet of music and inspected it, and another, and another. A pattern of no pattern emerged. Each page had similar markings within the stanzas, but none were the same.

Eva decided they weren't a misprint but were placed there for some purpose. She returned to Hattie's bedroom, brought David's satchel to the living room, and reviewed the other music sheets, most of which were

Hattie's recorded songs. Only the batch from Karl's gift contained the markings.

"What are you up to, Karl?" she said.

Her ex-husband had been cagey for years about how he spent his time away, which had compounded Eva's mistrust of him, culminating in their civil divorce. He had changed after his posting in Germany, collecting and reading the writings of that madman, Hitler, and socializing with Nazi diplomats beyond what was required of his job. No matter how he tried to explain himself, the armpit tattoo he returned with proved he had become one of them.

Whatever he hid in the sheet music, he had involved Hattie, which was unforgivable. Now, it was up to Eva to protect her. She had to know what was behind those markings. She grabbed a pencil and some writing paper, listed each song, and copied the markings from every page, including the spaces and moving down a line to represent a different stanza. When she finished, another pattern emerged. The markings appeared to be a series of dots and dashes resembling Morse code, suggesting they contained hidden messages. Since Karl had gifted the music to Hattie, he either knew about the secret code or had added it himself. Knowing his past associations and what the FBI had arrested him for, whatever the messages were, they likely had something to do with Nazi Germany, and that infuriated Eva. Karl had tried to justify his actions by telling Hattie in her backyard months ago that things weren't as they seemed, that his being a Nazi was only part of the truth, but Eva didn't believe him for one minute. She'd lived with Karl's lies for too many years and would not let him drag their daughter into his world of deception.

Eva put the music away and returned the satchel to its original position. After returning to the couch, she folded her notes, placed them in the pocket of her slacks, and silently debated what to do next. She could investigate what was concealed in the sheet music, but that would be time-consuming. She had a gut feeling that Hattie was in danger, requiring immediate action.

Soon, Hattie and David appeared in the backyard, walking through the breezeway connecting the garage to the main house. Eva waited for them to drop things off in their room and come into the living room, pretending to read the morning newspaper so as not to appear anxious. The trick was getting Hattie alone without worrying David until Hattie wanted to involve him.

David entered first. "Hi, Eva. I'm heading to the kitchen. Can I get you anything?"

She hoped he would stay there long enough for her to speak to Hattie. "I'm fine, thank you," Eva said, concealing her uneasiness when Hattie came into the room as he left. She put the paper on the table. "I'm glad you're back, sweetheart. I have something to show you."

Hattie looked frazzled. "Can this wait, Mother? I need to speak to you about something important."

David reentered the room with a glass of water in his hand.

"We can talk in my bedroom. I wanted to show you another stage dress in my closet that would look great on you." Eva stood and started walking without waiting for a response from Hattie. She knew it was rude and made her appear selfish, but it was the only way to get her daughter alone.

Hattie huffed and followed.

Eva closed the door after they entered her room and ushered Hattie to the bed. "Let's sit, sweetheart. I also have something important to tell you about your father."

Hattie froze briefly before cocking her head. "What about him?"

"When you couldn't sleep last week, I discovered you in the living room looking through a collection of sheet music you said he gave you for Christmas. I remembered some titles and wanted to play one on the piano today, so I took them from David's satchel in your room."

"What about it?" Hattie appeared curiously fidgety.

"I noticed something different about the stanzas and looked at them more closely."

"What did you find?"

"I found markings on every page of every sheet of music."

"Could it have been a printing error?"

"That's what I thought at first, but the markings weren't the same from page to page." Eva pulled her notes from her front pocket and unfolded the paper in her lap. "I pored through the sheets and recreated what I found. I think it's Morse code."

Hattie grabbed the papers. "Like some type of hidden message?"

"Yes, and I think your father put them there."

"Why would he do that?"

"Don't act surprised, Hattie. We both know this has to do with his arrest, and I'm afraid possessing the sheet music has put you in danger."

Hattie flopped back on the bed, crying while holding a hand over her eyes. "I hate lying to you, Mother. You've been so kind to me since I arrived."

Eva straightened her spine. She could not stand having someone she loved being dishonest with her. "What have you been lying about?"

"Everything."

"What do you mean by everything?"

Hattie popped up and wiped the tears from her face. "Where do I start?"

"The beginning is always a good point."

"A month after Father's arrest..." Hattie explained how the FBI fed stories to the media to tank her career and threatened to haul in Olivia and her husband if Hattie didn't come to Brazil to flush out her father. Eva restrained her anger, allowing her daughter to continue. Hattie detailed how an agent in Rio, who was now nowhere to be found, had strong-armed her into ferreting out information about Heinz Baumann, but she didn't mind after discovering he was behind the kidnapping of the missing women, including Anna Reyes. She locked eyes with Eva. "When Baumann held a gun to my head, he threatened to kill me if I didn't give him the lists."

"What lists?" Eva asked, still holding back her outrage over how Karl had endangered her.

"I'm not sure, but I suspected they were in the sheet music. Father cautioned me about never letting them go when he gave them to me."

"That son of a—"

"Mother, don't. I don't need you badmouthing him when I have more important things to worry about."

"More important than your life being at risk?"

"Yes. I'm afraid Olivia might be in danger."

"But you said the FBI agent is missing. Doesn't that mean the threat to Olivia has passed?"

"No. I'm talking about her arriving in Rio by ship in four days."

"Olivia is coming here? Why? What about the kids? Are they coming too?"

"No. Just her. Frank hired a nanny to help while she's away. She wants to see for herself that I'm okay after the ordeal at the plantation."

"That's so like Olivia. She lets things stew for a while before going all in. But why do you think she's in danger?"

"I know you don't want to hear this, Mother, but it concerns Frederick."

"Not this again."

Eva sprang from the bed and stomped to her vanity. Hattie was never happy with her seeing Frederick romantically, and her daughter's lingering resentment over her infidelity hurt more than Eva would ever admit. Showing weakness was never her way. Showing strength when she had none was the only way she knew how to survive. Regrettably, this friction arose from a relationship that could never progress past informality. Her civil divorce from Karl may have legally ended their marriage, but in the eyes of the church and God, she was still married, meaning she would forever live alone.

Hattie followed and locked gazes with Eva in the mirror. "Please, just listen, Mother." The look in her eyes conveyed genuine fear and made Eva pause and nod her understanding. "I overheard Frederick in his study on the night of the gala..." Hattie explained Frederick and some men, whom she suspected were from the Italian contingent, had discussed sinking a passenger ship to drive a wedge between Brazil and the United States to prevent a naval base from being built in the north.

"This is preposterous, Hattie." Eva was convinced Hattie must have misunderstood what she had heard. Frederick was a Swiss ambassador and would never engage in matters of war.

"Listen, Mother." Hattie placed her hands atop Eva's shoulders and squeezed. "At the party last night, I sneaked into his office."

"For heaven's sake."

"I found documents in a hidden compartment written in German and a map of the bay. With everything Father has been involved in, I fear Olivia's ship might be a convenient target, a way to send me a message about Father's lists."

Eva gasped. Hattie would never lie to her about something this important. She was always protective of Olivia and would move mountains to ensure her safety. Some of what Hattie said made sense, but Eva had difficulty reconciling the Frederick she knew and the one her daughter had painted. She could believe what Hattie saw but hoped Frederick had an explanation for his involvement.

"We need to do something." Eva squeezed Hattie's hand on her shoulder.

"I've already spoken to Commander Bell at the embassy. The security chief promised to share the information with local authorities and the State Department but doubted they would act with nothing specific to go on."

"But what about the documents? We need to tell the police about them so they can stop the attack." Eva's stomach twisted at the thought of her baby girl being in danger. She'd do whatever it took, pay any price, to ensure she was safe. "I can bribe them to look into it."

"He's a diplomat. The police can't search his home."

"There has to be something we can do." Eva felt helpless. Desperate.

"Get me into Frederick's mansion again. If I can take photos of the documents, we can find someone to translate them."

"Tell me where they're at." Eva turned and clutched both Hattie's wrists. She could not risk putting her daughter in harm's way if her suspicions about Frederick were correct. "I'll call and tell him I'm spending the night. I'll take pictures while he's sleeping."

"No, Mother. It's too risky. You'll have no one covering your back. If you're caught, there's no telling what he might do."

"I'm sure the man is in love with me. He won't hurt me."

"If Ziegler is who I think he is, love has nothing to do with it. He's using you to get to Father."

Eva cocked her head back, recalling some questions Frederick had about Karl. Individually, they seemed innocent, but in total, they could be construed as probing. She also rethought the frequent late-night visitors to Frederick's home and quiet whispers. Eva had believed he was conducting diplomatic business as he had claimed, but now she thought Hattie's suspicions could have been true.

"What do you have in mind?"

"Arrange to take me over to scout the grounds for our wedding. That will justify bringing my camera. You keep him busy. I'll get into his study and take the pictures."

"I don't know, sweetheart." Eva turned to face Hattie.

"We have to." Hattie clutched Eva's arms, and the two stood, holding each other. "Olivia could be killed. How many servants will there be in the house tomorrow?"

"The cook, one maid, and a gardener. The driver stays in the garage guest room until he's called."

"Good. We can have the gardener with us while we walk the grounds. After I excuse myself, I'll send the maid on an errand. That will leave the cook to evade, but I doubt she will go upstairs. I should have plenty of time to get the pictures."

"You're sure about this?" Eva asked, feeling unsure about the whole thing. If anything happened to Hattie, she would never forgive herself.

"Yes. Now, make that call, but make the invitation for just the two of us."

"What about David? And what about your father's sheet music?"

"The music can wait. It's secure for now. We need to focus on Olivia, but David can't know about this. He might think it too dangerous and try to stop us."

Eva thought it strange that Hattie kept secrets from her fiancé but didn't question her. The important thing was doing everything they could to keep Olivia safe.

14

The following day

Yesterday's camera debacle had Hattie suspicious of everyone and everything and back to compounding lies to do what must be done. Yesterday, she had revealed much of the truth to her mother, which provided some relief and, in a way, had brought them closer. However, she left out several aspects for selfish reasons and to improve the odds of getting to those documents in Ziegler's study. Telling Eva about the logbook and photos meant explaining why she trusted Maya over David, a conversation she wasn't prepared to have. And until she was certain how the micro-camera had become broken, the less information she shared, the better.

David sipped his morning cup of coffee at the kitchen table. "Are you sure you don't want me to come along? I can drive."

Eva placed her mug in the dishwasher. "I'm sure. Ladies' brunch and a little shopping. You would be bored to tears. I'll have your fiancée back in no time." She faced Hattie. "Ready, sweetheart?"

Hattie downed the rest of her coffee and added her cup next to Eva's. "I need to grab my bag."

"Don't forget your camera," Eva said. "The mosaic sidewalks are spectacular."

"Of course." Hattie turned to David. "We should be back in a few hours."

He nodded after she kissed him on the cheek. His expression was hard to read, but Hattie guessed he was skeptical about why they were shopping while the sabotage plot hung in the air. She ignored his pouting, because Ziegler was expecting her and Eva soon.

While Eva went to the garage, Hattie popped into her room and grabbed her handbag and the Kodak camera she kept atop the dresser. She slid out the private entrance, joined Eva in the car, and patted the camera on the seat next to her. "Now I'm ready."

Eva drove through her neighborhood, down the rolling hills of Rio, and through the thick midmorning weekday traffic until they were at the mansions on Embassy Row. She pulled up to the entry gate of Ziegler's home and pressed the gray metal speaker box button.

A woman's voice sounded in Portuguese. "May I help you?"

"It's Eva Machado. Mr. Ziegler is expecting me."

The two-panel wrought iron gate swung open. Eva steered up the cobblestone path and parked even with the front door. When Hattie reached for her camera on the bench seat, Eva clutched her hand with worry in her eyes. "Be careful, sweetheart."

Emotion swelled Hattie's throat. "I will. For Olivia."

"For Olivia," Eva repeated.

Hattie squeezed her mother's hand and felt her love. As they did during their stage appearances together, they would team up today and put on a remarkable performance for Ziegler's sake. They exited the car and ascended the steps.

The door opened, and the maid greeted them in Portuguese. "Good morning, Miss Machado. Mr. Ziegler is in his study and will join you in the garden."

"Wonderful. Can you ask the groundskeeper to accompany us? I'm sure we'll have some questions."

"Of course, miss." The maid gestured down the hallway. "I have brunch waiting for you on the veranda."

"Thank you, Isabella," Eva said, linking arms with Hattie as they followed the maid to the back of the house. Her mother's extra-tight hold while walking communicated her anxiety about their plan.

Two months ago, Hattie, like her mother, would have been a nervous wreck sneaking into a place she wasn't supposed to be and taking pictures of something she wasn't supposed to see. However, after everything she endured with Baumann to find Anna, she'd discovered that covert activities and weaving a believable cover story came naturally to her. Years of concealing her love life in darkness had readied her for the spy world.

Hattie patted Eva's forearm and whispered, "We'll be fine. I got this."

They reached the back patio, where the maid had laid out servings of pastries, cheese, and fresh fruit on a table. They could choose from coffee, juice, and water. "I'll let Mr. Ziegler know you're here, miss," Isabella said before scurrying upstairs.

Hattie fixed a plate and sat at the dining table but didn't eat or drink, recalling she was drugged the last time she was near her target for intelligence gathering. Instead, she cut and pulled at her selection to make it appear she'd been nibbling. She considered warning her mother, but Eva had already popped some fruit into her mouth.

Minutes later, a local man of Brazilian descent with darker hair and skin color dressed in work clothes walked up the concrete pathway from the garden and approached their table. He removed his wide-brimmed straw hat and spoke in Portuguese. "Isabella said you wanted to see me, Miss Machado."

"Yes, Abilo," Eva said in Portuguese. "My daughter and I are here to scout the grounds as a location for her wedding."

Abilo grinned and bowed his head toward Hattie, speaking in English, "Congratulations, Miss James."

"Congratulations, indeed," Ziegler said in English as he emerged from the French doors onto the patio. "I was surprised when your mother called yesterday. I was under the impression you weren't ready to set a date." He kissed Eva on the cheek, and Eva flinched. She was never very good at hiding her emotions, which was endearing sometimes, but that flaw might get Hattie caught today.

"My mother reminded me that we need to think about having the ceremony before my nephew starts kindergarten in September," Hattie said. "Would that timeframe be convenient for you?"

"I'm sure I can make it work."

Hattie wiped the corners of her mouth with a cloth napkin to further the ruse she'd been eating, pushed back in her chair, and stood, grabbing her Kodak from the table. "I hope you don't mind if I take some photos."

"Of course not. Feel free to take pictures of anything you want, but I'm afraid I only have an hour before I have to leave for a meeting. If you don't finish today, I'm happy to have you back another day." That was Ziegler's subtle way of saying they were not welcome there when he wasn't.

"We better get started," Eva said, pushing back her chair. "Let's start with the lawn. I'd like to get an understanding of the winter color palette of the surrounding flowers." She linked her arm around Ziegler's and guided the group away from the house.

Eva was a master at controlling a conversation and taking over event planning like nobody's business. She had the gardener pace off areas for the altar and guest chairs for the ceremony and angling the arrangements to backlight the seating area by the setting sun, bathing the bride and groom in an angelic glow.

"I was thinking about having the groom and his best man enter through the north trail," Eva said. That was the distraction Hattie needed. Eva would pull them deeper into the garden while Hattie would make her break. "Remember, it's vital that the wedding theme and flora complement one another. Come, everyone."

"You go ahead. I need to use the restroom after that cup of coffee," Hattie said.

Eva squeezed her hand before retaking Ziegler's arm.

Hattie walked across the lawn toward the veranda and met the maid at her station near the food table. "Could you ask the cook to prepare me some hot herbal tea with honey and bring it to the patio while I use the bathroom?"

"Of course, Miss James. I'll see to it after I escort you to the downstairs powder room."

"Thank you, Isabella, but I can find my way."

"I'm sorry, miss, but we have orders to escort guests around the home."

This was more than a stumbling block. It was Mount Everest unless Hattie devised something to pry the maid away. "I understand, but this is quite embarrassing."

"Miss?" Isabella squinted in confusion.

"It's my time of the month, and I came unprepared."

The woman nodded her comprehension. "I can get you something from my purse."

"That's very kind of you, but I need a change. Understand?"

"Yes, miss. I'm sorry I can't help you with that."

"No, no. I'm not explaining things right. My mother and I use the guest room next to the powder room to dress for our performances. We kept products and a change of clothes there, so everything I need is upstairs."

"I can take you."

"I really need some detergent and a wax bag to take things home. Could you get those for me?"

"Of course. Please wait here. It might take me a few minutes to gather them."

"I'm afraid I might miss too much of the tour. We're here scouting the grounds for my wedding this winter."

The maid grinned. "Yes, I heard."

"I need to get back quickly." Hattie squeezed her clasped hands. "Please, Isabella. This is important to me, and to show my gratitude, I'd like you and a friend to be my guests at the Golden Room for a dinner show. Would you like that?"

The woman beamed with a broad smile. "Yes, Miss James. I would like that very much."

"Thank you." Hattie pressed the maid's hands again. "I'll see you upstairs in a few minutes."

While the maid entered a door nearest the kitchen, Hattie used the other door leading to the main corridor. Once inside, she ran up the winding staircase, clutching her camera, and hit the second floor without breaking stride until her hand landed on the doorknob of Ziegler's study. She shut the door behind her, dashed to the desk, and placed her camera atop it. After fetching the nail clippers from the top drawer, she jiggled and turned the file in the lock, but she was rushing and didn't feel it move. She took a deep, calming breath, closed her eyes briefly, and tried again. Shifting the file at a different angle, she finally got the lock to turn.

She opened the lower drawer, trying not to jerk it and make too much noise. Her heart raced as she wiggled the fake back. She had maybe a minute longer before the maid would come upstairs. This was her last chance to get the plans and potentially save a hundred lives, her sister's being among them. Time was not her friend. There wasn't enough to take the pictures and return the pages to their hiding place.

Hattie had one choice.

She grabbed the leather roll, replaced the false panel, and closed the drawer. After snatching her camera, she bolted toward the door, secured it, and hurried to the bathroom. Her heart beat so fast she thought it might seize.

A knock on the door made her jump.

"Miss James? I have the items you requested," Isabella said through the door.

"One moment." The choking thought of being caught gripped her. She had to hide the documents. The pedestal sink had no storage compartment, leaving only one possibility. She stuffed the roll in the narrow space between the wall and a colonial pillar in the corner, straightened her blouse, and opened the door.

Isabella stood outside, holding a wax bag, a tiny bowl of powder detergent, and a small nail brush. "I thought the brush might help."

"Yes, it will." Hattie accepted the items and gave the woman a brief hug. "Thank you. I'll leave your name with the assistant manager at the club. If you call ahead, I'll ensure she seats you near the front."

"You are so generous, Miss James." The woman bowed a fraction.

"It's my pleasure."

"I'll wait for you."

"If you could see to my tea so it's ready when I get downstairs, I'd be grateful. I have to perform tonight and feel a scratch in my throat." Hattie pursed her lips into a thankful smile, praying she had sweetened the pot enough.

Isabella bit her lower lip in a clear battle of conscience. "Yes, miss." She bowed her head again and hurried down.

Once Isabella was out of sight, Hattie closed the door loudly to ensure the maid heard. She didn't have time to take in her profound relief. The priority was getting the documents out of the house with no one seeing them, but she also had to make her cover story appear authentic. She splashed water on the counter and poured some detergent down the sink. After stuffing the wax bag into her purse, she grabbed her camera and the leather roll and slipped her heels off to not make any noise on the marble floors.

Hattie flew down the stairs on the balls of her feet and sneaked out the front door. Hiding the documents in the trunk would have been ideal, but she didn't have the key. Eva never locked her sedan, so Hattie opened the rear passenger door, slid the container under the passenger side of the front bench seat, and closed the door. She returned inside, redonned her shoes on the fly, and walked slowly and calmly, acting as if nothing had happened.

Hattie went to the veranda with her camera and purse, met Isabella at her workstation, and accepted her hot tea and honey. "This is perfect. Thank you." Her heart was still beating hard, and she sipped the drink several times, exaggerating the fantom tickle in her throat when Eva and Ziegler appeared on a garden path with the groundskeeper. Hattie returned the teacup to Isabella, squeezed her arm, and waited for Eva and her group to reach the patio. "I'd like to get more pictures of the lawn and fountain. Would you mind coming with me, Mother?"

"Yes," Eva said. "I'll show you where I think David should enter."

Once out of earshot of the others, Hattie unsheathed the leather covering over her camera lens, snapped several photos, and leaned close to her mother. "We need to leave now. I'll explain in the car."

Eva gave her a curious look before checking her wristwatch. "Look at the time," she said loud enough for the others to hear, then led Hattie back to the patio. "Frederick, it's almost time for your meeting, and I have a singing lesson to give in a bit."

He checked his pocket watch. "That it is. I hope you got everything you wanted, Hattie."

"I'm sure I did." Which was why she needed to get out of there.

"I'll see you out," Ziegler said.

Hattie grabbed her mother's handbag from the dining table, hooked her arm around Eva's, tugged hard, and followed Ziegler to the car. "No, no, no," she whispered to herself after noting an inch of the leather roll was protruding from underneath the bench seat. She was looking for it, but if luck was with her, Ziegler would keep his eyes on Eva, not the stolen documents that she was sure he would kill to get back.

Hattie hopped into the sedan on the passenger side and rolled down the window while Eva said goodbye to Ziegler. They chatted about when they would see each other again, but Hattie was too nervous to sit still for Ziegler's pleasantries, so she stuck her head out. "We must get going, Mother. Frederick has important business to tend to."

After receiving Ziegler's kiss on the cheek, Eva got in the front seat and drove toward the road. Someone inside the house usually flipped a switch that opened the gate before they made the turn around the driveway, but this time, it remained closed, sending Hattie into a panicky pant. She thought the worst: someone had seen her in the study or with the documents and intended on keeping her and Eva there until Ziegler sorted things out.

Eva slowed, gripping the steering wheel tighter. "What did you do, Hattie?" Agitation was in her voice.

"I took the plans. They're under my seat."

"You did what?" Eva snapped her head toward Hattie. "What were you thinking?"

"What was I supposed to do? The maid had orders to follow me around the house. I got away from her for a few minutes but didn't have enough time to take photos. Would you rather I left them with Olivia's life hanging in the balance?"

"No, but..." Eva looked over her shoulder, and Hattie followed her gaze. Ziegler was standing in the same spot on the driveway, giving what Hattie perceived as an unnerving death stare. That he knew what she had done and had her in his snare.

The pit in Hattie's stomach grew as she feared for Eva and Olivia, not herself. She had spent years hating her mother, but now she wanted to protect her. Motion in Hattie's peripheral vision caught her attention, and she glanced toward it. The gate panels were arcing open.

"Drive, Mother. Drive!"

15

Eva drove to the street and prepared to turn right to go home, but Hattie said, "Go left."

Eva did and settled into the traffic lane. "Where are we going?"

"The papers are in German. Someone from the US Embassy can translate them."

Eva pulled over and parked along the curb. "Are you crazy?"

"Why is it crazy?"

"You have stolen documents from the Swiss ambassador," Eva said. "Once you hand them over, we'll never see them again. The American bureaucracy is like walking through a tar pit. There's no telling if they'll act before Olivia's ship arrives. I have a better idea."

"What's that?"

"Marta Moyer. She's German. I know she'll help us."

Hattie trusted Leo Bell to help and do the right thing, but Eva had a point. Leo's boss, Jack Lynch, was the definition of a bureaucrat and would likely slow the process until it was too late. But after what Marta endured in the basement of Heinz Baumann's plantation as his captive, Hattie was certain the woman would do anything to help.

"Let's call her," she said.

Eva drove home, leaving her car at the top of the driveway. After Hattie retrieved the leather roll from the floorboard in the back seat, they stepped through the gate and walked the path bisecting the lush, colorful flora. Its perfectly manicured appearance got Hattie thinking. If she stayed in Rio, Eva might occupy her time with her, not her garden. Hattie never thought this possible, but she would like that.

Once inside, Hattie called out for David, but he didn't answer. She followed Eva to her office. Eva thumbed through her index box of clients and pulled out the card she needed.

Hattie paused for a moment, considering that her mother had a phone in all the primary rooms in the house—a luxury by any measure. Her mother was more well off than Hattie realized, which meant she taught music and sang occasionally to provide her purpose, not for the money.

Eva picked up the receiver and had the operator connect her to Marta's number. "Hello, Marta. This is Eva Machado." She explained she had some papers that required translating from German to English by someone she trusted would show discretion. "I have a lesson to give. Would it be all right if my daughter Hattie brought the documents over? ... Marta? Are you okay? ... Thank you. She'll be over soon." Eva hung up the phone and turned to Hattie. "Her son isn't feeling well, so she can't leave the house, but you can head over there after he finishes his lunch, say in an hour."

"That's perfect." With her mother gone, Hattie could collect the logbook photos from Maya and also have them translated today. Since Baumann had watched the docks while looking for her father, the book might provide insight into Ziegler's plan to sink the passenger ship.

"Whatever you're up to, you're not going there alone," David said, walking into the office.

Hattie snapped her stare toward the door, hiding the leather roll behind her back on instinct. He had overheard them talking, and it was clear he would not leave without getting answers. Her idea of keeping David out of this and getting the logbook translated was moot, but translating the plans in that roll was not. "Don't get mad, but Mother and I didn't go shopping."

"I guessed as much. Where did you go?"

"Ziegler's home to get those papers."

"So you took pictures and already had Maya develop the film?"

Eva narrowed her eyes. "Maya Reyes? Why would she develop them?"

"I'll tell you later," Hattie said, turning to David while holding up the roll. "I didn't have a chance to take photos, so I took the documents."

His eyes widened. "Are you nuts? What happens when he discovers them missing?"

"I had no choice. Time is running out. If we're lucky, we can get them translated and return them before Ziegler knows they're gone."

"Then I'm definitely taking you to the Moyers. In fact, I'm not leaving your side until those papers are back where they belong."

"You two will have to go. I have a lesson in an hour but should be back in time to cook you an early dinner before your show. I'm eager to hear what Marta says."

"Me too. I'll let you know right away if we find anything definite." Hattie kissed her mother goodbye on the cheek and walked her to the door.

Once Eva was outside, David put his hands on his hips. "What the hell, Hattie? Sneaking about Ziegler's house with only your mother to back you up. What were you thinking?" He gripped her forearm too hard to show concern. She'd never seen him this angry. "You're going to get yourself and everyone around you killed if you're not careful."

Hattie glanced at his hand before fixing her stare on his face. For the first time, he appeared threatening. "You're hurting me, David, and scaring me."

He released his grip and stepped back, appearing to calm himself. "I'm sorry, but I can't protect you if you go off like that." He lowered his head. "If anything happened to you."

Hattie felt guilty for leaving him out of the loop on so many things and telling lie after lie. Experience had taught her that David was her friend and should be worthy of her trust. However, the broken camera, the missing logbook, the absent Agent Butler, and her AWOL father had made her situation so convoluted that she wasn't sure what to do.

She reached out and caressed David's shoulder. "I'm sorry, too. It's just that I'm worried about Olivia."

"Let me help." He cupped his hand on her cheek. He'd touched her like this several times before, but this instance had more emotion behind it. His confession that he loved her in a way that she could not reciprocate complicated things more. She was sure his feelings for her colored much of his reaction, but she had difficulty reconciling his aggressiveness with her, the confusion making her head pound.

"David," she said softly. "I appreciate everything you've done for me, but I can't be that kind of girlfriend."

He sighed. "At least not with me. Two months ago, you thought you would be better off abandoning a satisfying sex life for conformity."

"Do you realize how hard that would be on us, on me, knowing I didn't love you the way you loved me? I couldn't do that to you. I'd rather live another lie than hurt you like that."

His eyes misted with tears. "Okay."

Hattie hoped this conversation would end their emotional discomfort so they could concentrate on being friends again and unearthing Ziegler's sabotage plans.

Hattie knocked on the Moyers' front door an hour later with David by her side. Marta had vanished the last time she was on this stoop, and her husband was exhausted from worry. Questioning him on one of the worst days of his life had felt like an intrusion, but it had helped her piece together that Baumann was behind the missing women.

Hattie had spoken to Marta and glimpsed her through the cell doors when they were hostages at the plantation, but this visit marked their first official meeting. The anticipation made her uneasy. Though her name was kept from the news account of what happened that night, Eva had conveyed Hattie's involvement to Marta in the weeks following, at least the part Hattie had shared with her.

The door opened.

Hattie had only seen the police photo and a profile picture of Marta from her evening at the Golden Room to see Eva's performance—the night Baumann abducted her—but she could tell Marta was once glowing and pretty. The woman standing before her appeared haggard with pale skin, gaunt cheeks, and dark circles below her eyes. She looked thinner than the woman in the photos and had dull, lifeless eyes.

Marta's expression pinched as if fighting back tears. She said nothing and spread her arms, inviting Hattie in for a hug. Hattie pulled her in tight, allowing her to melt in the embrace. Marta's body shook as she wept. Hattie hadn't realized the physical and emotional aftermath had levied such a toll on Marta, and she wondered if the other three of Baumann's surviving victims were as broken.

Hattie let her take control, so they stood in the doorway for several moments. The terror Marta had endured from being drugged, interrogated, and held captive in darkness for weeks, not knowing when it would be her turn to be taken from her cell, never to return, poured from her. Hattie absorbed the woman's pain and felt weaker by it until Marta quieted and pulled away.

"I'm so glad you're here," Marta choked out, gesturing into her house. "Please come in. I put out refreshments."

After quick introductions, Marta offered an ice-cold sugarcane juice and suggested they sit in the living room. "I made it fresh this morning. Tobin and my son love to drink it when they get home from work and school." Her words were pleasant, but her tone was flat and vacant.

"I'm fine, thank you," Hattie said, sitting in an armchair. Marta sat next to her. "I spoke to Tobin when you were missing. He seemed like a good man and father." Tobin had tried to appear strong, but the pain in her husband's eyes had torn Hattie to pieces that day. Now, seeing Marta drowning in a living hell, Hattie wondered if death would have been kinder to her and to him.

"Yes, a good man." Marta's distant look was a sign she was lost in thought, grappling with her emotions.

David stood. "I hate to bother you, but may I use your bathroom?"

"Yes, yes," Marta said. "It's down the hallway, second door on the left."

Once David exited, Hattie reached out and patted Marta's knee. "Are you sure you're up for company?"

"Yes, yes. The nightmares were keeping me awake." Marta went to the corner tray cart stocked with vodka and cocktail glasses and fixed a drink.

"I'm so sorry you went through that." Hattie also had horrible dreams from her one night on the plantation and could only imagine the visions haunting Marta in her sleep.

"I thought we could use something stronger." Marta returned with two cups of clear liquid and offered one to Hattie. She accepted the glass but placed it on the coffee table a foot away. "The newspaper and police said nothing of your involvement, but your mother told me about your investigation, how it pointed to Baumann, and what you went through that night. I'm so sorry he took you too, but I'm forever grateful for what you did."

"Thank you for your discretion. I must keep my name out of it for safety's sake."

"I understand." Marta squeezed Hattie's hand before taking a large gulp. "But because of you, half of us survived."

Hattie's lips quivered because her family caused all of this. Baumann had taken Marta and the rest of the women as part of a bloodthirsty search for her father and those damn lists. If only Hattie had acted faster and respected the FBI's instructions to document Baumann's spy operation sooner, lives could have been saved and survivors spared further trauma.

"Yes, survived," Hattie said, fighting to keep it together. If she hadn't auditioned at the Halo Club, Baumann would not have followed her there, and Anna Reyes would still be alive. The ugly truth would always stay with her. Whenever she heard a loud sound like a dish being dropped in the Golden Room or a car backfiring on the street, Hattie flinched, reliving the snap of the gunshot that killed Anna. Sometimes, like now, the guilt was overwhelming, and escaping down a bottle sounded better than having it swallow her whole. The nearby drink grew increasingly enticing.

Hattie picked up the glass, swirling its contents several times before bringing it to her mouth. The subtle scent of potato told her the Moyers could not afford the expensive vodka that filtered the impurities. Cheap vodka was Hattie's weakness. It was plentiful at any bar, and the smell didn't linger long on her breath, making it easier to hide her indulgences.

"Hattie," David said, reentering the room. He sat across from her, extending his cupped hand—his silent urging for Hattie not to go down that rabbit hole and to give him the tempting drink at her lips. One sip was all it would take to get through this meeting with Marta. One sip to take the edge off, to not feel the guilt.

But.

Hattie needed a clear head. She couldn't spiral again when Olivia's life was in danger, so she handed the glass to David and mouthed, "Thank you."

Marta sat up straighter and patted Hattie's knee, preparing to stand. "I'll pour you another."

"I'm fine." Hattie wasn't fine but was strong enough to endure this.

Marta returned to her seat. "Eva said you have something that needs translating from German."

"Yes." Hattie grabbed the leather container and placed it on her lap. "I need to ask for your discretion first. To not discuss what I'm about to show you with anyone or ask any questions. Can you promise that?"

"Of course. Anything for the woman who saved us."

Hattie's throat swelled. It was hard to swallow, so she responded with a rapid, grateful nod. She unfurled the roll and tipped the pouch to remove the papers. A key fell out. She was sure it wasn't there before, so she returned it to the holder and made a mental note to inspect it later. "We came across these documents and need to know what they say. Can you translate them for me?"

"Yes, of course. I haven't read anything in German in years. Everything here is Portuguese or English." Marta took the pages and the map and flipped through them. Most contained a few brief paragraphs, but others were fuller. "These talk about the American military building a Navy base in Natal. Since when—" She looked up but stopped in mid-sentence. "Sorry, no questions."

"Thank you," Hattie said.

"This one talks about severing ties between the United States and Brazil by blaming them for the sinking." Marta's eyes got extra round. "Sinking?"

"Does it say what ship or when?"

Marta scanned the page more. "The ship's name isn't mentioned, but they say the engine room is the intended target, and there will be at least six guards." She reread it. "They say Sunday traffic will be light in the city, making escape easier."

"Sunday." Hattie gasped. Olivia's ship was scheduled to arrive at the Rio port on Sunday. "Is there anything that will tell us when and where this will happen?"

Marta sifted through the documents again. "This one mentions having a man assigned to the crew, and this says a hundred passengers." She threw a hand over her mouth. "My God."

"Anything else?"

Marta shook off the shock before returning her attention to the papers. "One more thing. There's mention of a warehouse to store a shipment from Hamburg for three days." The delivery must have been for the materials needed for the attack, likely explosives.

"Three days? You're sure." The shipment should have arrived today if the sinking was slated for this Sunday. Hattie's heart rate increased as she realized the plan may have already been underway.

"Positive."

She clasped Marta's hands. "Thank you for helping me. We'll make sure the authorities know about this, but please, keep your word and mention this to no one."

"I will. You will let me know what happens, won't you?"

"Of course." Time was running out. Hattie had to get this information to Leo Bell. "May I use your phone, Marta?"

"Yes, it's in the kitchen. I'll show you." Marta walked Hattie to the next room and left, giving her privacy.

After receiving no answer at Leo's direct line, Hattie asked the operator to connect her to a number on his business card, which he gave her when she was at the embassy.

A woman answered.

"This is Hattie James. I need to speak to Lieutenant Commander Bell or Mr. Jack Lynch. It's urgent."

"I'm sorry, Miss James, but they are not at the embassy today. I can try to get a message to them, but they will return to the office tomorrow."

"Yes, please." Hattie passed along Eva's phone number, home address, and when she would be working. "Tell them it's a matter of life or death." When she finished the call, she was sure her ending plea was not an exaggeration and prayed they would get her message in time before Hattie had to leave for the Golden Room to warm up for her show.

16

Frederick's appointment with the embassy staff had gone longer than expected. Frankly, the entire event had bored him to tears, but tending to his official duties was essential to providing cover for his true agenda. By the time his driver pulled onto the grounds of his mansion, the Italian Embassy sedan was already parked at the end of the curved driveway. He was late for his next meeting, which he never liked. Not being on time was disrespectful.

Once the car stopped, Frederick bolted up the steps as fast as his protruding belly allowed, not stopping to greet the maid, who was dutifully awaiting him at the open doorway with his mail sitting on a silver tray. He tossed his hat at her and kept going up the interior stairs until he reached the doors of his study. He paused to catch his breath, swiped back his dark hair, and adjusted his round-rimmed glasses before pushing open the right door.

The two men inside stood.

"Sorry to keep you waiting, gentlemen. It couldn't be helped." Frederick stepped toward them and shook their hands. "May I offer you a drink?"

Both visitors waved him off like his tardiness was nothing and declined refreshments. The more senior man spoke. "The shipment of explosives arrived this morning. We personally saw to their delivery at the warehouse you designated. Are you sure your man will have enough time to build the devices?"

"Yes, the detonator timers came in last week. We now have everything we need to get him started today."

"What about the key you were waiting for? Unless your man can place the primary bomb belowdecks, our effort won't have as much impact as we'd hoped."

"Yes, I acquired that yesterday. We'll have unfettered access throughout the engine room. After the explosions, the ship will sink fast, leaving no time for rescue. However, the media at the dock will have ample opportunity to capture photos to shift the tide against the Americans." Frederick had thought everything through carefully. The president's assassination would shock the local people, but nothing would enrage them more than seeing a symbol of power and wealth burning and sinking to the ocean floor.

"Splendid. Are things set to point to them?"

"Yes, the apartment was rented months ago in the name of Leo Bell. Documents and uniforms have been placed there. When the Brazilian nationals conduct their investigation after the murder, the evidence will implicate the American Embassy. The country will be outraged after losing a president to an American assassin." Only then would the government be pressed into turning its back on the United States and withdrawing its plans to build the naval base in Natal—the one task Berlin had made clear was critical he accomplish.

"Good, Herr Ziegler. If your plan fails, we will all be shot."

"Do not fret, gentlemen. Everything has been planned to the finest detail. By this time on Sunday, the president of Brazil will be dead, and we will celebrate our victory." Frederick poured them each a finger's worth of his best whiskey, and they toasted to the Third Reich and the German-Italian alliance. "To a new world order."

After going over more details of Sunday's attack, he walked the Italians to their car and held onto the open passenger door after his associates boarded. "I assure you. Things will go well."

"We will hold you to it," the younger man said, closing the door before they drove away.

A lot was riding on the success of this plan. Baumann's death and the massacre of his entire Rio contingent had come on the heels of losing Karl James and the list of American spies in Germany and German spies in America. Securing the Atlantic's linchpin was his sole opportunity to redeem himself in Berlin's eyes and bring honor back to the Ziegler name.

He returned to his study to review the timing and sequence of events he'd carefully planned to leave nothing to chance. After inserting the key to unlock the lower desk drawer, he knew something was wrong. The lock wasn't in the correct position. He opened it without turning the key, removed the false back, and slid his hand inside to retrieve his leather document roll, but he felt nothing. He sent his hand searching deeper from side to side, but still nothing.

Panic roared.

In his frantic search, Frederick shifted hard in the chair and tore at the files, tossing them haphazardly, but the satchel still didn't appear. He ripped the drawer from its railings and dumped the remaining contents onto the desk but had no luck. Falling to his knees, he searched the drawer cavity, but dread overtook him. The satchel was gone. He could easily recreate the information on the papers from memory, but losing the ship's key was a devastating blow.

Anger fired in his head like a machine gun as he realized everything he had worked toward for months was unraveling. It had taken a month for him to locate and persuade the person to give him the unreproducible key to the engine room. Three days was insufficient to source another. Without it, the Brazilians would not witness the carnage and might not force their government's hands.

Frederick slumped in his chair, retracing the day's events. He had looked at the documents earlier that morning and returned them to their hiding spot before joining Eva and Hattie on the patio to tour the grounds for Hattie's insipid wedding. The staff had the opportunity to break into his desk for months, making it unlikely that one would choose to act today. Since Eva was with him the entire time, Hattie James must have been the culprit, but a nagging issue remained: How did she get into the study? He had given the maid strict orders to not let guests roam the house unescorted. Isabella had failed at her duties and would soon meet an untimely death.

He rang the servant bell and waited, stewing in a bubbling puddle of anger. Other than killing a boat worker and stealing his key, assuming he could find a man who had one of the remaining three keys in existence, he had little choice but to retrieve what was stolen from him.

Minutes later, Isabella appeared in the doorway. "You rang, sir." She was the mousey type who seldom looked him in the eye, displaying a coddled child's confidence on the first day of kindergarten.

"Close the door, please."

The woman's eyes widened, and her body seemed to shrink even smaller, making her already petite frame seem cartoonish in size. She went rigid while closing the door.

"Do you know why I need to speak to you privately?" Frederick asked, hoping the implication would pry the information from her with little difficulty.

"No, sir." She kept her head bowed.

"I know someone was in my study earlier today because a file is missing." He paused when she shifted her feet twice. The nervous sign said he was on the right track. "Tell me what happened with Miss James. Otherwise, I will call the police since you are the only one allowed here alone."

"I escorted her inside..." Isabella explained how Hattie had convinced her to let her use the powder room upstairs and sent her on an errand to retrieve some cleaning items from the kitchen before bringing her tea to the patio. "But I swear, sir. She was alone for only a minute or two."

"It was long enough for her to leave with one of my files."

"I don't know what to say, sir. She didn't have any papers with her when she returned outside. Could the file have been misplaced?"

"When have I ever misplaced my papers?" Frederick rose from his chair. "Collect your things and never come back. I'll have the cook deliver your final wages."

Her chin quivered. "Please, sir. I need this job."

"You should have thought of that before you ignored my instructions." He waved his hand dismissively. "Go." He would deal with her another time.

Once the door closed, Frederick rang the chauffeur bell, alerting Riker to pull the car up. He gathered his briefcase and checked the pistol hidden in the shoulder holster under his suit jacket. It was fully loaded, with the safety on, but that would not last long. Hattie James had to pay up before she paid for what she'd done.

As he descended the stairs, Isabella was hurrying from the kitchen toward the front door, clutching her handbag close to her chest with one hand and covering her sobs over her mouth with the other. It was a shame she had to die. He'd grown rather fond of the way she doted over him.

His car awaited him at the bottom of the entry steps, and Riker opened the rear passenger door as Frederick stepped closer. He had handpicked the man from the embassy staff for his strength, discretion, and skill with almost any type of weapon. Frederick was aging, had put on several extra pounds, and no longer trusted his body to get himself out of dicey situations. Riker was his insurance policy.

"Where to, Mr. Ziegler?" Riker said in German.

"Eva Machado's home, and quick."

Riker pulled around the curved driveway, passing Isabella on the cobblestone.

Frederick said, "Before I forget, I had to let Isabella go. You need to take care of her." The implication was clear.

"Of course, sir." Riker pulled off the property and sped through Rio's crowded city streets in the afternoon traffic.

Frederick sat in the back seat, rubbing his temples to stop the pounding in his head as he explained to Riker what Hattie James had taken. He didn't say it, but everything from his honor to the war effort was riding on finding that key. When they arrived at the top of Eva's driveway and exited the car, his headache had worsened.

"I need Hattie James alive. The rest can die." Frederick sent Riker to climb the fence and enter from the back. Meantime, he pulled from his pocket the key to Eva's home, which he'd lifted and had copied one night while she was sleeping. He unlocked the garden entry gate, walked on the path through the lush plants and flowers, drew his Luger from its holster, and used the key again to open the front door to the house.

Frederick stepped inside, walking deliberately to avoid being caught by surprise. The living room was unoccupied. He'd visited the house only once when dropping off Eva but had memorized its layout. Eva's bedroom and greenery room were to the right, and the kitchen and hallway leading to the guest bedrooms were to the left. Eva should have been at her studio, giving a singing lesson, eliminating the need to subdue her.

He headed left, thumbed his pistol's safety to the ready position, and entered the kitchen, but no one was there. The two coffee cups on the counter suggested someone might have been in the house. He heard a noise coming from the back bedrooms, so he backtracked and started down the corridor, squeezing the butt of his gun tighter. The first room was empty, so he proceeded toward the bathroom, where he detected another sound. Footsteps made him pause one step before reaching the doorframe, so he held the pistol upright. He wheeled it level as he stepped into the opening, ready to pull the trigger.

The man flinched and turned, staring down the steel barrel. "No one is here, Mr. Ziegler," Riker said in German and holstered his sidearm.

"We can't wait for them to come home. There's no time to waste. We have another stop to make."

They hopped back into Frederick's sedan and doubled back through town, racing through traffic. Riker parked the car at the back of the building where fewer eyes might see their getaway and stayed there while Frederick circled to the front and entered the studio. He quietly approached a secondary door and heard singing and another voice shortly after. Time was limited, but he couldn't afford to draw attention from passersby, so he waited at the door. He fidgeted and paced, unable to get a hold of his anxiety that everything would unravel if he could not force Hattie James to turn over the key.

The music stopped.

The secondary door swung open, and Eva stepped out with her arm over the shoulder of a girl no older than twelve. The child seemed taken by Eva's doting, soaking in the praise from South America's once most famous performer. Aside from Frederick's social events and the rare Golden Room appearance, Eva Machado was not in the spotlight often these days, but her fame and wealth still yielded much power in Brazil. If he could not use her as bait for Hattie, he would leverage her connections to find another way to gain access to that ship.

Eva glanced up at him. The smile she typically greeted him with wasn't there, replaced by a frightened deer look. She barely acknowledged him and continued walking the young girl to the glass door, speaking to her in Portuguese. He'd picked up enough of the language to discern she was giving her words of encouragement about her singing, not telling her to get help or the police.

He let out one snicker, thinking he cared more about missing the doting of a servant than he did about this woman, whom he'd let into his bed for the last six weeks.

Once the student left, Eva shut the door and forced a grin. "Frederick, what brings you here? I thought you had meetings at the embassy."

"I did, but now I need to show you something. Please come with me to my car."

Eva fluffed her perfectly styled hair, but she still appeared nervous. "I'd love to, but I must prepare for my next lesson." She opened the door for him to leave.

Frederick shook his head, gently closed the door, and locked it. Eva's fingers trembled when she brought her fingers closer to her mouth. She was right to feel nervous, because he would not stop until he got what he wanted.

He lowered the blinds on the glass door and the adjacent window. "I had hoped to do this the easy way." He drew his Luger but did not point it directly at her. "Go out the back door and to my car. Otherwise, I'll have to shoot you and torture Hattie until she returns what she stole."

"What are you talking about?" Eva's voice was brittle with fear. His turning on her could explain her retiring reaction, but she had been acting like a nervous cat from the moment she saw him.

He gripped her upper arm like a vise and pulled her into the back room. "Come now, Eva. You distracted me while she sneaked into my study. Now, I need that satchel."

"What satchel? Why would she steal something from your study?" If not for her earlier nervousness, Eva almost sounded convincing, though he was onto her. Years on stage taught her to mask her sadness or upset behind a false front.

"I'm not buying this act for one second, Eva. Now, tell me where she hid it."

"I still don't know what you're talking about."

Frederick placed a note he'd written there atop the piano and dragged her out the back toward his car as she struggled to break free of his grip. Despite his age, she was no match for his strength. Riker opened the back passenger door.

"Riker, do something!" Eva shouted. "He's hurting me."

"I'm afraid he'll hurt you more," Frederick said, "unless you cooperate. Now get inside before I knock you out with the butt of my pistol."

Eva glanced back and forth between both men. The painful look of betrayal in her eyes could not be helped. It was inevitable, since Frederick only got close to her to locate Karl James and get those lists.

Eva's expression turned from frightened to enraged in an instant, but she complied and slid into the rear compartment. Frederick would retrieve the key, no matter what.

17

When David pulled into the garage at Eva's home, Hattie was still numb from the emotional meeting with Marta Moyer and nearly falling back into an alcohol quagmire. She remained in the car for a moment, thinking she had to pull it together. Peeling back some lies with Eva and David was helpful, but until the truth behind all the lies between her and the people she loved surfaced, she doubted whether she had the strength to come back from the edge again.

"Are you coming?" David asked.

"Yeah." Hattie shook off her melancholy and walked with David inside the house.

David entered the kitchen to pour them something to drink while Hattie peeled off to the living room. She laid out the documents from Ziegler's roll and took pictures of each page, including the map and ship schematic. After securing the case around her camera, she returned the items to the satchel and removed the key she'd discovered. She had seen nothing like it. It was longer than traditional keys and had more complex cutting and indentations, appearing impossible to duplicate.

Since it was hidden with the papers, she deduced it had something to do with the sabotage plan. It could have been to a secure facility or even the ship Ziegler intended to sink. Whatever it opened, it was important enough to store with the plans. She figured the key *was* the key to the attack and would not let it out of her sight until she handed it directly to Leo Bell, so she stuffed it in her bra between her breasts.

David returned with the cold drinks and gave her one. "Did you get the photos taken?"

"All done. Now, we can hand the documents to the embassy and use the pictures to figure this out after Maya develops the film. I plan to ask her tonight at work."

"What about the key you found?"

Hattie patted her chest. "It's in a safe place."

"Then we have nothing left to do but wait until we have to head to the Palace," David said, plopping down on the sofa and putting his feet on the coffee table.

"Mother would kill you if she saw you like that."

"What she doesn't know won't hurt her." He laughed, but she didn't join him.

Hattie was never very good at waiting, doubly impatient if it meant sitting around. She willed Leo Bell to respond to her call and for Eva to return from giving singing lessons. If David hadn't been there, she would've gone to the library to pass the time and found a book on Morse code to decipher Eva's notes from her father's sheet music. Instead, she grabbed the documents from the pouch and studied them, looking for any more information she could glean despite the language barrier. She stared at them for what seemed hours, but nothing jumped out at her. Unfortunately, the schematic didn't show dimensions, which could have helped her narrow down which ship Ziegler was targeting. It would have been relieving if she could have ruled out Olivia's ship, but all the circumstantial evidence—the conversations she'd overheard and the target ship's Sunday arrival—made it impossible. As far as Hattie knew, Olivia's ship was the objective.

When her stomach grumbled, she checked the time on the wall clock. It was after five o'clock. Leo still hadn't returned her call. Since the embassy had closed a while ago, she figured he would contact her first thing tomorrow. But it was more troubling that Eva should have been home two hours ago.

"Mother is really late. I'm calling her studio," Hattie said. She used the phone in the living room and asked the operator to connect the call. It rang and rang, but no one picked up. "She's not answering," Hattie said. "I'm starting to worry about her."

David lifted his feet from the coffee table and stood. "She's likely wrapped up with a student, but let's go to the studio to make sure."

"Thank you." Hattie sighed in relief. She could always rely on David to protect her, whether from an external threat, her worries, or the demons that threatened to drag her back to the bottle. Why, then, didn't she trust him enough to know about the logbook photos? Maybe it was his occasional overprotectiveness rooted in his feelings for her, but she realized it was something deeper that she could not put her finger on. It was a debate about who she trusted more—David or her father—but she already knew the answer. Despite him not answering her signal, Hattie knew her father would keep his word. It was blind trust, pure and simple.

She grabbed the document roll and placed the film from the camera into her purse. A bad feeling told her not to let them out of her sight until this ordeal ended. The slow drive into the Lapa district during the traditional rush hour had Hattie biting her fingernails. Every minute wasted in the traffic jam was another minute she wasn't sure if her mother was safe.

When they reached the street where her mother worked, Hattie spotted her mother's Ford Coupe one shop down. "There's her car. She might still be here."

David found a parking spot a block from Eva's studio, and Hattie ran the entire way to the glass front door with her purse slung over her shoulder and the leather document roll firmly gripped in her left hand. She discovered the blinds were drawn. Out of breath and pulse still racing, she tried the knob with her free hand but found it locked. She rattled the door, but it would not budge.

"Damn it." She thought they might have missed Eva by minutes if she had car trouble. David's idea that she had stayed with a student made sense until Hattie saw lights through the blinds. Something was amiss. Her mother never left the studio without first turning off the lights. Since Hattie was a child, Eva constantly harped about not leaving them on when anyone left a room.

"We need to get in there, David. Something is wrong."

He tried forcing the door open, but it was too solid to budge. Getting in would require breaking the window or picking the lock. "I remember seeing a back door," David said. "Let's try it."

A tightness built in Hattie's chest as they walked to the corner and turned down the back alley. She could not help but think that her stealing the documents was why she hadn't heard from her mother.

They reached the back of Eva's studio, and David tried the door. It opened, another bad sign that something was terribly wrong. Eva always locked it. She would never risk her cherished baby grand piano from her early days as an artist and her prized photographs with celebrities and government elites by not securing them.

Hattie entered first, flying through the doorway and calling, "Mother, are you here?" But she received no answer. The practice room was unoccupied. She dashed toward Eva's office, hoping she'd fallen asleep after a long afternoon of teaching. It was open, but when Hattie reached it, she gasped. Eva wasn't there, but her purse was. That woman went nowhere without it. She had a handbag in all shapes, sizes, and colors for every occasion. The purse wasn't merely a convenience or accessory to her. It was a fashion statement.

Hattie stepped to the desk and opened the handbag. Eva's car keys and wallet, with a significant amount of cash, were still there. Even if Eva had popped out of the studio for a few minutes to grab a coffee at the corner shop, she would have brought her wallet. Hattie racked her brain to think of where her mother might have gone without her purse, but nothing made sense. She had vanished like those missing women Baumann had taken in the middle of the night.

Hattie grabbed her mother's bag and went into the practice room, clutching it close to her chest with the leather roll. Tears flooded her eyes, clouding her vision as she walked. David stood nearby, looking on with curiosity.

"She's not here," Hattie said, wanting to disbelieve the words. If they were true, something horrible had happened to her. She plopped down on the piano bench to gather her bearings and wipe her tears.

"She could be back home by now," David said.

Hattie shook her head, holding out her mother's purse. "She would never leave without this."

"Was she robbed?"

"No. Her wallet is still there." Hattie's gut twisted at the thought her mother was missing because of the leather satchel she held in her hand. She shifted on the bench and looked at the sheet music clipped to the stand above the keys. One of Hattie's hits from last year was on top. She dreaded the possibility that something terrible had happened to Eva. If it had, the thought of Hattie's song being Eva's final performance after a lifetime devoted to singing made her cry even harder.

A piece of paper atop the piano caught her eye. She picked up the handwritten note and read it. Her heart nearly stopped. "My God."

"What does it say?" David said.

"It's from Ziegler. He knows I took the plans and has taken Mother." Hattie threw a hand over her mouth, knowing she had caused this. She cleared the horror settling in her throat before continuing. "He wants to trade her for the documents and the key. I'm supposed to meet him at his table at the Golden Room tonight after the show."

David let out a loud sigh. "What can I do to help?"

Hattie studied the rest of the note. "Ziegler said not to go to the authorities, or he'll kill Mother." Pure fear struck her. She was in way over her head and had no way of protecting herself. "Be with me when I meet with him, for starters. Do you still have Eva's gun?"

He patted his side beneath his suit jacket. "I always have it with me when I leave the house."

Knowing David had a firearm made Hattie feel much better about tonight's meeting. She'd learned her lesson with Baumann and would never again meet an adversary without armed backup next to her, nor would she eat or drink anything once she met up with Ziegler.

"To be clear, you'll hand everything over to him, right? I mean, we have the photos," he said.

"I doubt Ziegler will let us go after kidnapping my mother, so I plan to stall until we can enlist some help."

"Then we should leave for the Palace. We scheduled a rehearsal with the band since we added two new songs," David said.

"I forgot something at the house. We need to cancel and go home first."

David checked his wristwatch. "I'll call the band leader. What do you want to do about the set? The manager is expecting a ten minute longer performance tonight."

"I trust you. I'll follow your lead." Hattie trusted him with her music but not with her father. It was a dichotomy she had yet to fully understand.

Fearing Ziegler had someone watching her, she could not go to the police or the embassy for help. However, her father was the one person with the right skills to save her mother. Hattie needed to signal him one more time with the edelweiss. If he didn't answer the call, she would be on her own, abandoned and surrounded by a sea of spies and killers.

18

Hattie used her key to open the gate to the private entrance to her dressing room in the parking lot at the Copacabana Palace Hotel. The same key unlocked the building door. David followed and placed his satchel on the sofa, the case containing their set music and the ones her father gave her to safeguard. Though she had the undeveloped film from the photos she'd taken of the sheet music the day she returned from the plantation ordeal hidden in her underwear drawer at home, she was glad David took her father's gift to every performance. The original sheet music potentially contained more concealed text than the photos might have captured or what Eva had uncovered.

"I'll meet up with the band," David said. "Make sure they're good with the new song order."

"Thank you. I need to check with Maya to see if Ziegler has made a reservation tonight and where he will be seated."

Once David left with his satchel, Hattie used the house phone in her dressing room to ring the restaurant's reception desk. She asked the head waiter to send Maya back for an urgent matter. The dining room was open for food service, so it might take some time before Maya joined her.

Arriving too late to call the stylist from the hotel's beauty salon, Hattie sat at the vanity table to get ready for the show. She cleaned her face with cream and applied makeup the way her mother had shown her the evening of the gala. Eva had mastered applying the correct shadows and highlights to make the lights love her, and Hattie had to admit that her mother's method was superior to hers or that of the hotel's stylist. She didn't have time today to curl her hair the way she preferred, so she chose a straight look tonight and hit it with spray to keep it in place.

The day was so hectic she hadn't thought about which gown to wear on stage. She stood staring in her closet, thinking which dress might be best suited for running through a plantation at night while being hunted by a madman. Given her past encounter with an adversary at a nightclub, her conjecture wasn't too far-fetched. She settled on an item that would not hinder her if she needed to make a fast getaway. It was loose around the waist, provided more coverage for her chest, and hit right at the knee.

After removing and hanging up the slacks and blouse she'd arrived in, Hattie put on her stage dress and adjusted the key hidden in her bra. While affixing the stem of edelweiss she'd picked from Eva's plant room through the top buttonhole, she silently prayed her father would see her signal tonight. So much was riding on the outcome of her meeting with Ziegler after her show.

Before she could zip up the dress, a knock on the door startled her. She opened it, hoping Maya had come, and she wasn't disappointed, especially by her slight grin. Seeing Maya again made the memory of the brief kiss they shared yesterday morning in the darkroom tingle her lips. Maya had more healing to do before they could get back together, but Hattie trusted that day wasn't too far in the future.

"Please come in." Hattie swung the door further, letting Maya into the room.

As Maya passed, she paused and inhaled. "I like your perfume."

"Thank you." Hattie closed her eyes momentarily, feeling the electricity flowing between them before closing the door and turning her back to Maya. "Would you mind zipping me up?"

Maya moved close and worked the zipper. "Was this the urgent matter, Hattie? I was busy out there." And the magic was gone, replaced by her curt tone. "I don't like being played."

Hattie spun around, frustrated by having wiped out all their progress in the last few days. "No, no. That's not it." She clutched Maya's forearms. "Something horrible has happened."

Maya blinked, and her cross expression turned into a look of concern. "What happened?"

"I returned to Ziegler's place this morning with Mother and sneaked into his study but didn't have time to take photos, so I took the file and some key."

"What key?"

"I'm not sure what it's to, but I found it in the pouch with the documents. Strangely, it wasn't there the first time I discovered the plans. It must be critical to pulling off the attack. Otherwise, he wouldn't have asked for it back."

"Wait. Ziegler asked for it?"

"That's the horrible thing. Ziegler knows I have it and has taken Mother. He wants to exchange her for the documents and key."

"My God, Hattie." Maya's eyes got wider with shock. She gripped Hattie's forearms in an extension of their undeniable bond. "You're going to give them back, aren't you?"

"Yes, but I have to play it smart. I doubt he'll let us walk away after this."

"What do you plan to do?"

"I need to stall until I get some help."

Maya glanced at the flower on Hattie's dress and released her grip. "You mean your father. You've been trying to reach him for days."

"Yes. I can't do this on my own." Hattie recalled the horrifying massacre at the plantation compound, where her father had slain those who had posed a threat. "You saw what he's capable of."

"Which is why I want him nowhere near me."

"Maya, I'm desperate. I can't go to the police, and I tried contacting the US Embassy, but they haven't returned my call. I know my father can help."

"Still." Maya closed her eyes and pursed her lips, clearly struggling to come to terms with Hattie's dilemma.

"I know he upsets you, but I have no choice."

Maya let out a weighty sigh. "What do you need from me?"

Hattie grabbed her handbag and handed Maya the roll of film she'd stuffed there for safekeeping. "I took pictures of what I found. Can you develop them?"

"Of course."

"Next, I'm supposed to meet Ziegler at his table tonight to discuss the exchange. Did he make a reservation?"

Maya nodded. "He requested seating for two in the back corner."

"I need you to seat him in the middle of the room at a table for four so we won't have a repeat of what happened at the Halo Club with Baumann."

Maya's lips quivered at the mention of that madman's name. She shook her head and choked out, "Okay."

"Do you know if Leo Bell will be here tonight? He's a friend from the embassy and might help us."

"He wasn't on tonight's list."

Hattie sighed. "Then, if my father doesn't show, we're on our own. Do you have your gun with you?"

"What do you think?"

Hattie took the stage, wearing her edelweiss, while David had the leather document roll stuffed into his music satchel at his feet beneath the piano bench. They performed flawlessly. The band segued effortlessly through the added songs toward the end. The table Maya had set aside for Ziegler in the middle remained empty until a waiter escorted him to his seat when Hattie started her traditional closing song. He sat there, looking regal like he did every time she saw him, but his expression was flintier than she'd ever seen. The center table, not the corner as he'd requested, would give Hattie an advantage, thanks to Maya.

Once Hattie sang the last note and took her bow to roaring applause, David hurried her off the stage, carrying his satchel. Hattie guided him through the wings. "Follow my lead," she said. "I'm going to stall for time."

"I hope you know what you're doing."

So did Hattie, but she had only one play to save her mother, Olivia, and herself.

Moments later, she emerged from the stage door into the main dining area with David. Audience members murmured as she walked past, but unlike at the Halo Club, they remained polite and did not rush her for autographs and photographs. It helped that Hattie took long, fast strides, looking like she was on a mission. And she was. Life or death.

She reached Ziegler's table, feeling more anxious than she'd expected. Hattie needed to appear calm and in control to get him to flinch, which meant she had to set the tone by showing strength she wasn't sure she had. She sat in a chair before being invited or waiting for Ziegler to stand. David settled beside her.

"Where is my mother?" Hattie said in a low, demanding inflection.

"Safe for now," Ziegler said, adjusting his round eyeglasses. Hattie had seen him do that several times and thought it might be his nervous tell. He was as anxious as Hattie. "Where is my property?"

"Safe for now," Hattie said. She could play his game.

Ziegler slid his hand under the table and its white cotton cloth and pressed something hard and cold against her leg. Its size made her suspect it was the muzzle of a pistol, and a quick glance confirmed it. "Don't play with me, Hattie James. Give me what I want, or your mother and your feckless boyfriend will die." He glared at David before returning his attention to Hattie.

"If you hurt either of them, you will never get those documents."

"And the key, Miss James."

"Yes, that too."

"Then hand them over, and I will send your mother home."

"We know that won't happen because we have discovered your plan for Sunday." Hattie bluffed, not knowing the specifics other than a day of the week, but his eyes widened, confirming she was on the right track. So the attack *was* planned for this Sunday, which meant her sister's ship could be the target. "And you need that key. It seems I hold all the cards."

"It might seem that way, Miss James, but you don't."

"I'm willing to test that theory." Unsure when her father or Leo might respond to her calls, Hattie needed ample time to devise a plan and hoped two days would be enough. "I will give you everything on Saturday, the day before you need that key. If anything happens to David or me, I've arranged for the items to be delivered to the authorities, so I suggest you remain patient. I will call you with a place and time for the exchange." Hattie rose. It was time to exaggerate and put some fear into the man's head, so she leaned closer to stress her point. "You have stirred a hornet's nest, Herr Ziegler. If you hurt my mother, you will not be safe. My father has trained me well. I will enjoy having you meet the same fate as Baumann and his men, but I won't rush it this time. I will savor it."

Ziegler sprang from his chair, adjusting his glasses. She had him on the ropes. "Saturday, or you all die." He huffed and marched out of the dining room.

David cocked his head, staring at her with curiosity. "What the hell was that?"

"That was me buying us time." Hattie's hands shook. She never knew she had it in her to go toe-to-toe with the enemy and come across just as ruthless. Confrontation had been her nemesis, leading her to move to New York and dive into a bottle when the heartache of betrayal had become too much. Staying to fight was utterly foreign to her, but it was exhilarating.

A waiter stopped by their table and asked, "Can I get you anything, Miss James?"

A drink sounded more tempting than it should have, but Hattie could not afford a single setback. She needed to lean forward and control the battlefield. "No, thank you."

David raised his index finger. "Scotch." When the man left, he asked Hattie, "Was any of that true about what happened at the plantation?"

Hattie considered telling him it was all a lie, but she realized a bit of mystery, keeping the people around her guessing, might keep her alive long enough to save her mother. "I'll leave that for you to decide." She grabbed his music satchel with the leather roll of documents Ziegler desperately needed and stood. "I'm heading to my dressing room. Don't get drunk. I'll need you sober if Leo or my father come."

"Don't worry," he said. "I'll be ready."

Before turning to walk away, she saw Maya at a nearby table, speaking to a customer. They locked stares. Maya gave her a questioning look, and Hattie nodded, sending the message that it had gone well.

She retraced her steps toward the stage door and stopped to greet a few guests who made eye contact with her. The exchanges were brief, polite, and complimentary. Once backstage, Hattie shook the hands of band members lingering in the corridor and thanked them for an excellent performance.

"You make our job easy," one said.

Hattie smiled as she shook his hand. "Likewise, and I'm very grateful."

She continued down the hallway and entered her dressing room to change out of her stage dress, but once she saw the couch, she plopped down, burying her face in her hands. The weight of this nightmare hit her like a tidal wave. Only ten days ago, Hattie told her mother she loved her after more than a decade of despising her, and now she would lose her if she didn't hand over the documents and key. If she gave Ziegler what he wanted, her sister's ship might sink with her on board. No matter which path she chose, someone she loved could die.

"Songbird." The male voice coming from the right startled her. Hattie snapped her head toward it. Karl stepped from the closet, dressed in a waiter's uniform.

Relief washed over her. "Father." She sprang to her feet and wrapped her arms around his torso. "You're here."

"I saw the edelweiss," he said.

She pulled back, releasing her hold. "Where have you been? I've been signaling for days."

"Scouting. It's a long story, but if I find what I'm looking for, it could make a difference if the United States enters the war." Karl focused on Hattie's eyes. "Is something wrong, sweetheart? I saw you with Ziegler tonight without Eva. Don't trust him. You need to stay away from him."

"I took something from him, so he took Mother." Hattie's eyes filled with tears, and her words came out sounding frantic.

"You're not making sense." Karl gestured toward the couch. "Sit and tell me what happened."

Once seated, Hattie explained what she'd overheard outside Ziegler's study the night of the gala, how she sneaked back and tried to photograph a hidden file she found the following week, and her signaling him without success. "But the micro-camera I had from the FBI was broken." The second she mentioned the FBI, she cringed at the slip. "Oh, Father. I'm so sorry about the FBI, but they forced me, threatening to arrest Olivia and Frank for your escape if I didn't lure you out of hiding."

He squeezed her hand. "I know their tactics, sweetheart. Leverage anything and everyone to break the case. Now, how did the camera get broken?"

"I don't know, so I told Mother what I'd heard because Olivia might be on the ship they want to sink."

"I'm confused." He scrunched his expression. "How is Olivia involved in this?"

"She's coming to Rio to see for herself that I'm okay after what happened with Baumann."

Karl shook his head in frustration. "That is so like her. What makes you think her ship is the target?"

"After filling in Mother, she took me back to Ziegler's this morning. I sneaked up, took the plans, and hoped you could translate them from German, but—"

"I'm sorry," he said softly.

"I took them to a friend of Mother's, a survivor from the plantation, so I trust her. The papers didn't have the ship's name, but they mentioned Sunday. Olivia's ship is arriving this Sunday and is carrying some political bigwig with security."

Karl rubbed his clean-shaven chin. "I see. So that's why you signaled me."

"Originally, yes." Hattie sniffled and stifled a sob. "Ziegler knows I took the pouch containing some key, and he's angry. Now he's taken Mother and wants a swap. I told him I'd do it, but he would have to wait until Saturday. I needed time to reach you."

"He'll never let either of you live." Karl formed a fist and set his jaw. She hadn't seen his eyes narrow in an ice-cold rage before, and it was chilling. "Who else knows about this?"

"David and Maya. I tried to take what I knew to the FBI, but the security chief at the US Embassy said Agent Butler has been missing for weeks."

"Weeks, huh? That means he's dead. Does Jack Lynch know Eva is missing?"

Hattie blinked at the mention of Lynch's name, but she remembered he would have known who was assigned to the embassy. "Not yet. I tried to reach him, but he was out of town."

He stood and kissed Hattie on the forehead. "All right, sweetheart."

A knock.

They both turned their heads toward the door when it inched open, and Maya appeared, saying, "Hattie, are you okay? How did it—" She froze, locking her eyes on Hattie and Karl.

Hattie dashed to Maya and pulled her inside, closing the door after her.

Maya kept her stare on Karl and sneered. "You finally showed up. Some protector."

"I'm here now."

"To slit more throats, I'm sure." Maya's look of disdain vibrated in the room.

"Can we not do this now?" Hattie said, pulling Maya toward the couch. She told Maya how the meeting with Ziegler went and her stalling tactic for Saturday.

"What's next?" Maya asked.

"I'll find her," Karl said.

"I'm coming with you." Hattie stood and asked Maya to unzip her before going to her closet to change clothes.

"It's too dangerous, sweetheart."

"You're going to his house, right?" Hattie poked her head out the doorway. "I've been there. You haven't."

"Does he have armed security?" Karl asked.

"Only during events. There's a tall wall surrounding the property, but you need me. I know the layout and where the servants might be." She finished changing and returned to the room. "Don't argue. I'm coming."

Karl gritted his teeth. "Fine."

Maya locked eyes with Hattie in an intense stare. Worry was in them. She hiked her skirt to her knees, pulled her pistol from her leg holster, and handed it to Hattie. "Take this." She cupped Hattie's hands and squeezed. "Be careful."

Hattie rubbed her thumbs against Maya's hands. "I will."

"We need to get going, Hattie," her father said.

Another knock on the door. "Are you dressed, Hattie?" David said through the door. "I want to head home."

David would disapprove of her going with her father, but Hattie was not ready to argue the point. Not knowing how long this would take, she needed a cover story for the entire night. "I'll get rid of him." Without caring how it might look, she opened the door enough for him to see Maya standing behind her but not her father. Saving her mother was more important than her privacy. "I'll see you in the morning."

David nodded his understanding but looked disappointed. "Do you want me to pick you up?"

"No. I'll find my way home."

"What if your father or Bell come around?"

"Leave a message at the hotel front desk." Hattie kissed David on the cheek, thanked him, and closed the door before turning to Maya. "Do you mind staying in here until he leaves? Our car is right out back, so you should hear it."

Maya looked uncomfortable with her father standing there and glanced at him before saying, "Sure."

Karl snapped his stare between the two women with a confused look. "Either of you want to tell me what's going on here?"

"I'll tell you later, Father." Hattie expected an awkward conversation, but it was long overdue. "First, we have to find Mother."

19

After she hopped into Karl's sedan, Hattie's father didn't grill her about what had transpired between her, Maya, and David at her dressing room door. Thank goodness. She needed time to come up with the right words to explain that her relationship with David was a sham because she slept with women. Karl remained silent driving from the beachfront area and settled into the light midnight traffic to the Botafogo neighborhood. Quiet, though, did not equate to acting at ease. He constantly rolled his neck, suggesting Hattie had shocked him, but that discussion would have to wait until they had more time.

As Hattie directed him to Ziegler's mansion, she explained about the gate, wall, and general layout of the house and property. "He has three regular servants. A driver and cook who come and go daily and a maid who sometimes spends the night when he has overnight guests."

"Do I want to know how you know the last part?"

"No, you don't."

Hattie told him they were getting close and to slow the car. When they passed the compound, she noticed the front porch lights were on, but the upper floor was dark.

"Park at the end of the block. You'll need to climb a tree to get over the wall. There's a walk-through gate near the driveway that opens from the inside. Let me in, and I'll show you how to enter the house undetected from the back garden."

He rolled his neck again after parking the sedan. "All right, Hattie, but stay close. I go inside the house first."

"I'm not the same person I was in New York, Father. I'm getting pretty good at sneaking around."

"That much is apparent." He opened the driver's door.

Hattie held up Ziegler's leather document roll. "Before we go, we need to secure this. They're the papers Ziegler is looking for."

"Give it to me." Karl got out and opened the rear door. He lifted a false flap at the bottom of the back bench seat and slid the satchel beneath it. "It will be safe here after we lock up."

Hattie got out, placed Maya's pistol inside the waistband of her slacks at her back under the trailing edge of her blouse, and waited for her father to circle the vehicle. "If you go in without me, I'll never forgive you, and I'll come in after you."

"I know." Karl kissed her on the forehead and locked the car. "I'll meet you at the front gate."

When he scaled the tree and disappeared over the wall, Hattie walked the sidewalk to the gate, passing two streetlights. A minute passed before she worried her father had gone into the house, leaving her behind. She fumed, thinking he had decided to make her stand on the sidelines until Eva was safe. After the second minute, she considered circling back and climbing the tree. Finally, the small gate opened, and Hattie stepped through.

"What took so long?" she asked.

"I'm not as young as I used to be," he said, rubbing his hand against his lower back.

"Are you okay?"

"I'll be fine." He placed both hands on his back above his bottom and stretched until a crack sounded. "Old injury."

"I never knew."

"When was I supposed to tell you I nearly broke my back being tossed from a moving truck in Toronto?"

Hattie shook her head, realizing she knew little about the man she'd known and loved all her life. "When this is over, we have much catching up to do."

"Yes, we do."

"Follow me," Hattie said, waving him forward.

Light from the waxing gibbous moon provided ample illumination to make their way around the property's perimeter and stay close to the wall until they reached the vast back garden. She took a pathway lined on both sides with the lush greenery she'd seen from the second-story study balcony. The route camouflaged their approach to the center fountain, where she crouched to assess her surroundings. The back of the house was completely dark, but, considering the time, the lack of lights didn't mean no one was there. It could have meant the occupants were asleep.

"The balcony on the left is Ziegler's office," Hattie said. "The one on the right must be Ziegler's room. The windows in the middle are secondary bedrooms and a hall bathroom." She lowered her stare to the first floor. "Center on the bottom is the ballroom. To the left is the music room. The dining room and kitchen are to the right. The servants hang out there when they're not needed."

"I doubt this place has a basement. The soil isn't conducive until you get out of town," Karl said. "Where do you think he might be holding her?"

"Downstairs is strictly for entertaining and food prep. Mother says he spends most of his time upstairs."

"That's where we go first. How do we get inside?"

"The kitchen entrance. The cook leaves the door unlocked for the gardener and driver. We can use the servants' stairs to the second floor."

"Eva certainly knows a lot about Ziegler's house."

"Like I said, you don't want to know why." Cloaked by darkness, Hattie stepped lightly from behind the fountain and headed toward the far end of the covered patio. When she reached the building, her father placed a hand on her shoulder and drew a pistol from his waist holster.

"Me first, sweetheart."

Hattie readied the handgun Maya gave her. "After you, Father."

He tested the doorknob and smiled at Hattie when it turned. They slipped into the mansion. The room lacked enough light to move around without accidentally hitting something, so Karl unclipped a handheld flashlight from his belt and brought it to life, producing a faint glow.

Hattie gestured toward the open stairwell on the other side of the refrigerator. As they climbed to the next floor, the stairs creaked in three spots, but they were a better choice than the broad, sweeping staircase in the front entry area, where they would have been easily seen approaching.

They landed at the top nearest what Hattie assumed was Ziegler's suite. Karl shined the light down the corridor long enough to see all the doors were closed. He turned and whispered to Hattie, "Cover the hallway."

Hattie nodded.

Once their eyes adjusted to the darkness again, Karl eased the bedroom door open. When he slipped inside, holding his gun out with both hands, Hattie moved to the doorway to observe the hallway and bedroom. She held her weapon the same way as her father, ready to fire. The bed was empty, and Karl disappeared deeper into the room, which she assumed led to a private bathroom. He returned seconds later, shaking his head.

"Not here," he whispered.

They tiptoed from room to room, quietly searching but yielding the same results. They reached the double doors of the study at the top of the main stairs. If Ziegler was in the house, he likely would be in his office. Hattie readied her handgun when Karl placed his hand on the knob. This time, she would follow him in to better their odds.

He pushed through the dark room, and Hattie was on his heels. She wheeled her pistol toward the desk, where she hoped he was, so she could put a bullet into Ziegler's arm and watch him writhe in agony until he told her where he had her mother.

Moonlight shone through the balcony's glass French doors, somewhat illuminating the room. When Hattie saw Ziegler seated at the desk, Karl called out, "Don't move, Ziegler. Where is Eva?"

Hattie's heart pounded at the thought she might be seconds away from getting her mother back.

Ziegler didn't flinch and remained silent. His desk was in the shadows, so it was impossible to tell whether he had a pistol.

Hattie took a chance, reached behind her, and flipped up the wall switch, turning on the overhead lights. Karl immediately reissued his command, and Hattie gripped her gun extra tight, but her hands were sweaty from nerves. She pointed the muzzle at the man who had betrayed her mother in the worst way—using her life as a bargaining chip.

Her father approached the desk, pointing his pistol at Ziegler. The man didn't move, but Hattie noticed his head slumped to one side like he was asleep. Suddenly, Karl lowered his weapon, making Hattie blink in confusion.

Karl circled and kicked the chair. Ziegler fell against the desk. "He's dead."

Hattie stepped closer, feeling numb. She lowered the hand with the gun to her thigh. The blood spatter and brain matter on the chair and bookshelf behind the desk didn't bother her. However, seeing their only link to Eva lying there with a gunshot wound at his temple made her tremble. How were they supposed to locate her? "What do we do now, Father?"

"Turn over every stone until we find her."

"In two days? Where do we start?"

"By starting with whoever would be desperate enough to kill Ziegler for that key."

The word *kill* hit Hattie like a slap in the face. Whoever did this was also turning over every stone. Her thoughts focused on David, alone at Eva's house. "David could be in danger. We need to go."

A quick run through the bottom floor confirmed Eva was not on the premises. Hattie and Karl rushed to his car, where he ensured Ziegler's document satchel was still in its hiding place. He drove like a madman through the mostly empty streets and up the steep slopes of Rio's hills. Karl was making record time, but it felt like an eternity to Hattie. David could have been hurt and bleeding, and every second on the road could have meant losing another drop of blood.

The moment Karl parked at the top of Eva's driveway in front of the garage, Hattie flew out the passenger door, carrying Ziegler's document roll. She had her key to the house ready, but her hand shook as she tried to unlock the solid garden door.

Karl stepped beside her, steadied her hand without saying a word, and helped her insert the key. A twist of the knob opened the door. She dashed down the path while her heart pounded violently at the possibility David might be dead. One more door stood in her way of knowing his fate.

Her hand still shook, but it was not enough to miss the keyhole this time. She twisted the knob but paused, readying herself for the worst outcome. Despite her growing mistrust of David, the only thing he had done to earn it was to be overly protective of her. Their two years of faking a relationship had turned into a genuine loving friendship in New York, but once she arrived in Rio, entangled in the world of Nazi spies, she began seeing duplicity everywhere, perhaps where none existed.

Hattie opened the door and discovered the lights on and the ceiling fan swirling the cool evening air. She gasped, focusing on the askew couch cushions and a room that appeared to have been combed through.

"David?" Hattie called out but received no answer. She stepped farther inside, walking cautiously to see what was on the other side of the mess.

Her temples throbbed at the possibility of a horrible outcome. She barely had time to picture a gruesome scene when David's arm lying motionless on the tile floor came into view. Her breathing labored in short, dizzying exhales as she took another step. David was face down with his arms and legs in awkward positions.

"God, no," she whimpered and rushed to him, landing on her knees and throwing down the document satchel within seconds. She turned him over, discovering blood coming from his temple at the exact location where Ziegler had been shot. Tears flowed like a swollen river. "David, no." She cradled his head, not caring if blood stained her beautiful clothes.

Then.

His arm twitched. He was alive, and Hattie's breathing shortened more in profound relief. "David. David." She stroked his cheeks until his eyes fluttered open.

"The house is clear," Karl said. Hattie hadn't realized he'd left the room and scoured every inch of the house in the time it took her to learn whether David was alive or dead. She looked up with tears blurring her vision but could tell Karl's chest was heaving from exertion.

Hattie returned her attention to David. He raised a hand to his head and groaned.

"Can you sit?" Hattie asked. "Is anything broken?"

She pulled him forward by his jacket lapels when he tried to push up from the floor and eased him into a sitting position. Hattie glanced at her father. "Can you get a wet towel and a bowl of water so I can tend to his wound?"

Karl nodded and entered the kitchen.

Hattie nudged David across the tile until he leaned against the couch. She inspected the gash on his left temple an inch above his hairline. It appeared to be relatively deep.

Karl returned with the towel and bowl and handed them to Hattie. She dabbed at his wound and discovered it was still bleeding. "Father, Mother keeps a first aid kit in the drawer by the refrigerator. Can you get it for me?"

"I'll be right back," Karl said.

Hattie continued to clean the wound as David became more alert. "Can you tell me what happened?"

"Two men came through the patio door and took me by surprise. They were looking for the key."

Karl came back with the supplies and handed the kit to Hattie. "Can you describe them?" he asked David.

"Not really." David looked at Karl with skepticism in his eyes, which Hattie expected. This marked the first time the two men had crossed paths in Rio and since all this business of her father's arrest began. David had every reason to mistrust him, just as her father had mistrusted David. "They hit me over the head from behind, and the blow blurred my vision. They kept asking about the key."

"This is all my fault." Hattie pursed her lips while applying an adhesive bandage over David's wound. "First, Mother. Now you."

"I'm fine." He gripped Hattie's wrist and gestured his chin toward her father. "What is he doing here? What happened with Maya?"

"Father came to my dressing room." When David released his hold, Hattie fixed the cushions and helped him onto the couch. "We needed to act fast and find Mother, but we found Ziegler dead in his study."

David drew his head back. "Ziegler is dead?"

"Yes, from a gunshot to the head," Hattie said. A sense of helplessness flooded her again. "Now we have no way of finding her."

"It's not safe here, sweetheart," Karl said. "Pack what you need. I'll take you two to a place where they won't find you until we figure out what to do next."

After throwing some clothes and toiletry items into two travel bags, they headed to Karl's car. David slid into the back seat, and Hattie held on to his music case and Ziegler's document roll and sat in the front. Karl drove through town in the dead of night, taking many turns to lose anyone who might have been following them. He entered the favela close to the docks where Hattie and Maya had located the families of several of the women whom Baumann had abducted and parked in front of a run-down shack at the end of a street.

Dogs barked in the distance.

"We're here," Karl said. He got out and grabbed the travel bags Hattie and David had packed. Hattie secured the satchels and secrets they held and guided David to follow her father into the shanty. A damp, musty smell saturated the room.

Karl lit two kerosene lamps. The wooden structure was in disrepair, with broken slats on the floor, walls, and roof. Otherwise, the room was well kept. Towels and shirts hung from a clothesline stretched across one wall. A bed with a worn, lumpy mattress and gray wool blanket was in one corner, and a scratched table with two chairs sat in another. A rickety dresser was between them.

"Is this where you've been staying?" Hattie asked. She hated to think her father had to endure squalid conditions while she had been living a life of luxury at Eva's and the Golden Room.

"Sometimes. The favela dogs bark at everything, so it's easy to know if someone is sneaking up on me."

"And when you're not here?" she asked.

"I move from hotel to hotel in town under different names."

Hattie settled David in the bed so he could rest. She checked the bandage on his wound, noting the bleeding appeared to have stopped.

Karl stepped to a shelf behind the table and grabbed two canteen cups and a sealed jug. He popped the cork and poured some water. Hattie joined him at the table, and he handed her a cup. "There's an outhouse across the street," he said. "Otherwise, I have a piss bucket. I know this isn't much, but it's safe enough for us to regroup and get some sleep."

"It's fine, Father, but I don't think I can sleep until we come up with a solution to find Mother." She glanced over her shoulder toward the bed. David had closed his eyes.

"Let's start from the beginning. Tell me everything you know about this assassination plot to sink a ship."

"Mother and I went to Ziegler's gala to perform..." Hattie spoke of everyone she was introduced to that night and of overhearing voices when she returned upstairs to change from her stage dress. "I thought they sounded familiar but couldn't place them. I remember thinking one might have been the Italian colonel I'd met earlier."

"Do you recall a name?"

Hattie shook her head. "I'm sorry, Father. I'd met so many people that night, but Leo might know him."

"Who's Leo?"

"Lieutenant Commander Leo Bell. He's a naval attaché assigned to the US Embassy. I'd reached out to him first after overhearing about the plot."

"How do you know him?" Karl's question sounded like he was suspicious.

"He's come to my show at the Golden Room a few times, and we met at the bar one night. We've been friends since, two Americans in a foreign country and all. Leo likely knows of his military counterparts at the other embassies. We can call him first thing in the morning."

"Do you trust him?" he asked.

"Yes," she said without hesitation.

Karl nodded. "At least we have a stone to overturn." He glanced toward the bed, and Hattie followed his stare. David appeared to be sleeping. "Care to explain what happened in your dressing room earlier?"

Hattie closed her eyes, unprepared to have this awkward conversation. "I do, and I will, but not tonight. Not here. We need to figure out our next move."

Her father sighed deeply and remained silent for several beats. "Okay." He crossed his arms, slid his bottom closer to the edge of the chair, and slouched, preparing to get some sleep.

Hattie had hidden the truth about her love life from so many people, and for so long, she wasn't sure where to begin or how he would take it. However, she was certain her life would never be the same once she did.

She slipped into bed beside David, ensuring she did not disturb him. She lay there on the edge of sleep, wondering whether the truth would improve her life or make it worse.

20

At ten in the morning, the bar was already full. Hattie had been in some sleazy low-rent bars in New York City, especially after her career nosedived when the FBI leaked the story about her father being an accused traitor and murderer to the papers. The Boteca da Boa Vita on the outskirts of the favela where Karl rented a shack was in the same class. While local Brazilian music played from a radio in the background, the pungent smell of stale beer, urine, and cheap cigarettes hit her the instant she walked inside. The odor stayed with her despite her being farthest from the bathroom next to an open window.

"He's late," David said, sitting beside her in the booth and sipping a glass of watered-down whiskey.

"He'll show." Hattie drank from her can of cola. She didn't trust the water here. "He said he'd come."

David remained quiet for a moment before saying, "I don't understand why you didn't call me at the house when your father showed up last night. I would have helped."

"I know you would have, but my father was insistent, and as it ended up, having you there wouldn't have made a difference." Hattie could not bring herself to say that she had kept him out of the loop because of a lack of trust, especially after he took a beating because of her. "It won't happen again."

"I hope not, because I'm tired of it." David winced and touched the bandage on his temple.

"How is your head?"

"I'm a little sore and have a nagging headache, but I'm okay."

Hattie kept her eye on the bar entrance and smiled when Leo Bell appeared, wearing a casual long-sleeved tan shirt and dark green pants. "He's here."

Leo spotted Hattie and approached. He acknowledged David with a nod and sat in the booth across from Hattie.

"I'm glad you came." Hattie let out a sigh of relief.

"During your call, you said it was a matter of life or death and to tell no one. Of course I came."

Hattie leaned closer and explained the events of the last twenty-four hours, since taking the documents from Ziegler's home, detailing Ziegler's ransom demand at the Golden Room and finding him dead in his study the previous night. She left out the part about her father's involvement until she knew he would help, but her shaky voice painted her desperation to rescue her mother. "Eva is still missing. We need to find someone involved in the assassination plot. I think one of them might be an Italian colonel I'd met earlier the night of the gala."

"I know who you're talking about. His name is Franco Santoro." Leo nodded. "What do you want me to do?"

"We need Santoro to talk. He might know who has my mother now."

"And if he doesn't want to?"

"We'll make him."

"You're talking about beating and torturing a diplomat."

Hattie steeled her eyes to convey her determination and clutched his hand across the table. She squeezed hard to stress her point. "I'm talking about getting the truth out of the enemy. War is on the horizon for the United States. Otherwise, you wouldn't have come to Brazil to scout locations for American naval bases. Italy is the enemy."

"I can't argue with that." Leo leaned back in the booth when Hattie released his hand. He rubbed his chin, clearly torn over the dilemma she had laid at his feet. "If I do nothing, Eva dies, someone important might be assassinated, and a hundred innocent people might get caught in the path of Ziegler's plot. If I help you and we're wrong about the Italian, my Navy career is over, and I'll likely face a court-martial."

Hattie's lips quivered when he shook his head. "I know I'm asking a lot, Leo, but I'm desperate."

"How sure are you about Santoro?"

"I could lie and say that I'm positive he's involved, but considering what's at risk for you, I won't. I've just reconnected with my mother and can't bear losing her again."

Leo released a weighty sigh. "All right, Hattie. I'll help you. What's the plan?"

"I don't want to involve you any more than we must. Just get Santoro here, and we'll do the rest." Hattie still wasn't ready to reveal her father's involvement since he was still one of America's most wanted fugitives.

"If Santoro is part of an assassination plot, he's likely armed and dangerous. You'll need more than just the two of you."

"We have another man," Hattie said, "who is just as dangerous."

Leo cocked his head to one side, raising his eyebrows. "You're talking about your father, aren't you?"

"Yes." Hattie gauged his response and saw curiosity, not anger. "I truly believe he is innocent, caught in the middle of something huge."

"I have a confession, Hattie."

She took in a rattled breath, fearing the worst scenario: Leo Bell was a covert spy and had been chasing her father.

"I asked for a copy of your father's file after we met, and some things don't add up."

Hattie reserved her judgment that Leo might not be on her side. "Like what?"

"If he killed those FBI agents, why would he get on a ship to Rio, where his ex-wife lives? He would have known our intelligence assets would have been looking for him here. The entire case against him smells like cow dung in the summer heat."

Hattie's shoulders slumped in relief. "You're the only American in a position of authority I've come across who believes he's been set up."

"After my experience with my father, I like to get all the facts before I judge a man."

"He's a good man, Leo, and he still loves my mother deeply. He won't stop until he finds her."

"Which is why I need to be there when he questions Santoro. Your father might take it too far." Leo let out a loud breath. "In fact, this entire plan might be a bit too far."

David leaned and whispered in Hattie's ear. "Do you really trust him? He could turn on your father."

The question made Hattie finally understand why she trusted Leo Bell more than David. Leo had said aloud that he didn't believe the charges against her father, but David had yet to say anything of the sort.

"Yes, I do," Hattie said to David before turning to Leo and telling him that her father had a place nearby. "We'll take Santoro there and interrogate him together."

Leo's expression was unreadable. He could leave or call the US Embassy and have them search for her father in the favela, yet Hattie trusted his instinct to do what was right, not what the rulebook dictated.

Leo stood from the booth, extended his hand to Hattie, and said, "Let's find your mother."

Two hours later, after leaving to call the Italian Embassy, Hattie and Leo came back to the Boa Vita and occupied a different booth, sitting side by side. This location was nearest the bathroom and offered the worst experience regarding smells, but it was also closest to the rear exit for an easy getaway.

Hattie didn't worry about making a scene while they forced Santoro out the back door once he arrived. As the afternoon wore on and the patrons had their fill of drink, three short-lived scuffles had broken out since she and Leo returned. Only one had garnered much attention, but that was to allow onlookers to lay down bets on which participant would be left standing.

They sipped on the sodas the waitress had dropped off minutes earlier.

Leo swirled his beverage, settling the ice lower in the glass. "You know, Hattie, when I saw you perform at the Copacabana in New York, I never envisioned we'd be sitting together in a dive bar in Rio, waiting to kidnap an Italian Army officer."

"You and me both."

Hattie recalled that last show at an A-list club in the States. Professionally, she'd been living the life she'd dreamed of with a recording contract, a wildly popular hit song, and an abundance of performance offers at trendy venues. Money was never an issue, but her private life was. She hid her romantic life in exchange for public acceptance and lived with scars from the women who betrayed her. Eva had broken her family, and Helen Reed had broken her heart. She never expected to be involved in espionage like she was now. But here, surrounded by spies, Hattie second-guessed everything and doubted everyone around her except for Leo. She had lost her innocence, a naivete she missed and would never get back.

Leo laughed. "Though, I gotta say, I've been in naval intelligence for a decade, and you're the prettiest spy I've worked with."

"Tell me, how many spies *have* you worked with?"

"Only a few. I'm an analyst and spend most of my time behind a desk making sense of information, not in the field collecting it."

Hattie laughed. "I'll still take it as a compliment."

A man dressed in a light suit approached their booth. It was Santoro, and he gave Hattie a long, piercing look. She glanced across the aisle and locked eyes with her father. He nodded that he was ready.

"You said it was important, Commander Bell," Santoro said in English in his thick Italian accent, standing even with Leo.

"Not here, Colonel Santoro." Leo stood, as did Hattie, and both slipped from the booth.

"I don't have the time for games." Santoro sounded impatient. "What do you want?"

Hattie raised Ziegler's document roll for Santoro to see. "A trade for the key that was in here."

Santoro focused on the pouch and arched his eyebrows. "That key will get you killed."

"It already got Ziegler killed, but I'll trade it for my mother. Who has her and where?"

"You'll be contacted tonight at the Golden Room. I suggest you do as instructed." Santoro turned to leave, but Karl slid from his booth and stood behind him.

"Now I know we don't need you," Karl said, poking the muzzle of his pistol in Santoro's side. "I suggest you come with us. Otherwise, I'll put a bullet in your back, and not a single person in the bar will bat an eye."

Leo grabbed one of Santoro's arms, and Karl took the other. The man struggled, but Hattie's father punched him in the kidney, doubling him over in pain. They ushered him toward Karl's waiting sedan, where David was at the wheel. One bystander stared at them as they exited, but Hattie bribed him with a few coins to look the other way before jumping into the front seat.

Anywhere else in Rio, a man being forcibly removed at gunpoint would have resulted in numerous calls to the police. However, as Hattie had learned while questioning family members of Baumann's victims, people in the favelas kept to themselves and showed no interest in getting involved.

Leo and Karl yanked Santoro into the back, and David pulled away, driving several blocks to the shack. After dragging the Italian officer inside, Karl and Leo tied him to a chair in the center of the room, binding his wrists to the chair's arms. Santoro strained against the ropes but didn't make a sound. No one in the neighborhood would heed his screams if he did. Instead, he spat at Leo's feet.

"My embassy will file a formal protest against the Americans for this," Santoro growled.

"That's fine," Leo said, "but first, you will tell us where Frederick Ziegler was holding Eva Machado."

"I don't know what you're talking about," Santoro said.

"It looks like we'll have to do this the hard way," Karl said to Leo before turning to Hattie. "I need you and David to wait in the car. I'll get you when it's done."

"Not on your life." Hattie knew from experience how far her father would go to get what he wanted, but she didn't want Leo dirtying his hands more than he already had, so she could not let that happen unless it was a last resort. "I can't let you two have all the fun." She walked up to Santoro, straddling his legs, and raised his head by the chin. "The massacre at Baumann's plantation was the warmup act for what my father and I have in mind for you if you don't tell me where my mother is. I'd hate to have the Italian Embassy ship your body home part by part."

The man swallowed hard.

Now that Hattie had his attention, she needed to give him a reason to cooperate. "If you tell us what we want to know, we'll turn you over to your embassy after this is over. If you don't, my father might get a crack at you if you don't die before I'm done with you. Choose."

Santoro swallowed hard again. "Wagner has her."

"Strom?" Karl asked. He clearly knew the man.

"Yes, Strom Wagner," Santoro said. "He plans to contact you right after your show to arrange an exchange."

Hattie forced his chin higher, making him look her in the eye again. "Where is he keeping her?"

"He didn't tell us, but he had us open our warehouse overnight for another delivery."

Hattie pressed her thumb and index finger around his throat, adding pressure until his pulse throbbed against them. Before her eyes were opened to the horrendous brutality of the Nazis, Hattie would have never thought herself capable of violence. However, with her mother's life in the balance, she had yet to find her limit as to how far she would go to save Eva. She was becoming more like her father every day. That should have been something to fear, but it wasn't.

"Where?" she asked.

He choked out the address, and Karl nodded that he knew where it was. "You said another delivery. What did Ziegler have shipped there?" Karl asked.

"Explosives."

Karl gestured for the others to join him in the corner, out of earshot of Santoro. "I've seen that warehouse. It's surrounded by a block wall and armed guards. We'll have to go in after dark."

"Will three guns be enough?" Leo asked.

"If we distract the guards, it should be," Karl said.

"Four guns," Hattie said with a sharpness in her tone, insulted by how Leo assumed she could not handle a gun. Technically, she had never fired one, but David had shown her how to use it. She'd practiced holding, loading, and unloading it enough that she no longer feared it.

Leo's narrowed eyes suggested he was skeptical.

"Count her in," Karl said. His sense of sureness made Hattie feel like an equal participant, not a helpless thing who needed her father to do the heavy lifting.

Leo offered Hattie a nod of respect.

She glanced at the Italian. "We need him to tell us about the attack. What ship are they targeting, and when? We still don't know if it's Olivia's."

"And who they plan to assassinate," Leo said.

"Yes, of course." A tinge of guilt crept up the back of Hattie's neck. She'd been so wrapped up in protecting her sister and rescuing her mother that she'd forgotten about the assassination angle.

Motion to the group's left caused everyone to snap their heads in that direction. Santoro had worked the bindings loose on his wrists and sprang toward the only window. Leo lunged, tackling him to the floor. Karl also darted as they rolled on the ground. David disappointingly remained still. Legs and arms moved so fast in a frantic scuffle that Hattie could not distinguish whose limbs they were.

A gunshot.

Hattie's breathing halted. The three on the ground stopped moving, frozen as if all were shot. Fear pushed up her throat, locking her jaw in place. Unable to move or make a sound, she stood statuesque, waiting to learn which man had been shot.

Karl lay on top with Santos beneath him, and Leo was on the floor, crushed by both men.

Her father moved first, pushing himself up from his knees.

Hattie dashed toward him, her heart pounding so hard it ached. "Are you hurt?"

"No, I'm fine." He rolled Santoro off Leo, exposing bloodstains on both men.

Hattie gasped. Leo was a good man merely trying to do the right thing.

If he got shot, she would never forgive herself. But if Santoro was mortally wounded, they wouldn't find out if Olivia was still in danger.

Then.

Leo stirred, letting out a long breath. "Holy Moses, that hurt. Get him off me."

"Are you shot?" Hattie kneeled in front of him. "You're bleeding."

"No. I'm okay." Leo glanced at his torso. "Ah, heck. I liked this shirt."

Hattie let out a nervous laugh and stood.

Karl flipped Santoro off Leo and examined the Italian on the ground. He still wasn't moving. The stain on his shirt was expanding, and blood was pooling on the wooden floor. "He's dead."

Leo sat up, palming his forehead. "Why did he go for my gun?"

"It's not your fault." David finally said something and helped Leo to his feet.

"I doubt the local authorities will look at it that way," Leo said. "How are we going to explain a dead Italian diplomat shot by my gun in a favela?"

"We dump the body," Karl said. "I know a place where the jungle will swallow it, and the cougars and jaguars will feast on it."

"You can't be serious." Leo looked at Karl as if he was a lunatic.

"Remember, Wagner plans to contact Hattie tonight at the Golden Room," Karl said. "If she isn't there to meet with him, he'll know something is up and will move Eva. We're running out of time, Bell. We need to spend what little we have to devise a plan to infiltrate that warehouse, not answer questions at a Rio police station."

Leo sighed. "You're right."

Searching Santoro's pockets yielded no further intelligence that might help find Eva.

Once Leo changed into one of Karl's shirts, they wrapped Santoro's body in a blanket and stuffed him into the trunk of Karl's car. Hattie sat in the front seat with her father, clutching his hand. So many lives were riding on their actions over the next few hours, including those of her mother and sister.

During the long drive north of town through the tall, lush mountains, the four agreed on a plan to overtake the Italian warehouse where Wagner might be holding Eva. They would meet in Hattie's dressing room after her performance, and it didn't matter whether Wagner contacted Hattie for the ransom demand. They would try a rescue after midnight.

Karl turned off the highway onto a dirt road and drove for some time before stopping at a stretch where the guardrail protecting motorists from the sheer cliff below was missing. He and Leo pulled Santoro's body from the trunk and laid it on the ground, still wrapped in the now bloodstained blanket. They both rolled him down the embankment, sharing in the complicity.

Hattie watched the jungle swallow Santoro's body as her father had described, without leaving a stitch of evidence for passersby to discover. The large predators would fight over his flesh, devouring it within hours. Hattie felt no remorse, which should have bothered her. Before witnessing Baumann's depravity at the plantation, she had considered any unnatural death a travesty. However, that ordeal and this one with her mother had taught her some people didn't deserve the life they'd been given. She included Ziegler and Santoro among them. And she expected to add Wagner to the list after tonight.

21

The low hum of hundreds of voices rose from the audience as Hattie waited in the wings to begin her show. David and the band were already in position. She peeked through a break in the curtains before the stage lights came on, looking for someone who might fit her father's description of Strom Wagner—tall, square jaw, graying dark hair, matching full eyebrows, and two prominent dimples when he smiled. He could have been any of a dozen men she spotted in the crowd who didn't have their backs to her, but she hoped her father, who was floating around the room disguised as a waiter, officially this time thanks to Maya's cooperation, might spot him.

When the announcer's voice came over the club's speaker system and introduced Hattie's name, she rolled her neck and straightened her posture, preparing to focus for the next ninety minutes to put on a memorable performance. A dinner show at the Copacabana Palace Hotel Golden Room was not cheap. While most patrons were frequent, wealthy attendees, Hattie poured everything into her performance each time she stepped onto the stage. She realized some guests had saved their money for weeks or months to see her sing, so she considered it her responsibility to ensure they had the time of their lives.

She walked out to booming applause, waving to the crowd and stopping for David to kiss her hand before walking to her mark at the center. When the band music started, she cupped the microphone as if she were caressing a lover's cheek and sang her first note. The blinding spotlight made it impossible to distinguish the audience members' features except those closest to the stage, but her task was to perform, not search for a kidnapper.

Hattie moved across the stage to make eye contact with a few guests for a more intimate experience for them. She spotted bright blond hair in the audience, focused on two familiar faces, and smiled broadly through the chorus, pointing and waving at her old friend and manager. Finishing the song, she realized she had a golden opportunity to return a favor and turned to the band, giving them the pause sign so she could speak.

"Thank you for coming, everyone. It's an honor to sing to you tonight." Hattie placed a hand over her brow to shield the spotlight's glare and found her friend again. "We have a special guest in the audience. Please give a round of applause for America's singing sensation, Miss Maggie Moore."

Hoots and whistles filled the room.

Maggie spun on her heel to wave to the packed house for their warm welcome. She returned her attention to Hattie and gave her a playful "don't you dare" look.

But Hattie ignored it and stared her in the eye. "A few months ago, I was sitting in this audience during the governor's birthday celebration, and Maggie invited me to perform with her on stage. Maybe we can entice her up with me with a little encouragement." Hattie glanced at the crowd, inviting applause by raising her hands. "What do you say?"

The people roared.

Maggie laughed, rose from her chair, and approached the stage as the guests cheered louder. They knew they were in for a treat. Hattie hurried to David at the piano. "Switch to the Moore set, but same ending song."

"Got it." David turned and informed the band members of the set change as Hattie returned to center stage.

Maggie cupped the microphone and whispered to Hattie, "Nicely played. I guess this makes us even."

"I'll always be in your debt, Maggie," Hattie said. After Hattie signed with RCA Records, Maggie went all out to assist her career, emphasizing the need for women to support each other in a male-dominated industry.

Her selflessness raised the bar for how women should comport themselves in this business, which cemented their friendship.

"Same set?" Maggie asked.

"What else?"

For the next eighty-five minutes, Hattie James and Maggie Moore put on a show the audience would not soon forget. Their flawless choreography and harmonies made it seem like they had performed together daily for months. And that was the foundation of their friendship. It didn't matter how long they had been apart. They picked things up like they had seen each other only yesterday.

When it was time for Hattie's signature closing song, Maggie improvised, which was her strong suit, singing the chorus and background. The performance would have generated an instant number-one hit. They took their bows, laughed, hugged, and left the stage arm in arm to join Maggie's agent at their table. David followed with his music satchel before the curtains closed.

"Hattie, you remember George Wade?" Maggie said.

"Of course." Hattie clutched his hands and let him kiss her on the cheek.

"You two were incredible up there," George said before shaking David's hand. "We should put together a South American tour. I can see it now." He made a box sign with his thumbs and index fingers. "The Rio Rhapsody."

Hattie accepted a towel from a waiter who had come to their table. She took it without looking at him.

He whispered into her ear, "Wagner is here. Upper corner past the bar."

She turned, nodding her understanding to her father, knowing she couldn't glance in that direction and chance revealing she knew who Wagner was. No, she had to wait for him to make contact, which was torture since waiting always made her edgy.

Once her father left, Hattie let David scoot her chair in when she sat. She thanked him and squeezed Maggie's hand atop the white tablecloth. "It's so good to see you. Why didn't you call or telegram saying you were coming?"

"I wanted to surprise you." Maggie patted her hand before letting go. "I was thrilled to read in the rags that you were performing here in residence. I knew you'd bounce back and make an even bigger splash."

"Thank you. Rio has given me an incredibly warm reception." Hattie qualified her reply and glanced at George. She recognized his slight at the mention of a South American tour, not one in the United States. He didn't say it, but he'd made the point that he felt Americans weren't ready to forgive the daughter of an accused traitor and murderer.

Maggie touched Hattie's forearm. "Before I forget, my lawyer secured the rights to our unreleased duets from RCA. Of course, they destroyed the master recordings, but I've been busy building a studio at my Upper East Side brownstone. Whenever you're up for visiting the States, I want us to rerecord them like we perform them on stage."

Hattie's lips trembled with joy and gratitude. She clutched Maggie's hand again as tears fell down her cheeks. "You are the best friend anyone could ask for, Maggie Moore."

"And so are you, Hattie James." Maggie leaned closer and whispered so only Hattie could hear, "Find a lady here to heal your broken heart?"

Hattie pulled back in shock. Over the years she'd known Maggie, she never disclosed her romantic interest in women. Yes, she'd discussed in vague terms the painful breakup she went through after Helen Reed cheated on her, but she was careful not to reveal too much. "You know?"

"For some time."

"And you're okay with it?"

"It makes no difference who you invite into your bed," Maggie whispered, patting Hattie's hand. "And to hell with anyone who thinks otherwise."

Hattie felt hopeful as her head spun from the revelation, envisioning a future where she would not need to conceal her true self from friends, family, or the world.

"You handled yourself well after our last show at the Copacabana club in New York," Maggie said. "If I had my way, I would have pulled Helen by the hair and dunked her head in the toilet."

Hattie laughed. "I would have loved to have seen that. So, what brings you to Rio besides surprising me?"

"I'm here for a special Mother's Day performance."

Someone touched Hattie's shoulder. She turned, finding Maya with concern in her eyes and a folded slip of paper in her hand. "It's urgent."

Hattie opened the note. It read, "A gentleman requests your presence at his table on the upper level to discuss your mother."

"Thank you." She returned the sheet, feeling the blood rush from her face. Maya pointed toward the upper corner, the same area where her father had spotted Wagner. Hattie focused on Maggie again. "I'm sorry to cut this short, but I have a pressing matter to tend to."

"Is everything all right?" Maggie asked. "You look pale."

"I'll be fine." Hattie pushed up and whispered to David, "I'm about to meet with Wagner. Tell Leo." He nodded and walked toward the stage door. Hattie kissed Maggie on the cheek. "I hope to see you again before you leave the country."

"Count on it. After my performance, I'm staying at the Palace for a few extra days." Maggie looked at Hattie with narrowed eyes full of worry. "Whatever this is, be careful."

"I will."

Hattie made a straight line to the bar, not stopping for fans who tried to get her attention. Under normal circumstances, she would shake their hands, take photos with them, and chat briefly while providing her autograph, but tonight was far from ordinary. The lives of her mother and sister hung on what Wagner had to say.

Hattie continued toward the upper level, lifted her stage dress a few inches with her left hand, and climbed the three steps. She stopped at the small table in the corner. One man occupied it, his back against the wall.

"You have information about my mother?" Hattie asked without waiting for pleasantries.

"Please sit, Miss James," the man said.

"I never share a table with strangers."

"Then please call me Strom." Wagner gestured toward the chair across from him.

Hattie took a seat. "Do you have my mother?"

"Right to the point. I like that, Miss James. Yes, I have your mother, and you have something I need. If you want to see her alive again, bring the key to the Statue General Osorio in one hour."

"That's impossible." Hattie sensed a trap and needed to stall to give her team a chance to rescue Eva from the Italian warehouse tonight. "It will take me half a day to retrieve the key from its secure location."

Wagner stood and threw out some cash for his drink. "Nine o'clock tomorrow evening. If you're one minute late, Eva Machado will die, and I will find you and slit your throat." He walked away, leaving Hattie stunned. She slumped in her chair, thinking Wagner had selected the ideal setting for this meeting. Hattie felt cornered. If their rescue attempt failed, she had to hand over the key and risk her sister being killed.

Hattie glanced at the table. Wagner had left a cocktail glass that appeared untouched in the center. She lifted it and gave it a sniff. The lack of any scent except for the crisp smell of alcohol suggested it was vodka, Hattie's weakness. It could have been a coincidence, but she no longer believed in them. A chill traveled down her spine when she thought he had ordered it to taunt her into giving in to her demons. Wagner knew too much about her, but how?

Hattie retraced her steps through the dining room, walking between the tables and stopping to shake a few hands. Once through the stage door, she spotted Maya waiting in the corridor, and she appeared nervous.

Maya grabbed her by the arms, worry flavoring her expression. "What happened? Does he have your mother?"

"Yes, but I don't have time to explain. I have to get to my dressing room."

"Your father is there, which means something is about to go down. I'm coming with you." Maya raised an index finger when Hattie opened her mouth to object. "Don't argue."

Despite everything they had been through at the plantation with Anna's death, Maya wanted to help beyond staying in the wings, and that was the best sign yet that she was getting closer to forgiving Hattie.

"I know what it's like losing someone you love, and I don't want you going through that." The pain of Anna's death was still heavy in Maya's voice.

Hattie had yet to admit it to herself, but she was sure she loved Maya and that Maya loved her. Hattie had seen her through her worst at Anna's funeral, and now she had offered to spare her that pain. If that wasn't love, she didn't know its meaning. She would be a fool to turn down Maya's offer.

"Okay." Hattie took her by the hand down the hallway, passing two band members smoking cigarettes. With graver things to worry about, she didn't care if they saw their display of affection and entered her dressing room.

Everyone was in place—Karl, Leo, and David—and each issued her a curious look.

"Maya is here to help," Hattie said.

"Are you still packin'?" Karl asked.

"Of course. Several." Maya added a slight snarl. "There are too many men like you in Rio."

"Glad to have you on board." Leo issued her a two-finger salute.

Karl asked about the meeting with Wagner.

"The exchange will be at the Statue General Osorio. He wanted it to be in one hour, but I stalled. We have until nine tomorrow night."

"I'm not familiar with that location," he said.

"I am," Maya said. "It's in a park across from the Imperial Palace near the post office and ferry terminal."

Karl rubbed the back of his neck, a sign he was anxious. "All right, we might not need to go there if we're successful tonight."

"What's tonight?" Maya squinted.

"A rescue," Hattie said. "We learned this afternoon that she's being held in a warehouse in the industrial section north of Rio. We're going there after I change."

"What can I do to help?"

"Be with Hattie in the car when she distracts the gate guard so she's not alone," Karl said.

Maya turned to Hattie. Her stare was like a soft caress when she said, "She won't be alone."

22

The idea of hurting innocent men to get to her mother had Hattie's stomach in knots. She had no problem doing what was necessary to villains or the enemy to get inside, but not to three local night watchmen, as her father had described them. "They likely have families to go home to," Hattie said from the back seat of her father's sedan as they drove north to the industrial area along the dark, empty streets.

Karl glanced over his shoulder from his position behind the wheel. "I agree. We incapacitate, not kill."

"That won't give us much time," David said, sitting beside Hattie.

"We won't need a lot," Karl said. "The warehouse is only big enough to store equipment, supplies, and a dozen vehicles for the embassy. Once we break in, working in teams should get us out within minutes. Does everyone understand their role?"

"I'll get the guard on the northwest corner between the warehouses." Leo glanced at Karl from the front passenger seat.

"I take out the one on the southeast end near the street." David glared at Leo, perhaps sizing up his motive for helping Hattie.

"And Maya and I entice the watchman out of his shack at the entry gate while you sneak up on him." Hattie glanced at Maya next to her. Her distant stare out the window suggested she was anxious about tonight.

"Once the guards are neutralized, I remain at the gate, providing cover," David said, "while the rest of you go inside."

"We search in twos." Karl slowed the car and parked a few blocks from the warehouse, clear of streetlights to camouflage their activities. "Hattie, when we go inside, you're with me. Maya, you're with Leo."

Hattie didn't like being separated from Maya, but cutting their search time in half was necessary.

"Set your watches," Karl said. "It's eleven forty-five. Hattie and Maya will drive up to the gate at midnight. Leo. David. Knock out your guard, tie and gag him, and make your way back to the gate. The one in the shack will have the key. We go in, grab Eva, and get the hell out of there."

Everyone adjusted their watches and climbed from the vehicle. The night air smelled of engine fumes, damp, urban rust, and concrete and contained a rare chill—a foreboding that something of grave consequence was about to transpire.

Karl kissed Hattie on the forehead and said, "Let's get your mother, sweetheart."

The three men, each armed with a handgun, hurried on foot down the street, disappearing around the corner of another warehouse. Hattie and Maya returned to the car with Hattie as the driver. A lost foreigner seeking directions was more believable than a local-looking woman.

The stifling air inside the car's cabin from five people having ridden in it for the last half hour had refreshed when the doors opened. Hattie checked her watch. They had another ten minutes before they had to be in place. She removed the small revolver Maya had given her and stuffed it at her right hip on the bench seat cushion with the grip still visible next to a roadmap she found in the glove compartment. Maya hiked her skirt, earning Hattie's attention, pulled her pistol from the strap around her thigh, and placed it at her left hip in a similar fashion.

They were ready.

The air surrounding them grew heavy again as anticipation of the impending danger shallowed their breathing. Hattie twisted the vinyl on the steering wheel for several minutes and finally broke the silence, "Thank you for coming. I feel a lot better with you here."

"Hattie," Maya said as soft as a whisper. She paused until Hattie craned her neck to look her in the eye. "I couldn't let you do this alone." She turned her hand upside down, resting it on the bench seat and inviting Hattie to hold it. "I don't know what I'd do if I lost you."

Hattie locked gazes with her and took her hand, feeling Maya's rapid pulse beating her fear. She drew Maya's hand to her lips, letting the caress linger before pulling away. The urge to say "I love you" hit her harder than the euphoria from their first kiss, but she resisted. Emotions were high, making this the wrong time to declare such a thing. Perhaps if she and Maya were in a better place after this ordeal and after they'd spent more time together...

Stop it, Hattie told herself. *You're getting way ahead of yourself.*

"I feel the same," Hattie said, releasing Maya's hand. She looked at her watch. "It's time."

She started the engine, depressed the clutch, put the sedan into gear, and drove toward the Italian warehouse, glancing at Maya often. When the guard shack came into view, she checked her watch again. It was one minute until twelve, so she slowed to time her arrival and sell the cover of being lost and needing directions. The hand on her watch clicked to midnight.

It was go time.

Hattie maneuvered the car parallel to the watchman on the wrong side of the road, aiming to appear confused and position herself near the gate. The uniformed guard was inside and kept his eyes on their vehicle. She stopped about fifteen feet from the structure, rolled down the driver's window, and butchered her Portuguese. "Perdoe-me, senhor. Eu sou...sou... lost."

Maya giggled.

The man slid the window open and shouted, "O que?"

Hattie lifted the roadmap from the seat bench, unfurling it and hanging her upper body out the open car window. She switched to English. "I'm supposed to pick up my friend's brother at work, but she's too tipsy to help with directions."

He shook his head. "Eu não consigo ouvir você."

Hattie rattled the map for emphasis. "Pode me ajudar?"

The man said something in Portuguese and closed the window, making

Hattie wince in doubt. She wasn't sure if she'd played her role well enough until he opened the door. He exited the shack and walked toward her vehicle. At the same time, Karl emerged from a row of nearby bushes and approached.

"He's coming," Hattie whispered to Maya. They both gripped and readied their pistols.

When the guard reached her car and bent to Hattie's eye level, she said, "I'm looking for Rua da Industria. He said to look for a red building. Vermelha."

"Ah, Industria." He nodded that he understood. Karl stepped directly behind him and struck him on the back of the head with the butt of his pistol. The man looked dazed, his knees wobbled, and he fell to the ground.

Hattie leaned farther out, confirming he wasn't moving.

Karl tied his feet together at the ankles and his hands at his back with rope, covered his mouth with a strip of masking tape, and unclipped the set of keys dangling from his belt. While Hattie drove the car forward to the cyclone gate, her father dragged the unconscious guard to the shack, turned off the light, and closed the door.

Leo and David appeared from opposite corners carrying their firearms and hurried toward the gate. Hattie and Maya joined them with their guns.

"Are we good?" Karl fumbled for the gate key.

"Yes," Leo and David said.

Based on Karl's memory of the storage facility, they had eliminated the guards, and unlocking the doors was the only obstacle remaining. Hattie's breathing labored as she watched her father try one key after another without success. Finally, the lock clicked, making Hattie flinch. They were almost through.

Karl rolled the gate open five feet and slid through first, dashing ten yards across the parking area toward the warehouse door. The others followed while David stayed to provide cover in case anyone stumbled into their operation. After a few tries with the keys, Karl opened the warehouse door. Everyone readied their weapons, and Leo and Karl pulled out their flashlights.

Hattie lined up behind Karl, Leo was next, and Maya brought up the rear. They were ready to break out into their teams. Karl gestured for Leo and Maya to go left and that he and Hattie would go right.

Karl and Leo turned on their flashlights, and Karl pushed through the door first. Hattie's heart thumped harder as she followed him into the dark facility. Her stare fixated on the cone of light her father was casting. Looking to her side, she noticed another cone speeding through the opposite end of the warehouse.

They quickstepped between tall metal shelves, passing stacks of office supplies, uniforms, and file boxes. The end of the aisle opened to a larger area housing six sedans and two cargo trucks. They checked each vehicle, one by one, but found no sign of Eva. Beyond the carpool were several wooden crates with their lids off. Karl stopped to inspect the markings written in German. This was a good indication that the Germans used this facility.

They were running out of real estate. Leo and Maya caught up, signaling they had yet to locate Eva. The only unsearched area was an office with curtain-covered windows at the far end of the building. Karl reached the door first, but Hattie placed her hand on the knob before he could. She was why her mother had become a pawn in this plot. Hattie should be the one to risk her life by going through first.

She gave her father a determined look, refusing to relent. He let out a weighty breath but signaled for her to wait until he readied the flashlight. Once Karl lined up behind her, she tightened her grip on her pistol and twisted the knob. Her heart pounded in her throat, like a warrior drum calling her to battle, giving her the courage to rush into danger.

In unison, he shined the light, and she pushed the door open. A chair was in the middle, and food wrappers and rope surrounded it on the floor. A woman's white sweater lying among the trash proved the dead Italian officer was right. Eva had been there. If only he had lived long enough to tell them where to look next and which ship was their target.

Hattie slumped against the door, holding back her tears. They were too late.

Eva was already gone.

Karl turned on the office ceiling light and pulled Hattie into a brief, tight hug. "This isn't over, sweetheart. We'll find her, but we need to get out of here before the guards free themselves."

Hattie tucked away her disappointment and stood straighter. "Let's go."

Everyone funneled out the warehouse door and into the car after Karl tossed the keys through the guard shack window. He drove through the empty streets without speeding to avoid earning the attention of the police cars hiding in the shadows of their night shift.

Hattie sat in the middle of the back seat with Maya and David on either side. On instinct, she clutched Maya's hand in the dark, drawing enough strength to fight off falling apart.

"Did you learn anything in there?" David asked.

Leo craned his neck to speak to David in the back. "We saw signs that she was held there."

"Which means Santoro didn't lie," David said.

"He was also right about the explosives," Karl said as he turned onto a main boulevard. "I saw empty crates with German markings. I recognized the coding. They contained dynamite. Whatever ship they intend to sink, the plan is already in motion."

They were steps behind Wagner and had no choice but to meet with him for the exchange. Hattie needed to keep it together for two more days —one to get her mother back and another to save her sister.

Karl looked into the rearview mirror and held his gaze. "Maya, can you direct me to the statue where the exchange will be tomorrow?"

"Sure." Maya guided him through town until they reached Tiradentes Palace, the seat of Brazil's federal legislative government. "The next building is the central post office in the old Imperial Palace. Beyond that is the general's statue." Maya pointed when greenery came into view.

Karl slowed.

"The square is street accessible on this side and at the corner." Maya directed Karl to take a right. After he turned, she said, "The statue is surrounded by trees and bushes with four access points."

"Where do those points lead?" Karl asked.

"One to the post office, one toward the ferry terminal, and the other two to the cross streets."

Karl drove past without stopping to not draw attention to the fact that they were casing the park. "We need somewhere to regroup and get some sleep before the exchange tomorrow. Eva's place isn't safe. We could check in to a hotel."

"Go to my house," Maya said, squeezing Hattie's hand. "I doubt anyone would look for you there. I have two beds, a couch, and a stocked pantry." She gave Karl directions and held Hattie's hand the rest of the way there.

Once inside, the men took turns using the restroom, with David and Karl taking showers. Maya and Hattie worked in the kitchen, preparing food for the group. Hattie suggested baking a breakfast casserole for its simplicity.

"What's in it?" Maya asked.

"It's easy." Hattie pushed up her sleeves, grabbed a mixing bowl from a lower cupboard, and pulled eggs, linguica, peppers, onions, and cheese from the refrigerator. She started by chopping the meat. "Can you cut up the vegetables?"

"Sure."

As they prepared the food, Hattie remembered the morning after the time she and Maya shared bodies. They had danced to music and exchanged long, sensual touches and kisses while preparing breakfast. It was the most playful and erotic encounter she'd experienced. And from Maya's frequent glances and looks filled with longing, Hattie guessed she had recalled the same memory.

Hattie browned the meat and poured it into the mixing bowl. Maya scooped the vegetables she'd prepped into the frying pan and stood at the stove for several extra beats, touching Hattie's side from shoulder to thigh. The contact was subtle but so electrifying Hattie could think of nothing else.

"I think they need turning," Maya said.

Hattie looked at the pan, noting the vegetables were about to burn. "Oh, crud." She shook herself from her daze and saved the food from sure death.

Once she'd mixed the ingredients, poured them into a baking dish, and put the concoction in the oven, they cut up fruit and a loaf of bread Maya had bought from the bakery yesterday and set plates on the counter so everyone could serve themselves. When Hattie turned to check on the oven, Maya slipped an arm around Hattie's waist and pulled her closer until their abdomens pressed together.

Maya said just above a whisper, "I've missed being this close to you."

"I have, too." Hattie closed her eyes and exhaled, enjoying the feeling again. After eleven days of fearing for Olivia's life and now Eva's and enduring the chaos to save them, this moment of intimacy was a needed respite. The built-up anxiety drained from her like a popped spring losing its tension.

Hattie inhaled. Though Maya had worked up a bit of a sweat at the warehouse and in the kitchen, Hattie still smelled the faint scent of the perfume she had worn at the Golden Room for work last night. Its intoxicating floral aroma had become so familiar that Hattie would know Maya was in the room without opening her eyes.

Maya fiddled with the stray strands of Hattie's hair, staring at them as if they held a vital secret. Her gaze shifted to Hattie's lips, and they parted involuntarily, tingling at the thought of a coming kiss.

Hattie focused on Maya's lips and raised a hand, caressing her soft cheek. "I've missed you," she said softly.

A floorboard creaked, and someone cleared their throat.

Hattie and Maya startled and snapped apart. The only plank that made that sound was the transition from the hallway to the kitchen. Hattie tensed, suspecting they'd been caught by her father or Leo—the only two in the next room who would not understand. It was so unfair. If she and Maya were of different genders, there would be no need for explanation, but societal judgment tainted their natural connection, turning it into something dirty and sinful. Love between two adults, no matter its stripes, should be celebrated, not spat on.

Hattie waited for the shock, followed by outrage. Instead, she heard David say, "Are you crazy? Leo and your father are in the other room." He sounded more like a scolding parent than a concerned friend.

Hattie's shoulders relaxed before she turned, giving him a grateful look. "Thank you."

Leo appeared in the opening behind David. "Whatever you have cooking in here, Maya, it smells like my mama's kitchen on a Sunday morning," Leo said.

"That would be Hattie's casserole," Maya said. When Leo reached for a slice of fruit from the tray on the table, she slapped his hand and winked. "Breakfast will be ready soon."

Karl walked in. "That smells like Hattie's cooking."

"You would be right," Hattie said. She opened the oven and forked her creation to test its doneness. "I guess we're eating now, but it won't be crispy on top."

Once everyone filled their plates and Leo pulled in an extra chair from the living room, they ate at the kitchen table. Hattie's placid mood became somber when they discussed their approach for tomorrow's hostage exchange, and Leo drew a diagram of the designated location.

"Ideally," Karl said, "we should have eyes on each access point to the park, but Wagner will expect David to be with Hattie. That leaves us with three people to cover four exits."

Leo made three X marks on his sketch. "Then we place someone inside the tree line here and here to cover the streets and a third on this corner to cover the exits to the post office and ferry terminal."

"Agreed," Karl said.

"I thought the goal was to get Eva back," David said. "Why do we need to guard the exits?"

Karl gave him a look that implied he considered the question naïve. "First, I doubt Wagner intends to let anyone get away alive. SS officers aren't known for leaving loose ends. Second, we can't let him have that key. My other daughter might be on the ship he plans to sink. The goal is to get Eva back without losing that key and have everyone in this room walk away in one piece."

David nodded and shrunk back as if he'd been slapped on the hand.

"We still need to narrow down which ship might be the target." Hattie grabbed Ziegler's leather roll from the counter and laid the papers on the table. "Something in here might tell us which one."

Leo examined the documents. Since they were written in German, he scanned them but studied the diagram of the ship's lower compartment while Karl pored over the pages containing text.

Leo looked up at Hattie. "What ship is your sister sailing on?"

"The SS *Brazil*."

"Then her ship is not the target."

Optimism took root, perking up Hattie. "How can you be sure?"

Leo turned the schematic around and placed it in the center of the table. "If this is to scale, the engine room is too small. The SS *Brazil* was refitted with a turbo-electric propulsion system. Its two generators, motors, and propeller shaft take up half of the engine deck space running from stem to stern. The room in this diagram is half that size."

Karl craned his neck to see the illustration. "Then how big is this ship?"

"It's not a transoceanic passenger liner, for sure. It could be a smaller steamship for local runs or a large yacht."

Hattie and Karl let out loud breaths woven with profound relief.

"The documents mention Sunday," Karl said. "Do you have any contacts with the Brazilian navy or the merchant port who can tell us if any ships of that size are scheduled to dock on a Sunday anytime soon?"

"I might." Leo checked his wristwatch. "I can make a few calls after sunrise."

"We should get some sleep," Karl said. "It's already been a long night, and we might have another."

Maya turned to Hattie. "I'll call in to the Palace Hotel when we wake and tell them we've both fallen ill and you can't perform tonight."

"Good," Hattie said. "I can't even think about singing today."

They divided up, with Karl and Leo opting for Anna's old bed, Hattie and David taking Maya's bedroom for appearances, and Maya taking the couch. Hattie rolled over on her side, facing away from David. She would toss and turn for another hour, relieved her sister was safe but worried about her mother. Once on the edge of sleep, her mind drifted to Maya and the incredible night she and Hattie spent in this bed. She would dream of sharing their bodies again and finally saying, "I love you."

23

After everyone got some sleep, Maya called the Golden Room in the morning, telling the manager to cancel Hattie's performance and bring in her backup act. When the phone was available, Leo called the port. Karl remained quiet in the corner living room chair, dividing his attention between her and Hattie. His piercing stare made Hattie feel exposed, as if he had realized her secrets and was judging her. The feeling was heartbreaking. Losing her father's love and respect would be like losing both lungs. She couldn't breathe without them.

Leo hung up the phone and spoke to the group. "My contact at the port says the only ships scheduled to arrive this Sunday are the SS *Brazil*, two cargo freighters from East Asia, and one from the United States. All are too big to be the ship in the diagram. He mentioned two passenger ships that fit the steaming capacity I gave him, but those vessels aren't due to arrive until midweek."

"What does that leave us?" David asked.

"Unless there's a special charter ship my contact doesn't know about, it could be a substantially sized yacht," Leo said. "I remembered seeing a few in the harbor and marinas that could be potential candidates, so I asked my buddy to research it, but it will take some time to get back to me."

The group tried to get more sleep, but most tossed and turned, anxious to set up for the exchange with Strom Wagner.

Hattie checked the wall clock. She had fifteen minutes before the group would depart, so she retreated to the kitchen to wash and put away her empty drink glass. While she was at the sink, her father entered the room and sidled next to her with two other cups in his hand.

"Do you mind?" he asked.

"Happy to." Hattie gestured for him to place them in the water.

"Now that we know Olivia is safe, no matter what happens tonight, you and Eva are the priority. Understand?"

Hattie hated to voice it now that she was certain Olivia's ship wasn't the target, but preventing the assassination and attack no longer took precedence. Their focus was to save Eva and walk away alive. If Wagner got away with the key, so be it. "I understand."

He cupped his hand over her suds-covered one. "We all come home today."

Hattie leaned against his tall, sturdy frame as she had done many times over the years. As a little girl, she had viewed him as an unflappable pillar of strength. She also knew she had her mother's talent as a singer but didn't want her self-centeredness, envying her father's mettle for serving and protecting his family. The last few days had shown her that she possessed the perfect mix of the people she loved and admired most.

"Hattie," he said and paused until she met his eyes. His look of worry and nervousness was concerning. "About Maya."

She wanted to tell him everything. Tell him she experienced love and passion like everyone else, just not with whom he might expect. He might not have liked Helen, who didn't know the meaning of monogamy, but she could tell he respected Maya for sticking by Hattie's side despite the events at Baumann's plantation. If he knew how much she loved Maya and how she felt in her bones that the feeling was reciprocated, maybe he could overlook the part his religious teachings considered sinful.

"Father." After several silent beats, she rubbed her temple with her dry hand and whispered, "I've wanted to tell you the truth for a long time."

He swallowed hard. "Just tell me you trust her."

"With my life."

Leo entered the kitchen, carrying more dirty plates and glasses. "This is the last of them. We should get ready to leave."

"Thank you," Hattie said. "We'll be right out."

Once Leo left and Hattie started washing the remaining dishes, Karl said, "We need to talk when all this is over."

Hattie placed another dish on the drying rack, wiped her hands, and turned to him. "No matter what you think—"

"Hattie? Karl?" David yelled from the living room. "Are you coming?"

Karl kissed Hattie on the forehead. "We'll talk later."

Hattie rehung the dishtowel on its hook and joined the group with her father.

Maya appeared from the hallway leading to the bedrooms. "Bathroom is free."

The last-minute takers took care of their business and returned. Everyone checked and concealed their pistols in waistbands, shoulder holsters, or, in Maya's case, her thigh band. Hattie and David got into Leo's car, which he'd picked up earlier in the day, and the rest boarded Karl's sedan. If Wagner had men watching the exchange location, they wanted to keep Karl, Leo, and Maya's presence unknown.

It was eight thirty.

The sun had gone to bed hours ago, but the moon was exceptionally bright. They had a half hour before they had to be at the statue. If things panned out as expected, her mother would be home safe within an hour, Wagner would be dead, and the attack would be averted. If they didn't, Hattie and everyone she loved in Rio, along with Leo Bell, might meet their demise.

The two cars took different routes toward the Imperial Palace, but Karl's vehicle left first so they would be in place well in advance of the meeting time. Hattie and David took off ten minutes later. He maneuvered in the evening traffic, remaining quiet behind the wheel.

Hattie had difficulty discerning his mood. Before coming to Rio, he never wore his emotions on his sleeve, but Hattie had learned his tells in New York and could always distinguish his sullen moods from simply being preoccupied. However, he'd become more challenging to read since admitting his feelings for her. She didn't know whether he was upset with her or was merely going over his role in the exchange in his head. Frankly, she preferred not knowing at the moment.

Karl took a direct route to the Imperial Palace and glanced at Maya in the front seat. From what he could tell after seeing her and Hattie together on several occasions, their affection for one another went beyond friendship, and he didn't know what to think about it. As a teenager, Hattie was intelligent, talented, and growing into her beauty. Karl had expected to beat off potential suitors with a stick, but she had been preoccupied with singing and school and could not be bothered with boys. He did grill her prom date —the only time a boy came calling.

He'd always thought her interest in men ran thin, as it often did with hardworking women, and he was surprised when Hattie introduced David as her boyfriend last Christmas. The man's overly firm handgrip at their first meeting made Karl suspect he was trying to prove something, but he never imagined it was a lie about his relationship with Hattie. While Karl now suspected their courtship was a sham, he wondered whether they were both faking. The bigger question was why David would stand for such a thing if they were. Whatever he was hiding likely explained why he deeply distrusted the man.

Karl put aside his concerns about David and refocused on Maya. However inappropriate he considered her friendship with Hattie, he trusted her intentions more than David's. Maya had every reason to hate Karl and Hattie and blame them for her sister's death, yet she opened her home to them and joined in the rescue effort without batting an eye. That was pure devotion.

Leo leaned forward from the back seat, folding both arms atop one another across the top. "You should know that I read the case file against you, Karl, and something smells wrong."

"Besides Hattie, you're the only one who believes I'm innocent."

"I'm not saying you're innocent, but the evidence doesn't add up, which is why I didn't turn you in the first time I saw you. That, and I trust your daughter."

Karl harrumphed. He liked this man. Leo was honest and grounded in integrity and selfless service. If he hadn't known that Leo was married and had doubts about Hattie's interests, he would have considered the commander an ideal suitor for her.

"But I give you forewarning," Leo said. "When this is over, I have to report that I've seen you."

Karl locked eyes with him in the rearview mirror. "I would expect nothing less."

"However, the number of details I provide will depend on how all this works out."

"I appreciate that," Karl said.

"Don't thank me yet."

Karl parked around the block from the exchange location. It was close for a quick return and getaway but far enough away from the plaza that they wouldn't be spotted arriving together. Once on foot, they split up before turning the corner. Maya carried a camera case and posed as a photographer interested in getting pictures of the statue and palace in the moonlight. Leo had a bag of stale breadcrumbs, looking like a tourist feeding the seagulls still scavenging for food. Karl brought nothing, preferring to stay alert, and sat on a park bench facing the courtyard.

They were in place, ready for the exchange.

Within a minute, he'd spotted two blond men dressed in suits appear and linger in the area steps outside the streetlight's glow. They were clearly Germans waiting and watching for Hattie and David to arrive. He suspected there might be more and kept scanning in the bright moonlight.

Strom Wagner wasn't a military man with gobs of combat training. Still, he posed a tremendous threat. He was a well-connected government official and diplomat whom Karl had first met during his post in Germany fifteen years ago while still gaining the Nazis' trust. Even then, Wagner had a reputation for being thorough and ruthless, which explained why he climbed the ladder so quickly. Karl expected him to have every avenue of escape covered and enough firepower to overcome a significant opposing force. However, Wagner could not gauge Karl's resolve and willingness to sacrifice himself for the woman he loved. And always would.

~

It was after hours, so David parked their car a half block from the statue courtyard adjacent to the post office inside the historical Imperial Palace. He turned to Hattie and said his first words to her since leaving Maya's house. "I have a bad feeling about this, Hattie. If something goes wrong, I want you to know that everything I do is to protect you."

Hattie blinked at David's phrasing. He had spoken in the present tense, meaning whatever he'd done was ongoing, perhaps based on his feelings for her.

"That's why you are such a good friend, and I love you for it." Hattie patted his hand, hoping the boundary she'd set would stick. "Let's go get my mother." She grabbed the leather document roll from the bench seat, tucked the key deeper into her bra between her breasts, and exited the car.

David also got out, offered his arm, and they walked toward the court-yard. Streetlights and a bright moon lit their path down the sidewalk in front of the old palace. The pedestrian and vehicle traffic around the government buildings was nonexistent this time of night on the weekend, but the faint sound of honking horns and truck engines trumpeted in the background.

Hattie turned the corner and noticed the plaza was sparsely populated. Maya was taking photographs, Leo tossed breadcrumbs to the gulls, and her father was on a bench. Two groups of two men stood between the trees close to Karl, drawing her suspicions.

Hattie checked her wristwatch. It was five minutes before nine. She continued with David through the courtyard, consciously trying not to look at Maya, Leo, or Karl and draw attention to them. They stopped at the three-foot-high wrought iron fence surrounding the statue.

Everyone was in place.

A foreboding hung over Hattie as she remembered her father's worry that Wagner would not let her, David, and Eva walk away from this alive. Her father had warned that Wagner could have other men there to prevent their escape, so she scanned the area for others besides the four she'd already spotted. She touched the handgun stuffed into her waistband, anticipating one of those men would force her to pull its trigger for the first time.

Her watch clicked to nine o'clock. It was time.

She swiveled her head, scanning for Wagner and her mother. Minutes later, a car arrived at the corner of the courtyard. The driver got out, opened the street-side rear passenger door, and pulled a woman out, holding her by the elbow. Then, the front door opened, and a tall, trim man emerged.

The trees and well-manicured shrubs made it challenging to distinguish the people, but they had to be Wagner and Eva. The three stepped slowly toward the statue. When they passed through the opening between the greenery, Hattie recognized her mother. Eva appeared haggard with dirty clothing and mussed hair. The man clutching Eva's arm was Riker, Ziegler's driver. Wagner was on Eva's left, and when they got closer, his hate-filled, determined expression sent a chill down Hattie's back. Her father was right. He didn't intend to let them leave this courtyard alive.

David stepped forward when Wagner and the others reached the iron fence, putting himself in a position to take a bullet intended for Hattie if needed. "That's far enough, Wagner." They stopped about ten feet away, well out of arm's reach and the glow cast from the nearby streetlight.

Eva didn't struggle to break away from the other man's grip. The terrified, worn-out look on her face told the tale that her fight was gone. Hattie flashed back on the women held captive and drugged in Heinz Baumann's basement. After a week of captivity, Anna Reyes still had a fire in her belly to fight back. However, Marta Moyer appeared emotionally beaten, still reliving the horrible experience two months later. If Marta's state after enduring Nazi imprisonment was a preview of what Eva had experienced, Hattie hoped her mother's defiance had been drugged out of her, not ripped away through unspeakable acts.

"Mother, are you okay? Have they hurt you?" Hattie clutched the document roll tighter, her bargaining chip for Eva's life.

"Oh, Hattie, I want to go home," her mother said, slurring her words as if she'd been drugged. In a way, it was a relief.

"We're here to take you there, Mother." Hattie focused on Wagner and raised her hand with the satchel. "I have the documents."

"Show me the key," Wagner said. Hattie tossed the container to Wagner. He caught it and examined its contents. "Nice try, Miss James. The key."

"After you let my mother go."

Wagner whipped a pistol from beneath his suit coat flap and pointed it at Hattie. "Or maybe I'll shoot you right here."

"Then you'll never find it. Let Eva go, and I'll tell you where it is." Hattie chose her words wisely to give the impression that she didn't have the key with her.

Wagner flipped the document holder to the man holding Eva, who snatched it in midair with his free hand. Wagner jerked Eva close to him, mashing the muzzle of his pistol to her temple, reminiscent of how Heinz Baumann had held Hattie captive on the plantation while getting Karl to show himself. The unnerving memory made Hattie shudder.

"Enough with the games, Miss James. I want our attack to succeed tomorrow, but I can always plan another. You have five seconds to turn the key over. Otherwise, your mother dies, and I return to the drawing board. Show it to me."

When he pressed the gun harder, forcing Eva's neck to strain against the pressure, tears filled Hattie's eyes. She was out of time and hoped the others had moved closer. "All right, Wagner." She reached into her bra, grazing nervous sweat on her breastbone as she pulled out the key. "Here it is. Now let her go, and I'll toss it over."

Wagner released his hold on Eva and pushed her toward Hattie. "No tricks. The key on the count of three or I shoot her in the back." He extended his left hand with the palm up while pointing the gun at Eva's back. "One, two—"

Hattie tossed the key, her heart thumping at a wild pace. "Hurry, Mother. Hurry!" She reached for Eva's flailing hand.

Out of the corner of her eye, David pulled the revolver from his waistband and wheeled it toward Wagner a second before he caught the key.

Gunfire rang out.

The streetlight near the statue went dark.

Bright eruptions of light sparked in the darkness, coinciding with each shot.

Seconds earlier

"No, no, no, no, no," Karl mumbled at David's boneheaded move. David was supposed to wait for Karl, Leo, and Maya to take out Wagner's backup, but he'd made his charge too early. The others in the courtyard would now fire at will.

Karl drew his weapon, trusting Leo and Maya had done the same.

Footsteps clomped but were drowned out by gunshots. Multiple muzzle flashes gave away the enemy's positions, so Karl was judicious with his attack, firing once on the run at the bursts of light, hoping to hit the target.

The blasts echoed in the dark, making determining where they came from impossible. However, Karl knew Leo's and Maya's locations before the streetlights were shot out and hoped they attacked the closest bright bursts as he did.

Between shots, he followed the sound of footsteps and a loud voice. "We have everything!" someone yelled in German. It must have been Wagner. Those words sparked panic in Karl. Did everything include Eva and Hattie? Instinct told Karl to follow him, so he pivoted toward the street, where Wagner's sedan had stopped.

Karl's chest heaved with each breath as the fear that everyone he loved was in greater danger than when this night started. He stretched his legs to their limits, dodging a bullet that whizzed past his ear in the dark.

A car door slammed.

Tires screeched against the pavement.

Footsteps advanced rapidly from behind him.

Karl turned and fired, not knowing who was in his crosshairs.

24

Hattie's breathing sped to a dizzying rate until she found her mother's hand and yanked it toward her. Eva stumbled, and Hattie fell with her. Someone approached them at a rapid pace. The direction wasn't from where Hattie expected Leo, Maya, or her father to be, so she yanked her gun from her waistband at the small of her back and pulled the trigger three times without being sure of a target. A grunt and the thump of a body falling to the ground said she had hit someone. But who?

A man yelled something in German.

A car door slammed.

Tires screeched against the pavement.

More gunfire but no visible muzzle flashes.

The click of shoes on the concrete established several people were running, but Hattie could not discern their direction of travel.

In her drugged stupor, Eva got to her knees and pushed up like she was about to run, but that would have been a grave mistake. The darkness made it impossible to tell where the shooting was coming from. Hattie pulled her mother to the ground and shielded her with her body. "Stay down, Mother!"

The gunfire and rapid footsteps stopped.

Then, horrifying silence.

Hattie poked her head up, dreading to find the people she cared about lying on the ground, but the shadows created by the trees played tricks with the moonlight. The smart move was to remain quiet, but she could not stand the waiting...the damn waiting. She had to know their fate.

"Maya!" Hattie called out. Her heart pounded at the possibility that Maya was lying in a pool of blood somewhere nearby, fighting for her life, perhaps by the bullets Hattie had sent flying in the dark. "Father!" She waited several seconds. "Leo! David!" But no one answered. The worst probable outcome flooded her mind. They were all dead, and Wagner's men were waiting for the right moment to finish off her and Eva.

Hattie felt like falling apart, but she had to stay strong and in control long enough to get her mother to safety. She picked up her weapon and pointed it as she scanned the area, ready to fire. Her eyes finally adjusted to the lower light, and she discerned no one was standing or walking in or near the courtyard. Three, maybe four bodies lay on the ground motionless, but with their dark clothing, it was impossible to tell who they were.

"I'll be right back, Mother."

Eva clutched Hattie's arm. "Don't leave me, sweetheart." Fear was in her voice.

Hattie was afraid, too, but she had to find out who was lying there and whether they were hurt or dead. "Stay here and don't move. I'll be back."

She ran to the first one and held her breath while rolling over the body. It was Riker, the one who had dragged Eva from the car. The man Hattie had shot and killed. The idea of taking a life hit her hard, but she didn't have time to wallow in the gut-wrenching finality. She picked up his gun and hurried to the second and third bodies, discovering they were men she didn't know. After retrieving their weapons and stowing them at her waistband, she returned to her mother. It was too unsafe to stay there, so she decided to inspect the fourth body closest to the street on their way to safety.

If they were caught by the police, whoever was lying dead by that statue and possibly the missing Italian military diplomat would be tied back to her and Eva. The plan was to return to Maya's house if they got separated, so Hattie had to make it back to the road, find a taxi if the car was gone, and evade the authorities.

"We have to go, Mother." Hattie pulled Eva to her feet and shoved a gun in her hand. "I need you to carry one of these." She wrapped an arm around her mother's waist and steered her toward the street where David had parked their sedan. Eva was sluggish but kept up with Hattie's pace.

Hattie's pulse raced, but she was so focused that her surroundings took on absolute clarity. She saw the swirls in the concrete pathway and the lines of the bark on the tree trunks as they passed them. Smelled the faint scent of gunpowder lingering in the night from the shootout. Tasted the coppery flavor of the blood in her mouth from when she fell to the concrete and bit the inside of her cheek. Felt the cool night air enter her nose as she inhaled. Keenly alert, she was prepared to face any of Wagner's men and save her mother.

As they neared the fourth body on the ground, Hattie slowed. "I need to see who this is."

Eva whispered, "Okay," and stopped a few feet short of it.

The size made it clear it wasn't Maya, but it could have been either of her male companions. She kneeled and took a deep breath before rolling it to its back. When David's face appeared, she gasped.

He moved, bringing a hand to his head.

"Are you shot?" Hattie frantically inspected his clothing for signs of bleeding.

"No," he said. "I was trampled and knocked out."

"Can you walk?" Hattie helped him to his feet.

"Yeah, I'm good. Is your mother okay?"

"She's fine. We have to get to Maya's house."

"What about Karl and the others?"

"I don't know."

"Karl?" Eva said, staggering closer to them. "Is he involved with this?" Her disdain for the man bled through loud and clear.

"Yes," Hattie said, holding her frustration in check. "We need to go." She got to the car and placed Eva in the back seat. When David moved toward the driver's door, she said, "You have a head injury. I'll drive, and don't argue."

Once on the road, Hattie shifted gears expertly and maintained an average speed to not attract attention, though every passing minute of not knowing whether Maya, Leo, and her father were alive was agony. She hit traffic traveling through the Lapa district, Rio's center of nightlife, but it thinned out after reaching the area around the police headquarters. After a few more blocks, she drove past Maya's house. The interior lights were off, and there was no sign of her father's car, but that didn't mean they weren't inside. They could have been waiting in the dark for Hattie to come back.

After parking alongside the house, she guided her mother along the sidewalk and up the walkway to the front door. David followed. She kicked at the loose wooden slat underneath the frame and retrieved the hidden key behind it.

"Wait here," she said to David and Eva. They were still groggy from their injury or the drugs, so she took charge to make sure it was safe to enter the house. Neither objected. She unlocked the door, placed the key back where it belonged, and inched the door open while holding her gun in a ready position.

The house was dark and quiet. She tiptoed down the hallway and carefully peeked around the corner. There were no indications of movement. She searched the kitchen and the bedrooms without turning on the lights, discovering no one was home. Hattie slumped against the wall, letting her imagination get the best of her. She'd examined all the bodies in the courtyard but might have missed more if they were bullet ridden, lying in the gutter. Tears threatened to overtake her.

But.

Eva and David needed her. She had to keep it together.

Hattie pushed herself upright, returned to the front, and ushered them down the dark corridor after securing the lock. She turned on a lamp in the corner next to the couch and settled Eva onto the sofa. David appeared more alert and sat in a chair. Hattie hurried to the kitchen without activating the switch since the window over the table faced the side street. She fumbled in the scant light to fill two glasses of water and wet a small hand towel. She returned to the living room and handed one glass to David and the other to Eva.

"Drink this. You need to flush the drugs from your system." Hattie sat beside her mother, studying her for a moment. Her eyes were droopy, she had difficulty keeping her head upright, and her face was smudged with dirt and mascara.

Eva cupped the glass in both hands and drank at Hattie's continuous urging until it was empty. "Thank you, sweetheart." She looked around and asked, "Where are we? Why aren't we home?"

"It's too dangerous to go there tonight. We're at Maya Reyes's house."

"That's sweet of her to open her home to us. Where is she? I'd like to thank her."

Hattie dabbed at her mother's cheeks with a damp towel, cleaning the streaks and telltale signs of what she'd been through over the last forty-eight hours. "I don't know." Her heart sank at those three words. "She, Father, and a friend were in the courtyard for the exchange. We were supposed to meet here if we got separated."

Eva's expression turned sad. "I'm so sorry, sweetheart." She patted Hattie's leg, appearing too weak to offer more solace. "What day is it?"

"It's Saturday night."

"Oh my. I've lost two days." Eva shook her head as if trying to knock out the haze. "What about Olivia? Her ship is due to port soon. Is she still in danger?"

"No." Hattie cleaned more streaks from Eva's face. "Leo figured out the target is much smaller, not a passenger liner the size of the SS *Brazil*."

Eva widened her eyes, wagging her head in disappointment. "Leo? You mean Commander Bell, the third wheel in your engagement."

"He is not a third wheel." Hattie snapped her hand back and stood. "How many times do I have to tell you he's just a friend?"

"A friend who risks his life to save your mother."

"Because it was the right thing to do." Hattie slammed the towel on the table. "I can't believe you're quibbling over the motive of the man who helped save your life."

"I'm sorry, sweetheart. It must be the drugs. I'm grateful for what everyone did and hope they make it back safely."

Hattie sucked in a calming breath. "It's fine, Mother. I'll find you something to eat and get you more water."

She entered the kitchen, keeping the light off. Until they were out of danger, she would keep the lights to a minimum. After placing the glass on the counter, she removed the loaf of bread from the box and butter and some sliced fruit from the refrigerator. While buttering two slices, Hattie recalled the last meal she and Maya made before departing for the exchange. Everyone was anxious and not too hungry, but Maya insisted they eat something since they weren't sure when the next opportunity might present itself. Leo had sat at the kitchen table, so their subtle touches were limited to standing side by side at the stove and sink. She remembered the fresh tropical smell of Maya's hair after she'd showered and how light-headed she'd felt, dying to be closer. She would have given or done anything to get one more chance to hold her again.

Hattie shook off the memory and longing and put the plate of fruit and bread on the table. She went back to the sink and turned on the water to fill the glass.

The kitchen light came to life, and someone released a breathy exhale. Hattie didn't have to turn to know who it was. Maya's scent smelled like home.

Hattie dropped the glass in the sink, shattering it into pieces. She rushed to Maya, enveloping her in her arms. Holding back the dam was a waste of energy. She let the tears stream down her cheeks, grateful Maya was alive.

"Hattie?" Her father's voice tore them apart instantly. A moment later, he entered the room.

Hattie hurried to him, melting in his powerful hug. "I thought you might have been killed."

"We're all fine. Thank goodness you're okay. We thought Wagner took you and Eva with him," her father said, pulling back from the embrace. "We followed his car after taking out most of his men, but we lost him at the German Embassy."

Hattie shook her head. "After the shots stopped, I found David unconscious near the street. I got him and Mother and came here, making sure we weren't being tailed."

"That must have been before we doubled back to get you. You were gone, so we came here." He pulled her into another hug. "The important thing is that you and your mother are safe."

Hattie looked to her side. Maya's lips trembled. Hattie reached for her hand. Maya took it and squeezed it before letting it go. Hattie loosened her hold and focused on her father. "I need to get some food for Mother. She probably hasn't eaten in days."

"I'm sure that glass of water was for her," Maya said. "I'll get her another."

"Thank you, Maya." Hattie nodded but said "I love you" with her eyes. She followed her father into the living room with the plate.

Leo was on the couch beside Eva but stood when Hattie entered the room. She laid the food on the coffee table so her mother could reach it, turned, and wrapped her arms around Leo's torso. "I'm so glad you're safe."

He pulled back. "Same here, young lady. After we doubled back, and you weren't there, we thought Wagner had taken you and Eva into the German Embassy. I was ready to call in the Marines to storm the gates."

Hattie laughed. "I'm sure you would have led the charge."

"If it meant saving your pretty little face." Leo winked.

Maya came in with the water, and Hattie sat with Eva again. "Can you tell us what happened to you, Mother? Did they hurt you?"

"As far as I remember," Eva said, "no one laid a hand on me."

"Did they keep you drugged?" Hattie asked.

"Yes. As soon as Frederick manhandled me into the back of his car, he covered my face with a sweet-smelling handkerchief." Eva took a bite of the buttered bread.

"That would have been chloroform," Karl said. "It has a sweet smell similar to ether."

Eva harrumphed. "I don't want to know how you know that tidbit." She turned back to Hattie. "The next thing I know, I'm tied to a chair in an office."

"That was the Italian Embassy warehouse," Hattie said. "We searched it and found where you'd been held."

"The Italians?" Eva said. "It makes sense. They were thick as thieves with Frederick, holding meetings at all hours of the night." She shook her head in disgust. "I can't believe I let that man touch me."

"He fooled all of us, Mother." Hattie bent the truth that she'd been onto him for quite a while, to comfort her mother.

"Speak for yourself," Karl said. "I never trusted Ziegler from the first time I met him."

Eva narrowed her eyes at him. "Maybe if you had said something back then, I wouldn't have gotten into this mess."

"Please, Mother," Hattie said, "let's not argue. I just got you back. Why don't you finish your food, get cleaned up, and get some rest?"

"You're right. I'm sorry."

"Yes, Senhora Machado," Maya said. "We're about the same size. While you use my shower, I'll pull out some clean clothes for you. You're welcome to sleep in my bed."

"I'm not sure if I can stand long enough for a shower."

"I'll help you," Hattie said, offering Eva her arm.

Once Eva showered and changed into Maya's lounge clothes, Hattie brought her to Anna's old room instead of Maya's. The idea of her mother sleeping in the bed Hattie had shared with Maya gave her the shivers. Hattie tucked her in and sat on the edge of the mattress, holding Eva's hand. She finally let tears flow about having rescued her.

"I'm so sorry I got you into this," Hattie choked out.

"You have nothing to apologize for. We both thought your sister was in danger." Eva held her hand tighter. "I'd walk through fire to protect either of you girls."

Hattie nodded, unable to speak past the guilt and relief battling for dominance.

A knock on the door drew their attention. Karl poked his head into the doorway. "Mind if I come in?"

"For a moment," Eva said. "I'm quite tired."

"I won't stay." He approached the bed, kissed Eva on the forehead, and cleared his throat before speaking. "I'm so relieved you're safe, Eva."

"Thank you for helping rescue me. I understand everyone put themselves into harm's way, but none more than you."

"Just because we're no longer married," Karl said, "doesn't mean I don't care for you."

Eva looked as if she might cry. If Hattie hadn't known her better, she would have thought her mother still had feelings for her father. Despite

Hattie's expectation of disappointment, they felt like a family again, at least for that moment.

"Is there anything else you can tell us about Ziegler and Wagner's plot?" Karl asked.

"I'm sorry, but no," Eva said. "They kept me drugged most of the time."

"All right. I'll let you get some sleep." He kissed her again and said, "Schönen Muttertag."

The last word sounded familiar to Hattie, but she could not place where she had come across it recently.

Eva formed a slight grin. "Thank you. It's been a while since you've wished me a happy Mother's Day."

Hattie also kissed her, wished her the same, and left the door cracked open so she could hear Eva if she needed anything. She walked out with her father, feeling something momentous had transpired in that bedroom. It was time to have a heart-to-heart with him, so she invited him into Maya's room, shut the door, and leaned against it. Yesterday, she had gone over in her head what she would say to him, but now that she was standing in front of him, she had no words.

She had told no one who wasn't like her about her romantic life. Maggie Moore was the first to reveal she had figured it out, and thankfully, it made no difference to their friendship. For years, she'd wanted to be honest with Olivia and her father, but the thought of them shunning her paralyzed her, leading to a life of secrecy. She realized now that the lies had to stop, but the fear of seeing disappointment and disgust in her father's eyes still had her frozen.

"This is about Maya, isn't it?" he asked.

"Yes, Father." Hattie's hands shook.

He cupped them in his. "You love her, don't you?"

Tears flowed freely. He knew. He'd figured it out. Now, she waited for the shoe to drop. That he only held her hand to say goodbye to the daughter he could no longer accept. But Hattie never again wanted to deny who she was.

She nodded and said through the tears, "Yes, I love her."

"I can tell she feels the same about you."

She dipped her head. "I hope she does."

He took a loud, deep breath. "Does David know?"

She looked him in the eye, knowing he wanted to see if she'd been unfaithful like her mother. "Yes, he knows because our courtship is a sham."

"Why would he agree to such a thing?"

"Because he's like me."

"I see." He let out a weighty exhale and turned away.

She reached out and spun him around, forcing him to face her. "Please don't turn your back on me. I'm the same little girl you raised into a strong, independent woman. It hurts that you're ashamed of me."

Tears filled his eyes. "I'm not ashamed of you. I understand creating a narrative for public acceptance, but I'm ashamed I didn't make you feel safe enough to tell me the truth." He lowered and shook his head. "With all the lies I've lived, I thought the one bright spot of truth was with my girls, but I have failed you as a father."

"Oh, Father." Hattie cried. Of all the ways she envisioned their talk going, this wasn't it. It was more than she could have asked. "You haven't failed me. I'd become so good at hiding who I was because of my job that it was easier to hide it from everyone, including you."

He shook his head again. "But you should have trusted me with your secrets."

"I could say the same about you. We both hid who we were from each other, but it's time to rip off our masks."

"You're right, sweetheart."

They sat on Maya's bed, and Hattie told him how she first knew she loved differently, how Helen Reed broke her heart, and how she almost fell to her death off the roof of her apartment building in a drunken stupor.

"That's why you stopped drinking," he said through tears.

"Yes. I didn't like who I'd become when I was, and I never want to be that person again."

He squeezed her hand. "You are so much stronger than I thought."

"I learned it from you."

"And your mother."

Hattie swallowed the emotion in her throat. "I'm realizing that."

"I guess it's my turn." Karl took another deep breath. "After the war, I was assigned to the Black Chamber and realized I had a knack for intelligence gathering."

Hattie nodded. "In order to shock me into helping them find you, the FBI told me you worked at the Cipher Bureau and transferred to the War Department's Signal Intelligence Corps. I held out until they threatened to jail Olivia and her husband for aiding your escape. They'd found some official diplomatic papers in her home, Father."

He ran a hand down his face. "The file Matthew took from my briefcase and hid from me."

"Tell me about you becoming a Nazi officer," Hattie said.

"It was part of my cover when the War Department sent me to Germany as a diplomat. My job was to infiltrate and gain their trust. The only way was to become one of them, so I joined the Nazi Party. The SS recruited me to spy for them."

"So you're a double agent."

"Technically, a triple agent. I've always been loyal to the United States. While I've provided Germany with classified information to further my cover, I made sure no American would be in harm's way."

"I'm certain of it," Hattie said. "Tell me about the sheet music. Mother found the Morse code you hid in it."

"Of course she did. That woman could spot anything odd having to do with music."

"It contains the lists Baumann was looking for, doesn't it?" Hattie asked.

"Yes."

"What are they?"

"My insurance policy. I was supposed to compile a list of American spies in Germany for the Nazis. At the same time, the War Department tasked me to put together the same list across all government agencies. The requests came within a day of one another, which meant the War Department had a traitor in its midst, and the Germans were onto me. I couldn't trust anyone, so I told both sides I had compiled a list of each nation's spies in the other's country and altered the originals so I was the only one with the lists. After I hid them with you, I was going to flush out the turncoat but was arrested, broken out of custody, and put on a ship to Rio before I could. That told me both sides are desperate to get their hands on those lists."

"But how are they your insurance policy?"

"It's the threat of them getting into the wrong hands. Both sides want me alive to tell them where they are."

"But who is the professor? You said to only turn over the lists to her."

"She got me into this work." He paused, taking on a wistful look.

"She's important to you, isn't she?"

"Yes. She's like an older sister and has been retired for several years. I can say she is the only person I trust other than you. She has the cipher to decode the lists." Karl gripped her arms. "Promise me something, Hattie."

"Anything."

"If the US enters the war and I'm dead, get the lists to the professor. Your mother will remember who she is and can help find her." Never had he appeared more serious or desperate. Whatever doubt she had about his loyalty to the United States was erased at that moment.

"I promise."

"Tell me," he said. "Does David know about the sheet music?"

"No, he doesn't," Hattie said.

"Good. Keep it that way."

"But why?" Hattie sensed that what she had told him about David had tainted his impression of him. However, her own lingering doubts about David stemming from his feelings for her had colored her objectivity for months.

"I know he's your friend, but I don't trust him. He's been overpowered by Wagner's men twice and walked away each time. He could be the luckiest man on earth, but I've learned there's no such thing as luck in this business."

"Or coincidence," Hattie said.

"You've learned the most important lesson quickly, sweetheart."

"Yes, I have."

25

Sunrise was half an hour away, and Hattie had gotten no meaningful sleep. She tossed and turned much of the night, discovering her mother snored. Loudly. Eva was still sleeping next to her, as she should have been. Having been held captive and drugged for two days had taken a physical and mental toll, and recovering from it would take some time. Besides, her mother didn't need to worry whether Leo was wrong about the attack plan target and whether Olivia was still in danger. Hattie had worried enough for them both.

The first slivers of light cut between the curtains of Anna's old bedroom, prompting Hattie to slip out of bed and dress without waking her mother. Leo's contact would be back at work soon and might have information on large yachts expected to be in use today. If he did, Hattie could rest more easily, believing that Olivia was likely not in Nazi crosshairs and that they could do something to prevent the attack.

Hattie eased the door open and heard Leo's voice. This man amazed her. He continued risking his life with little sleep out of nothing more than a friendship he'd struck with her months ago. Leo Bell reminded her much of her father. He was guided by duty and loyalty and never backed away from a challenge.

As she walked down the hallway, the bitter, aromatic scent of freshly brewing coffee called her and got stronger with each step. She tiptoed into the living room, discovering Leo on the telephone, David asleep on the floor, and Maya sitting on the couch sipping from a mug.

After smiling and mouthing "Good morning" to Maya, Hattie followed the tempting aroma to the simmering pot on the stove, poured herself a cup, and sat at the kitchen table. The morning paper was unfurled, displaying the headline in Portuguese, "Swiss Ambassador Found Dead." She read a few lines of the article, which said the police were investigating but hadn't ruled out suicide.

"How did you sleep?" Maya asked, stepping into the kitchen, still holding her mug.

"Mother snores." Hattie laughed.

Maya joined her at the table. "We all heard. This house has very thin walls." Maya laughed before turning her expression serious and reaching for Hattie's hand across the tabletop. "I was worried sick when the gunfire started."

"I was too," Hattie said, squeezing Maya's hand. "But we're safe." The moment between them was perfect. They were both vulnerable, and Hattie felt closer to Maya than she had in months.

"For now," Maya said. "I'm afraid Wagner will come after you and Eva again if his attack doesn't go as planned."

"We'll have to make sure that doesn't happen," Leo said as he entered the room.

Hattie and Maya yanked their hands apart, and their connection was gone.

Hattie's father came in behind Leo.

"What did you learn from your contact?" Maya asked.

"He couldn't narrow it down. Private crafts don't have to file departure and arrival plans, but security at the largest marinas reported that today is particularly busy because it's Mother's Day. Many owners are taking their boats offshore and into the bay."

Hattie cocked her head, trying to recall where she had heard the holiday reference. She'd known for almost two weeks that Olivia's ship was due into the Port of Rio on Mother's Day and had wished her mother a happy holiday last night, but someone else had used the term more recently. The days had all blurred together since Ziegler had taken her mother, making it difficult to remember who had said it and when. She recalled meeting with Ziegler in the Golden Room after performing, breaking into Ziegler's house, and finding him dead. That led to enlisting Leo's help to find the Italian colonel, who died in a struggle with Leo after leading them to Wagner. She later met Wagner after her show the night she saw Maggie Moore.

Maggie. That was it.

"Wait," Hattie said. "Maggie mentioned she was in town to perform for a special Mother's Day event. We know it's not at my club, so maybe it's being held aboard a yacht." She turned to Maya. "She's staying at the Palace Hotel. Can you call and have the desk clerk connect us to her room? Maggie usually leaves orders to not be disturbed when she's sleeping. You might have some luck reaching her agent, George Wade. He's traveling with her and should be in a room on the same floor."

"I'm on it," Maya said.

They all assembled near the couch. While Maya asked the operator to make her call, David woke, rubbing his eyes. "What's going on?"

"We're trying to reach Maggie or her manager at the hotel," Hattie said. "The attack might have something to do with a Mother's Day celebration she's performing at." She racked her brain to recall any other references to the holiday. Then she remembered her father saying something to Eva last night. Hattie asked Karl so only he could hear, "What is Mother's Day in German?"

"Muttertag. Why?"

"I remember where I saw that word." Hattie turned to Maya, whispering while she waited for the call to connect, "Are the logbook photos under the floorboard?"

Maya nodded and spoke to someone at the desk, asking them to ring Maggie's room. "I understand, but this is an urgent matter. I need you to send someone up there and wake her ... I'll take full responsibility ... Yes, I'll wait." Maya cupped the receiver and relayed the conversation to the people in the living room. "There's no answer on her room phone, so the clerk is sending a bellhop."

"I'll be right back," Hattie told the others. She hurried to Maya's room and closed the door to ensure no one could see what she was about to do. After lying on the floor, she reached under the bed near the head, lifted the loose floorboard, and pulled out two manila envelopes, curving them lengthwise to fit through the narrow opening. Once Hattie replaced the board, she returned to the living room, where everyone waited anxiously for the clerk to return to the phone with news about Maggie Moore.

Hattie sat on the couch beside her father and laid the pictures on the coffee table. "These are photos of Baumann's logbook." She flipped to the images of the pages toward the end of the book, found the one she was looking for, and showed it to Karl. "Here." She pointed. "Muttertag. What else does it say?"

Her father squinted, reading the page. "It's a surveillance entry from one of Baumann's agents at the marinas. He sent agents to them and the ports daily, collecting intelligence on the movement of cargo and people." Karl returned his attention to the photo. "This says two men at the Gloria Marina spoke of a large Mother's Day event and mentions the Southern Cross."

"Could that be the name of the yacht?" Hattie asked Leo.

"An excellent chance. I'll call my port contact when the phone is free."

Eva wandered into the room. Hattie rushed over and guided her by the elbow. "How are you feeling, Mother?"

"I have a bit of a headache."

"It's likely a hangover from the drugs they gave you," Hattie said. "I'll get you some water."

Maya kept her hand cupped over the receiver. "I have some aspirin in the bathroom medicine cabinet."

"I'll get it," Leo said, heading down the hallway.

After helping Eva onto the couch, Hattie hurried to the kitchen, filled a glass, and returned as Leo reentered the room with a bottle of aspirin. "Here, Mother, take these."

Eva swallowed the medication and swigged more of the water. "What is everyone doing up so early, and why so glum?"

Before Hattie could explain, Maya spoke over the phone. "Thank you for trying. Please let Mr. Costa know that Miss James and I should return to work tonight, but I'll call the club in the afternoon if anything changes."

She finished the call and handed the handset to Leo so he could reach his contact at the port.

Hattie turned to Eva. "We're trying to figure out what ship is the target of Ziegler's plot. We think it will be today, on Mother's Day, involving a large yacht."

"That would be President Narciso Garza's boat," Eva said. "He's going all out to impress his supporters by having the celebration off Copacabana Beach since his mother's ninetieth birthday falls on Mother's Day this year."

Everyone snapped their stare toward Eva and froze.

"Are you sure?" Hattie asked.

"Of course I am." Eva harrumphed. "He invited me, but as a guest. Can you believe it? A guest!" She waved her hands with the zest of a scorned diva. "He hired Maggie Moore to perform for his aging Brazilian mother, not Brazil's brightest star, who is also a mother."

"Do you still have the invitation?"

Her mother raised her chin in indignation. Any ill effects from the drugs were clearly gone. Eva was back to her old self. "I threw it in the trash weeks ago where it belonged."

Hattie sucked in a frustrated breath. "Do you remember the time of the event or where you were supposed to board?"

Eva shook her head. "Sorry. I only recall that it was a traditional Mother's Day brunch."

"Brunch?" Hattie focused on her father. "That would explain why we couldn't reach Maggie. She's already preparing for her performance."

Leo hung up the phone and rejoined the group. "My contact said the *Southern Cross* is a yacht registered to President Garza. I heard what Eva said. We need to call the police."

"If we go to the police," Karl said, "we'll open a can of worms."

"What about my embassy?" Leo said. "They can help."

"Do you want to explain about the dead Italian? He was shot with your gun." Karl shook his head. "Our best option is to convince the president's security team to cancel the party."

"What dead Italian?" Eva asked.

"Later, Mother," Hattie said.

"And if they don't?" David asked.

"We do what we can," Karl said.

"We better get a move on." Leo gathered his weapon and a light jacket from the coat tree in the corner.

The others did the same.

"You can't be serious, Hattie," Eva said. "It's too dangerous for you to go."

"Dangerous like rescuing you from a madman in a shootout?" Hattie peppered her response with a little too much impatience and corrected her tone. "We'll be fine, Mother. I have to stop my friend from getting on that boat."

"I'm coming with you," Eva said. "The authorities might listen to me."

Karl asked Eva and Hattie to go to Maya's bedroom to discuss something in private. After closing the door, he placed both hands on Eva's shoulders. "I know you've figured out I hid something in the sheet music."

Eva's eyes turned dark and fiery when she threw off his grip. "Whatever you hid in those pages, you've endangered our daughter by giving them to her."

"I had no choice."

"You always have a choice," Eva snarled. "But you took the easy way out by hiding your dirty little Nazi secrets with Hattie."

"There are much bigger threats at play here, Mother," Hattie said. "After everything I've learned from the FBI, I believe him."

"He's brainwashed you into thinking he's something he's not, sweetheart. Don't trust him."

"After he risked his life to save you? I think not," Hattie growled back. "I'm tired of not trusting the people I love enough to tell them the truth." She glanced at her father, who gave her a sympathetic look. He shook his head, conveying that this was not the time to come clean about her romantic life. Hattie pivoted. "Like it or not, we are a family and must trust that we are doing right by one another."

Eva huffed. "Fine. What do you need me to do?"

"Stay here," Karl said. "If something goes wrong and we don't make it back, I need you to keep the sheet music safe and get it to the professor if—"

"The professor?" Eva sneered. "I never liked her."

"Well, she never liked you, either." Karl laughed. "If the United States enters the war, the information on those pages could make the difference between winning and losing. Promise me you'll find her."

Eva rolled her eyes. "I will."

Karl let out a weighty breath and kissed Eva's forehead. "Thank you."

They returned to the living room, where everyone was ready to go. With much at stake, the tension in the room was thick. They'd figured out that the Brazilian president was the target of an assassination plot and that a hundred guests, including Maggie Moore, were in danger of becoming collateral damage. They were on their own since calling for help wasn't an option.

Eva pulled Hattie into a hug. "Be careful, sweetheart."

26

Leo eased his sedan to the front of the house. David and Maya climbed into the back seat. Eva stood at the door, holding Hattie's hand. To Hattie's surprise, her mother also grabbed Karl's hand.

"Bring my daughter back to me," Eva said.

The three leaned in until their heads touched. Hattie and Karl joined hands, completing the circle. The chasm forged from past hurts and intricate webs of lies had no bearing right then. They were a family, a bond that was never truly broken.

"I will." Karl pulled back, raised Eva's head by her chin, and kissed her on the lips.

Surprisingly, Eva didn't snap back or slap him across the cheek. Instead, tears formed in her eyes. "You come back too, Karl."

He winked but said nothing, sending a chill through Hattie with the implication that he would sacrifice himself to make sure she made it home.

Hattie took his arm as they headed down the concrete walkway to the curb. He opened the rear door so she could sit next to Maya in the back seat. The gesture was subtle but showed his support for Hattie and her relationship with Maya. After Hattie climbed in and held Maya's hand against the cushion so as not to be in Leo's view if he glanced back, Karl joined Leo in the front.

"Let's go save the president," Karl said.

Hattie glanced past Maya at David. He didn't appear nervous or anxious, only lost in thought as he stared out the window.

Leo put the car into gear and drove through the light early morning traffic toward the Gloria Marina. He slowed, reaching a line of cars waiting to enter the main parking lot, and inched ahead until he got to the access point, where two armed guards controlled entry. He cranked down the driver's window, letting in the briny scent of the ocean air.

"Convite, por favor," the guard said.

Maya leaned forward and spoke in Portuguese. "Miss Hattie James and company. She's part of the entertainment."

The guard checked the pages on his clipboard and said, "Her name isn't on the list. I'm afraid I can't let you through."

Hattie angled toward the gap between the front seat headrests next to Maya and spoke Portuguese. "Maggie Moore recruited me and my crew to perform today." She glimpsed the people milling about the end of the parking lot and focused on a batch of men stacking cases resembling those musicians often carried. "She should be with the band and can clear this up."

The guard looked at the growing line behind Leo's car and sighed. He waved over the other sentry, whispered something, and gestured toward a group of people at the dock's edge. The other man took off jogging. "Pull over to the side and wait."

Hattie repeated his command in English, and Leo pulled forward.

When Hattie leaned back, Maya said softly, "You've been holding out. Your Portuguese is excellent."

"I was rusty at it when I first came to Rio, but it's come back." She smiled at Maya and gave her hand a furtive caress with her pinky. "Especially since spending time with you."

Silence filled the cabin for several minutes until the other guard approached with Maggie and her agent. Hattie got out to head off her questions and odd looks. When the two got closer, Hattie kissed Maggie on the cheek and whispered, "Please play along. I'll explain later."

Maggie pulled back. "Hattie, I'm glad you came."

"Of course I would after your gracious invitation. I couldn't let Brazil's president down." Hattie gestured toward the car. "I brought my stylist and a few people to help with the preparations."

"What's going on, Maggie?" George Wade said. "You mentioned nothing about Hattie joining us."

"After you said something about a South American tour, we thought a presidential performance was the best way to kick it off." Maggie waved her hand dismissively and turned to Hattie. "Good thinking. They can help get the instruments on board for my band." She shifted and focused her attention on the sentry. "They are with me, officer. How can I get them aboard?"

The man appeared confused, so Hattie translated. He replied in Portuguese with Hattie's translation. "He'll need our names to add to the list."

Hattie gestured for the clipboard, telling him she could write the information. She added their names, writing Joseph Fuller instead of Karl James to leave no paper trail of her father's presence in the country.

The guard handed Maggie the board, and Hattie explained she needed to sign for everyone. Once she did, he instructed Leo to park in the corner with the staff. While he did, Maggie told George to go ahead and they would meet him at the gangway. She locked arms with Hattie and guided her toward the dock where her band had staged their equipment.

"Not that I'm unhappy to see you," Maggie said, "but what the hell is going on, Hattie?"

"This is going to sound crazy, but trust what I'm about to tell you is the truth."

"This sounds ominous."

"It is," Hattie said. "When I was at an ambassador's home, I stumbled across a Nazi assassination plot involving the sinking of a ship. A lot has happened in trying to figure out the target. My mother was kidnapped, and the ambassador was killed after I stole the plans."

Maggie stopped, gripping Hattie by both arms. "My God. That's why you acted strange the other night. Is Eva okay?"

"Yes, she's fine, but we couldn't stop the attack. That's why we're here. We think the president and his yacht are the targets."

Maggie jerked her head back. "Have you contacted the police?"

"There isn't enough evidence for them or the American Embassy to act on, so we're on our own if we can't convince the president's security to call off the event."

"This is crazy, Hattie. How do they plan to attack the yacht?"

"It's a long story, but we sneaked into a warehouse and found evidence of a dynamite shipment large enough to destroy the boat."

Maggie's eyes widened with shock. "We can't let anyone on that ship."

"Do you know when the yacht is scheduled to embark passengers?"

"They board at nine for a ten o'clock departure. My show is at eleven."

Hattie checked her wristwatch. "That gives us an hour to find the bomb and prevent the attack."

"You can't be serious."

"More than anything, which is why I came to stop you from going aboard."

"What can I do to help?"

"Get us on that yacht. We'll do the rest," Hattie said. The others caught up, and Hattie said that she had explained the basics to Maggie and passed along the timeframe facing them.

Maggie eyed the group. "Who are you?"

"You know David," Hattie said. "This is Leo Bell, a naval attaché from the American Embassy. Joseph Fuller is his helper, and Maya Reyes is the manager from the Golden Room."

"I thought you said the embassy wouldn't help," Maggie said.

"Not officially," Leo said. "I believe Hattie and want to help."

Maggie pulled Hattie a few feet back and spoke softly. "Isn't she the luscious one from Friday night?"

"Yes, but that doesn't matter."

"Oh, yes, it does"—Maggie pressed a hand against Hattie's chest—"if it means healing this." When Hattie blushed, Maggie said, "I'm happy for you."

"Can we table this discussion until later?"

"Of course. Let's get your group on the boat."

Maggie led everyone to the pile of gear and introduced them to the band members, explaining that Hattie would perform with her today and the men would help carry and set up the instruments.

The security guards at the gangway leading to the yacht inspected the instrument cases, patted down the men, and looked into the women's handbags. Since Brazilian male police officers never searched women unless they were accused of a crime, Hattie and Maya were weighted down with everyone's handguns in their waistbands.

Once aboard, George directed the men to set up on the bow deck at the raised platform, which was brought in for today's performance. Maggie pulled the event organizer away from overseeing the caterers hopping around the decks, decorating and setting up tables and chairs. She introduced Hattie and Maya and explained she had added Hattie James to her set.

The man ran his fingers through his thinning hair and spoke Portuguese so fast that Hattie had difficulty keeping up, but Maya calmed him down, reassuring him that other than the introductions, nothing else would change. Maggie would split her pay and perform for an hour, including the songs the president and his mother requested.

"You're getting two performers for the price of one," Maya said in Portuguese.

However, it was a performance that would likely never happen. If they could not locate the bomb and alert the president's security team, they would create a commotion to evacuate the ship. Hattie hated to think it, but setting fire to the boat while only the crew was aboard would have a much better outcome than having it explode. Hattie would rather risk arrest for arson if the explosives weren't on board than see bodies being fished from the water if they were.

The man smiled, shook the women's hands, and walked away, shouting something to the caterers assembling a food table.

Minutes later, once the instrument cases were all in place, the men joined the women, and everyone ducked into the stateroom set aside as Maggie's dressing room. Hattie and Maya distributed the guns.

Hattie turned to Leo for his expertise with ships. "How should we proceed?"

"I'm betting the main bomb will be placed below the waterline in the engine room to disable the yacht. Placing it there would cripple the boat and make it take on water rapidly. It would sink well before help could arrive. I suspect they might plant a second device close to the president to ensure his death and keep him from jumping overboard. We'll need to spread out and search from top to bottom."

"No one is to be alone. We work in teams," Karl said. "I expect heavy resistance below, so Leo, David, and I will take the lower deck. Hattie, you and Maya look topside. When you find it, get the president's security team."

"It will go much faster if I join you," Maggie said. "We have only thirty minutes before the guests will be allowed on board."

"I can't ask you to endanger yourself, Maggie," Hattie said. "You and your band must get off the yacht if we can't stop this."

"She's right, Hattie," Karl said. "This is a big boat."

"You're not asking, Hattie. I'm offering." Maggie winked.

"But we don't have a weapon for you if it gets dicey."

"Here." Maya hiked her skirt and removed a derringer from her left thigh, keeping a larger pistol on the other. "I brought two."

Maggie accepted the small gun and whispered to Hattie. "I like her."

Hattie grinned.

They filed from the stateroom, dividing into their teams. The men headed downstairs while Hattie, Maya, and Maggie explored the other rooms. Each was trimmed in rich, glossy mahogany and adorned with crisp white fabric with splashes of green, yellow, and dark blue—the colors of Brazil's flag. They searched in the closets, under the beds, and in the private bathrooms but came across nothing resembling an explosive.

Nearby voices dictated they be cautious while continuing down the corridor to avoid appearing suspicious. They sauntered to appear like they were searching for a particular room and soon entered the narrow but sizable galley that seemed to run the width of the boat. Six workers in white cook's uniforms were busy at the stoves and prep counters. Hattie scanned the area, looking for anything unusual, but too many food boxes for the party were stacked inside to make a decent assessment.

"May I help you?" one woman in uniform said in Portuguese while wiping her hands on a dish towel.

Hattie had to create a cover story. She said in Portuguese, "Yes, Maggie and I are singing at today's celebration. Can you have a pot of hot tea and two cups sent to the band area ten minutes before the show?"

The bright glint of recognition sprouted on the woman's face. "Of course, Miss James. We didn't know you would perform today."

"Thank you," Hattie said. "We're missing a large makeup case. I wondered if any odd boxes or suitcases ended up in the galley this morning. Can you look for me?"

"One moment," the woman said. She went to the kitchen's far end and spoke to another worker.

"Good thinking," Maggie whispered.

"I've learned to improvise."

The woman returned moments later. "I'm sorry, Miss James, but it's not here. Everything here is for today's lunch."

"Thank you for looking," Hattie said.

They went back to the corridor and searched a nearby storage room. Hattie cracked the door open to leave when a man wearing a black-and-white catering uniform passed by, pushing a handcart with a box on it. His lighter skin and hair meant he was of Anglo descent, which was odd. She expected the waitstaff to be of Brazilian heritage, like all the others she'd encountered since arriving in Rio.

Hattie remained hidden behind the door to avoid the man noticing her and waited until he reached the end of the corridor before peeking her head out. He entered the main dining room, the location for today's lunch. Hattie pulled her pistol from beneath her waistband.

"Wait here," she said. "Something is off about that waiter. I want to see what he's doing."

Three months ago, before being ripped away from her life in New York City, Hattie never would have considered going toward the danger. She would have called those paid to do such crazy things and run in the opposite direction. But the deeper she got into her father's world, the less she feared taking risks when the greater good hung in the balance. She was becoming more like him every day.

Hattie clutched the revolver waist-high in front of her with both hands and stepped down the corridor. Her breathing picked up, and her heart raced faster, but a hundred people might die if she didn't remain calm. She entered the dining room. The man was kneeling at the table of honor and fumbled with something underneath it. Hattie raised her gun higher, aiming at the center of the man's back.

"Senhora James?" a woman called out from behind Hattie.

Hattie lowered her pistol and held it at her thigh and out of sight a moment before the man turned toward the voice. They locked gazes. He narrowed his eyes at her, giving her a fuming look and broadcasting that he knew she'd seen what he was doing. Hattie noticed a chain dangling from the man's neck. She gasped. The unique key Ziegler and Wagner were willing to murder Eva for was at its apex.

Her hunch was correct. She'd stumbled on the explosive being planted.

Hattie had a choice. She could raise her pistol again and chance he would not kill her and the cook before she could get off a single shot, or she could play it safe. She reasoned the man was there to plant a bomb in secrecy, and shooting two women where he'd hoped to snare the Brazilian president in a deathtrap would foil his plan. Wagner's determined search for the key made it imperative for this man to leave no trace of blood in the room. This created an opportunity for Hattie to save the innocent woman.

"Senhora?" the woman repeated.

"Sim?" Hattie turned, slipping the pistol into her waistband so the man could not see.

"Shall I send out lemon and cream with your tea?" the woman from the galley asked in Portuguese.

"Sim por favor." Hattie shooed the woman off, getting her to exit the dining room and out of harm's way.

Before Hattie could turn to face the man again, he came behind her and placed a hand over her mouth. "I wish you hadn't seen that," he said in English.

Hattie strained against his hold but didn't call out, fearing the woman might return out of curiosity.

"Smart woman, Fräulein James. I'm going to remove my hand. If you scream, I'll kill everyone who gets in my way, escape, and carry out our plan another time. Now, come quietly. We're both getting off this boat."

Hattie was a loose end and knew he would shoot her at the first opportunity, but she could not risk endangering more people by making a scene.

She would have to bide her time until the right opportunity presented itself for her to act.

She nodded.

The man lowered his hand and grabbed her upper arm with a viselike grip. When he shoved the business end of his handgun into her side, she glanced at it. The pistol was longer than she expected and had a metal cylinder attached to the muzzle. She'd seen a few gangster movies and knew it was likely a silencer to muffle the gunshot sound.

He snatched the revolver from her waistband and led her from the dining room toward the side of the yacht facing the harbor, not the dock, giving her the impression he planned to shoot her and throw her overboard. Hattie had to make her move. "You'll never get away with this," she said. "Others know about the plot, including the American Embassy."

"Too bad no one will believe them when they discover their new attaché is behind everything." He pressed the gun harder. "Now go." He clutched firmer when a crewman dressed in a white uniform shimmied past them on the side deck.

As they reached a spot not visible from the forward or aft decks, he stopped Hattie. "It's a shame," he said. "I rather enjoyed your records."

Hattie's pulse raced because she had run out of time and options. Making a commotion would put more people in danger, so she looked for anything she could use as a weapon but saw only hooks fastened to the railing.

A woman's laughter came from the bow area and got louder when Maggie and Maya appeared on the side deck, walking arm in arm. They smiled at each other and laughed as Maggie regaled the story about how she enticed Hattie onto the stage of the Golden Room months ago and how they brought the house down with the performance.

Hattie deduced they had planned a distraction to catch Hattie's captor off guard, and she was ready to react. Maggie and Maya walked irregularly, acting like they'd had too many drinks. When they were about to pass the man, Maggie shoved Maya toward him.

This was it.

Maya reached for the man's left hand and placed him into an agonizing thumb hold, the same maneuver she had used on an unruly customer the day she and Hattie first met. Then Hattie grabbed the end of the gun, pushing it downward. Several sharp claps sounded, and corresponding splinter holes formed in the deck's wooden slats, the spot where the pistol had fired. The smell of gunpowder was faint, and Hattie felt the silencer grow hotter.

The attacker appeared to refocus, straining to break Hattie's grip on the weapon, but he groaned and arched his back as Maya applied more pressure on his thumb and twisted hard. At the same time, Hattie pushed harder, forcing the muzzle back toward him. He leaned forward, pressing against Hattie.

Another sharp clap.

His eyes rounded extra wide, and he stopped struggling, appearing to be processing the fact that he'd been shot.

Maya and Maggie turned him to face the railing, gripped him by the belt on both sides, and lifted him. The chain around the man's neck dangled precariously over the water below when his upper torso angled toward the water. If her mother had been taken hostage and almost killed for the key fastened to that chain, Hattie surmised it was vital to stop the bombing.

She reached for it.

Her fingertips grazed the chain's tiny metal balls, but Maya and Maggie continued to lift, pushing him farther over the rail. Hattie leaned farther. Her balance was off, and she had to steady herself with one hand on the beam while snatching blindly in the air, hoping to salvage what might be their only hope of success.

Her hand cupped the key as the man flipped over the railing. Hattie yanked. As the man tumbled, hurtling toward the water, the ends of the chain dangled from Hattie's hand. Once his body splashed into the harbor, Hattie felt her center of gravity shift and feared she and the crucial key were about to join her attacker.

She teetered.

Her foot slipped, preventing her from getting traction to stop the fall.

Then.

A hand latched onto the fabric of her blouse near her bottom, and an arm wrapped around her waist. Both tugged hard, pulling her to safety and thumping her backside on the deck.

That will leave a mark, Hattie thought. She opened her hand. The key in it meant whatever bruise might appear tomorrow was worth the result.

Maya helped Hattie up and yanked her into a trembling embrace. "Thank goodness." She pulled back, inspecting Hattie from head to toe. "Are you hurt?"

Hattie grazed Maya's cheek and felt her melt into the brief touch. "I'm fine." They had found one bomb and had the key. It was time to do as her father instructed. "We need the president's security team to evacuate the ship."

27

Karl hated being separated from Hattie, but it was the only way to better their odds of stopping the attack before security let passengers on board. Before his daughter came to Rio, he thought she was much like Eva—talented, independent, and smart as a whip—but he never considered her capable of navigating the dangerous waters enveloping them. However, several events—the deadly hunt on Baumann's plantation, breaking into Ziegler's mansion and the warehouse, entrapping the Italian officer, and serving point on Eva's hostage exchange—showed him that Hattie was full of surprises. She was as much like him as her mother, which made him prouder than he thought possible. He was confident she would find the other bomb and get the people off the boat.

Once they left Maggie's stateroom, Leo led Karl and David down a ladder to the lower level housing the engine room. The corridor was humid from the heat of the machinery and musty from the smell of diesel and lubricant oils. Dim bulbs hung every few yards on the walls in metal cages and lit the way. Several compartments separated by hatches comprised the deck. Since they were in dock and the threat of taking on water was low, each door was open, providing a clear path to the aft section. The farther they traveled toward the rear of the yacht, the louder the hum of equipment.

Soon, Leo took point. At the next compartment, he suddenly stopped, crouched, and gestured for the others to stay quiet. He raised two fingers, indicating that two men guarded the entrance.

They would need a distraction to overpower them.

Karl stowed his weapon behind his back in his waistband, snatched a clipboard with several sheets of paper from a wall hook, and signaled David to wait there. He whispered to Leo, "Follow my lead."

Leo nodded and hid his gun.

Karl climbed over the hatchway transom and walked toward the sentries while flipping through the pages on the board. As he and Leo approached, the guards on either side of the open hatch became more alert, sliding their hands into a slit at the belly of their gray overalls, which was likely standard for workers on the engine level.

Karl was sure they were readying their weapons. He stopped short of the door and waved them closer to avoid being seen by anyone inside the engine room. They didn't budge, so Karl flipped a page and waved again while speaking German. "Mr. Wagner wants to know if everything is in order. Are we on schedule?"

Both men stepped forward. The guard on the left cocked his head but kept his eyes on Karl. The one on the right looked at his companion, making the other the leader. Taking him out first was critical.

Karl trusted the machinery noise would mask the sounds of what was to come. He showed the leader the clipboard and pointed to the paper. When the man averted his stare to the board, Karl flipped it up, smashing it against the leader's nose. Since the maneuver would only temporarily daze him, Karl punched him in the throat, bringing him to his knees. At the same time, Leo headbutted the other guard and pummeled him with rapid punches to the face, sending him to the floor. Karl and Leo snatched their pistols, striking them both on the head until they lost consciousness or died. Karl could not tell which.

He waved David forward and gestured for him to help drag the bodies a few feet away to the wall so they would not be visible to the others farther inside. Karl searched them and discovered each man was armed with a Luger equipped with a suppressor.

Ideally, changing into the guards' overalls would have provided the best element of surprise, but they were running out of time before security would let guests aboard for the party, so the silencers would have to suffice. Unfortunately, the silencers added length and weight to the pistols, likely affecting their balance. Unless the Nazi agents re-zeroed their weapons and adjusted the sights after attaching the silencer, the bullet's trajectory might be altered. Karl would have to be closer to his target to compensate, and he hoped Leo knew to do the same when he handed him the second Luger.

"Use these first," Karl whispered. He was first through the hatchway, with his pistol at the ready. Leo followed, and David brought up the rear. The boat engines were off, but the hum of power generators and compressors was strong. A maze of metal pipes decorated with valves, wheels, and levers crisscrossed the room. The compartment was larger than Karl expected, a testament to the grand size of the yacht.

Three men, all wearing gray overalls, were in the room. Their fair complexion told Karl they were likely of German, not Brazilian, descent. They turned, drawing long pistols through the open slit in their uniforms near their bellies.

Karl pulled the trigger once as he climbed over the transom, aiming at the man in the center. His shot was off target and penetrated a metal pipe, sending steam spewing into the air.

The three scattered. One dipped behind a piece of equipment for cover, another rolled to the metal gangway, and the third retreated deeper into the compartment down one of the three narrow pathways running the room's length.

Karl pushed farther inside, adjusted his aim to account for the silencer, and fired before the man on the floor could upright himself and ready his weapon. The shot hit him center in the chest, and he dropped backward, arms limp.

Leo moved forward and focused on the generator, the source of gunfire coming at them. He signaled Karl that he would go right toward the hull to flank the attacker.

Sharp claps sounded.

Bullets whizzed past Karl's head, plinking off the steel hull. He crouched, fearing the ricochets as much as the initial shots. When he looked up, Leo was moving, but he should have waited until Karl was ready to draw fire. Leo was either crazy for going out in the open or the bravest son of a gun for drawing the gunman's focus away from Karl.

More claps, dings of rebounding shots, and hissing steam.

Leo ducked behind a pipe barely wide enough to shield his profile.

The lack of cover made this a horrible idea, but Karl crouched and inched forward, even with the equipment to crowd the gunman and force his attention back. He fired but missed and dropped to the deck.

A clap.

A sudden, sharp pain besieged Karl's left upper arm when a bullet pierced the back of it. *Damn ricochet*, he thought. He'd never been shot and was surprised that once the initial sting passed, an intense burning sensation engulfed him.

Leo spun around the pipe and lunged forward, pulling the trigger twice and hitting his target in the chest. The man jerked and fell, dropping his pistol through the slats over the metal floor. Steam hissed as Leo approached the body. He turned it over using his foot while aiming his gun at the man and wagged his hand under his chin, signaling he was dead.

Leo glanced at Karl's arm and mouthed, "Are you okay?"

Karl nodded and gestured to continue moving aft. He could not give in to the pain with at least one attacker remaining.

David stayed in the hatchway, ready with his handgun. Karl expected nothing less. The man had shown no interest in confronting danger unless Hattie was involved, but the timid musician persona seemed to have been more for show than self-preservation. The pianist appeared more complex than he let on, so Karl signaled David to wait there and cover the center aisle.

Karl and Leo would go down the aisles along the hull, searching for the third attacker among the engine and power equipment. The steam pouring into the compartment made the air oppressively hot and partially obscured the area in moisture clouds.

Karl wiped the sweat dripping from his forehead with a forearm as he stepped down the metal walkway. Pain from the gunshot wound had become somewhat bearable. Other than being slightly winded, he was surprisingly calm. Before the professor recruited him into this world, he never envisioned situations like this. Karl had been a paper-pushing diplomat at home behind a desk, not someone who knew every aspect of his sidearm and trusted his skills with it more than those paid to protect and serve. However, he thrived on missions like this, getting through them because he knew his instincts and training were good. They had yet to fail him.

Three bloodstained bodies were piled on the path. The men were dressed only in skivvies and undershirts, appearing to have been stripped of their uniforms. Death no longer bothered Karl, but he envisioned Hattie sinking to the bottom of the harbor if he didn't eliminate the third attacker, and he could not let that happen.

Karl accidentally kicked a wrench on the pathway when he sidestepped the bodies. It tumbled off the platform, hitting the metal hull and creating a piercing, echoing clank. Not much real estate remained in the engine room, but the third adversary had plenty of spaces between the equipment to hide.

A sharp clap and more hissing signified another shot.

This had morphed into a cat-and-mouse game, but Karl liked the odds. David was an adequate safety valve at the hatchway, but Leo was his secret weapon. As a naval officer, he was trained with weapons, but Karl got the impression that his Texan background made him an excellent hunter. Stalking prey, whether animal or man, required the same skills—patience, determination, and deadly accuracy with a firearm. Leo possessed all three in spades. However, the conditions could not have been more dangerous. They found themselves trapped in a confined space with only one exit with an attacker who was desperate to survive. Maybe reasoning might defuse things.

Karl spoke in German and continued pushing deeper into the engine room. "You're all alone now. You are outnumbered. There's no way out. You can resist and die in the effort or give yourself up and take your chances with the Brazilian police. Choose now."

A sharp clap. Another steamy hiss.

Karl received his answer. Whoever this man was, he would rather sacrifice himself than surrender to the enemy, a Nazi mindset Karl never understood. Living to fight another day had a more significant impact than needless sacrifice. Nevertheless, Karl was happy to oblige the man.

Passing the last piece of equipment along his path, Karl spotted the third attacker crouched by a secondary door near a large compressor. Sweat covered the man's face, but his calm look meant he was determined to see this through, not afraid of meeting his fate.

Based on the boat's configuration, the hatch didn't lead to a way out but to a dead-end compartment. Slipping inside would have provided an excellent defensive position, but the man appeared to be guarding the door, making Karl think the cache of explosives was hidden there.

His location didn't offer him a clean shot. To hit the target, Karl would need to leave the cover of the mechanical equipment, putting him in the open and vulnerable to gunfire. He needed to rattle his opponent, so he clanked his gun against the steel hull, creating a cracking echo. The man swiveled his head and gripped his pistol harder. A series of noisy clanks from the opposite side of the compartment, likely Leo serving up a similar distraction, forced the man to pivot toward the sound. Karl stepped forward from his concealment, steadied his aim, and pulled the trigger twice.

The man twitched with each shot and slumped to the metal grating.

Karl rushed over, stuffed his weapon into his waistband, grabbed him by the lapels of his overalls, and spoke in German, "Where is the explosive?"

A loud, piercing gunshot rang out and echoed in the steel chamber, making Karl flinch and snap his stare to the front of the compartment. David had moved inside and held his gun at the ready. He must have fired, but at what?

Two sharp claps followed. David fell to the floor. A fourth man darted from the opposite side, scurried out the hatch, and slammed it shut.

Leo stomped down the center aisle, leaping over the two dead attackers, and tried the hatch lever. He pushed harder, straining to open it, but quickly abandoned his effort. "It won't budge."

Karl returned his attention to the man in his grasp and repeated his question, "Where is the explosive?"

The man smiled, blood smearing his teeth. "You're too late. No one can get to it without the key."

28

Maggie acknowledged Hattie with a nod. It was time to involve the authorities and get off the boat. Hattie squeezed Maya's hand, and the three cut through the dining room. Stepping onto the dockside deck, Hattie collided with a man dressed in gray overalls. They both stumbled to their knees. Something fell from the man's uniform. She locked stares with the man, noting fear in his eyes before glancing at the floor. A pistol with a silencer had fallen out. The man snatched the gun, scrambled to his feet, and ran toward the gangway, stuffing his weapon back into his overalls.

A sense of dread swept through Hattie. She feared something had gone horribly wrong in the engine room, and David, Leo, and her father were in mortal danger. She turned to Maggie. "Get your band off the ship and tell security about the device at the president's table so they'll evacuate the boat. I'm going to find my father."

Maggie jerked her head back. "Your father? He's here?"

Hattie could have kicked herself for the slipup, but the minutes were dwindling. "Yes, he is. I'll explain later. Please get your people to safety." She turned to Maya. "You need to go with her to talk to the security team."

"Don't be a hero, Hattie." Maggie gripped her hand. Worry was in her eyes. "Come with us."

"I'll be right behind you. Now, go." Hattie kissed Maggie on the cheek and pivoted to Maya. Fear swirled in the woman's eyes. "I have to save him."

Maya clutched both of Hattie's hands. "Be careful."

Hattie smiled and squeezed them before letting go. She retraced her steps inside and descended the ladder leading to the lower deck. Instinct told her to be ready for anything. After pulling her revolver from her waistband, she kept it prepared for another attacker as she went down one more level, deeper into the yacht's bowels.

Lights in the metal cage sconces flickered like they were shorting out. Something felt wrong. She expected it to be cooler below the waterline, but the air was steamier, warmer, and thicker with the smell of diesel fuel and mechanical oil. Condensation trickled from the overhead pipes.

She walked faster, following the wall markings to the engine room while clutching her gun in one hand and the key in the other. Stepping over one open hatchway and another, she slowed after spotting something on the floor at the far end of the corridor. She slipped the key into her pocket, held her pistol with both hands to steady her aim, and approached cautiously.

Two bodies dressed in the same gray overalls as the man who had bumped into Hattie were piled atop one another in the corner. At first, she feared they might be David, Leo, or her father, but a closer inspection revealed they were not.

Hattie proceeded to the hatch marked "Engine Room" in Portuguese and tested the door, but it was locked. Unsure of who might be on the other side, she pressed her ear against it, listening to the rhythmic hum of machinery. Time was running out, so she pounded on the door. "Father? Are you in there?"

"Hattie?" The voice was muffled through the thick metal, but she recognized the Texan accent.

"Leo?"

"We're trapped. Can you open the door? Work the wheel, then the lever."

She tried spinning the wheel and moving the lever. "They won't budge. I think it's locked."

"Sometimes there's a locking mechanism. Look for a smaller lever or latch."

Hattie inspected the door, running her hand along the seam and every inch of steel, but nothing stood out. "I can't find it. I'll get help. Maybe someone can get it open with a blowtorch."

"I'm afraid David doesn't have that much time. He's been shot and is losing blood fast," Leo said.

Hattie gasped. "What about my father? Is he hurt?"

"Yes, but not as badly. David's in awful shape, though. We need to hurry. The explosives are here, but we can't get to them without the key."

"I have it." Hattie dug it from her front pocket and held it up as if he could see it. "I have the key." But it did them no good behind the door. She rubbed a hand through her hair, horrified by the circumstance. By the time she found someone and they broke through the door, David would likely be dead. If the rescue didn't work fast enough, the explosives might go off, killing Leo and her father.

"It's no use, Hattie!" her father yelled. "Get help!"

"Wait a second." Hattie gripped the key harder, recalling the lengths Ziegler and Wagner went through to get their hands on it. All along, she believed the key was crucial to stopping the attack.

"The key is the key," she said, inspecting the door again. She looked for a keyhole in the typical locations but found nothing. Hattie expanded her search to the steel panel housing the hatch and discovered a small metal flap. She raised it, revealing a cylinder seated near the locking mechanism. The tiny hole in the middle resembled a keyhole. She put the key in and turned, but nothing happened. She tried to spin the wheel again, and this time it moved. Hattie remembered the rule for plumbing—righty tighty, lefty loosey—and spun it left until it stopped and pulled the lever in the same direction. The sound of metal scraping against metal echoed in the corridor.

"Try opening it now!" Hattie yelled.

The door opened to Leo's harried expression and a release of hot, steamy air. "We need to get David topside," he said.

Hattie glanced at the floor, several feet inside the room. David lay writhing on the walkway with a tourniquet circling his left leg. His clothing was bloodstained, and his skin looked ashen. Blood had pooled beside him.

"Dear God, no." She rushed to his side and kneeled, not caring if blood stained her slacks. She touched his cheek, discovering it was cold and clammy. "He needs help now." She looked at her father, noting the strip of Leo's shirt wrapped around his arm. "You're hurt."

"I'm fine," Karl said. He and Leo lifted David through the engine room hatch, and Karl held David upright with his uninjured arm. David appeared weak but could stand with assistance.

"Go. Get him medical aid," Leo said. "I know my way around an engine compartment. I'll find and disable the bomb."

Karl looked at Hattie. "Let's go, sweetheart."

"Go, Father. I know how to open the lock. We'll be right behind you." Hattie clutched her father's shirt lapel, knowing he didn't trust David. She dreaded the thought but wasn't sure how far he would go to get David out of her life. "Don't let him die."

Sweat dripped down Karl's cheeks. His expression said her accusation hurt him. "I won't," he said in a flat tone.

"We got this," Leo said, placing a hand on Karl's shoulder.

Karl looked him in the eye. "Bring her back to me."

"I will."

While Karl helped David down the corridor, Leo grabbed a flashlight from a wall hook and led Hattie down the center aisle, stepping over the bodies of dead attackers. Steam hissed from pipes, requiring her to duck several times to avoid being burned. When they reached the end, Leo dragged a body blocking a secondary compartment hatch out of the way.

"I'm not sure how to get in, but before he died, this guy said we needed the key to access the bomb."

"I think I know." Hattie inspected the door and the surrounding area. The hatch didn't have an obvious lock. However, a tiny metal flap was on the ridge dividing the nearby steel panels. She flipped it up, inserted the key, and turned it to the left. "Try the wheel now."

Leo twirled the wheel and smiled. "You are a genius, Hattie James." He pushed the lever up and opened the small hatch that was not much bigger than a porthole. After shining the flashlight inside, he said, "Holy hell."

Leo shifted to let Hattie peek into the compartment. It was the size of a water closet but was half the height and packed with dynamite. "I'm guessing this is bad," Hattie said.

"About as bad as it gets." Leo shook his head. "This would take out the entire aft end and sink the boat within minutes. There wouldn't be time to man the lifeboats."

"What do we do?"

"I doubt anyone would stay on board to detonate the bomb, so there has to be time pencils. We disable those, and it should be safe."

"Should be?" Hattie gulped.

"Unless a spark sets off the detonator."

"You mean like the lights blinking in the passageway."

"We better hurry." Leo peeked inside again. "I think I see the detonator." He reached in, stretching his arm, but pulled back. "I can't reach it." He repositioned to crawl through the opening, but Hattie stopped him.

"You'll never fit," she said, "but I will. Let me do it."

Leo sighed. They both knew it was dangerous, but Hattie was the only option to disable the bomb. "All right, but I'll talk you through it."

Hattie placed her pistol on the metal walkway, grabbed the flashlight, and slipped headfirst into the dark compartment. The confined space was oppressively hot, and sliding her torso over dynamite that could obliterate her at any moment made her uneasy, yet her hands didn't shake. She trusted Leo to instruct her correctly on how to make the explosive inert.

She shined the light into a gap in the sticks of dynamite. "What am I looking for?"

"The detonator should be a brass cylinder the shape of a pencil."

"Shouldn't be too hard to find." Hattie shimmied deeper inside and felt around until her hand hit something sleek and smooth. She touched a second and a third. "Hey, Leo, how many detonators are there supposed to be?"

"Two. They're usually used in tandem for redundancy."

"I feel three."

"Stupid Nazis," Leo said. "That's overkill. There's likely a fourth."

Hattie passed Leo the detonators one by one through the opening before slipping farther in until she teetered on the ledge and was in danger of falling in. She shined the flashlight between the dynamite and moved the sticks around methodically. Finally, in the corner along the edge of the compartment, her hand hit another brass cylinder. "Got it." She handed it backward to him and shimmied out.

"We need to get these into soda ash or baking soda," Leo said. "There should be a water bucket in here."

"I'll find one," Hattie said. She hurried down the center aisle, scanning left and right until she found a tool workbench. She located two metal pails among the wrenches, hammers, and rags and took them to Leo. "I thought two would be safer. Less to explode at a time."

Leo laughed, carrying the buckets. "We think the same way, missy. Let's get out of here."

They stepped over the engine room transom and started down the passageway, led by the flickering wall lights. Clomping footsteps down ahead made them stop. If Maggie and Maya had done as Hattie had asked, the president's security team would likely have been racing toward them.

"We're gonna be in a world of hurt if we don't do as the police say," Leo said.

"We think the same way, mista," Hattie said.

Leo laid down the buckets, and they both kneeled, placed their handguns on the floor, and raised their hands behind their heads, waiting for the officers to take them into custody.

"I hope your Portuguese is good," Leo said.

"It should be good enough."

"Should be?" Leo gulped.

Hattie laughed.

Four men in dark gray uniforms, matching five-point caps, and black leather boots appeared in the corridor. Each carried a pistol and raced toward Hattie and Leo.

"Stop! You're under arrest!" the first one shouted in Portuguese.

"We found the main bomb," Hattie said in Portuguese, pointing to the buckets. "Unless you want to blow up, we must get the detonators into soda ash from the laundry."

The cop peeked into one and sent a man up one level. He directed the other two to handcuff Hattie and Leo.

"Five are dead, and there's a cache of dynamite in the engine room," Hattie said. "I trust the boat has been evacuated."

"Quiet," the officer said, pulling Hattie to her feet. He turned to his men. "Take them out."

The others took Hattie and Leo up two ladders to the main deck. When she stepped out of the dining room, the parking lot came into view. It was teeming with police cars and fire trucks, and sirens sounded in the distance, bringing the seriousness of the ordeal back into focus. While descending the gangway, she darted her eyes back and forth, scanning the dock and parking area for David and her father, but the dozens of officers, firefighters, and yacht staff members milling about made it impossible to locate them.

Once at the bottom, Hattie spotted Maya and Maggie struggling to get past the cordoned-off line. Maya cursed in Portuguese and flailed her arms but settled down after catching Hattie's gaze.

Hattie shouted, "Where's David?"

"In the parking lot." Maya shook off an officer's grip on her arm. "An ambulance is coming."

Hattie turned to the officer clutching her arm like she was a criminal. "Please, my fiancé was shot. May I see him before he's taken to the hospital?"

"I have my orders," he said in Portuguese.

"I beg you." Hattie had remained calm until then, knowing they were doing the right thing. However, not seeing David after witnessing the gravity of his wounds sent her to pieces. Tears streamed down her cheeks at the thought that he had no one else in Rio to worry about him. Hattie knew his mother was still alive but did not know how to contact her if the worst happened. "I just want to see him."

The other officer escorting Leo whispered something to him, and the one holding on to Hattie loosened his hold a fraction. "I'll give you one minute."

Hattie sagged her shoulders in relief.

He guided her behind a fire truck where David lay on a portable military-style stretcher on the pavement. Hattie fell to her knees beside him. Her hands were still cuffed at her back, preventing her from holding his hand or caressing his cheek. "Help is coming, David. You'll be at the hospital in no time."

He stirred and fluttered his eyes open. "Hattie," he croaked. "You're safe."

"Yes, I'm safe. We disarmed the bomb. Everyone is safe."

"Good." David closed his eyes again. He looked weaker than he did inside the boat, and his clothes appeared to have more blood on them.

An ambulance entered the parking lot, and another police officer directed it toward the fire truck.

"It's here, David. You'll be in expert hands." Hattie let more tears flow. David was fighting for his life, and she was handcuffed, unable to do anything to help.

The officer pulled Hattie up when the ambulance attendants approached and grabbed David's stretcher. When they shoved him inside, an awful feeling swept over her. This might have been the last time she would see David, and her heart snapped in two. Not long ago, he told her that everything he did was to protect her, and that was precisely what he was doing when he got shot. She could not stand by and see innocent people hurt, so he bravely risked his life to save her from a lifetime of guilt and regret.

After the attendants slammed the back doors, Hattie focused on her father sitting on the fire truck's bumper with an officer observing his every move. He was watching her with his hands cuffed in front of him.

"Are you all right, Mr. Fuller?" Hattie asked.

"I'm fine, Miss James," Karl said, but he didn't look fine. Similar to David, he appeared paler than he did earlier. Hattie glanced at his wound. He had the same makeshift dressing on his arm, and his clothes also looked more blood-soaked.

Hattie turned to her police escort and spoke in Portuguese. "Is another ambulance coming? He looks ill."

"I don't know," the officer said, turning her to the police cars.

"Hattie," Karl said.

Hattie craned her neck over her shoulder in time to see her father wobble and tumble to the pavement. "Nooo!" she screamed, lurching toward him, but the officer yanked her back. She could not break free. "Help him! You need to help him."

A firefighter laid her father flat on the ground and checked the bandage on his arm. Moments later, another ambulance pulled into the parking lot. As the attendants placed Karl onto a stretcher, officers forced Hattie and Leo into the back of a police car and slammed the door. She was powerless to do anything but watch in horror from behind the glass.

Hattie thrashed in her seat, struggling to loosen her restraints while looking out the window, searching for Maya, but she could not find her. She had never felt more frustrated or angry for doing the right thing. They had prevented an attack of enormous proportions, saving the president's life and those of a hundred guests, yet she could not hold her father's hand before he was carted away. Her solace lay in the assurance that he would be cared for and this mess would resolve once the truth surfaced. That was until...

The back door of the police car flew open. "Hello, Miss James. You can't seem to keep yourself out of trouble."

"Chief Inspector Silva." Hattie spat his name. Just when she thought the day could not get any worse, he appeared.

29

Hattie studied the black-and-white checkered floor. The illumination cast through the bar-covered, dirt-smudged window onto the tiles had shifted, telling her the noon hour had come and passed. She and Leo had been waiting in the narrow interrogation room since Chief Inspector Silva had officers bring them through the back entrance of police headquarters.

The room was more intimidating than the modern, clean one in Washington, DC, where the FBI had taken Hattie following her father's escape. This space clearly had history, starting with the dent in the metal dome light hanging above the table to which she and Leo were handcuffed. The depression was suspiciously head-shaped, as was the indentation on the wall near the window.

But none of those things fazed Leo. He remained at ease, which Hattie understood. He was assigned to the American Embassy and had the power of the United States government behind him. Conversely, Hattie had Eva Machado in her corner, a force to be reckoned with. However, she didn't have the security that came with diplomatic immunity. Six men were dead, two bombs were on the president's yacht, and Hattie was a foreigner with a gun. Luckily, the explosives didn't detonate with passengers on board, but she still had to explain things to a detective with whom she had a rocky history.

Unsure who might have been listening, she and Leo agreed in the back of the police car not to discuss anything about what had happened until his embassy supervisor arrived. Leo hummed one of Hattie's songs to pass the time. Hattie sang a verse, and Leo even belted out the chorus. He had an exceptionally pleasant voice. Toward the end of the song, Hattie was less anxious about waiting.

The door opened.

Hattie and Leo stopped singing.

Inspector Silva and Jack Lynch, the chief of security at the US Embassy, walked into the room. Neither looked happy in their tailored suits, and both looked out for blood. They needed someone to blame for the events on the yacht, and Hattie feared she might be their convenient target.

"It's about time, Jack," Leo said, raising his chained hands a few inches. "Tell him to get these off me and Hattie."

"This is one hell of a mess, Leo, but they are releasing you into my custody until things are sorted out."

"Is there any news about David Townsend and Mr. Fuller?" Hattie asked, looking back and forth between Silva and Lynch.

"Nothing yet." Silva unlocked Leo's cuffs and slid the chain from the bar on the table. "No leaving town until we've concluded our investigation, Commander Bell."

"What about Hattie?" Leo rubbed his wrists once the restraints were off. "She's the hero in all this."

"We have many questions for Miss James," Silva said, turning to her. "Are you willing to answer them now?"

Hattie opened her mouth to respond, but Leo stepped forward and said, "Hold that thought, Hattie." He turned to Silva. "I can tell you that Miss James brought her concern to me twelve days ago about a vague plot to sink a ship she overheard at the Swiss ambassador's home and possibly assassinate a government official at an event."

Silva snapped his stare at Hattie. "Why didn't you bring the information to the police?"

Hattie raised her eyebrow at the man's audacity. "Why would I trust you after how you handled Anna Reyes's disappearance? Not to mention the rest of Heinz Baumann's victims."

Silva harrumphed. "Still, you are required to report evidence of a crime to the police."

"The threat was vague," Leo said, "and we had nothing to go on but an overheard conversation."

"Yet," Silva said, "you sneaked onto the president's yacht uninvited. Now, six men are dead, and our navy is still removing explosives from a hidden compartment that needs a special key that Miss James had. That's too much of a coincidence."

"It's quite simple, Inspector," Leo said. "Maggie Moore told Hattie she was performing at a Mother's Day party for the president on his yacht. It was a long shot, but we thought the conversation Hattie had overheard was about this event, so Hattie agreed to perform with Maggie. Hattie asked me and a few friends to come for moral support. While helping set up the band equipment, we observed a group of suspicious men. We split up to follow them. Hattie stayed with the women on the main deck."

"Is that true, Miss James?" Silva asked.

"Yes. I followed a suspicious-looking man into the dining room and saw him placing something under the president's table. He caught me and held me at gunpoint until Miss Moore and Miss Reyes distracted him. There was a struggle for the gun, and he was shot before falling overboard. I found the key on the deck after he fell and thought it was important, so I left to find Commander Bell while the others got help."

Silva turned to Leo. "So you left the women topside to fend for themselves while you did what?"

"I grabbed the other men and followed the group below deck. When I saw them loading a suspicious-looking box into the engine compartment, I thought something was off when they posted sentries at the engine room hatch. I felt the ship was in imminent danger, so I took action."

"Which was?" Silva asked.

"We distracted and overpowered the guards, took their guns, and entered the engine compartment. More armed men were inside, and we had to defend ourselves. Five were killed, but we believe one assailant got away."

"Can you describe him?" Silva asked.

"I'm afraid not. I was a little busy. But it would be safe to say he was German like the other attackers."

"What makes you think they were German?" Silva said.

"I heard them yelling at each other in German."

Silva removed a notepad from the inner breast pocket of his suit jacket and flipped to a page. "I'm familiar with David Townsend. Tell me about the other man."

"His name is Fuller. I met him in the navy."

"And he just happened to be in Rio when this went down."

Leo shrugged. "Men of the sea tend to travel, Inspector Silva."

"And you trusted him enough to bring him aboard with you?"

"Serving together forms a special bond." Leo looked Hattie in the eye. "I can honestly say that Mr. Fuller is a patriot, a man of honor. I would trust him with my life."

Hattie wanted to thank him, but she nodded and swallowed past the growing lump in her throat. Her father had proven himself innocent to Leo without a shred of evidence, giving her hope that one day, he could emerge from the shadows, cleared of the charges against him with his reputation restored.

Leo returned his attention to Silva. "Is there anything else, Inspector? Can I take Miss James to the hospital to check on her fiancé?"

"I'm afraid it's not that easy, Commander Bell," Silva said. "We need to verify your stories. Miss James must remain in custody until we speak to Fuller and Townsend."

The door swung open, and Eva appeared in the entryway. A short man dressed in a double-breasted dark suit followed her into the room. His academic appearance and stiff posture screamed bureaucrat.

"Sweetheart." Eva opened her arms and stepped toward Hattie, but her companion put up his hand to stop her.

The man reached into his breast pocket, handed Silva a business card, and spoke in Portuguese, "I'm Cesar Tavares, President Garza's chief of staff. Miss James and her associates single-handedly prevented the assassination of our president and saved the lives of his family, guests, and countless others. She is a national hero. I'm here to secure Miss James's release and take her to the hospital so she can be there when her fiancé is out of surgery."

"The investigation is still ongoing." Silva clenched his teeth. "We have yet to corroborate her story."

"You are done here, Inspector," Tavares said. "Miss James will be available for an interview once she knows her fiancé is okay." He waved his hand dismissively toward Hattie. "Now, unlock those."

Silva cursed under his breath and did as he was told.

Hattie stood, rubbing her wrists. "I'd say it's been a pleasure, Inspector, but it never is with you."

Eva threw an arm around her. "I'm glad you're all right, sweetheart, but let's get you to the hospital."

Leo swiveled toward Lynch. "I need to go with them. Those men were wounded on my watch."

Lynch flapped his hands in frustration. "Go. This entire event has been bizarre."

Eva led Hattie from the interrogation room into the corridor, and Leo and Tavares followed. Once they reached the detective's squad room, all heads turned in their direction. Hattie and Leo were suspected presidential assassins when officers dragged them into this office earlier. However, walking out, they were heroes, but she didn't feel like one. She had done the right thing, but David and her father were hurt and might die, an outcome for which Hattie would never forgive herself.

Hattie and Leo said nothing, stepping into the elevator. Eva did all the talking. She was cautious not to mention Karl's name and went on about the news reports she heard on the radio. "When they broke in with an emergency bulletin and said an assassination attempt had been foiled, I knew that was you. I thought you might be in a pickle, so I called Sophia."

"Sophia?" Hattie asked as the attendant closed the gate and sent the car downward.

"The first lady, of course." Eva waved her off like she was silly not to have known the name. "I explained things to Sophia, and she told her husband, who got me in touch with this scrumptious man." Eva hooked her arm around Mr. Tavares's.

He blushed, adjusting his tie. The wedding ring on his finger likely had everything to do with the sweat rolling down his forehead.

The elevator attendant worked the levers to stop the car on the first floor and opened the scissor gate, letting the group off into the busy main lobby. Several uniformed officers turned their heads, whispering to one another, as Hattie and Leo passed. The attention could have stemmed from her and Eva's celebrity, but she suspected they were still under the impression that she and Leo were would-be assassins.

The low hum of dozens of conversations and the squeaking of a half-dozen ceiling fans filled the large open area. As their group approached the exit, a voice called, "Hattie, wait!"

Hattie spun on her heel to follow the woman's voice. Seconds later, Maggie and Maya emerged through a group of people queued in line. When the two caught up to their group, Hattie wanted to pull Maya into a full embrace, but it wasn't the right place. Instead, she gave Maggie and Maya brief, loose hugs and asked, "Did they question you?"

"Yes," Maggie said. "We asked to see you, but they told us to wait here. That was over an hour ago."

"We're on our way to the hospital to check on the others," Hattie said. "Do you want to come with us?"

"I need to find my agent and the band members first, but I'll call you there later," Maggie said.

Maya touched Hattie's arm. "With everything going on, I'm sure you've forgotten, but your sister's ship will dock within the hour. How should we handle her arrival?"

Hattie smiled and turned to Mr. Tavares. "Do you mind giving us a moment alone?"

"Of course," he said. "I'll be at the door."

The group huddled and whispered.

Eva looked at Hattie, wagging her eyes at Maggie.

"Maggie's fine, Mother," Hattie said. "She knows everything. I don't want Olivia seeing Father. That woman can't keep her mouth shut if her life depended on it."

Eva sighed. "You have a point, but I want her with us if something goes wrong."

"Maya and I can pick her up at the dock and bring her to the hospital," Leo said. "We'll tell her that David has been hurt and keep her in the waiting room until you tell us what to do next."

"Thank you, Leo," Hattie said.

"You are wonderful friends." Eva hugged Maya and Leo. "I can't thank you enough."

"Yes, I have wonderful friends." Hattie clutched Maya's hand with her left and Leo's with her right, grateful she had these two in her life.

30

The driver weaved the shiny black government sedan through Rio's thin Mother's Day traffic, laying on the horn several times in the restaurant district to nudge slower cars out of his way. Hattie used a straight arm against the passenger headrest in the turns to avoid being tossed around like a rag doll.

Mr. Tavares wiped beads of sweat from his forehead with a handkerchief, sitting beside her mother on the opposite end of the back seat from Hattie. Without question, Eva made him more nervous than the zigzagging ride through town.

Road signs guided the driver to the entrance of Mercy Hospital. The driver stopped short of the main doors. Before he could exit to let out his passengers, Hattie pushed the back door open, stepped to the curb, and offered Eva her hand. "Hurry, Mother."

Eva got out and leaned into the back compartment. "Thank you, Cesar. I'll take it from here. Please give Narcisco and Sophia my best." She slammed the car door, hooked her arm around Hattie's, and entered the building at the lobby and primary waiting area. People packed the two dozen seats. Men sat quietly, and women cooled themselves with hand-fans or tended to their children. Three nurses dressed in white uniforms staffed a reception desk.

Other than the day after her sister was born, Hattie had visited a hospital once to see a friend who had their appendix removed and remembered that every room was clean and whitewashed with a prominent antiseptic scent. This hospital was much older and not as well maintained, but the smell was the same. She didn't know what to think about the facility's conditions but reserved her judgment.

Hattie stepped to the welcome desk, placing her hands palm down on the counter. A rush of anxiety hit her as she envisioned David and her father in operating rooms with a crew of doctors and nurses working feverishly to mend their injuries. Her Portuguese escaped her, and she reverted to English. "David Townsend and Karl...I mean Fuller were brought in."

Eva gently placed her hand atop Hattie's and spoke to the nurse in Portuguese. "Two men were brought in with gunshot wounds from Gloria Marina. One is my daughter's fiancé. The other is a close friend. Do you have information on either patient?"

The nurse checked a clipboard. "Yes, one is still in surgery. The other made it through. He lost a significant amount of blood, so we brought him to a room to rest."

"May we see him?" Eva asked.

"Yes." The nurse rattled out a room number and direction, pointing down a corridor.

Eva thanked the nurse and asked her to send word about the other victim as soon as his condition was known.

Hattie and Eva walked down the hallway and up a flight of stairs before locating the room where the reception nurse had said one man was taken to recover after surgery. Despite feeling horrible for thinking it, she hoped the man in the room was her father. Losing David would be awful, but losing her father would crush her. She paused at the door, took a calming breath, and entered the room. She stopped. Her knees wobbled when her father's profile came into view as he lay asleep on the first bed. An immaculately wrapped bandage covered his left upper arm.

Eva came forward, squeezed Hattie's hand, and whispered, "Thank God."

Hattie stepped closer to his bed. She reached out to touch his arm but didn't want to disturb his peaceful rest, so she pulled back. The man sleeping in the other bed had no visitors, so she took a chair from the far side and placed it next to her father's bed.

Moments after Hattie and Eva sat, a nurse dressed in a crisp white uniform entered the room and appeared surprised to see guests. "Are you family?" the woman asked in Portuguese.

"In a way, yes," Eva said. "The man is American. We're the closest thing he has to family in Brazil. My daughter was swept up into the same ordeal that resulted in his injury."

The nurse offered a slight grin. "I'm glad he has someone."

"What can you tell us about his prognosis?" Eva asked.

The nurse grabbed the clipboard hanging from the metal frame at the foot of the bed. "They got the bullet out and successfully repaired his wounds, but he'd lost a lot of blood before going into surgery, so he received two units."

"He should be okay, right?" Hattie asked in Portuguese, turning her stare to her father. His wound had been wrapped, and his bleeding was under control when he left the engine room, so he must have aggravated his injury while saving David. Hattie couldn't have been more grateful.

"Yes. We have him on more fluids to help him get his strength back." The nurse checked the intravenous tube and bottle connected to his arm. "Do you know the patient's name? No one knew at the accident scene."

Hattie kept her gaze on him, hoping his alias would not set off red flags. "Joseph Fuller."

The nurse jotted down the information in his chart. "What about the other man who came with him? Do you know his name?"

"David Townsend," Hattie said. "He's my fiancé. Can you send word of his condition?"

"Of course," the woman nodded.

"How much longer will he be asleep?" Hattie asked.

"It's hard to say," the nurse said, "but he should come around within the hour. Get me when he wakes." The woman checked his blood pressure and pulse, noted the numbers in the chart, and left the room.

Hattie was oddly content waiting in silence for her father to wake, comforted that his color was returning. However, quiet was not in Eva's lexicon. Her mother talked about how worried she was after turning on Maya's radio and hearing the reports of the thwarted assassination attempt at the docks.

"When they said several were injured and dead and a man and woman were taken into custody, I couldn't sit by and wait for you to return."

"I'm glad you didn't," Hattie said. "Otherwise, I would still be hand-cuffed in that interrogation room."

"You and Commander Bell seem to be growing closer." Eva had the subtlety of a buzz saw.

Hattie rolled her eyes. "I told you, Mother. Leo and I are just friends."

"Are you sure he thinks the same way? A man doesn't risk his life for a woman without good reason."

"The only reason he needed was that it was the right thing to do. Leo Bell is a good man. He had every opportunity to turn Father in to the embassy, yet he didn't. He looked at the evidence the FBI gathered against Father and believes he was set up."

"That all might be true, but the eyes don't lie. I could tell from a mile away that he considers you more than a friend, as does Miss Reyes."

Hattie snapped her stare toward Eva, afraid of what she might have figured out. "Excuse me?"

"You heard me. I heard the rumors about her when she first took over the Halo Club but didn't want to believe them. You need to keep your distance from her."

"After what we endured at Baumann's plantation, I will do nothing of the sort." Hattie raised her voice from a whisper, unable to rein in her protective side. "Maya is a good friend."

"The affection she shows you is unnatural, Hattie. People will talk."

Hattie's anger boiled. After everything they went through to rescue Eva, this was the thanks she gave—judging Maya, and by extension Hattie, as unnatural and immoral. "You mean people like you. God forbid that someone loves in a way you don't. God forbid that someone refuses to go along to get along. God forbid that someone refuses to live a lie any longer."

"Lower your voice, sweetheart. You're making a scene." Eva glanced behind her to ensure no one was listening. The door was shut, and the man in the next bed was fast asleep. The only person Hattie could upset was her mother, and at this point, she didn't care.

She let out a maniacal laugh but lowered her voice. "Sweetheart? If you only knew."

"Knew what?"

"That David and I are just friends. We have never been lovers and never will be. That the person who broke my heart was a woman. That Maya makes me happy, and I love her the way you think I love David." Before Hattie knew it, she had spewed her entire reality to her mother.

Eva had a dazed look, her mouth hanging agape. "Are you saying this to hurt me?"

"Pettiness is your department, not mine."

"Hattie?" Karl stirred in the bed. His eyes fluttered open. "She won't understand."

Hattie rushed to his side, cupping his hand. The anger she felt a moment ago melted into profound relief. "Father, conserve your energy. You lost a lot of blood."

"Good." He struggled to push up to a reclining position in bed. "I was afraid all that blood was David's."

Eva looked at Karl, eyes wide. "You knew?"

"She's still our daughter," he said, shaking his head to make himself more alert.

Eva's lips quivered. "I'll get the nurse," she said before leaving the room.

Hattie helped him to a more comfortable position. "Try not to move so much."

"Any word on David?" he asked. His voice sounded tired.

"Nothing yet." Hattie fluffed his pillow to distract herself from the awful possibility that David might not have been as lucky as her father and that she had just spilled her life's truth to her mother.

Eva returned with the nurse but kept her distance from Hattie and Karl.

"You're looking well," the nurse said in Portuguese.

"He doesn't speak the language," Eva said in Portuguese. "I can translate for you."

The woman asked how Karl was feeling and about his pain.

"Like I've been shot, but I've felt worse." Karl sat up straighter.

While the nurse checked Karl's bandage and vitals, Hattie stepped back, even with Eva. "I love you, Mother."

Eva stiffened her posture to express her anger and disappointment in Hattie, which hurt more than Eva likely realized. She whispered, "The nurse's station sent a note. Leo and Maya arrived with Olivia. They're in the waiting room. Livvy will wonder where we're at."

Hattie nodded.

"What time is it?" Karl asked.

"It's almost two," Eva said, moving closer to the bed. "You gave us quite a scare."

Karl became uncomfortable and fidgeted with his blanket. "When can I get out of here?"

Eva translated his question and the nurse's response. "The doctor wants to keep you overnight to make sure you've regained your strength."

"That won't do," Karl said. "I'm feeling fine."

"You need to rest, Mr. Fuller," the nurse said, with Eva translating. "I'll let the doctor know you're awake."

Once the nurse left, Karl ripped the IV from his arm, using enough care to not send blood spurting.

"What are you doing, Father?" Hattie asked.

"Getting out of here." He threw his blanket off, exposing more of his hospital gown. He flopped his legs over the bed's side and stood, wobbling slightly.

Hattie steadied him. "You should lie down."

"I recognized the man security caught in the parking lot. He's an SS agent, which means he likely recognized me. He might use me as a bargaining chip for a lighter sentence." Karl stood straighter and hobbled toward the man in the second bed.

"What are you doing?" Eva asked.

"He's about my size." Karl opened the wall closet on the far side, pulled out a shirt, trousers, and a pair of sandals, and returned to his bed. "Do you mind turning, ladies?"

Hattie and Eva turned until he asked for help to put on the button-down shirt.

"This is crazy," Hattie said, slipping his injured arm into the sleeve. "You just got out of surgery."

"And if I stay, I'll likely end up in handcuffs," he said, wincing.

"There's no talking sense into him," Eva said, folding her arms across her chest. "He's the most stubborn man on earth when he gets something in his head."

"You used to like that about me." Karl grinned, buttoning his shirt.

"That was before..." Eva trailed off without finishing her thought.

Karl had regret in his eyes. "I know." He kissed her on the cheek. "Can you get me out of here?"

"Livvy is here," Eva said. "She'll expect us to sit with her, waiting for news of David."

"I don't want you leaving alone, but I have an idea," Hattie said.

Minutes later, Hattie and Eva sneaked Karl past the nurse's station when it was unoccupied and went down the stairs they had taken earlier. The steps were tricky, but Karl took his time with a woman on each arm and made it to the main floor, albeit sweating buckets.

"Stay here," Hattie said, leaning her father against the stairwell wall. "I'll be right back."

Eva and Hattie put aside their anger and disappointment and entered the lobby waiting area. Hattie heard someone calling her name before she could look for her sister.

"Hattie!" Olivia sprang from a chair, waving them closer so hard that Hattie thought she might sprain her wrist.

"Not a word about Father," Hattie said to Eva. They crossed the room and greeted her sister with a firm hug.

"Your friends filled me in." Olivia pulled back, holding Hattie at arm's length with worry in her eyes. "Any update on David?"

"He's still in surgery," Hattie said.

"Mother." Olivia opened her arms, pulling Eva into another long embrace. "It's so good to see you."

Four uniformed police officers entered the main doors and rushed to the reception desk. After speaking to a nurse, they dashed toward the stairwell where Hattie had left her father. She panicked, realizing her father was correct about the SS officer using his identity as leverage. They were looking for him.

Hattie glanced at Leo and Maya standing nearby and gave them a worried look. "I need to speak to my friends for a minute." She gestured for

Leo and Maya to follow and led them to the stairs, but her father wasn't there. She slumped against the wall. "They took him."

"Took who?" Maya said, rubbing Hattie's arm.

"My father." Hattie buried her face in her hands. She was too late. After everything he'd done to get her mother back and risked his life to save people he had never met, the police had taken him.

"I'm right here, sweetheart." Karl struggled to climb the stairs from the basement level.

"Thank goodness." Hattie and Leo helped him up the last few steps.

"I saw them coming, so I ducked down a flight," her father said.

"We need to get you out of here." Hattie turned to Leo and Maya. "Can you take him to your place so he can rest?"

"Of course," Leo said. He handed Maya his car keys and slung Karl's arm over his shoulder. "Pull the sedan around to the service entrance on the side. The police should be watching the front."

"I'll see you soon." Maya nodded, squeezed Hattie's hand, and slipped out the stairwell.

"I'll be in touch, sweetheart," Karl said before kissing her forehead. "Signal me if you need me before then."

"I will." Hattie stood straighter to hold back more tears as she watched Leo take her father down the stairs. If she didn't, they would never stop.

Hattie returned to the waiting room, enduring Eva's snide looks and her sister's barrage of questions. She gathered Leo had stuck to the story he had told Inspector Silva and left out many of the details they could not afford to be made public, like her father's involvement and her mother's abduction. Doing otherwise would only tie the Italian officer's disappearance to them.

"Are your friends coming back?" Olivia said. "They have my luggage."

"I'll arrange for your bags to be sent to my home, Livvy," Eva said.

A nurse approached their group and spoke in Portuguese. "I understand you're waiting for word on David Townsend." Her expression was unreadable, making Hattie more anxious.

Hattie, Eva, and Olivia stood.

Hattie clutched her sister's hand, bracing herself for the worst.

"He made it through surgery and is asking for Hattie."

31

Twelve days later

Nearly two weeks with Olivia highlighted one salient point for Hattie: she missed her sister. Touring the city and countryside and laughing with Olivia nightly was the medicine she needed after the harrowing last two months. However, their relationship wasn't always the best. Seven years separated them in age, and when Olivia was little, Hattie considered her the annoying tagalong, but after their mother returned to Brazil when Olivia was twelve, and it was just them and their father, they had become closer than any two sisters could get.

Hattie would have to say goodbye today. A melancholy hung with her from the moment she woke and remained with her through breakfast and the car ride to the dock. Depressing silence and long, sad looks replaced the witty banter and uncontrollable laughter she'd looked forward to every day since her sister's arrival.

Eva pulled up to the dock valet, instructed him to fetch Olivia's bags from the trunk, and said she would return for her sedan in less than an hour. He helped her out while another attendant tended to the luggage. David eased out of the front seat and stood using his cane. Hattie and Olivia slid from the back. Before Hattie could link arms with her sister, Eva circled, slipped her arm around Olivia's waist, and guided her toward the boarding line at the dock. The slight was subtle but loud and clear to Hattie.

She and David walked together, forgoing the linked arms or hand-holding they once displayed to further the public perception of their loving relationship. Since telling her parents the truth about her romantic interests, Hattie felt less inclined to put on a show for appearance's sake when she wasn't in the spotlight. And once Olivia boarded the ship, she could stop pretending at home.

Hattie scanned the hundreds of passengers in the loading area. Maggie Moore stood out with her bleached-blond hair and formfitting bright red dress. Hattie hurried a bit more and caught up with Eva and Olivia. "I see Maggie and George."

"She's hard to miss," Olivia said.

"The woman doesn't know the meaning of subtle," Eva said, drawing laughs from the group.

"That's rich coming from you," David said, earning more laughter. Eva Machado was always dressed to impress and rarely let anyone outdo her in a crowd.

Maggie Moore spotted them and waved them closer.

George shook hands with David. "It's good to see you walking around."

"Bed rest was driving me crazy." David rolled his shoulder, which he still favored since being shot. He must have injured it falling to the floor in the engine room.

Maggie greeted the women with hugs, saving Hattie for last. "I'm going to miss you, my friend."

"And I will miss you," Hattie said. "I can't thank you enough for staying on a few extra days to travel back to New York with Olivia after the police cleared you to leave the country."

"It's nothing to give you a little peace of mind."

"Still, it means a lot to me."

"We still have to set a date for you to return to the Big Apple. Construction on my studio should be finished by October. Besides recording our duets, I've been sent several songs I think would be perfect for you to record."

"You're serious about starting your own label," Hattie said.

"Dead serious. We could give RCA and Columbia a run for their money."

Maggie Moore was a force of nature and an incredible friend. Hattie would be crazy not to take the woman up on her offer to kick-start her recording career.

"My six-month contract is up in September. Can we hold off making a decision until then?"

"Take all the time you need." Maggie leaned in and whispered, "I know you have a lot to work out with Maya."

Hattie smiled with gratitude and focused on Olivia and Eva. Both women had tears, and Olivia was a blubbering mess. Neither was good at goodbyes, but her sister took the prize at losing complete composure.

Olivia turned to Hattie, wiping her nose with a handkerchief. "Christmas isn't too far away, right?"

"The time will pass quickly, you'll see," Hattie said. "Though I feel bad about missing Matthew's and Sarah's birthdays."

"I have their presents." Olivia glanced at the porter tagging and loading her bags onto a cart. "I'll tell them that Auntie Hattie sends her love." Another wave of tears hit her.

Hattie wiped her sister's cheeks with her thumbs. "You better get going before you flood the parking lot."

Olivia giggled through the tears. "I can't believe Maggie is letting me stay in her suite. First class for twelve days. I'll be spoiled by the time we dock in New York."

"As it should be."

The drive back to Eva's home was awkwardly silent. Until now, Olivia had acted as a buffer, delaying an uncomfortable conversation that had to happen. After David was released from the hospital, Hattie told David about spilling the truth about their relationship and her love interests to Eva, yet her mother hadn't confronted him about it. Hattie suspected that talk would be forthcoming once they stepped through the front door of her house.

Once inside, Eva walked straight to her kitchen, put on her apron, and began whipping up a grand feast for lunch. She had two outlets for her nervous energy—gardening and cooking. Hattie supposed Eva first needed to process Olivia's departure before she dug into her other daughter's failures. At least the woman was an excellent cook.

Soon, the house was filled with sweet and savory aromas, making Hattie's stomach growl. She'd been hungry for an hour but didn't have the guts to go into the kitchen and face her mother's inquisition. Instead, she stayed in her room, picking out her dress and accessories for tonight's performance at the Golden Room.

She was excited about the show. Things with Hattie and Maya had improved dramatically after the ordeal on the yacht. Facing the danger together had brought them closer and put the bad blood between them further in the past, but Olivia had been a virtual magnet since her arrival, clinging to Hattie and making alone time with Maya impossible. They'd shared one other kiss, but Hattie hoped to change that tonight after her show.

After picking out her stage dress, Hattie checked on David in their bedroom. The doctor said he could return to work playing the piano in another two weeks, so he stayed at home for her performances, following orders to rest as much as possible. She found him packing his things.

"What are you doing?" Hattie asked.

"Since your sister is gone and we no longer have to pretend, I thought it best to move into the other guest room until we figure out a long-term solution."

"You're probably right." Hattie could not argue with him. Since Eva knew they weren't really a couple, their nightly banter had disappeared and sharing a room with him had become awkward. Airing the truth had broken their friendship. "But the doctor said no lifting anything heavy until you return to work. Just grab things from your drawers. I'll get your bags when I get back after tonight's performance."

"Are you hungry? Your mother's stress reliever has me starved."

Hattie laughed, remembering Eva's cooking sprees before her divorce from Karl. "I suppose the house will smell like this for days, but I'll eat something at the club."

"You can't tap dance around her forever, Hattie. If she doesn't want us here, we'll have to find our own place until your contract ends. It's not like we can't afford it."

"You know what? You're right." Their combined income from the Golden Room was enough for any rental in Rio for the next four months. With her FBI business exposed to Eva, she could stop pretending her assets were frozen and needed to save money by living with her mother. "Let's speak to her."

They entered the kitchen, where the aromas were strong and enticing. Eva was seated at the table, eyeing her creations while rubbing her hands together as if deciding which one to dive into first to eat away her sadness.

"Can we talk, Mother?" Hattie asked.

"I suppose adding ten pounds can wait." Eva gestured for Hattie and David to sit. She focused on David. "Explain why you went along with her elaborate lie to deceive me."

"There's no need to grill him, Mother. David and I think it's time to make our own living arrangements until my contract is up."

"That's it?" Eva folded her arms in her defensive posture. "You set off a bombshell in that hospital room, and now that you have an opportunity to explain, you turn tail and run."

"I told you everything that needed saying."

"I think not. Even if I put aside the immoral aspects of what you said, you two have been lying to me since the day you walked through my door. I deserve an explanation."

Hattie rolled her neck at the coloring of her romantic life as immoral. How could love between adults be immoral? From an early age, she'd known that she loved differently and thought nothing abnormal about it until Sunday school taught lessons spouting otherwise. If not for the church getting into her head, she might have spent her teenage years loving, not loathing, herself.

"She's right, Hattie," David said, turning to Eva. "She is my friend. I'd do anything to help her."

"There's more to it. A mother knows these things. I can tell you love her, but for the life of me, I can't figure out why you would be part of this pretense. Do you deny loving her?"

David glanced at Hattie. Pain was in his eyes. "No. I love her, but I know I'll never have her heart."

Eva turned to Hattie. "So you took advantage of the man's feelings for you to appear normal. That's cruel."

"Right there, that's the problem. Who I love should not be considered normal or abnormal. David entered our agreement with his eyes open for acceptance's sake. So close-minded people like yourself wouldn't judge me based on something I wouldn't change if I could. This is who I am, not something I do for pleasure's sake. I'm still the daughter you raised to be confident, kind, and compassionate."

"I also raised you to be honest and to follow the church teachings."

"You mean like thou shall not commit adultery?"

Eva appeared hurt. "I regret hurting you and Olivia. If I could change that, I would."

Hattie rolled her neck again. Attacking her mother for something Hattie already had forgiven her for was wrong. Her mother's affair was a byproduct of her believing Karl had become a Nazi. While Eva's reason didn't excuse her infidelity, Hattie understood why she had strayed and should not hold it against her.

"I shouldn't have brought that up, and I'm sorry. I know you did your best."

Eva's lips trembled. "Thank you."

Hattie took a moment to form the right words before meeting her mother's gaze. Eva was hurting, which wasn't what Hattie wanted. "You and I are survivors. We fight for our place in the world, showing people what they want to see. That we are just like them, living happy lives, but underneath, we are a mess. We find our happiness where we can in order to hold on. Maya makes me happy and want to face a world that would rather hate me than understand me."

"I'm suddenly not hungry." Eva's lips quivered more. "I'm going to lie down." She pushed herself up and started toward the living room but stopped, looking over her shoulder. "Don't feel like you have to rush to find a place to live."

Eva disappeared down the hallway, and Hattie sat, feeling numb.

"That went well." David laughed.

"Like a train wreck." Nothing had been resolved. How could it with words like immoral, unnatural, adultery, and cruel having been tossed around like weapons?

~

Eva was numb when she left the kitchen. She loved her daughter more than life itself but could not reconcile her sexuality with a lifetime of Catholic teachings. Besides being against the law, her lifestyle countered everything she'd been taught about moral principles. Eva hated thinking Hattie would never know the joy of being a mother. Of raising a daughter and watching her grow into a kind, caring woman with a family of her own. The thought that Hattie's bloodline had no chance of continuing broke her heart.

Eva felt a headache coming on while walking down the hallway. Every negative outcome of her daughter's lifestyle pounded in her temples. She closed the bedroom door behind her, but not from the battle raging between her heart and her head. She'd been taught to turn her back on sin, but the last two weeks of pent-up anger and confusion had shown her that shutting out her daughter would break her. There had to be a way of convincing Hattie to change her ways.

Eva turned the corner to enter her bathroom but jumped, startled by a shadow. "You scared the life out of me."

"I saw Olivia off at the dock," Karl said, stepping forward.

"You're looking better. How is the arm?"

"Other than it being stiff in the morning, it's healed well." He rolled his left shoulder. "We need to talk about Hattie now that Olivia is gone."

Eva buried her face in her hands and wept, fearing she would lose her daughter for good over this.

"Let's sit." Karl guided her to bed and sat beside her. "I'm sure you have questions."

Eva wiped her tears with her fingers. "How long have you known about her?"

"She told me the night we rescued you."

"And you said nothing?"

"When was I supposed to tell you?" he said. "We had our hands full, and I knew how upset you would be."

"Of course I would be upset. What Hattie is doing is wrong."

"Is it? Other than Maya's sex, she's exactly the life partner we'd hoped for Hattie. She is strong, smart, responsible, and most of all, she makes our daughter happy. It seems we were the ones who have done something wrong."

"I agree. Where did we go wrong in raising a child with unnatural desires?"

Karl sighed. "This is going to be harder than I thought." He shifted to look directly at Eva. "We were wrong by not raising her to trust us with her secrets."

"No parenting style could have prepared her to reveal something like that to us," Eva said. She gasped at the thought of never looking at Hattie the same again.

"Isn't there?" Karl shook his head in obvious disappointment. "It's called unconditional love, and we failed her."

"*We* failed her?" Eva's question came out a little too sharp. She realized this wasn't the time for defensiveness, but everything she knew about her daughter had been turned on its head.

"Yes," Karl said. "She should have felt safe enough at home to tell us anything and be herself around us."

"You're blaming me and the church, aren't you?"

"No, I'm blaming us. I should have been home more and not stressed so much about the public perception of my job. While I can't fault your faith, you could have made it clear that her happiness and well-being were more important to you than adhering to the church's strict teachings."

Eva opened her mouth to object but couldn't once she processed Karl's point. The church had been an essential part of her life since childhood, with priests and nuns drilling into her a moral code handed down through the centuries. She had her own crisis of faith when she gave in to an attraction before legally divorcing Karl. And later, her priest's refusal to grant an annulment made her question the church, not her faith. She should have seen that faith and church weren't synonymous, but knowing no other way, she continued going through the motions as any good Catholic would.

Eva wept for teaching her daughter to keep secrets. To not trust her. "We failed her."

"Yes, we did."

Eva wiped her eyes again. "What now?"

"I won't lie and say I'm happy about this," Karl said. "A part of me still wants grandkids from her."

"Me too."

"But I won't cut her out of my life for simply being herself." Karl cupped Eva's hand and squeezed it. "I will be patient, get to know Maya, and love my girl like always."

"I'm not sure if I can do that."

"Then you will lose her forever, Eva."

That was an outcome Eva wasn't prepared to accept. She recalled the incredible feeling she experienced moments before going on stage with Hattie at the gala when Hattie had said she loved her. Other than holding Hattie in her arms for the first time after giving birth, Eva had never felt such pure joy. She could not bear losing Hattie again after having been lost to her for so many years.

32

Later that evening, Hattie pulled Eva's Ford into her reserved parking spot at the Copacabana Palace. She sat at the wheel, replaying the conversation with her mother. Barring a miracle, she didn't see Eva coming around any time soon. When she and David moved out, they would need a used car to get about town for a few months until her contract expired. And unless they found something furnished, they would have to buy a host of things. Perhaps she should speak to the hotel manager about renting a suite or two rooms and deducting a negotiated price from their pay.

She pushed aside her disappointment and entered her dressing room through her private patio. As she opened the closet door to hang the new stage dress she'd bought during a shopping spree with Olivia, Hattie half expected her father to spring out and surprise her with a hug. He always had a sixth sense of knowing when she needed him.

After pouring a glass of water, she picked up the phone, dialed the Golden Room's host station, and asked the bar to send in her hot tea and honey. "Right away, Miss James," the head waiter said.

"Can you also send a club sandwich and salad from the kitchen? I didn't have time to eat before arriving."

"Yes, senhora. I'll have everything sent on the same tray."

Hattie sat at the vanity and turned on the bright lights to do her hair and makeup. Deciding to forgo the in-house stylist, she used her mother's techniques when they prepared for the gala event and could not hold back a smile. That evening would always be special to Hattie. It marked the first time she and her mother appeared on stage together and the first time she told Eva she loved her since her parents' divorce. And Hattie wept, thinking she might never get back the bond she felt that night.

A knock on the door.

"Come in!" Hattie yelled, wiping her tears with a tissue.

The door opened, and the server walked into the room.

Hattie didn't look up, dabbing a makeup sponge below her eyes to hide that she'd been weeping.

The server placed the food tray on the coffee table, and a moment later, Maya appeared in the mirror. She put a hand on Hattie's shoulder and crouched until their heads were even. "You've been crying. Missing your sister already?"

"Yes, but that's not it."

"What then?"

Hattie rested her hand over Maya's. "I talked to Mother about us today, and it didn't go well."

"What did you expect?"

"I'm not sure, but I'd hoped to walk away knowing she still loved me."

"Did she say otherwise?"

"No, but—"

"Then give her time. If she didn't order you out of her house and her life, there's a chance she might come around."

Hattie turned to face Maya and caressed her cheek. "I'm so glad you're here." She wanted to say she was happy to have her back but didn't want to risk her pulling away by pushing too quickly.

"Me too." Maya pressed her lips against Hattie's with tenderness, letting the kiss linger longer than their last one.

Hattie tried not to read too much into it, but the feeling of their lips touching stirred memories of their one night of passion together. A moan escaped—Hattie's and then Maya's. She drifted a hand but caught herself before grazing Maya's breast. Maya had to first overcome her association of Anna's death with Hattie and take the next step, though Hattie was running out of self-restraint. Imagining her fingers and lips on Maya's skin would soon not be enough.

Another knock on the door. "Thirty minutes, Miss James," her band leader said through the door.

Hattie dreaded breaking the kiss but needed to answer and rein this in. Otherwise, she would take the lead. She pulled back and yelled, "Thank you!"

"I better get going so you can get ready." Maya smiled, an auspicious sign.

Hattie grinned, confident that they were back on track. "Before you go, I know the insurance company paid out, but you didn't get the expected amount. Since you still have a few months until you have to decide what to do with the Halo Club property, I was thinking I could loan you the rest to rebuild."

Maya stood and stepped back, looking a bit rattled. "I don't want money to be between us." Her words came out brittle.

Hattie felt she'd set back all their progress and needed to fix it. "It doesn't have to be. We could draw up a contract. I would leave that up to you to determine how we proceed."

"This is very generous of you, Hattie, but I'm afraid this would change things between us."

"Of course things would change. We would be partners." Hattie moved closer and grazed Maya's cheek. "I was thinking we could reach out to the families of Baumann's victims and the other survivors and offer them jobs at the new club."

Maya smiled again—the reaction Hattie had hoped to receive. "I'll think about it."

~

Hattie smoothed her dress and climbed the steps to the stage wings behind the curtain. She glanced at the band leader, signaling she was ready, and shifted her stare to the piano player Maya had hired temporarily to fill in for David until he was cleared to return to work. The woman was a talented musician and held her own in an all-male band. She would make an excellent acquisition for the Golden Room after Hattie left or returned to the United States to resume her recording career or for the Halo Club once it reopened.

The band leader announced in Portuguese and English, "...proud to present the American songbird, Hattie James."

As the curtain retracted, Hattie crossed the stage, nodding to the band members moments before they started playing. She hit her mark right on cue at the microphone, looked into the sea of packed tables past the spotlights washing out their faces, and belted out her first note to a thunderous ovation.

Her ninety-minute set stretched into a hundred ten with applause and two encores, with her singing two Maggie Moore songs they had performed on stage together twice during Maggie's unexpected lengthy stay. The crowd roared when the curtains closed, allowing Hattie to leave the stage.

The piano player handed her a towel to wipe the sweat from her brow. "Thank you, Zoya. You played exceptionally well tonight."

"I missed two notes." Zoya shook her head, speaking in a thick Portuguese accent.

"Yet you didn't skip a beat. That's the sign of a true professional. Mr. Townsend will return soon, but I hope to work with you in the future."

"Thank you, Miss James. That means a lot."

As they walked down the private corridor behind the stage, a server handed Hattie a message and scurried away. Hattie unfolded the note. Leo had asked her to come to his table for an urgent matter.

"I'm sorry to cut this short, Zoya, but I must go." Hattie tossed the towel on a tray in the hallway, entered the dining room, and looked for Leo's table. Several guests shook her hand and took pictures, but all were respectful and thankful for the personal attention.

Maya caught up with her in the aisle. "What brings you out so quickly?"

Hattie showed Maya the message. "Can you take me to him?"

"Follow me." Maya led her through the crowd, dodging the servers delivering food and drinks to the tables, and walked toward the back of the room, which was perplexing. Hattie had left standing orders that the staff should seat Leo near the front whenever he came to her show, but she didn't question Maya's seating arrangement.

When they reached the back, Leo locked eyes with Hattie and waved her closer. The man sitting beside him looked up, stopping Hattie in her tracks. She touched Maya's arm, encouraging her to stop. "Oh, hell no."

"What is it?" Maya asked.

"That man with Leo."

"Who is he?"

"The biggest pain in the butt I've met." Hattie squeezed Maya's forearm. "Don't leave. I want witnesses."

"Witnesses?"

"You'll see." Hattie approached the table, and both men stood. When Leo kissed her on the cheek, she whispered, "What is he doing here?"

"He has something for you."

"Unless it's a public apology, I want nothing to do with him."

Leo laughed. "I don't blame you after reading your file, but hear him out." He held the chair for her and did the same for Maya.

"What do you want, Agent Knight?" Hattie asked.

The last time she saw FBI Special Agent Samuel Knight, she was stuck singing at the Playhouse in the squalor of the Five Points neighborhood of New York City. Performing at a place where fellatio was performed regularly under the tables was Hattie's low point after Knight single-handedly tanked her career. He had dropped stories in the *Times* and *Post*, labeling her the daughter of a traitor, and visited her at the club to strong-arm her into flushing out her father in Rio by threatening to arrest Olivia and her husband.

Knight looked at Maya and whispered something to Leo.

"She's cleared," Leo said. "Neither of us would be alive without her help."

Knight nodded and turned his attention to Hattie, looking as smug as the first day she had met him. "I have something from the attorney general for your heroics in recognition for thwarting a presidential assassination, which could have mired Brazil and the United States in controversy, perhaps pitting the two countries on opposite sides of the war. And for acquiring the photos of the logbook you gave Commander Bell, which proved to be a treasure trove of intelligence. The information we gleaned from it will give us a leg up if we enter the war. The British are using pieces of it as we speak to push back on U-boat attacks in the Atlantic. Your actions have and will save countless lives." He slid a small dark blue container across the table, resembling a jewelry gift box.

"What is this? Another threat to get me to do your bidding?"

"Just open it, Miss James," Knight said.

Hattie lifted the cover, revealing a bronze coin imprinted with her name and image. "What is it?"

"Congress held a classified closed-door session and voted to award you the Congressional Bronze Medal. I was instructed to convey the nation's gratitude."

Hattie closed the lid and shoved the box back to Knight. "You know what you can do with this medal."

Maya and Leo snickered.

"You have no idea how rarely this medal is given out," Knight said. "You should be honored."

"There is no honor in innocent people dying. Five women were killed, including Miss Reyes's sister, so I could get my hands on Baumann's logbook. I would be honored if you would take the next flight back and tell our government to show their appreciation by setting up a fund for the families of those who died."

Knight harrumphed. "I'll pass along your request in my next diplomatic pouch heading back to the States."

Hattie narrowed her eyes with confusion and turned to Leo.

"I only learned about it today, Hattie," Leo said, giving her a contrite smile.

Knight slipped the coin box into his inner breast pocket. "That's right, Miss James. I'm your new contact in Rio. We'll be working together until you hand over your father."

Hattie took in a rattled breath. "Peachy. Where is Strom Wagner? Will he come after us?"

"No one knows, but we wish we did. We had reports that Wagner was heading up something huge in the jungle that could change the direction of the war."

〜

Hattie pulled the car into the garage later that night and sat at the wheel, mulling over Maya's advice about giving her mother time to come around. Time usually healed most wounds, but Hattie's sexuality was more than a hurdle. It was a mountain. "Patience," Hattie told herself.

She entered the house through the breezeway door and dropped her purse in the bedroom she had shared with David for months. After using the bathroom, she peeked into the other guest room and discovered David snoring in bed. Moving his bags into his new room could wait until morning.

Closing the door, she heard a clanking sound coming from the front of the house, turned on the hallway light, and went to investigate. The kitchen lights were on, and the smell of more fresh cooking filled the living room. She stepped around the corner, finding Eva in her silk robe at the stove, flipping something in a pan.

"You're still up?" Hattie said.

Eva looked over her shoulder. "I thought you might be hungry."

Hattie stepped closer and saw the sandwich frying in the pan. "Misto quente." Since childhood, the ham and cheese sandwich had been her favorite morning and late-night snack. Eva would add whatever fruit or vegetable was on the verge of going bad and season it to bring out more of the flavors. Her sandwiches were seldom the same, which always made them enjoyable. She sensed...hoped...that tonight's offering was an olive branch.

"Peppers or bananas?" Eva asked.

The bananas had already developed spots, but the peppers looked like they still had a few days of life.

"Bananas," Hattie said, knowing Eva would add a dash of cinnamon—her favorite spice. While she filled two glasses with orange juice and set out some napkins, Eva plated the sandwiches and joined Hattie at the table.

"How was your show tonight?" Eva asked.

"Good." Hattie took a bite, letting the flavors invade every corner of her mouth before chewing and swallowing. "The replacement piano player has a wonderful future."

"She should. I taught her."

"Ah, that explains her striving for perfection."

When Hattie reached for her glass of juice, Eva cupped her hand over Hattie's but said nothing. She squeezed hard as a river of tears streaked her cheeks. The connection she experienced with Eva the night of the gala and after rescuing her from Wagner's clutches had returned, but it felt fragile, as if it could break any moment.

"I love you, Mother."

"I love you, sweetheart," Eva croaked through the tears. "I spoke to your father."

"Father was here? How is he?"

"He appeared well and fully recovered." Eva wiped away a tear with her free hand. "He made me see certain things."

"He did, huh?" Hattie forced back a smile.

"The past couple of months have shown me that Karl is a good man and an even better father."

"Yes, he is." Hattie nodded, barely grasping her mother's turnaround. Eva had hated everything about her father for years, believing he'd become a Nazi. But with the truth in the open, she had finally seen him for who he really was—a loving father, husband, and patriot.

"I'm not sure how long this will take," Eva said, "or if I'll ever get used to the idea of you being in love with a woman, but I want to try because I can't lose you again."

"I don't want to lose you either." She squeezed Eva's hand. This wasn't Hattie's dream, where Eva accepted her with open arms, but it was more than expected. It was a darn good start.

"I'd love you to continue living here but would understand if you feel you can't stay. Either way, I'd like to get to know Maya better."

Hattie's lips quivered. So much change had happened in the last few months. Her family had been turned upside down and spun around like a whirly top with all the secrets and danger, yet they ended up closer. Hattie could finally see a day when she sat at the dining table with her parents for family dinner with Maya by her side.

"You're going to love her."

After they finished their midnight snack, their goodnight hug was the longest they had ever shared. It was filled with hope, love, and honesty. For the first time, they embraced as themselves, with no lies between them. It was the most freeing experience Hattie had encountered.

Hattie entered her bedroom, feeling the world's weight had lifted. She still had to contend with FBI Agent Samuel Knight and the pressure to flush out her father. However, with her mother, Maya, David, and Leo in the know and waiting in the wings to help, Hattie believed she could put off Knight indefinitely.

The room seemed stuffy, so she opened the window to let in the late autumn air. The cool breeze felt nice, reminding her of the changing seasons in New York and Washington, DC. She didn't realize until then how deeply she had missed snuggling in flannel sheets under a cozy wool blanket. By the time she readied for sleep in the bathroom, her room had cooled too much. The light linens on the bed might not keep her warm, so she lifted the lid to the steamer to find her warmer sleepwear.

Hattie sifted through the collection of her and David's clothes and removed her nightgown, exposing the steamer's bottom. She noticed a small tear in the lining and inspected it. She had bought the trunk new for this trip, so a cut in the liner surprised her. As she ran a fingertip across the rip, she felt something hard between the fabric and the metal casing and touched it to determine its size. The object was slightly larger than her billfold, so she dug into the hole and pulled out the item.

Hattie gasped, unable to speak or make a noise. Breathing became challenging as she tried to wrap her head around what she had found. Why was Baumann's original logbook hidden inside her steamer trunk?

THE SECRET WAR
Hattie James #3

In a world of secrets, her greatest performance may be off-stage.

In a factory hidden deep in the Brazilian jungle, the Germans are developing a long-range bomber capable of reaching the United States—a weapon that could tip the scales of World War II in their favor. With the clock ticking down to a sneak attack on American soil, singer-spy Hattie James's mission becomes clear: she must gather intelligence and stop the Nazis before it's too late.

When a failed assassination attempt in Rio on the American Vice President puts her loved ones in jeopardy, Hattie realizes both developments are connected and that the price of failure is more than she can bear. With betrayal hiding around every corner, Hattie must confront the brutal reality of war as even those she once trusted—her fellow spies and closest allies—might have their own deadly agendas.

As alliances shift and enemies close in, she faces a desperate battle in the heart of the jungle—a fight to destroy the Nazi threat and save the lives of those she loves. The stakes are higher than ever, and Hattie must use all her wit, charm, and courage to survive.

Get your copy today at
severnriverbooks.com

ACKNOWLEDGMENTS

Thank you, Barbara Gould, my plotting partner in crime, for serving as the best sounding board I could ever ask for.

Thank you, Kristianne and Nancy, for slugging through my rough, rough, rough first draft and giving an unvarnished critique.

Thank you, Jacquelin Cangro, my amazing developmental editor, for helping me whip this story into shape.

Thank you, termites, for having a party at my daughter's home. Without you, I would have finished this book months earlier.

Finally, to my family. Thank you for loving me...and the endless snacks.

ABOUT THE AUTHOR

A late bloomer, award-winning author Stacy Lynn Miller took up writing after retiring from the Air Force. Her twenty years of toting a gun and police badge, tinkering with computers, and sleuthing for clues as an investigator form the foundation of her Lexi Mills thriller series, as well as her Manhattan Sloane novels. She is visually impaired, a proud stroke survivor, mother of two, tech nerd, chocolate lover, and terrible golfer with a hole-in-one. When you can't find her writing, she'll be golfing or drinking wine (sometimes both) with friends and family in Northern California.

Sign up for Stacy Lynn Miller's reader list at
severnriverbooks.com

Printed in the United States
by Baker & Taylor Publisher Services